The Third Question

By James Arendorf

Inspired by true events and real people

Tickling the impossible.

Contents

Chapter 1

A dream

Sunday, December 13th, 1891. The day after the Second Question.

Early in the morning. Dalya Bouvard slowly opened her eyes. While moving her fingers, she felt the soft cotton bed sheets, her cheeks touched the silk pillow, Dalya was lying down on a huge comfortable bed under a velvet bed cover.

Dalya stared at the ceiling for several minutes. And because of the little light escaping from the closed curtains, the enormous chandelier timidly shone in the dark, the ceiling seemed to be in carved designs, blue and gold. Dalya felt the warmth from a fireplace, only some steps away from the bed. A peaceful silence invaded the bedroom. Dalya closed her eyes to stay in her dream for a few more minutes.

Suddenly, someone opened the door and entered the room. When she opened her eyes for the second time, Dalya noticed her friend Amira Mounier. Amira was wearing a pretty pink winter coat. A small white cap covered her head. Her long braids fell over her shoulder. Amira walked inside the room in silent steps, eyes wide open and dazzled by the luxury of this place.

Suddenly, and without bothering to wake up her friend Dalya, Amira screamed with all her strength and she jumped in the room, swiftly turning around like a spinning top:

- IT'S INCREDIBLE!! IT'S INCREDIBLE!! IT'S INCREDIBLE!! IT'S INCREDIBLE!!

Amira ran to every corner of the bedroom, she half opened the curtains of the large windows with a quick movement, she ran to touch the precious and refined wood desk, she paused near the luxurious large fireplace, she ran to the adjacent bathroom, she opened and closed the dressing closets with a quick movement, she jumped on the lounge chairs beside, she came back near the large windows ... Amira couldn't hold back her happiness or her fascination screams:

- IT'S INCREDIBLE!! IT'S INCREDIBLE!! IT'S INCREDIBLE!! IT'S INCREDIBLE!!

Quickly, Amira jumped on the bed and she hugged Dalya tightly in her arms. It was only at that moment, that Dalya realized she was not dreaming. Amira squeezed Dalya's neck, in a strong hug. The pain in Dalya's neck confirmed that no, it was not a dream; Dalya was indeed in a room at the Grand Mansion!

The day before, the events unfolded so quickly. Dalya vaguely remembers what happened after the Second Question. Except that she left the grand Mansion, she walked with her Uncle Giorgi, toward her parents' old poor house. When the Lawyer, Mr. Sloan Wilfrid caught them up halfway and ... the next day, Dalya Bouvard woke up in a room at the Grand Mansion.

Her friend Amira stuttered happily:

- You ... you ... su ... su ... succeeded!!

Dalya had some hard time to realize what had happened the night before:

- I ... I don't know how I did it ...
- The answer t ... t ... that you gave, was right!! Amira exclaimed, jumping on the bed

Dalya remembered having been forced to answer the Second Question of the Excelbox, as it was ordered in the Will. Except that Dalya was sure it wasn't the right answer. In total confusion, Dalya thought aloud:

- But ... how ... how is that possible? ... my answer ... I ...

Amira managed to calm her excitement for a moment:

- Dalya ... How did you find the answer?

Dalya looked at her friend, and she explained:

- The one word in common with the 5 clues, it was the verb continue. And ... I remembered a word you said, after reading the story of the tortoise and the rabbit ... in the school Library ... the word Perseverance ... Thanks to you Amira, I found this word ...

Amira Mounier blushed. She squeezed Dalya in her arms, less strong than before, but just as warm, and she said with a trembling voice:

- I am ... so ... so pleased ... that you're staying with me ... at school!!

Dalya was happy too, to stay at school and to continue her education. When she released Dalya, Amira exclaimed joyfully:

- As soon as we complete our holiday homework, we can explore and visit the grand Mansion!!

Dalya jumped:

- ... Holiday homework?! What homework?

Amira was greatly surprised by her friend's question:

- Uh ... well ... the homework that the teachers gave us ... before the end of the semester ... you did write all the homework, didn't you?

Dalya was paralyzed for a moment:

- No ... I wrote nothing ... I didn't think I would come back to school!

Before Amira could answer, someone knocked on the door and entered the bedroom, greeting the two little girls sitting on the bed:

- Good morning, Mademoiselle Dalya ... Miss Amira!!

It was the maid of the grand Mansion, Cristelle. The young girl wore her usual work apron and a white bonnet. She displayed a big happy smile, all her white teeth appeared entirely. Dalya smiled back:

- Good morning Cristelle.

Straightaway, a magnificent creature walking on 4 legs, followed Cristelle and entered the room. A white tattooed fur, sapphire piercing blue eyes, large powerful legs, a long tail floating in the air, the snow Panther walked toward the fireplace, in quiet and serene steps. Amira Mounier jumped and clutched her friend's arm, her voice and her body trembled:

- What ... what is ... a tiger ... here ... but it's ...

The snow Panther lay down on a Persian rug in front of the fireplace, and looked at the two little girls sitting on the bed, with a serene gaze. Dalya explained to her friend:

- It's a snow Panther ... her name is Séraphine ... she was the Late Governor's pet ...

Amira didn't let go of Dalya's arm:

- And ... this ... she lives in this house?

Cristelle displayed an amused chuckle, observing the animal:

- Yes, and she acts as Master of the house. I have to follow her every day to clean carpets and floor after her!

The young Cristelle tried to appease Dalya's friend:

- Séraphine is docile and quiet ... she will do you no harm ... be reassured!

Amira released Dalya's arm, her concern faded somewhat, but her astonishment remained. She had never seen such a remarkable and big animal, so closely and especially so free. Cristelle asked Dalya, in a cheerful voice:

- And besides that ... have you slept well, Mademoiselle?

In fact, Dalya had slept very badly last night. Although the covers were soft as cotton, pillows in silk and the bed comfortably lightweight. Except that several times during the night, Dalya woke up, she didn't realize where she was, she didn't know if it was a dream or a reality. Dalya didn't dare to tell Cristelle, she simply answered:

- Yes, thank you.

Cristelle came close to the bed, and she whispered to Dalya, with a very emotional proud voice:

- I'm so happy that you are here among us, at the grand Mansion. You have achieved a success, Mademoiselle!!

Dalya couldn't help blushing. She didn't know how her answer has been correct, without her being sure. Cristelle continued:

- And I am thrilled and honored to serve you, Mademoiselle. If you need anything, let me know, please.
- Thank You, Cristelle.

The maid approached the many large windows of the room, and she fully removed the velvet curtains, inviting the sunshine inside. The bedroom was huge, and it illuminated with luxury. The very large bed was set up on beams with golden motifs, covers and blankets were of softer and warmer fabrics, the office was in light brown precious wood, the adjacent lounge blue and gold chairs were refined, rugs on the floor were in beautiful Persian pattern, the massive crystal chandelier shone in all its splendor, the room wallpaper displayed beige and blue delicate designs, the near bathroom was in luxurious gray marble and silver tools, towels as fluffy and white as a cloud, a large adjacent dressing room contained wardrobes and cupboards in shiny wood, upright all along the wall, the big fireplace stood majestically in front of the bed, and everywhere dazzling crystal vases decorated the corners of the room .. . It was a luxurious and refined bedroom. Dalya and her friend Amira, remained speechless, amazed and intimidated by this splendor.

Cristelle said to the girls:

- In a few minutes, breakfast will be ready for you, Mesdemoiselles. In the dining room.

Dalya hesitated a moment before saying:

- It's just ... I have a lot of homework to catch up ... and a few days only before going back to school... I prefer to skip the brea...

Immediately, Cristelle interrupted her:

- Oh ... but that won't be possible, Mademoiselle!! You must absolutely have breakfast and eat well!! ... My responsibility as of now, is to watch over you, Mademoiselle!!

Approaching the fireplace, and under the serene stare of the snow Panther, Cristelle added 2 pieces of wood inside the fireplace, before continuing:

- If you wish, Mademoiselle ... I can serve you breakfast in the Library ... so you can eat there and work your homework, all at the same time.

Amira immediately exclaimed, in astonishment:

- There is ... a Library ... here!
- Of course. Cristelle laughed. A vast Library, that is sure to please you, if you are passionate about books, Miss Amira!

Still, for a moment, Dalya was confused:

- We ... we can have breakfast at the Library? ... Would that be possible? ... I don't think Mr. Ernest Laszlo will ever permit it ...

Approaching the bed of the little girl, Cristelle let out an amused laugh:

- Oh but, Mademoiselle ... as of today, the grand Mansion is yours!

At this announcement, Dalya was shocked:

- The Grand Mansion is ...

Cristelle finished Dalya's sentence, with a proud tone:

- Yours ... Yes ... you are the new owner of the grand Mansion now.

On that moment, and with all pride and pleasure, the maid Cristelle bowed in reverence in front of the little girl:

- Lady Dalya Bouvard.

Dalya was paralyzed by the words and gestures of Cristelle. Sitting on the bed next to her friend, Amira was too, very surprised by this news. Amira straightened up on the bed and she immediately repeated to her friend in a stunned voice:

- The Grand Mansion is yours, Dalya!

Dalya remained silent, shocked and confused. Cristelle realized that this news surprised the little girl, Cristelle then went on to explain:

- And so you can dispose of the grand Mansion, as you like.

At this moment, Amira jumped out of the bed, and under the stare of the snow Panther, the maid Cristelle and her friend Dalya, Amira ran around the immense bedroom, jumping and turning around like a spinning top, yelling with all her might:

- THE ENTIRE GRAND MANSION IS YOURS!! IT'S INCREDIBLE!! IT'S INCREDIBLE!! IT'S INCREDIBLE!!

Cristelle laughed her heart out, amused by the happy reaction of Amira Mounier. The snow Panther lying down near the fireplace, watched the jumps and the screams of Amira, and one could have almost seen Séraphine smile. Dalya smiled too, a nervous and a confused smile. Because no ... it was certainly not a dream.

Chapter 2

Tickling the impossible

Monday, December 14th, 1891. At the Law Firm.

Sloan Wilfrid joined the Law Firm, like all the previous mornings, happily humming a melody. Except that within his first steps inside the Firm, the young Lawyer could immediately feel that there was tension in the air. All employees were nailed to their desks, no one dared to move or speak, and they were all strangely silent and motionless.

When Sloan Wilfrid placed his coat on his office chair, he came out to make himself coffee in the counter. When he took a mug, a deafening and piercing yell was heard from the office of Mr. Ernest Laszlo, the Lawyer.

- VERMIN!! A VEGGY SELLER!! A GUTTER RAT!!

This scream paralyzed all employees of the Firm, except Sloan Wilfrid. The young Lawyer displayed a big cheerful and innocent smile, while serving himself coffee. Lyor Laszlo, the son of the Lawyer Ernest, joined Wilfrid in the counter. Lyor seemed to have not slept a wink of the entire night; he was confused by what was happening around him. Dark circles under the eyes, a very pale face and badly arranged hair. Lyor informed Wilfrid in a whispered voice:

- Mr. Ferdinand Edelmen ... the Governor's nephew ... he is in my father's office ... since this morning ...

Sloan Wilfrid smiled happily back at him:

- Yes, I heard his enchanting voice through the walls of your father's office.

Lyor seemed lost. And one thing that almost never happened to him, Lyor was wearing, for the first time in the Law Firm, a wrinkled blouse and a badly made tie. Wilfrid couldn't help teasing him with a sympathetic smile:

- You seem like you haven't slept all night, Lyor ... everything's alright?

Lyor Laszlo was troubled:

- What happened? ... The other night … But ... Wilfrid ... how ... how did she do it?

A scream shook a window glass, near the counter:

- MY FORTUNE!! THIS BEGGAR!! SHE HAS NO RIGHT ON MY MONEY!!

Wilfrid hummed a jovial and amused Musical tone, while adding some milk to his coffee:

- Ah ... we have a beautiful sun today ... isn't it a beautiful day for a ride in the park, Lyor?

Lyor Laszlo couldn't understand the joyous mood of his mentor Sloan Wilfrid. The young Lyor whispered in a stressed voice:

- Nobody could understand what happened the other night!! ... All the Law Firm is shocked ... The entire city is wondering how did she do it? ... We thought the first time was a pure beginner's luck ... but to be repeated for the second time?! ... Nobody believed it!!
- I WANT MY FORTUNE ERNEST!! MY RIGHT!! THIS VERMIN IS STEALING MY FORTUNE!! AN IDIOT!! A VEGGY SELLER!! A GUTTER RAT!!

Wilfrid stopped humming, and he asked Lyor in a very serious tone:

- Don't you think there is a taste difference between white and brown sugar?

Lyor was stunned and confused by Wilfrid's reaction. The lungs of the Governor's nephew seemed about to burst:

- HANDLE IT ERNEST!! I WANT MY FORTUNE BACK!! I CANNOT LOSE WHAT IS MINE!! DO SOMETHING ERNEST!!

Sloan Wilfrid finally decided:

- I prefer the brown sugar, it has a more caramelized flavor, I think ...
- IDIOT!! VERMIN!! GUTTER RAT!! BEGGAR!! VEGGY SELLER!!

Sloan Wilfrid took his cup of coffee, and he walked toward his office, followed by the young Lyor Laszlo. As soon as he closed the door, Lyor insisted in an anxious pleading tone:

- Wilfrid ... but what happened?

Given the confused look of the young Lyor, Wilfrid decided to explain to him, while sitting on the chair in front of his office:

- Everything happened legally, Lyor ... the little girl gave a correct answer.
- But ... Mr. Ferdinand Edelmen was already pronounced Heir to that fortune! Lyor exclaimed desperately.

Wilfrid let out an amused laugh:

- A mistake, my dear Lyor... a simple innocent little mistake ... The little girl had provided a correct answer before midnight, the deadline for the Challenge!! ... The appointment of Mr. Ferdinand Edelmen was made too early ... and so this appointment is invalid!

Lyor thought for a long second:

- So ... Mr. Ferdinand had to be nominated after midnight ... and only if she had given a wrong answer!

Wilfrid laughed:

- Exactly!

Screams shivered the windows of Sloan Wilfrid private office.

- I WANT MY FORTUNE IMMEDIATELY!! ERNEST!! WHAT HAPPENED IS IMPOSSIBLE!! IT'S A SCAM ERNEST!! THIS FORTUNE IS MINE!! MINE ONLY!!

Lyor Laszlo remembered something:

- But ... she wasn't sure of her answer ...

Wilfrid put down his coffee cup:

- Apparently, it was the right answer!

Lyor lay back on the chair, more troubled and disturbed than before:

- She ... she passed the Second Challenge ...

Wilfrid confirmed with a big defying smile:

- She passed the Second Challenge!

Despite the enraged screams of the nephew Mr. Ferdinand Edelmen, the paralyzed silence of the Lawyer Mr. Ernest Laszlo, the confusion of his son Lyor Laszlo, the astonishment of the Firm employees, and all the residents of Georgetown city ... despite all this; Sloan Wilfrid was proud and happy. Because as he had promised it, Sloan Wilfrid had protected a little girl's right to answer this Challenge.

This little girl succeeded for the 2nd time.

This little girl ... she tickled the impossible.

Chapter 3

The dishes

Monday, December 14th, 1891. In the Grand Mansion.

Although it was the holiday period, Dalya woke up early that morning. She washed and changed quickly. Then, she opened the door to walk out of her bedroom.

When she met, right at the door, the snow Panther. The animal was lying down on a carpet of the corridor just outside the bedroom. As soon as she noticed the little girl, Séraphine got up quickly, her sapphire eyes sparkled, her long tail straightened up, and a smile appeared on the animal's face. It is to be said that since their first meeting, the animal had a strange attitude toward the little girl. Dalya got used to the stares and follows of the snow Panther. She greeted her gently:

- Good morning Séraphine!

The snow Panther gave back a happy little meow. Dalya went on her way; she turned to the right of the corridor, down to lobby stairs, and walked to the Library.

Amira Mounier was busy on that day to study with Dalya. But she gave her all the questions to be answered for the Mathematics homework.

When the snow Panther entered the immense Library of the grand Mansion, Séraphine walked in with quick steps toward the large fireplace of the room and she lay down on the carpet in front.

The Library of the grand Mansion was Dalya's favorite place. The immense oval room was in 3 floors, filled with millions of books and volumes, to the delight of the little girl. Comfortable and luxurious chairs and couches were dispersed everywhere. The oval ceiling in transparent and colored glass, illuminated the Library in a clear and fresh light. It was a quiet and beautiful place.

Dalya followed the Panther inside the Library and she sat down in front of a large desk. Right away, she opened her Mathematics books, to begin her homework. And although the Mathematics course was her favorite, Dalya stared at the very long list of equations to solve, and she laughed:

- 105 equation!! ... Professor Wyatt has offered us a mountain of homework as a Christmas gift!! ... It will take me the entire holiday to solve!!

Fifteen minutes later, when Dalya was about to solve the 7th equation, someone entered the Library.

- Good morning, Mademoiselle!! Exclaimed the maid of the grand Mansion, displaying a big happy smile.
- Good morning, Cristelle.

The maid placed a tray on the desk table, right in front of Dalya:

- And here is ... your breakfast, Mademoiselle ... to help you work better!!

Dalya removed away her books:

- Thank you for bringing me breakfast here, Cristelle.

 The maid laughed:

- This is my job, Mademoiselle!

The breakfast in the grand Mansion was copious; a large cup of hot chocolate milk, a bowl of oatmeal with honey, a full plate of scrambled eggs with cheese and grilled sausages, slices of toast, a large glass of orange juice, and a bowl of fresh fruits.

While Dalya ate, Cristelle added a few logs of wood in the fireplace, under the half asleep stares of the snow Panther. Wiping her hands, Cristelle spoke to the animal:

- Some people work ... and others are napping all day long!

Séraphine turned around her long tail in the air, in response. And the animal slowly turned to stretch on her back, and allow the heat of the fireplace to warm her belly. Dalya had milk, and laughed:

- Séraphine is funny ...

Cristelle also laughed, while approaching Dalya's desk:

- I will bring you lunch here, Mademoiselle. Just like yesterday. If you need anything else, let me know.
- Thank you, Cristelle.
- And please finish your plate ... the eggs are the brain's best food!! Cristelle said in a caring tone, before closing the Library door.

Dalya ate her breakfast quickly, and she finished her eggs and sausages plate, as requested. She removed the tray, and she resumed back to her Mathematics notebooks:

- So ... the 7th equation is ...

The little girl worked her holiday homework in the immense Library, and with the only company of the snow Panther, lying down in front of the large fireplace.

Several hours later, Dalya was well advanced in her Mathematics homework. The 34th equation yet seemed difficult to solve. After a while, Dalya loosened back on her chair:

- I can't find a solution for this equation ... yet I have used all the techniques ... I don't remember having like this equation before ...

After consulting some Mathematics books, Dalya closed them with a sigh:

- My head is heavy ... I need some fresh air, to complete this homework ...

In order to refresh her mind and move her legs, Dalya decided to bring the breakfast tray to the kitchen of the Grand Mansion.

Until that day, Dalya had a rare contact with the employees of the grand Mansion. She knew them only from afar, from the time she was living with her family in the annex house.

Cristelle briefly showed Dalya the rooms and the main parts of the grand Mansion. When she entered the kitchen, Dalya discovered this place for the first time. A large wood dining table, occupied the center of the kitchen. The long counter where the Cook was working, was in gray marble. Kitchen utensils were well-ordered and in their respective places. A huge oven and a big cooker occupied an entire corner of the kitchen. A small door opened into the Pantry filled with food and preserved ingredients. Several rectangular windows offered a view into the garden and the back of the house. The kitchen of the Grand Mansion was impeccably organized and orderly.

The Chef, Mr. Ferrero Lutché was stirring a soup that was warming on the stove. And the help cook, Océanie was peeling apples, sitting in front of the large dining table.

- Good morning!

At this moment, the Cook and Océanie froze in their moves. They were both surprised to see the little girl in the kitchen, and they were even more shocked to see her holding the breakfast tray in her hands. Given the silence of the two employees, Dalya stepped forward toward the sink, she placed the tray and she spoke to the Cook:

- Thank you for the meals you serve me, Monsieur. The cheese omelet was delicious.

The Cook still troubled by the presence of the little girl in his kitchen, he murmured:

- I ... good morning ... omelet ... yes ... I ... with pleasure ... Mademoiselle ...

The Cook and Océanie exchanged a confused look. But what Dalya was about to do, certainly would shock them even more. The little girl turned toward the sink, she opened the faucet and she began to wash her plate and her cup.

At this instant, the head of the grand Mansion Mr. Bûchebois and the maid Cristelle entered the kitchen. Cristelle was explaining to him:

- I have already cleaned the living room, Monsieur. I removed all the carpets. When the Gardener gets the big tree, I will sweep the floor a second time and I will put back the carpets.
- Perfect Cristelle! The tree will be delivered next we...

The head of the Mansion, and Cristelle froze up. They noticed an unusual person in the kitchen. Dalya was busy in her task. The head of the Mansion asked in a perplexed voice:

- What ... what's happening?

Dalya gently put down the washed plate on the counter, and she greeted the head of the Mansion with a smile:

- Good morning!

The little girl took her cutlery and her cup, and she slid them into the sink. The head of the Mansion came close to her, and he asked with a curious voice:

- What are you doing ... Mademoiselle?

Focused on her task, Dalya naturally replied:

- I am washing the dishes.

The head of the Mansion struggled to understand what was really happening:

- Why?

All the employees of the grand Mansion were asking the same question. The answer was however clear to Dalya:

- Because it's dirty.

The employees lost their words and had eyes wide open. The head of the Mansion insisted to understand:

- No ... I mean why are you washing the dishes?

Dalya Bouvard was surprised by the question. She hesitated a few seconds before answering:

- Because the dirty dishes should be washed.

The head of the grand Mansion looked at the Cook and Océanie, hoping that someone can explain why this little girl was doing the dishes. But the Cook looked just as shocked as he was. Océanie was cutting the apples in a slow movement, without missing the scene in front of her. Only Cristelle decided to act:

- Mademoiselle!! But ... it is not up to you to wash the dishes!!

Dalya put down her washed cup and cutlery over the counter, and she asked all curious:

\- Why not?

At this moment, Océanie let out a mocking laugh:

\- This is the first time I witness an employer washing himself his own dishes. These are silly manners coming from a Noble person!

Without really thinking about it, Dalya spontaneously replied:

\- If we have hands to eat, we also have hands to wash our own dishes. Don't Noble people do that?

This simple spontaneous answer surprised everyone in the grand Mansion; the Cook had eyes and mouth all wide open, Océanie became mute and blushing, Cristelle displayed a large proud smile because of Dalya's response, the head of the grand Mansion became pale. In fact, they never had an employer like this little girl.

The head of the grand Mansion walked to Dalya and he addressed her with a respectful tone:

\- We ... we take care of your dishes, Mademoiselle. That's our job.

Dalya dried off her hands. Facing the curious looks, the heavy silence that hung in the kitchen, and the motionless moves of all the employees, Dalya had the impression of having committed an offense, without really knowing what it is. She replied in a shy voice:

\- Yes, Monsieur.

The head of the grand Mansion dared to say:

\- Bûchebois, Mademoiselle.

Dalya immediately replied:

\- Yes, Monsieur Bûchebois.

The head of the employees seemed annoyed by Dalya's attitude. He explained in a formal and respectful voice:

\- You must call me Bûchebois, Mademoiselle. Only Bûchebois. That's what the employers call the aids and home staff ... by their first names only.

The little 14 years old girl thought for a moment. Then, she looked up at the head of the grand Mansion, her new employee, and she smiled at him:

\- I prefer to call you Monsieur Bûchebois. If you don't mind.

The employees of the grand Mansion had a new employer; a strange little girl with unusual manners, bizarre attitudes, a particular language ... And above all, a disarming politeness.

Chapter 4

Forced to sign

Tuesday, December 15th, 1891. At the Law Firm.

Lyor entered his office. He had several files to deal with that day. And a busy day should definitely start with a good strong coffee. While Lyor was preparing himself a cup of coffee at the counter, he was called by the secretary's voice:

- Mr. Ernest asks to see you in his office, Mr. Lyor.

Immediately, Lyor abandoned his coffee, and he went straight to the Lawyer's office. As soon as he opened the door, Lyor greeted his father with a respectful voice:

- Good morning, Monsieur. You asked to see me?

Sitting behind his large luxurious black wood desk, Mr. Ernest Laszlo was reading a document in his hand, with a curiously quiet and scary attitude.

Since the 2nd Challenge, the Lawyer Ernest Laszlo wasn't only defeated in this inheritance case for the second time, he also had to endure the anger of the late Governor's nephew, Mr. Ferdinand Edelmen. And since several days now, Mr. Ernest Laszlo displayed an angry and demolishing mood, in his own Firm. The Lawyer screamed, insulted and slaughtered everything that moved on his way.

With a little hand sign, Mr. Ernest motioned at Lyor to approach. When the young apprentice came close, his father Mr. Ernest handed him a document, and he ordered him:

- Sign at the bottom of this paper.

When he took the document, Lyor hold on a few seconds to read the paper that was handed to him. And Lyor was stunned at what he found:

- This is ... this is the dismissal order of 54 employees of the Gantt leather factory ... 54 employees!!

Without the need for any further explanation, Lyor was convinced that his father was pouring out his defeat anger in the 2nd Challenge, toward the employees of this factory. It was a rash and an impulsive decision.

Lyor continued to read the document:

- But ... they are employees with over 10 years of seniority in this factory!!

This remark stung Mr. Ernest's calm, who exclaimed in an icy tone:

- I asked you to sign, not to read!

Unintentionally, Lyor thought aloud:

- Shouldn't I read every document before signing it?

At this moment, Lyor realized that his answer would certainly awake his father's anger. Because Mr. Ernest Laszlo was not someone who accepted disobedience and questioning his decisions. Lyor outran his father in a second, and he defended his idea, in a respectful and determined tone:

- I am well aware of the difficulties of the Gantt factory ... I think it would be more profitable and right, to only reduce salaries ... or even work hours, instead of a dismissal of these 54 emplo...
- LYOR!! I AM NOT ASKING FOR YOUR DAMN OPINION!! YOU SIGN THIS DOCUMENT, AND YOU GET THE HELL OF MY OFFICE!!

Lyor returned to the counter to prepare his coffee. He came back in a very different mood than his arrival, a few minutes earlier. Sloan Wilfrid joined Lyor, and greeted him cheerfully:

- It looks like a beautiful day!! ... Blue sky and shining sun, it makes me want to work in the garden, not at the office!

Lyor remained silent; he filled his 4th teaspoon of sugar and melted it in his coffee cup. Wilfrid let out an amused laugh:

- And I thought I was the only one loving sweets!!

Lyor's face revealed a serious and worried look. And when Lyor filled his 5th teaspoon of sugar and emptied it in his coffee cup, this time, Wilfrid realized that something serious occupied the young apprentice's mind:

- Lyor ... is everything alright? ... What is going on?

Staring at his coffee cup in a lost gaze, Lyor appeared in a state of shock. After a few seconds of silence, Lyor looked at Wilfrid and he trembled:

- He ... he forced me to sign ... he forced me to sign the dismissal order of 54 employees of the Gantt leather factory ... 54 employees, having spent 10 years in this factory ... 54 employees will not have any work and cannot feed their families tomorrow morning ... and it's all because of his anger against her!

Wilfrid have never lacked words to reassure and cheer up Lyor ... except this time. Wilfrid understood the shocked state of young Lyor. For some long minutes of a heavy silence, Wilfrid froze standing, leaning on the counter, his smile disappeared and his face got serious, without finding any words to say. Lyor filled his 7th teaspoon of sugar, and he whispered in a trembling voice:

- I was forced to sign the dismissal order of 54 employees ... 54 families ...

Chapter 5

Chess Pawns: the Soldiers

Several hours later, in the office of the Lawyer Mr. Ernest Laszlo.

The end of the day went much quieter and heavier than Wilfrid had expected. The news that Lyor brought him, disturbed Wilfrid's mood, for the entire day. He struggled to finish a file, which would usually take him only a few minutes to correct it.

After completing his work, Sloan Wilfrid walked to Mr. Ernest Laszlo's office. And despite the stubborn and tough character of his employer, Wilfrid sometimes could still manage to make him back off his decisions. The dismissal of the 54 employees, deserved to be defended. Wilfrid had to try!

When he opened the office door, Wilfrid met a familiar face. Mr. Strauss came out of the office, at the same time that Wilfrid was going in. Mr. Strauss was a close acquaintance of Mr. Ernest Laszlo, since several years. And his presence in the Law Firm awoke Wilfrid's curiosity. According to the latest news, Mr. Strauss had no judicial concerns.

Sloan Wilfrid and Mr. Strauss greeted each other briefly, before a voice called the young Lawyer.

- Come in Wilfrid.

The young Lawyer walked into the office. Mr. Ernest was sitting on a chair near the fireplace. He motioned to Wilfrid to sit on the chair in front of him. Wilfrid complied:

- It was a long day, Monsieur Ernest ... we have finished all the upcoming court cases.

A small table which had a game of Chess, was placed between the two men. Mr. Ernest Laszlo replied while moving a pawn in the Chessboard:

- Good ... good ... but we should be ready for the hearing of the week after ... it's the most important case we have.
- And we are ready, Monsieur Ernest ... I reviewed the file myself, 3 times!

The two Lawyers often played the Chess game, after the work hours. And having played hundreds of times, Wilfrid could confirm the exceptional talent of Mr. Ernest in this game.

The rules of the Chess game are very simple. The Chessboard is composed of six types of pieces: Soldiers pawns, the Castle, the Bishop, the Knight, the Queen, and the King. Each piece has a strict rule of movement on the Chessboard. When the king of the rival is caught, the game is won.

The Chess game wasn't only a relaxation moment for Mr. Ernest Laszlo, but also a time when Wilfrid could discuss sensitive issues with his employer. Therefore, at the end of this afternoon, Mr. Ernest being more calm and rested, Wilfrid seized the opportunity to dare, while moving forward a soldier pawn:

- I have heard news about the Gantt factory. Your decision to dismiss 54 employees is a ... very interesting idea.

Mr. Ernest Laszlo moved a Chess piece to another square on the right. Wilfrid observed the Lawyer a few seconds to ensure of his good mood, before continuing:

- However ... I have a little concern, if I may speak to you about it.

This time, Wilfrid was determined to play all his soldiers' pawns, convinced that his new game strategy, will succeed. Wilfrid moved a soldier pawn to a third box. Mr. Ernest raised his eyes toward Wilfrid:

- What is worrying you?

Mr. Ernest moved a pawn and in a quick movement, he swallowed Wilfrid's soldier pawn in one shot. Despite this defeat, Wilfrid went on with a natural tone:

- I had previously met with the Union Leader of the leather industry ... someone called Mr. Liam ... at a Christmas party, at a Congressman's house ... Mr. Liam is a very tough man, stubborn and difficult to negotiate with ... I fear that the dismissal of 54 employees of the Gantt factory, creates you a few worries and confrontations with the Union Leader ...

Wilfrid attempted another attack; he moved forward a soldier pawn. Mr. Ernest remained silent thinking for a few seconds. Then, the Lawyer moved one of his pawns toward Wilfrid and he asked:

- And why is that?

Wilfrid displaced his pawn soldier to the right:

- As I know ... Mr. Liam is a strong advocate of the employees' rights ... such a mass layoff, could put you in an awkward position in the public arena ... Mr. Liam will cease this opportunity to harm and darken your image ... and certainly the image of the Law Firm, as well.

Silence filled the Lawyer's office, only the fireplace flames could be heard. After a few seconds, Mr. Ernest Laszlo finally decided; he swallowed Wilfrid's soldier pawn with a ruthless move, and he asked his employee:

- And what do you propose?

Wilfrid's heart tightened to the loss of his soldier pawn, but he grabbed the opportunity of Mr. Ernest being ready to hear his proposal:

- I suggest ... if possible, of course ... delaying the dismissal for a few more months ... by the time we find a more subtle and less damaging solution for your image, Monsieur Ernest.

A few minutes of thinking later, Mr. Ernest Laszlo stated:

- Granted! ... I postpone this dismissal ... I expect a report from you, for an alternative to lighten the staff expenses of the Gantt factory...
- Understood, Monsieur Ernest! ... You will have a detailed report in a week!

Wilfrid ventured and moved forward another soldier pawn. He had worked on this Chess strategy since several days. The soldiers' pawns are incredibly effective. In addition to their numerous presences on the Chessboard, the soldiers' pawns are an excellent line of defense and attack. This time, Wilfrid was very sure to win the Chess game with his soldiers' pawns.

Mr. Ernest displaced one of his pieces forward, and he let out a mocking laugh:

- Lyor seems to have opinions ...

Wilfrid was well aware of the characters' conflict between the father and his son; he tried to dampen down Ernest's anger:

- Lyor is an intelligent young man with a quick thinking, very organized, hardworking ... he needs a little more experience, for sure ... but he is on the good track.

With an unpredictable and agile movement, Mr. Ernest swallowed Wilfrid's 3rd soldier pawn:

- I don't appreciate him having opinions about BalthEnterprise ... he thinks he knows something about the business management ... but he knows absolutely nothing about it!

Shocked by the loss of a soldier pawn, Wilfrid tried to recover quickly:

- I ... I will make sure to speak to him, to temper his opinions ... Monsieur.

Mr. Ernest ordered, in a calm tone:

- Lyor should handle only his files in the office! And nothing else!
- Yes, Monsieur ... I will let him know.

A moment of silence and thinking settled between the two men.

- What do you think? Ernest asked in a serious tone, after a few minutes.

Wilfrid stifled a nervous laugh:

- Well ... I still have important pawns. Although I have lost some soldiers ...

Ernest interrupted him:

- About her?

Wilfrid looked up at his game rival. He knew immediately who Mr. Ernest Laszlo was talking about. Her ... it was Dalya Bouvard.

The Lawyer, Ernest Laszlo enjoyed the Chess game, not only because he was unbeatable. But also, because it relaxed him from all the pressure of his work. Except this afternoon, and for once, the Chess game failed to appease his concern.

Wilfrid forced himself to repress his satisfaction. He replied in a natural tone:

- I think everyone has underestimated her. She is smart.

Mr. Ernest moved a piece to the left:

- You're right ... we underestimated her ...

Wilfrid displaced a soldier pawn 2 squares away. Mr. Ernest thought a few moments before moving his piece. Wilfrid dared to say in a calm and serene tone:

- In my opinion ... whether she succeeds or fails, in both cases you would be the winner, Monsieur.

Mr. Ernest was curious:

- How so?

Wilfrid pushed his soldier pawn one box forward:

- If she fails ... your client and good friend Ferdinand Edelmen will inherit the entire fortune, and he will be grateful to you for it.
- ... And if she succeeds?
- If she succeeds ... well, it will confirm your credibility and integrity to apply the Law. Your public image will greatly benefit from it ... in both cases, you would be the winner.

Mr. Ernest froze in his place, for a long moment. He was not hesitating on his next Chess piece move, he perfectly mastered the Chess game. But, he reflected on what his right arm, Sloan Wilfrid was telling him.

After several minutes of thinking, Mr. Ernest decided to move his piece one box to the right. And he asked his employee, in a curious voice:

- And what do you think ... about the next Third Challenge?

Wilfrid felt that question coming for sure. And he had his answer ready in his mind, since a long time. He replied in a natural and confident voice:

- Well, Monsieur ... it is impossible to predict what will happen in the next 12 months ... however, I think we should be aware of the obvious; things might not always turn the way that we have planned.

Mr. Ernest Laszlo went all silent for a moment. He moved one of his Chess piece. Instantly, Wilfrid noticed a strategic error from the Lawyer. Without hesitation, Wilfrid moved his soldier pawn and he took his rival's Chess piece. At this movement, there was a shadow of a smile on Mr. Ernest Laszlo's lips. A strange thing for someone who had just lost an important Chess piece.

Except that, the Chess game wasn't over yet. Mr. Ernest slowly approached the Chessboard, and in that moment, he made one single move, as unpredictable as sharp. He displaced his Bishop piece diagonally 6 squares, and ... he swallowed Wilfrid Sloan's white king, announcing with an icy cold voice:

- Checkmate.

Wilfrid froze in shock because of his defeat for the fifteenth hundred times. His heart and his brain stopped working; he had not seen this attack move coming. Wilfrid had however learned by heart and applied the Chess strategy; he had practiced for days and days on his soldiers' pawns. He was sure to win this game!

Except that ... despite his overwhelming loss at the Chess game, despite all his soldiers' pawns have been lost, despite he had to endure the arrogant and haughty looks of Mr. Ernest Laszlo ... despite all of this ... Wilfrid relaxed back on his chair and he smiled. He may have failed in this Chess game, but ... he had managed to postpone the dismissal of 54 employees of the Gantt factory!

And in fact, Mr. Liam ... the Union Leader whose Sloan Wilfrid talked about ... he was indeed the Union Leader of an industry ... the fishing industry, not the leather industry. Everyone can make mistakes. The error is human.

Mr. Ernest Laszlo relaxed on his chair too, and he stared at the fireplace in front of him, before saying with a convinced voice:

- And I correct you, Wilfrid ... things always turn the way that I have planned. I never lose.

At that moment, Sloan Wilfrid realized that the Lawyer will prevent, by all means and possibility, the success of the Third Challenge. He was not a man to accept defeat so easily, let alone by a little 14 years old girl. Ernest Laszlo was determined to attack. And Sloan Wilfrid was determined to defend. The next 12 months will be of no rest for these two men.

Sloan Wilfrid smiled at the Lawyer:

- Understood, Monsieur Ernest Laszlo ... very well understood!

Chapter 6

An ordinary cuisine

Wednesday, December 16th, 1891. In the grand Mansion.

Cristelle entered the kitchen, and she put down the lunch tray on the kitchen table. When the Cook watched the tray still full and the food still intact, the Cook exclaimed in an outraged tone:

- Again?! ... But it's Imposibile!! ... Why? ... Perché!

The maid Cristelle sat in front of the lunch tray, she sighed all confused:

- I don't understand! It has been 4 days now, that Mademoiselle Dalya doesn't touch any lunch and dinner meals ...

The Cook was shocked:

- But ... I Cucinato my best dishes!! ... Duck pâté ... trout with lemon ... cheese with truffles ... lobster!!
- Yes, Mr. Ferrero ... your dishes are very refined ... But she hasn't touched any of it! since she lives here in the grand Mansion, she only eats breakfast ...

The Cook asked:

- Ma Perché? ... Why doesn't she eat lunches and dinners?!

Cristelle observed the tray still full:

- I have no idea, Mr. Ferrero ... Mademoiselle tells me to serve her meals. And as soon as I put the tray in front of her, she answers that she is no longer hungry ...

The Cook asked Cristelle:

- Is she sick? Or suffering?
- I don't think so, no.

After a few seconds of silence and thinking. The Cook tried to find an explanation for the girl's strange attitude:

- Perhaps with her parents ... They only ate one meal a day? ... They didn't have lunches or dinners?
- It's absurd, Mr. Ferrero! It's a family like any other one; they ate 3 meals a day! Cristelle affirmed.

The Cook sat near the maid Cristelle, and they both observed the untouched lunch tray. The Cook thought aloud:

- I Cucinato my best dishes ... I served her Brussels sprouts with cheese, sol fish with lemon, duck meat with fresh cream, bread spread with pâté ... a luxurious cuisine ...

Cristelle sighed, all in confusion:

- And yet ... she doesn't eat ...

The Cook stood up at once, in an angry attitude:

- I hate when someone is capricious!! ... I have yet Cucinato the finest ingredients!! ... I eat this, I don't eat that!! ... I hate capricious people!!

Cristelle was sure that the little Dalya Bouvard was not a capricious girl. Yet, the maid of the grand Mansion couldn't know why the girl wasn't eating her meals!

Later, in the afternoon.

In one side of the large garden, The Cook Mr. Ferrero joined the Gardener, and he asked him:

- Can I have some basil herbs for tonight's soup? ... few stems will be enough ...

The Gardener replied immediately:

- I was about to cut some ... to allow new ones to grow ...

The Cook had a question that concerned him since the beginning of that day. He hesitated to speak to the Gardener about it. But after a few seconds of thinking, the Cook decided that his head will explode out of curiosity, if he didn't ask the Gardener:

- The ... the little girl ... the new Heiress ...

The Gardener had cut a few stems, he handed them to the Cook, while encouraging him to formulate his question:

- Yes? ... What is it about the new Heiress?

The Cook continued:

- Well ... she ... Do you think she is normal?

The Gardener stared at the Cook for a long moment; he couldn't understand his question. The Cook decided to explain:

- Her attitude is strange for an Heiress ... she washes her own dishes, she calls us Monsieur ... and she doesn't eat any of my refined cuisine! I Cucinato for her steamed salmon with oregano sauce!! Yet she didn't even touch it!! I hate capricious people!! ... Do you think she is normal?

The Gardener smiled at the Cook, and he affirmed with a confident voice:

- This little girl is much more than normal ... she may have strange and unusual manners, in our opinion... but she is a very special little girl!

Even if the Cook didn't understand the exact meaning of the Gardener's words, Mr. Ferrero Lutché took his herbs and he greeted the Gardener, returning back inside the grand Mansion.

When the Cook opened the outside door to the kitchen, he was surprised to discover a small silhouette sitting by the kitchen table; Dalya Bouvard was alone, eating toast bread, filled with butter, and she served herself a glass of milk. The Cook greeted her with a confused smile:

- Mademoiselle ...

Instantly, Dalya froze in her movements. She hesitated a few seconds before greeting the big man with a nice smile:

- Monsieur Ferrero.

The Cook put down his herbs on the kitchen table, and he began cutting the roots, and arranging the leaves. Straightaway, a wonderful delicious fresh smell invaded the entire kitchen. The Cook felt Dalya's stares and curiosity, he explained to her:

- It's called the Roman basil ... it's a fresh and beneficial herb ... I asked the Gardener to plant it in the garden, so I can use it more often ...
- You use it in cooked meals? asked Dalya
- Yes ... and its taste is delicious!! ... I chop the leaves and I use them in soups, also to add flavor to meals, even with meat ... or vegetables ...

The Cook handed to Dalya a small green leaf:

- Here ... taste this leaf ...

Dalya took the green leaf without hesitation, and as soon as she chewed it; her eyes became wide open and she exclaimed:

- It's very very good!! It's fresh!!

The Cook laughed:

- Yes! ... And it is a beneficial herb as well!! ... in herb or oil, the basil contains many vitamins ... it reduces hypertension and stress, it helps in digestion, reduces fever, protects the memory ...

Dalya continued eating her bread and milk, while listening carefully to the Cook's explanation about this herb. When he finished, Dalya smiled:

- It's fascinating! ... I always see Monsieur the Gardener carefully cares about this part of the garden ... but I never thought about tasting this herb!
- Well, all herbs are not for eating, Mademoiselle ... only a few are good to eat! ... The rest of the herbs are not to eat!

The Cook and Dalya exchanged an amused little laugh, for a moment. Dalya finished her bread and milk. But before she could stand up to wash her plate and glass, the Cook asked in a respectful voice, yet hesitantly:

- Mademoiselle ... may I know ... why don't you eat the lunch and dinner meals?

Dalya froze in her chair; she remained silent, seeking an adequate answer to this question. The Cook encouraged her to speak:

- You are eating bread and milk, now ... and yet you haven't touched your lunch meal, earlier ... is there something you dislike in the meals that I cook?

Dalya tried to answer:

- Your cuisine is ... very refined, Monsieur Ferrero ...

The Cook tried to understand:

- I've prepared for you lamb chops with white sauce ... steamed choux ... and a coffee cream ... don't you like it?

Dalya went all silent; she didn't know how to phrase her answer without offending Mr. Ferrero Lutché. The Cook stared at Dalya for a long moment, she didn't look like a capricious girl, yet her behavior was strange. The Cook insisted to understand:

- Would you like me to cook something else for you, Mademoiselle?

She had to reply, Dalya couldn't keep on refusing lunches and dinners. So then, the little girl gathered her courage, and she tried to explain:

- It's just ... your cuisine is very refined, Monsieur ...Thank you for cooking for me ... it really looks very delicious ... but ... if possible ... I prefer ... if you do not mind, of course ... meals less ... uh ... a cuisine ...

The Cook completed Dalya's sentence:

- An ordinary cuisine!

Dalya sighed with great relief:

- Yes, please!! If possible, Monsieur.

The Cook jumped out of his chair, he finally understood:

-   You don't like the pâté ... the lobster ... the duck!! That's why you didn't eat the lunches and dinners!! ... You ate only breakfasts, because they were made of ordinary ingredients ... bread, milk, eggs, fruit!!

The little girl stifled an innocent laugh. The Cook relaxed back on his chair and he stared at Dalya, with an astonished look:

-   And all this time ... I was working my brain off, to cook you the most refined dishes ... I ordered the salmon especially for you ... I almost lost a finger while boning the duck ... all this time ... while you only hoped for ordinary cuisine! ... Vegetables, chicken, meat, and ordinary dishes!

The Cook thought the girl was capricious. He was surprised to know that he was wrong about her. Dalya just wanted simpler food, like what most people eat.

The Cook laughed all amused, because he had finally understood the Gardener's words:

-   Special ... very special ...

The very next day. Thursday, December 17th, 1891.

Cristelle came back to the kitchen, holding Dalya Bouvard's dinner tray. When the Cook looked at it, he was delighted to see the dinner plates empty. Immediately, Cristelle exclaimed:

-   She ate her dinner entirely!!

The Cook let out an amused laugh. Cristelle still couldn't believe her eyes:

-   She even asked if there was still some spaghetti pasta with tomato sauce!! ... And she wants some more meat balls!!

While reserving her the second pasta dish, the Cook whispered to Cristelle, in a proud and amused voice:

-   I finally understood what she wanted to eat!!

Chapter 7

A thin difference

It was a rainy day. The sky poured buckets of rain since early this morning. A smell of freshness and earth arose from the ground. A cold wind blew gently and frequently. Winter reigned over the city of Georgetown.

Dalya's parents had returned to live in the annex house of the grand Mansion, under the strict instructions of the Lawyer, Mr. Sloan Wilfrid. And that day, the little twins were happy to join their older sister, in the living room of the grand Mansion. And although Dalya still had a lot of homework to do, she decided to spend some time with Ari and Adi.

The 3 sisters enjoyed creating origami paper figures. Dalya had found a book in the Library of the grand Mansion, explaining the art of folding a paper and turning it into several amusing figures.

Sitting on the floor on cushions, in front of the fireplace, Dalya focused on the book instructions, while folding the paper:

- So ... turn it like that ... then I have to fold the paper ... that's done ... and this piece of paper to get here ... okay ... and then ... I have to fold it up from this side ...

The snow Panther was lying down on a large chair, half asleep. She watched the three girls having fun. The little twins were sitting on the cushions too, and they were watching their older sister's moves, with a focused silence.

- This end to join with this one ... and the last step is to fold this part ... so that at the end ... we obtain a bird! ... There, it's done!

When Dalya gave the bird paper to her little sisters, the twins exclaimed all fascinated, their eyes wide open:

- Ooh!! It's Zoli!! ... Bird paper!! ... Zoli!!
- We want another Dindin!! ... Another Dindin!!

Dalya turned a few pages of the book:

- So, we did a butterfly, a boat, a flower, and now a bird ... what can we still produce?
- That Dindin!! Adi exclaimed, while pointing out at the book.
- This is a fox ... it seems difficult to do. Dalya replied.
- And that ... Zoli fish!! Ari asked, pointing to a drawing on a page.

Dalya thought for a moment, studying the drawing:

- The fish also seems complicated ... its figures are round ...

On that moment, a silhouette entered the living room. It was Océanie, the help cook of the grand Mansion. She placed a tray on the table, and she addressed Dalya coldly:

- The Cook serves you hot chocolate with marshmallows.

Immediately, the little twins jumped out of their cushions:

- Socolate!
- Masmallow!

Dalya smiled:

- It's very nice, thank you Océanie.

Océanie's face didn't display any warm expression. For some reason that Dalya didn't know, Océanie didn't like Dalya, much less her presence in the grand Mansion. Since the first day she has arrived in the annex house, Dalya always felt the arrogant and haughty stares of Océanie Shell on her. And yet, Dalya kept a polite attitude toward the help cook.

Océanie served two cups of hot chocolate to the little twins, and she said in a cold voice:

- The Cook asks whether your sisters will join lunch with you today ... to prepare the cutlery in the dining room ...

Except that before Dalya could answer this question, someone entered the living room of the grand Mansion, by the garden back door. It was Dalya's father, Mr. Antman Bouvard. Without addressing a single glance at Dalya, Antman Bouvard asked the little twins, in a kind tone:

- It's time to go back home, my little ones!

The little twins exclaimed:

- Go home now?
- Play a more bit with Dindin?

Mr. Antman knelt in front of Ari and Adi, and he smiled:

- Your mother prepared lunch already. It will be served in half an hour.

The little twins quickly swallowed their last hot chocolate drops. Dalya asked her father:

- I can take them back myself to the ann...

Antman completely ignored Dalya's presence. He made the little twins wear small waterproof hats:

- Wear this ... I'll walk you under the umbrella ... it rains a lot today!

The twin adjusted the hats over their heads, they put on their boots, and they kissed their older sister:

- Goodbye Dindin!!
- Bisou Dindin!!

Antman Bouvard opened his umbrella, and he carried the twins out, under the pouring rain. Dalya remained silent observing her father, walking toward the annex house.

Since the beginning of the Challenges, Dalya's father had changed his attitude toward his daughter. He was upset not to have access to the inheritance's fortune, and especially as fast as he had wished for. And after the Lawyer Mr. Wilfrid's threats, Dalya's father either looked at her angrily, or he ignored her completely, pretending she didn't exist. Despite the many occasions where Dalya tried to approach her father and talk to him, she faced a wall of contempt and silence from Antman Bouvard.

The help cook Océanie took back her tray, and she left the living room, leaving Dalya alone, still sitting in front of the fireplace.

The same day. Several hours later, in the afternoon.

The Geography Professor gave his students a long list of 40 words to search for and explain. Dalya hardly managed to find the first 6 words from the list, and she still had 34 more words. And even though the class was difficult, Dalya's determination to pass the Geography course, only increased.

Comfortably sitting in front of a desk in the grand Mansion's Library, Dalya would sometimes flip through some big books on her desk table, and sometimes she searched for other books on the Library shelves.

At a moment, two silhouettes entered the Library. Instantly, Dalya greeted them politely:

- Good evening, Océanie... Good evening, Igor...

The young girl and the young man exchanged an amused look, and they saluted bowing their heads. Océanie and Igor headed toward the big fireplace of the Library. Océanie took out her towels and she began to clean up the edges of the fireplace, while Igor was arranging the wood inside.

And while Dalya used a small ladder to reach a Geography book on a top shelf, she heard the conversation of the two employees. Océanie murmured:

- She is strange and abnormal, that girl ... I knew it from the first day I saw her in ... don't you remember?

Igor let out a discreet laugh:

- Yes! You guessed right! But I had no idea that she would wash her own dishes ... I had a hard time believing it!

Océanie asked in a tone curious:

- You think she would have washed our dishes, too? If they were in the kitchen sink?
- Certainly, she would have done it!!

Dalya pulled out her book, and she returned to her desk, pretending not to hear the whispers and giggles of the two employees, a few steps away from her. Dalya focused on her homework:

- Urbanization is ... the growing concentration of ... the ... population around ...

Océanie took a second towel, and she spoke in a lower voice:

- And yet, her parents are far stranger than her!!

Igor giggled:

- Well, the mother is silent and calm ...

Océanie's eyes were widened:

- Calm?! ... This woman is a monster! ... She has a diabolic stare! ... Did you forget that she was beating her daughter like a dog in the garage of the annex house?!

Igor confirmed:

- Yes! Yes! I remember that! It took me some time to understand why that girl wore gloves under August's heat! ... Her mother is a demon!

Océanie whispered:

- I wonder what would have happened to this girl, if the Lawyer Wilfrid hadn't stopped the mother ...

Igor thought aloud:

- She certainly would have kept beating her, until her daughter would lose her fingers ...

Océanie was outraged:

- And the father is not an angel either! ... Apparently, he made his daughter work day and night, regardless of her classes at school! ... I even heard that he was taking the money of the bags she used to sell at the market ...

Igor was surprised:

- What kind of father takes advantage of his daughter, that much? He believed the inheritance's fortune belongs to him! Thankfully Mr. Wilfrid clearly explained that to him!

Océanie replied:

- It is quite normal Igor! What can you expect from an addict of card games? ... He lost his entire salary to the risky gambling; instead of feeding his family ... it is pretty obvious he will take advantage of his daughter!

Igor sighed in a surprised tone:

- What a family! ... They don't deserve to be paren...

When suddenly, a little voice interrupted Océanie and Igor's conversation. Dalya came close to the fireplace, and she spoke to the two young people, in a very calm and polite voice:

- My parents are not perfect people. It is true that they did mean things. Nevertheless ... they remain the parents who gave birth to me. Whether they are good or bad people, I would be grateful if you avoid talking about my parents, in a mean and inappropriate way ... at least in my presence.

Igor became pale, realizing instantly that his words were rude. But Océanie did not bother the slightest; she let out an amused and insolent laugh:

- But ... we have said only the truth!

Straightaway, Dalya looked at Océanie, and she replied in a sure voice:

- Except that this truth, I know it very well, for having already lived it ... there is no need to remind me of it.

And before leaving the grand Mansion's Library, Dalya turned back to the two employees:

- And Océanie ... there is a thin difference between telling the truth, and stirring the knife in the wound.

Chapter 8

The Christmas tree

Saturday, December 19th, 1891. In the grand Mansion.

Dalya had completed her Mathematics homework. She had only a few research questions left in the Geography and History courses.

Her classmate Amira joined her, almost every day in the grand Mansion's Library. And the two girls worked studiously all day, while being served lunches and snacks by Cristelle. And since her first day at the grand Mansion, the snow Panther followed Dalya everywhere. Séraphine used to lay down on the Persian rugs or the luxurious chairs, and she watched the two students work, until she would fall asleep.

- I need a break. My head is full. Amira sighed while lying back on her chair.
- I agree with you. We worked very well these days. Dalya closed her Geography notebook, before continuing:
- Would you like to take a walk in the garden? ... Have some fresh air?

Amira didn't need to be asked twice. She jumped out of her chair right away. The two girls left the Library, followed by the snow Panther. Barely have they walked outside the grand Mansion's door, Dalya and her friend met the Gardener. Mr. Rosenwald was pushing an immense tree over a carriage.

- Good morning, Monsieur. Dalya said, holding the door open for him.
- Good morning, Monsieur. Amira repeated, imitating her friend and holding the other door open.

The tree was very long, wrapped in a cloth and bound by ropes. The Gardener was a strong and robust man, and yet he struggled to push the carriage.

- Good morning ... to you ... Mesd ... Mesdemoiselles ...
- Where are you heading the tree to? asked Dalya
- Toward the ... living room ...

Dalya and her friend surpassed the Gardener, they opened the living room doors wide open, and they moved a chair and a small table on his way. The Gardener let in the carriage to the living room, hardly avoiding a vase. He stopped in a corner, near a large window.

After a few minutes, the Gardener managed to raise the tree, and release it of its strings. The Christmas tree almost touched the ceiling, it was huge, fresh green color, a smell of earth and pine immediately invaded the living room, stems and branches were robust. Never the two little girls have seen such splendor of nature.

- It's ... a beautiful tree!! Exclaimed Amira.
- Yes, magnificent!! Dalya was also amazed.
- And the best of the entire city. Replied the Gardener, proudly. The late Mr. Governor greatly enjoyed this holiday.

The Gardener picked up his carriage and was about to leave the living room, when a cheerful voice interrupted him:

- Ah!! Thank you for bringing the tree so early this year!! Cristelle exclaimed, adding:
- And especially thank you for not making a mess on the floor, Mr. Rosenwald. I still have not forgiven Igor, about the disaster he made on the carpet, when he entered the tree, last year!

The Gardener let out a discreet little laugh. He greeted Cristelle, and then he left the living room. Cristelle approached the two girls:

- Are you having a break, Mesdemoiselles?
- Yes, we have almost finished our homework. Amira said.
- Our heads were overloaded. We needed a pause. Dalya laughed.
- And you've earned it, both of you! Cristelle said. You worked very hard these past days!!

Cristelle walked inside the living room, and she took out of a corner, several boxes in different forms:

- Mesdemoiselles ... what do you think of decorating the Christmas tree yourselves?

Dalya and Amira exchanged a happily surprised look. Amira had a very small Christmas tree, for her and her father. And it took them five to ten minutes to put the ornaments on it. So to decorate this immense tree, Amira jumped joyfully, and she didn't need to be asked twice. She immediately opened one of the ornaments' boxes that Cristelle offered them.

Dalya Bouvard hesitated for a moment. In previous years, her father used to bring a skinny and almost nude little Christmas tree. And because they were poor, Dalya decorated the tree with her little sisters, by using ornaments she made herself; wood stars, cotton moons, figures in fabrics, picked up flowers.

Except on that day, it was the first time in her life that Dalya had to decorate an immense real Christmas tree, with precious and luxurious ornaments; gold and silver stars, crystal figurines, porcelain flowers. And despite having spent several days and nights in this house, the little Dalya Bouvard was still struggling to get used to her new life ... at the grand Mansion.

Suddenly, a loud noise entered the living room of the Grand Mansion:

- DINDIN!! DINDIN!! DINDIN!! DINDIN!!

The two little twin sisters ran toward Dalya and jumped to her neck. The Gardener followed them and he entered the living room:

- They were looking for you, Mademoiselle. I let them inside.

Dalya thanked the Gardener with a smile, before he left. The little twins were happy to see their older sister; they were jumping and yelling her name. These last few days, and because of her homework, Dalya could visit her little sisters only few times, and the 3 sisters missed each other.

- Dindin!! Dindin!! Play now with us, today?

Dalya laughed at her little sisters:

- Alright, we can play today. But first, you need to say hello to my friends.

Dalya approached her classmate:

- Here is Amira Mounier. She studies at the same school as me. Say hello to her.

Amira knelt in front of the little sisters. Instantly, the little twins hugged Amira in their little arms, letting out a merry laugh:

- Mia!! Mia!! Mia!!
- Amira ... it's Amira!! Dalya corrected them.
- Mia!! Mia!! The little twins insisted.

Amira exclaimed:

- Your little sisters are adorable!!! They are such cuties!!!
- It depends on the day ... they regularly make fooleries. Dalya sighed.

Amira laughed at her friend's answer, and then she whispered to the little twins with a cheerful tone:

- You can call me Mia ... it's a lovely name. So ... who's Ari? And who is Adi?

The twins jumped simultaneously:

- Me Ari!
- Me Adi!

It is true that the twins looked identical, always wearing the same clothes, and always speaking simultaneously. It was almost impossible to separate them one from the other. Amira stared at them for a long second, and as expected, she failed to tell them apart from each other. Dalya presented to her little sisters:

- Say hello to Cristelle. She works here at the grand Mansion.

The little twins approached Cristelle, who kneeled down in front of them, and they kissed her on the cheek, simultaneously. Cristelle exclaimed:

- Your little sisters are very polite and lovely, Mademoiselle.

36

Dalya could barely hold an amused laugh. The twins asked Cristelle:

- You live here istelle?
- It's Cristelle ... not istelle ... Cristelle!! Dalya sighed.
- I love istelle!! The maid of the grand Mansion laughed.

The afternoon in the living room of the grand Mansion went on in a cheerful tone. Dalya, Amira and the little twins decorated the immense Christmas tree. The maid Cristelle brought them hot chocolate and several plates of delicious cookies. And at every opened box, all the girls exclaimed and laughed, while discovering the beautiful ornaments and luxurious decorations.

At a moment, during laughs and exclamations, Cristelle announced to Dalya:

- Mademoiselle, Mr. Sloan Wilfrid came to see you.

Dalya stood up and she greeted him with a happy smile:

- Good morning Monsieur Wilfrid.

When he entered the living room, the Lawyer was amazed by the immense tree:

- Good morning Mademoiselle ... well ... well ... what a beautiful tree you have here!!
- Monsieur the Gardener brought it inside, today. And Cristelle gave us the boxes of ornaments to decorate it. Dalya replied while greeting him.

Immediately, Lyor Laszlo also entered the living room. He seemed in a very bad mood ... and especially he seemed to have accumulated several sleepless nights. And as usual, he didn't even greet Dalya. Lyor walked in and he sat down on a chair, he started reading his newspaper, ignoring everyone and everything happening inside the living room.

Dalya almost got used to the rudeness and unsociable character of Lyor. The lawyer Sloan Wilfrid asked Dalya:

- I am reassured to know that you are not bored. You have some good visits today, at the grand Mansion.
- Yes, Monsieur. This is my friend, Amira Mounier; she studies with me at school. And we work together on our holiday homework, here in the grand Mansion's Library.

Instantly, Amira greeted him. Wilfrid smiled back at her:

- I am delighted to meet you Miss Amira. And I am glad that Mademoiselle Dalya has a good friend.

Amira Mounier blushed at the compliment, and she whispered a thank you before returning to sit down and continue her decorating.

- And ... here are my little sisters ... Ari and Adi ...

Wilfrid knelt in front of the little twins:

- Ari and Adi ... I finally have the pleasure to meet them ... finally!

Dalya waved at them to approach, and the little twins obeyed. Dalya explained to her sisters:

- This is Mr. Sloan Wilfrid. He is a Lawyer, and he takes cares of us.

The little twins stared at the gentleman kneeling in front of them, for a long minute. Then they exchanged a strange look. Since always, Dalya's little sisters could understand each other, without speaking.

Suddenly, the little twins jumped, they hugged Sloan Wilfrid and they screamed joyfully:

- Frite!! Frite!! Frite!!

Wilfrid was taken aback by the reaction of the two little girls; however he hugged them back, happy to have a surprise cuddle.

- No! No! No! It's not funny! Yelled Dalya upset.
- Frite!! Frite!! Frite!!

Wilfrid let out an amused and a curious laugh:

- Why do they keep saying Frite?

Dalya grabbed her two little sisters' hands, and she was embarrassed to answer this question:

- It's ... it's you, Monsieur.

Still kneeling on the ground, adjusting his tie, Wilfrid looked up at Dalya:

- How? ... Frite?
- They are little, Monsieur. They enjoy inventing words for everything ... and everyone. But I try to teach th...
- Frite!! Frite!! Frite!! The little twins laughed their heart out, without succeeding to break away from their older sister's hands.

Wilfrid was surprised by this news. He addressed the little twins with an amused smile:

- The young Mesdemoiselles have decided I am Frite, instead of Wilfrid ... and therefore, it will be so!

The Lawyer stood up and he smiled at Dalya:

- I always thought my name sounded too serious ... Frite makes me look younger!

Dalya was embarrassed by her sisters' foolishness, but she laughed at Mr. Wilfrid's answer. When she let go of her little sisters' hands, the twins went back to their places, in the middle of the opened boxes, and they continued decorating the tree with Amira.

- I would like to talk to you, for a minute, Mademoiselle. Wilfrid addressed Dalya in a serious tone.

He moved away some steps from the immense tree, and he asked:

- I came especially to check on you, today. Is everything going well here, in the grand Mansion? Are the employees treating you well?
- Yes, Monsieur.
- The employees have strict orders to ensure your comfort. Their job is to serve you.
- They do, Monsieur. All the employees are very nice to me.
- When are you going back to school?
- January 04th, Monsieur. After the holidays. I have almost finished my homework.
- Good ... good ... and your parents? Has there been any problem with them?
- No, Monsieur. I had a lot of homework, so I have visited them a few times only. And ... they have not spoken to me, since I've been living alone in the grand Mansion.
- I understand. But a little distance will be beneficial to your parents. It's better that way, believe me.

A question was burning Dalya lips. Yet, she dared to ask:

- Monsieur Wilfrid ... I was wondering ... forgive my curiosity ... but how did you convince the Lawyer Mr. Ernest Laszlo to let me live in the grand Mansion?

Sloan Wilfrid barely held an amused laugh and an innocent pride:

- Among my many gifts, manipulating is my most productive quality. I convinced Ernest Laszlo to allow you to live in the grand Mansion, so as to keep an eye on you, and better predict your success or failure in the upcoming Challenges.

Of all the possible answers, Dalya could have never guessed this approach. A surprised giggle got away from Dalya. Wilfrid continued to explain:

- The only thing I forgot to mention to Ernest Laszlo ... is the main reason for keeping you in the grand Mansion ... to preserve you away from any harm and abuse. Protecting you is my mission, Mademoiselle Dalya Bouvard!

Dalya would be eternally grateful to Mr. Sloan Wilfrid for defending and protecting her. She smiled back at him.

Sloan Wilfrid stared for a moment at Lyor Laszlo who got up from his chair. Lyor seemed bored to death; the young apprentice approached the tree and he admired an ornament hanging on a branch. Amira and the little twins were opening a few more boxes, laughing and exclaiming while discovering the beautiful ornaments.

Wilfrid continued his conversation, still in a low and serious voice:

- And given your current situation, I prefer that you spend the Christmas holiday here, at the grand Mansion. The employees have already been notified to prepare everything for you!
- Yes, Monsieur.

Dalya felt a twinge in her heart. Spending Christmas alone in the grand Mansion? It sounded sad. But Mr. Sloan Wilfrid was right. It would be better for Dalya to keep some distance from her parents. And if Antman and Augustine Bouvard were determined not to talk to her, during the Christmas dinner, then it would be better for Dalya to stay alone.

- About ... the Third Question. I am aware that you still have 12 more months to submit to the Challenge. It is too early to be concerned. However ... it is important that you pay attention to all the clues that are offered to you. You did a great job during the two previous rounds. So keep it up!
- I will do my best, Monsieur.

At this instant, Wilfrid took out an envelope from his jacket and he gave it to Dalya:

- This is a little Christmas gift ... for you ... it's a bit too early to offer it to you ... but as the tradition goes, I prefer that you don't open it until the Christmas day ...

Dalya was moved and touched by the gesture and kindness of Mr. Wilfrid, she smiled at him:

- You have already done so much for me, Monsieur ...
- I have done nothing more than what you really deserve. Wilfrid interrupted her.
- Thank you, Monsieur ... thank you, very much. And I promise not to open it before!

Wilfrid observed the other people in the living room. The little twins were eating cakes with their hands. Amira filled their cups with hot chocolate. Lyor was standing alone in front of the Christmas tree, admiring the ornaments that the girls had hung. Sloan Wilfrid affirmed in a serious voice:

- Mademoiselle Dalya ... I would like to remind you, that I am always available for you ... in whatsoever ... I must be notified of anything that worries you!

Dalya hesitated for a moment, and then she dared to say:

- It's just ... the Panther ...
- Yes? What is it with her?
- The snow Panther follows me everywhere, Monsieur Wilfrid. Séraphine insists to sleep in the same room as me, on the carpet in front of the fireplace. Cristelle and the Gardener tried to move her ... but she doesn't let me alone, for a second.

Sloan Wilfrid smiled, observing the snow Panther half-asleep, on a divan in the living room:

- Séraphine doesn't seem to wish you any harm. I even think she insists on watching over you, and protecting you. A maternal instinct, I suppose. She followed the late Mr. Governor, in all of his trips.
- She doesn't frighten me. It's just ... being followed by a Snow Panther; all the time ... it's strange.

Wilfrid laughed:

-   Yes, I admit that this is not an ordinary thing! It doesn't happen to everyone to be protected by a Snow Panther! ... But, you'll get used to it!

Dalya smiled at Mr. Wilfrid and she offered him a cup of hot chocolate and cakes. He happily answered without hesitation:

-   Gladly!

The ornaments boxes didn't seem to end. There were hundreds of them. And the immense Christmas tree hasn't reach a quarter of its decoration. Amira stored the empty boxes in a corner, in order to open new ones. Dalya served Mr. Wilfrid a cup of hot chocolate. Lyor was still standing in front of the Christmas tree, admiring some ornaments. The little twins were busy examining a piece of ornament, and they seemed to have a serious discussion between them:

-   Is a butterfly?
-   No bird ...
-   But big wings
-   Yes ... has bird's beak too
-   Like butterfly
-   Looky ... has legs!
-   Butterfly has no legs?
-   Bird has legs
-   Ah yes ...

A serious and cold voice manifested itself for the first time since joining in, and interrupted the conversation of the little twins:

-   It's an eagle!

The little twins turned toward the source of the voice. Lyor returned to sit on one of the chairs, and he repeated his words:

-   It's an eagle ... it has big wings, legs and a big beak. The ornament is too small, it is not visible enough.

The little twins observed the young Lyor Laszlo, while he took back his newspaper to read. Sloan Wilfrid sat down on a chair near the little twins, and he made the necessary introductions:

-   Mesdemoiselles Ari and Adi ... I present to you Lyor Laszlo ... he is the legal guardian of your older sister.

Lyor sighed with an angry tone. Dalya coldly looked at Lyor, before serving cakes to Mr. Wilfrid. And in a whispered and amused voice, Sloan Wilfrid said to the little twins:

-   And Lyor is always in a bad mood. One should not provoke Lyor.

The little twins had their eyes all wide open, for a few seconds, they stared in silence at Lyor reading the newspaper. Then, in an instant, Adi and Ari jumped and screamed joyfully, pointing at Lyor Laszlo:

- Riri!! Riri!! Riri!!

Amira turned back to her friend:

- Dalya ... what do they mean by Riri?

Dalya couldn't dare to answer that question. Mr. Wilfrid instantly understood what the little twins meant. He didn't hide his amused laugh, while addressing Lyor:

- Lyor ... congratulations on your new nickname!

Lyor looked up from the newspaper:

- My nickna... what?

The little twins jumped around Lyor's chair, just like parasite bees, yelling with all their might:

- Riri!! Riri!! Riri!!

Lyor didn't like to be mocked:

- No way am I to be called Riri ... Lyor!! ... It's Lyor!!

Amira laughed at this scene, she whispered to Dalya:

- He asked for it, being rude and arrogant since his arrival in this living room.
- Yes, I admit that my little sisters paid him back his politeness!

And for the rest of the afternoon, Sloan Wilfrid, Amira Mounier and Dalya Bouvard, they all enjoyed decorating the immense Christmas tree ... and also watching Lyor about to explode in rage, while the little twins sang joyfully:

- Riri ... Riri ... Riri ...
- Lyor!! It's Lyor!! In how many languages should I tell you that?
- Riri ... Riri ... Riri ...

Chapter 9

Making your own bed

Monday, December 21st, 1891. The morning, at the grand Mansion.

Océanie was the last employee to finish her breakfast that morning. Still sitting in front of the large kitchen table, Océanie slowly sipped her favorite bowl of oats, honey and almonds. The Cook was already preparing the ingredients for that day's lunch. The Gardener went out to start his work in the garden. Cristelle picked up the breakfast's plates and cutlery, and she put them in the kitchen's sink. And Igor was reading the last few paragraphs of the newspaper.

When the head of the grand Mansion came into the kitchen, he announced:

- Cristelle ... the chimneys need to be cleaned of ashes, so that Igor could light the fireplaces tonight.

While placing the last plates in the sink, Cristelle replied:

- Understood, Monsieur! ... I will start cleaning them right away!

Continuing his guidelines of the day's work, Mr. Bûchebois addressed Igor:

- We need some shopping from downtown today ... the Cook will give you a list ... and then I will tell you what we more need ...

Igor closed his newspaper, and he replied:

- Right away, Monsieur ... I'll put my coat on ...

Océanie was waiting to know her work, and the head of the grand Mansion turned toward her:

- Since Cristelle will be busy cleaning the ashes of all the chimneys ... you'll take care of Mademoiselle's bedroom this morning ...

Swallowing her last spoonful of oatmeal, Océanie replied:

- Yes, Monsieur.

The day's work program been established, all the employees were getting busy at their tasks.

A few minutes later, Igor was back in the kitchen, wearing his coat and hat. He sat down at the kitchen table while the Cook dictated him the shopping needed from downtown. Cristelle had arranged her coal bucket, rags and brushes. She wore her apron and was about to leave the kitchen. The head of the grand Mansion was sitting in a corner of the kitchen, shining his shoes.

When Océanie came back to the kitchen, just a few minutes after receiving directions of the day's work, the head of the grand Mansion asked her curiously:

- You arranged Mademoiselle's bedroom already?

Océanie displayed a lost attitude. All the employees of the grand Mansion then turned around toward Océanie. They were all curious on why she returned to the kitchen, so quickly. Océanie finally said in a confused voice:

- It's just ... I ... I was in the girl's bedroom... but everything was tidy ... the bed was intact ...

Igor wondered aloud:

- But if the bed is intact ... where did she sleep then?

Cristelle lowered her head in her apron, and she tried to appear invisible. Except that Océanie could not hold back her curiosity, she asked Cristelle:

- You have been cleaning this little girl's bedroom, since the first day she came here ... where does she sleep?

Cristelle's cheeks blushed, and she tried to speak naturally:

- Mademoiselle sleeps in her bed, of course!! This is an absurd question!!

The head of the grand Mansion and the Cook exchanged a confused look. Cristelle was not very good at lying. The Cook asked:

- So ... how is it possible that the bed is intact?

Cristelle searched for any words to escape this situation. Except that Igor surpassed everyone, thinking aloud:

- If she sleeps in the bed ... and the bed is intact ... so ... she makes her own bed, after having slept in it!

Cristelle had firmly kept this secret, since the first night of Dalya Bouvard in the grand Mansion. She had realized this the very next day. Except that Cristelle didn't dare to tell anyone, fearing their reactions to this so unusual attitude.

The head of the grand Mansion jumped out of his chair:

- An Heiress who cleans her bedroom and make her own bed, herself!

The Cook choked:

- Never have I heard such a thing!! Mai qualcosa Del genere!!

Océanie let out a surprised laugh:

- An employer ... who washes the dishes and cleans her own bedroom!! ... It's ridiculous!! ... This little girl is years away to learn good manners!!

At this moment, Cristelle got angry toward Océanie:

- And what do you prefer? ... An employer who leaves her bedroom upside down, neglected and messy? ... Because making your own bed has become bad manners now?!

The head of the grand Mansion replied in a shocked tone:

- But ... still, Cristelle ... she is an Heiress ... she is not supposed to make her bed ... it's our job!

Cristelle lowered the tone of her voice, and she affirmed:

- Yes, Monsieur ... you are absolutely right, and I understand ... it's just that it would take Mademoiselle a little more time to learn the new habits of her new life ... just a little more time ...

Igor said to Océanie, in an amused laugh:

- Just a little more time to learn the new habits!

Océanie laughed loudly:

- This girl is years away to become a Lady!

Chapter 10

Christmas in the grand Mansion

Friday, December 25th, 1891. Christmas Day. In the Grand Mansion.

When Cristelle opened the bedroom's door, she found Dalya awake and already sitting in the little living room. The snow Panther was standing on her feet, admiring the large garden covered in snow, through the bedroom's windows.

- Good morning Mademoiselle!! Merry Christmas!!
- Good morning Cristelle ... Merry Christmas to you too!

Cristelle stepped toward the window, and she fully opened the curtains:

- It promises to be a great celebration day, today!!

Dalya was busy wrapping gifts. She told Cristelle:

- These are gifts for my little sisters ... I made them dolls in cotton fabrics ... and wool hair... I think they'll be pleased to have new dolls ...

The maid of the grand Mansion approached to observe one of the dolls:

- They will be happy with your gifts, Mademoiselle ... you are very good at making toys!! ... The dolls are very pretty!!

Dalya smiled at Cristelle, before finishing wrapping her gifts. Cristelle added a log in the fireplace, and then she asked:

- Where would you like to have your breakfast, Mademoiselle?
- In the Library ... please. I still have one History homework to finish, and I will be free for the next days.
- Alright, Mademoiselle.
- I'll take these gifts to my sisters now, and then I will go to the Library.
- Perfect! It will give me enough time to prepare your breakfast.

A few minutes later, Dalya Bouvard left the grand Mansion and headed toward the annex house, where her parents lived. The Panther was following her like a shadow. Once Dalya approached the house, two small silhouettes ran to greet her with joyful screams:

- Dindin!! Dindin!! Dindin!!
- Good morning Ari!! Good morning Adi!! Dalya hugged them firmly, before offering them their gifts:
- Here are your gifts ... Merry Christmas!!

\- Mici Dindin!! Mici Dindin!! Merry kissmas too!! Mici Dindin!!

The twins hugged and kissed their older sister, and they quickly opened their gifts. And by hearing their joyful yells and jumps, Dalya was happy that the made-up dolls pleased her little sisters.

At an instant, another silhouette came out of the annex house. It was Antman Bouvard, Dalya's father.

\- Merry Christmas father ... I came to bring Ari and Adi some gif...

Dalya didn't finish her sentence, her father looked at her with an icy stare, and then he headed to the garage. Dalya was sad that her father had become cold and formal with her. When a woman voice was heard:

\- Ari ... Adi ... come back home ... it's cold!! ... I don't want you to fall il...

Mrs. Augustine Bouvard, Dalya's mother appeared on the entrance door of the annex house. She was unaware that Dalya came to visit them. She froze in her place; her face went pale and her lips mute.

\- Good morning mother. Merry Christmas.

Dalya's mother hesitated a few seconds, and then she turned and escaped inside the annex house. Dalya wasn't expecting any greetings from her mother. Even when she lived with her mother, Dalya never received back greetings to her Good mornings.

Dalya knelt and she spoke to her little sisters in a serious tone:

\- Don't do any fooleries, alright? ... Behave well with mom and dad. Promise?
\- Yes!! Yes!! Promise!! Behave!!
\- Go on ... get back inside the house now ... and have fun with your dolls!! ... I'll come and see you tomorrow ...

The little twins kissed their older sister and ran inside the annex house, jumping joyfully, holding dearly their new dolls.

\- *Monsieur Wilfrid was quite right.* Dalya said to herself. *It would be better for my parents and my little sisters that I spend Christmas away from them.*

Few minutes later, Dalya returned back to the grand Mansion, and she opened the door of the Library. The large fireplace was well lit, warming the immense room. The snow Panther was lying on a chair. When Dalya sat down at the desk, she opened her History book. A heavy and weighing silence invaded the Library. Only the fire flames emitted a slight noise. Nothing announced that it was a celebration day...

After several long seconds starring at her book, Dalya had an idea. She picked up her papers, pens and her History book, and she left the Library of the grand Mansion.

In the kitchen, Mr. Ferrero Lutché was taking out of the oven a pudding dish, in a very prudent move. Océanie was sitting in front of the big table, busy cleaning the cutlery for the festive dinner that day. Cristelle was preparing a breakfast tray. Igor was polishing his shoes in the corner.

- I wonder how the Congressman's feast will be tonight. Océanie wondered aloud.
- Last year's Christmas party was so huge; they had to recruit help to serve all the guests! Exclaimed Igor.
- I was told that there were fish dishes. Said the Cook.
- Really? Cristelle exclaimed. A Christmas with fish dishes, it might be a strange festive dinner.
- Yes! The entire menu was in fish. Igor replied. There was shrimp soup, caviar amuse-bouche, tuna mini-sandwiches, sol ...
- But it's not Christmas then? The Cook blenched.
- Anyway, I am happy not to have a lot of work today. Océanie sighed, relaxing on her chair. Imagine if we had 200 guests, like in the Congressman's party of last year.
- It would have been terrible to serve 200 guests!! I would have certainly passed out!! Igor Laughed starting to polish his other pair of shoe.
- I wonder how many guests the Congressman will have again this year. Wondered the Cook.
- Probably the same number as the last ye...

Cristelle stopped at the presence of someone in the kitchen. The little Dalya Bouvard entered and she greeted all the employees with a friendly smile:

- Good morning. Merry Christmas to you.

The Cook, Igor and Océanie all answered simultaneously, in a whisper:

- Merry Christmas, Mademoiselle.

Cristelle approached the little girl:

- I was about to bring you the breakfast tray to the Library, Mademoiselle. It will be ready in a moment.

Dalya put her notebooks and pens on the dining table, in the kitchen:

- I thought maybe I could take breakfast here ... if you do not mind.

All the employees froze in their movements. No one dared to say a word. They were disturbed by the strange and unusual ways of the little girl.

Given the silence of all the employees, Dalya stepped forward and sat down on a chair, she opened her books and began her last History homework. Cristelle, all puzzled, began to warm the bread toast for Dalya. Océanie and Igor exchanged a surprised look, while continuing their work in total silence. The Cook sprinkled his pudding with caramelized sugar, throwing curious glances at the strange little girl sitting at the kitchen table.

- Igor ... I need you to fill the woods of the chimney in the Libra...

The head of the grand Mansion, Mr. Bûchebois entered the kitchen, and he froze in front of a very unusual scene before him. He came close to Dalya in slow steps, and he said in a respectful voice:

- Good morning Mademoiselle.

Dalya raised her head and she smiled back at him:

- Good morning Mr. Bûchebois ... Merry Christmas.

The head of the grand Mansion seemed struck by this attitude. His words stumbled:

- I ... yes ... Good morning ... Merry Christmas to you too, Mademoiselle. May I ask what you are doing?
- I am finishing my History homework, Monsieur. Dalya replied naturally.

Océanie could hardly hold back her amused laugh. It was a faraway response than what Mr. Bûchebois asked for. The head of the grand Mansion rephrased his question:

- Yes ... I understand ... but I wanted to know what are you doing here, in the kitchen, Mademoiselle?
- Oh yes ... sorry, Monsieur ... I am taking my breakfast here in the kitchen. While at the same time, I am finishing my History homework.

The naturalness and spontaneity of the little girl disarmed the head of the grand Mansion. Igor let out a giggle. And immediately, Mr. Bûchebois shot him with a threatening look. The head of the employees turned back to Dalya, and he resumed his question for the third time:

- Yes, I noticed that ... but I wanted to know why does Mademoiselle want to take her breakfast in the kitchen?

Dalya reflected for a long second. Then she pronounced the only answer she could find:

- Why not?

This time, the Cook himself could not restrain his laughter. The head of the grand Mansion seemed confused and deadlocked. He thought for a few seconds, and he spoke to the little girl in a formal tone, carefully choosing his words:

- Mademoiselle … the meals will be served to you, in the dining room, in the Library, in the living room, or even in your bedroom. You cannot take your meals, here in the kitchen.

Dalya stared at him with a confused look; she didn't understand the logic of Mr. Bûchebois. Instantly, Cristelle stepped forward and she spoke to the head of the employees, with an imploring voice:

- It is a holiday, Mr. Bûchebois. Couldn't she have her meal here? With us, instead of being alone?

The head of the grand Mansion answered Cristelle with a thoughtful tone:

- I am sorry, Cristelle ... but no ... she is the Heiress of the Late Mr. Governor ... her place is not in the kitchen with the employees. Please escort Mademoiselle, right away, wherever she wants to take her meal.

Dalya silently picked up her notebooks and pens, her throat tightened, and her cheeks went pale. Before leaving the kitchen, Mr. Bûchebois addressed Dalya:

- All the employees of the grand Mansion are at your service, Mademoiselle. From now on, if you need anything, it is unnecessary to come to the kitchen. Please let us know, by ringing the bell. There's one in every room of the Mansion.

In the Library, Dalya sat in front of the desk. She couldn't understand why he wasn't allowed to eat in the kitchen with the other employees. But she didn't dare to ask more explanations or upset the head of the grand Mansion. The snow Panther emitted a strange sad meow, while lying down by the fireplace. Without even talking, it looked like the Panther felt Dalya's sadness.

After a few minutes, Cristelle entered with the breakfast tray:

- I'm so sorry for what happened, Mademoiselle!!
- It's nothing, Cristelle. Dalya tried to smile.
- You are very kind and polite, Mademoiselle. But you must understand that your status has changed now. You are the Heiress of this grand Mansion. And employers never share meals with the employees.

Dalya didn't know what to answer. And Cristelle sighed sadly:

- I understand that the change is difficult and new for you. But you'll get used to it, Mademoiselle.

Dalya smiled back at her, before taking the cup of milk that was served to her. Cristelle left the Library, throwing discreet glances full of empathy at the little girl ... all lonely, in a Christmas day.

The rest of the day passed calmly. Dalya finished her entire History homework in a few hours. She ate her lunch. Then she chose a book to read, in order to spend the rest of the day. She lay on a divan in front of the fireplace. The snow Panther was sometimes stuttering, lying too, near the fireplace in the Library.

Perhaps because of the heat from the fireplace, or tiredness of having finished all her homework, or sadness to spend a holiday alone ... at least for one of these reasons, Dalya had a long nap this afternoon. And the dream she had, was very strange; Dalya dreamed of being replicated in 12 identical copies, they all were riding back horses of a beautiful brown color, holding in their hands a flag with purple and yellow patterns, crossing 12 bridges that were opening to them. The dream seemed vague and strange, but yet so real...

When Dalya woke up, the sun rays seemed less brilliant through the Library windows.

-   I'm glad to know that you are well rested, Mademoiselle. I didn't want to wake you up.

Cristelle entered the Library. Dalya slowly got up:

-   I didn't see the time passing ...

The maid of the grand Mansion smiled:

-   A well-deserved nap. I came to announce that the dinner meal will be ready in a few minutes. Mr. Bûchebois insisted to serve you in the dining room, as it is the Christmas tradition.

And leaning toward Dalya, Cristelle whispered:

-   And this year, the Cook surpassed himself! He prepared some delicious dishes!

Dalya thanked Cristelle with a smile. The little girl arranged her books and documents in her bag. She cleaned the office desk, of pens and papers. Then, she walked to the living room, followed by the snow Panther. After her long nap, Dalya felt well rested.

In the living room, Dalya stepped toward the immense Christmas tree. She had hung the envelope that Mr. Wilfrid handed her, a few days earlier. She opened it, wondering what gift he could have offered her. A small letter was inside, Dalya read:

To Mrs. Lancel, Owner of Haute Couture boutique.

I kindly ask you to provide Mademoiselle Dalya Bouvard, with a complete wardrobe that suits both her size and her taste. And if possible, promptly.

The cost of the wardrobe is entirely on me. Please send me the bill at my work office, in the Law Firm.

Master Sloan Wilfrid.

Dalya Bouvard must have read this letter at least fifteen times without stopping. The words were yet simple and clear. But the little Dalya Bouvard could not believe her eyes:

- A ... a wardrobe? ... For me? ... New clothes? ... For me? ... But ... it's ... new cloth...

The letter escaped from Dalya's trembling hands and fell to the ground. She bent down to take it back. Except that at this moment, a small item caught Dalya's attention. Under the immense Christmas tree, there was ... a strange little package. Dalya took Monsieur Wilfrid's letter, and she came close to the immense tree. When she took the little package, it was wrapped in a luxurious gift paper with a bow on top of it. A small card displayed retyped words on a typewriter:

For Mademoiselle Dalya Bouvard

Dalya thought aloud:

- A package under the Christmas tree? How strange ... but why Monsieur Wilfrid didn't give me this package, when he offered me the envelope?

Always curious, Dalya opened the package immediately. And what she found inside was ... dazzling. For the first time in her life, Dalya discovered that she was offered a jewel. It was a beautiful bracelet in yellow gold, a multitude of tiny crystals in different bright colors, the pattern was a flower with blue violet petals, and the inside yellow-orange, and green leaves.

Dalya didn't believe her eyes. In one hand, she held an entire wardrobe offered to her. And on the other hand, she held a magnificent bracelet. In all her life, Dalya had never received such gifts, neither new clean clothes to her taste, much less a precious jewel.

A voice startled Dalya:

- Everything's alright, Mademoiselle?

Cristelle came near Dalya, who was standing still in front of the immense tree. Cristelle worried:

- I called you several times, Mademoiselle, but you didn't hear me. Is something wrong, Mademoiselle?

Dalya had lost her words; it took her considerable effort to explain to Cristelle:

- I ... Mr. Wilfrid ... I received ... he offered me a wardrobe for me, just me, new clothes ... my size and my taste ... and this ... also a stunning bracelet ... Mr. Wilfrid ... under the Christmas tree ...

Cristelle hugged the little girl in her arms and she exclaimed happily:

- But it's amazing, Mademoiselle!! An entire wardrobe!! You deserve it, Mademoiselle!! And you need it very much now, since you live here in the grand Mansion!! ... I'm so happy that Mr. Sloan Wilfrid takes care of you!! I've always liked this man ... he is always polite and respectful, even to the employees!! ... And a bracelet too! It is dazzling Mademoiselle!! I have never seen a jewel of such beauty!!

When she let go of the little girl, Cristelle continued all excited:

- I felt so sorry for you, earlier on, having been banned from celebrating Christmas with the employees in the kitchen ... but now I'm glad you received these wonderful Christmas gifts!! ... I will always bring the best cakes to Mr. Wilfrid!! An entire wardrobe and precious jewels ... I'm so happy for you!!
- I ... it's really ... a wardrobe and a bracelet ... I must visit him, to thank him ... after the holidays ...

Dalya's head was dizzy, not only because of Cristelle's strong hug, but also by these unexpected gifts. A beautiful surprise.

Seconds later, when Cristelle opened the door of the dining room, Dalya was fascinated by what she discovered. It was a large room; several beautiful bright chandeliers were attached to the ceiling, a long varnish wood and luxurious table, symmetrical chairs, immense windows that offered a view into the garden, and ... a long buffet table was installed along a wall.

Cristelle realized the little girl's shock:

- It's the Christmas dinner that the Late Mr. Governor enjoyed ...

Dalya came close to the long buffet table; dishes and food of all kinds, types and forms. 4 large plates of various salads, 3 pots of different hot soup, a huge dish of baked vegetables, 2 gratin of potatoes with white sauce, a large lasagna dish with delicious cheese, pasta stuffed with spinach, minced meat with tomato sauce, turkey legs roasted, a stuffed entire chicken, a large basket of several types of bread, a full plate of many types of cheese, a jar of 5 sweet juices, 3 different pies, a strawberries charlotte, 2 flan au caramel, a large bowl of diced fruits, 2 ice cream cakes. The table cutlery were in brilliant silver, the dishes were white decorated with pine green patterns and red bells, glasses were in bright crystal.

In front of this buffet, Dalya asked:

- All this ... for me?
- Certainly, Mademoiselle!! Cristelle laughed. Serve yourself as much as you want!!

When Cristelle left the dining room, Dalya stood frozen, in front of the long buffet table. At an instant, Dalya laughed:

- Where to start?

Dalya took a plate, and she served herself some choux and raisins salad. Before she could take stuffed tomatoes with cheese and herbs, the formal and serious voice of the head of the grand Mansion interrupted her:

- Mademoiselle ... your friends would like to meet you.

Mr. Bûchebois stepped back to allow Alfie Jaq and Gus Maurice to enter the dining room. Dalya was surprised and happy to see her friends. Alfie and Maurice stepped inside with a slow and hesitant walk, their eyes examining the luxury of this place.

Before leaving the dining room, Mr. Bûchebois addressed Dalya:

- If there is anything you need and desire, please ring us.
- Thank you, Mr. Bûchebois. Said Dalya before putting back her plate on the table.

It will take a little much longer for the head of the grand Mansion to get used to the politeness of his new employer. When Mr. Bûchebois closed the dining room door, Dalya hugged her friends simultaneously in her arms:

- I am so happy that you came in to see me, today!!

Maurice was the first to recover from the luxury of the dining room:

- I ... we thought you might like to have some company for Christmas Eve ...
- And you did very well!! I didn't dare to ask you to spend Christmas with me, away from your families!! I'm so glad you came!!

Alfie froze in front of the long buffet table:

- And we have done well to come ... look at all this food, Maurice!!

Maurice approached the feast, his eyes wide open:

- Are you waiting for other guests?

Dalya laughed while offering her friends, plates and cutlery:

- No, I was having diner, alone. The employees of the grand Mansion prepared the Christmas dinner, as they did in previous years for the Late Mr. Governor.
- You mean ... all this buffet table is for you? Alfie nearly lost his mind.
- All alone? Just for you? Maurice didn't believe his eyes.
- Serve yourself!! Dalya invited them, holding back her laugh, with difficulty.

Maurice and Alfie exchanged one glance to understand each other. Seconds later, their plates were filled with food, their mouths were saturated, and their cheeks were puffed. The three friends sat around the long dining table, and they enjoyed their Christmas dinner.

Dalya laughed while observing her friends enjoying the magnificent buffet. She laughed her heart out, happy to have company on this festive night, happy to have received wonderful gifts, and happy that Christmas went on ... much better than what she had imagined!

Chapter 11

Getting prepared

A few days before the back to school. Saturday, January 02nd, 1892. In the kitchen of the Grand Mansion.

Lunch time was close. The plates and cutlery were all placed on the kitchen table. As soon as she entered, Cristelle exclaimed:

-   Ooh!! ... The smell is delicious Mr. Ferrero!!

The Cook appreciated the praises on his meals, he proudly explained:

-   Today I cooked lasagna with tomato sauce and minced meat!

When Cristelle settled first in front of the lunch table, Océanie and Igor appeared in the kitchen too.

-   I'm seriously hungry!! exclaimed Igor
-   You keep eating like an ogre ... but how is it possible that you never get fat! Wondered Océanie in a curious tone.

The two employees sat around the table, while the Cook was placing his big lasagna dish, near a large bowl of a varied salad. When the head of the employees and the Gardener entered the kitchen, they immediately settled into their chairs around the table. The head of the employees asked:

-   Mademoiselle's lunch tray?

Cristelle answered while serving herself some salad:

-   I didn't see Mademoiselle, in the grand Mansion ... she didn't return yet from downtown … but her lunch tray is ready ... as soon as she comes back, I will serve her!

Lunch at the kitchen table took place in the usual good mood. Cristelle was chatting with the Cook about the lasagna's ingredients. The head of the grand Mansion proposed to the Gardener to plant a few chives in some places. Igor filled his mouth, without caring to breath. And Océanie was slowly cutting her green salad.

The plate of buttered bread with garlic and herbs, emptied quickly. To get some more, Océanie stood up and she filled the plate of buttered bread placed on the counter. When, all of a sudden, Océanie froze. She noticed something through the kitchen windows. Not believing her eyes, Océanie discreetly called Igor, whispering:

-   Come here!! Look at that!!

Igor stood up with difficulty, his mouth and two hands were filled with food. When he looked through the kitchen windows ... Igor froze up, too. Cristelle noticed the strange attitude of Océanie and Igor, but she continued to listen to the Cook, explaining his method of preparing the lasagna pasta.

Suddenly, Océanie and Igor ran to sit back into their places around the lunch table, and they watched in a focused stare, the kitchen door that gave onto the garden. A second later, Cristelle was about to discover what caught their attention.

A small silhouette came through the outer door of the kitchen and she walked toward the door of the hall, crossing the kitchen.

- Good lunch!

Dalya greeted the employees of the grand Mansion house with a cheerful smile, while carrying in her hands a pile of clothes. Immediately, all the conversations around the table stopped.

- What are you holding, Mademoiselle? Océanie asked in an innocent voice, hardly holding her amused laugh.

Dalya stopped and she naturally replied:

- I washed my school uniform and some clothes very early this morning ... I am getting prepared for the back to school on Monday ... My clothes dried very quickly ...

The head of the grand Mansion choked on his bread bite, he coughed loudly and his cheeks became swollen and red. The Cook fell out of his chair and he crashed to the floor with a shocked look. The Gardener was confused; and he thought aloud:

- She ... she washed her own clothes?

While Océanie and Igor, they burst into an uncontrollable laugh. Instantly, Cristelle jumped and she ran toward Dalya to take the clothes from her hands:

- But Mademoiselle!! You shouldn't wash the laundry!! I'll take care of that!! I'll fold them and bring them back to your bedroom!!

Except that Dalya affirmed with a sure tone, firmly holding her laundry:

- No no!! I insist!! I will fold my own clothes!!

Cristelle begged the little girl, trying to take the laundry out of her hands:

- Mademoiselle!! I've already explained it to you!! The laundry is our job!!

And Dalya Bouvard persisted:

- I know, yes!! But I want to fold my laundry myself!!

Because for some people, the change in status does not affect their habits ... vegetable seller or Heiress, Dalya Bouvard was getting prepared for the back to school, by washing her own clothes!

The same day. In a modest house, on the South side of Georgetown city.

The scent of white musk invaded the air in this room. The walls were painted in cream color, giving off a gentle warmth. The clear and bright wood parquet offered a beautiful picture of the ground. The few furniture and chairs occupied the space in the room. Everything seemed quiet and serene, yet...

- She is not ready! Miss Haîyang defended her point of view.
- She must be! We are already in the Third Challenge! Mr. Shang said.

Being of the same Asian origin, Mr. Shang was a young man a few years older than Miss Haîyang. He was gifted with a robust and muscular physique, a handsome allure, straight black hair and an intimidating presence.

Miss Haîyang exclaimed:

- But she is only a child!
- Well ... She is not anymore! She was designated! The man replied in a firm tone.
- Against her will! Miss Haîyang raised her voice.
- She has no choice to accept or refuse! Mr. Shang also raised his voice.
- You cannot make her go through the traini...

Miss Haîyang stopped at the entrance of Master Fong Ka-Ho in the room. Mr. Shang and Miss Haîyang bowed in greeting him. Master Fong Ka-Ho sat down in front of the two young people, and he invited them to sit.

- You dong xi zai kun rao zhu ni, Haîyang? (*Something on your mind, Miss Haîyang?*)

The young woman hesitated a few seconds to find the right words, without offending the great Master:

- I ... I do not agree with Shang, Master. I think it is too early for her. We may arouse suspicions. And she is only at the Third Challenge, Master! Nothing is yet confirmed!

Master Fong Ka-Ho spoke to the man:

- Ni jué dé ni, Shang? (*What do you think, Shang?*)

The young man answered, with an assured and confident tone:

- It is never too early to get ready, Master. I prefer to make time my ally and start as soon as possible. We cannot risk she'll be weak, when she will have to confr...

Miss Haîyang interrupted him:

- She can defend herself! I've teached her!

Mr. Shang faced her:

- It is not enough! You seriously think that on due time, she will defend herself with a simple hands movement?

Miss Haîyang exclaimed:

- You don't realize we will be exposed?

Mr. Shang tried to keep his calm:

- Our goal is to prepare her for what she is about to go thr...

A strong and serene voice interrupted the lively conversation of the two young people.

- A weapon.

Mr. Shang and Miss Haîyang instantly fell silent and they turned toward Master Fong Ka-Ho. The great man smiled while repeating:

- A weapon.

Given the confused looks of Miss Haîyang and Mr. Shang, Master Fong Ka-Ho explained, always in a serene and confident voice:

- Since we cannot approach her without arousing suspicions ... then I propose a middle ground ... offering her a weapon ...

Master Fong Ka-Ho spoke to Miss Haîyang:

- You will continue to prepare her...

Master Fong Ka-Ho faced Mr. Shang:

- And you shall offer her the most precise of all weapons ...

Miss Haîyang and Mr. Shang exchanged a determined and agreed look. They answered simultaneously:

- At your orders, Master.

The coming months will be decisive and crucial. At the other side of Georgetown city, while the little Dalya Bouvard was busy folding her school uniform and was getting prepared to the back to school... Miss Haîyang and Mr. Shang were also getting prepared, as well!

Chapter 12

A poor Nobility

Monday, January 04th, 1892. Back to school, at the Royal Georgetown College.

Winter has settled in this month of January. The trees, nude of leaves, trembled on the rhythm of the cold and icy wind. The floor was is mud because of the recent rainfalls. The sun was less present, replaced by gray and filled clouds.

And despite the cold of the winter, all the students were happy to restart their classes, and they were well rested thanks to the holidays. The big stairs of the school were filled with students of all levels, some were sitting on the edges to discuss their Christmas presents, and others were standing complaining about the holiday homework they couldn't finish.

Dalya was glad to come back to college. As soon as she stepped in the hall, Dalya noticed her classmate, who was arranging her bag.

- Good morning Amira! Beautiful day to be back to school!

Looking up, Amira smiled happily:

- Good morning Dalya!! … Happy to see you!!

Dalya smiled:

- To think that a few weeks before, I was so sure I wouldn't come back in this school!!
- Yes!! It was unpredictable!! But a nice surprise for everyone!! Amira jumped.
- A surprise for me too. Dalya laughed.

The two students head toward the classroom of their first course of the semester. The Mathematics classroom was empty and clear of any white chalk cloud. Dalya and Amira took advantage of the calm, to settle into their usual chairs.

- Did you find the solution to the equation number 35? Amira turned around.
- With difficulty!! Exclaimed Dalya. And it wasn't even in the Mathematics manual. I consulted a book from the Library of the grand Mansion. It explained the process of...

Dalya was interrupted by an arrogant and upset voice:

- And I thought that this semester will be quiet ...

Eriem Eyelord entered the classroom, followed by her entire court. She walked toward the large windows, and she sat on one of the edges. While her court settled around her. Gael Benoble did the clown, as usual:

- We are forced to study with our employees' children ... this is a sign of the end of the world ... I will not be surprised when the roles are reversed between the poor and the Nobles ... tomorrow we will be asked to sell vegetables in the market ...

The entire court laughed. Dalya and Amira didn't dare to look or answer them. Gael continued in a serious and a faked female voice:

- Buy my potatoes, Monsieur ... would you like some carrots for a good soup, Monsieur ... the zucchinis are only 15 cents, Mons...

When a firm authoritative voice interrupted Gael's show:

- 2 cents, Monsieur Gael Benoble.

All the students, including Dalya and Amira, turned around toward the entrance door of the classroom. At the door, there was Professor Canfield. And as always, he wore a stylish checked suit, a pretty bow tie on the neck and a pocket watch. Professor Canfield repeated his sentence with a defiant smile and a firm voice:

- Zucchinis are 2 cents per kilogram, Mr. Gael Benoble. And not 15 cents. Maybe if you did grocery shopping sometimes in the market, you would be better aware of the cost of the current life.

Gael Benoble turned all red. Without daring to say a word, all the students settled in their chairs, in total silence. Professor Canfield watched them for a long moment before speaking to a particular student:

- Mademoiselle Dalya Bouvard ... follow me, please.

Dalya and Amira exchanged a curious glance. Dalya then got up and left the classroom. Just a few more steps down the corridor, Professor Canfield stopped and he turned around, addressing Dalya with a joyful and kind tone:

- I am very pleased to see you here again, Mademoiselle!! ... I was so happy to know that you succeeded the Second Challenge ... well done, Mademoiselle ... well done!!
- Thank you, Professor. Dalya blushed.

Professor Canfield handed her a paper:

- Here ... is your new program for this semester. Since I'm in charge of your training, I decided to add a few more courses, apart from those that you follow already. I think you should take advantage of your presence in the College, to receive the maximum training possible.

Dalya read the paper that was given to her:

- Physics class ... Chemistry class ... Latin class ...
- Yes, in addition to your previous courses; Mathematics, Music, History and Geography ... you have 7 courses now. Will this be a problem for you, Mademoiselle?

-   No, Monsieur. I will do my best to pass all these classes. Thank you to have me registered.

Professor Canfield smiled:

-   Good luck, Mademoiselle. And mostly ... don't stop impressing us!

Dalya blushed:

-   Understood Monsieur.

When she returned to the classroom, the Mathematics Professor Mr. Wyatt was already pulling some papers out of his briefcase. Professor Wyatt displayed a discreet and happy smile, while he observed his student Dalya take her usual place. Amira turned around to her friend, she was eager and curious to know:

-   So? ... What happened? ... What did Professor Canfield want from you?
-   Professor Canfield signed me up for more classes ... So in addition to Mathematics, History, Geography, and Music ... I will be taking the classes of Physics, Chemistry, and Latin. Dalya whispered, while opening her manual.
-   It's great news!! We will spend more classes together. The Physics course is easy ... I will bring you my last year's notes; it will help you to better catch up. In the Chemistry course, you must learn by heart the table of chemical elements. The Latin course ... I assure you, no one has ever managed to exceed 15/20!

Dalya held her laugh, before Professor Wyatt addressed the students:

-   Mesdemoiselles and Messieurs ... welcome to the 2nd semester of the Mathematics course ... I am delighted to welcome my students of last semester ... all my students!

Professor Wyatt threw a proud and happy glance at Dalya, before continuing:

-   And for this course, we will correct the list of equations that I have given you for the holidays!

The rest of the class went on peacefully. Professor Wyatt explained the answers of the Mathematics homework, and all the students took notes and corrected their papers. When the bell rang noon, Professor Wyatt addressed his students, who were already beginning to put away their notebooks:

-   Next week, we will start the new algebra lesson ... I suggest you read the lesson in your textbooks before our next course ... Good day Mesdemoiselles and Messieurs!!

Dalya and Amira left the classroom and they headed toward the college canteen.

-   If Professor Wyatt thinks I'll read the new lesson before the next course, he is wrong! Amira said, while taking her tray and cutlery.

- Why not? Dalya curiously asked, while placing her empty tray on the counter tail queue in the canteen, and following her friend.
- Simply because it is the first day of school and my brain is already saturated! Exclaimed Amira while serving herself some vegetable soup.
- Yes, I admit me too. Dalya laughed, before proposing to her friend:
- You can come at the grand Mansion, this weekend, if you're free. We can review the new lessons together.

Dalya served herself soup, while Amira took 2 slices of Corn bread.

- Will there be apple and cinnamon muffins? Asked Amira.
- Certainly, I will ask the Cook to prepare it for you. Dalya answered while putting a slice of Corn bread on her plate.
- So then yes! I'm free this weekend! Amira affirmed in a sure tone.

Both students laughed for a moment, waiting for their turn in the queue to serve themselves the chicken fillets. The canteen was full at this lunchtime moment, almost all students were present.

- How is the Professor of Physics? Asked Dalya while taking a salted caramel mousse.
- He is smart and awesome!! exclaimed Amira, filling her bowl with desserts, before continuing to explain:
- His course is difficult, certainly. But he explains very well the techniques; he is patient to repeat the lesson until everyone has assimilated. Since always, he is my favorite teach...

A mocking voice interrupted Amira:

- I guess the veggy seller is delighted to have food to eat, in our canteen!

Amira and Dalya turned around to discover behind them; Gael, Eriem and their entire court, on the queue line of the canteen, a few steps away from them. Amira whispered to Dalya:

- Ignore them!
- Can't they get busy about something else other than humiliating me? Dalya asked in a low voice.
- Don't listen to them, Dalya. They'll get bored soon and they will leave you alone.

Except that, it was easier said than done. Dalya hoped to spend a discreet semester without provocations and incidents.

- You should serve yourself some more chicken ... it is obvious that you don't eat enough of it at home! Gael said.

Eriem and her court laughed aloud. And Gael was happy to continue his mockery on Dalya:

- I guess you have never tasted the salted caramel mousse ... Probably not ... it's a dessert for the rich people onl...

A calm and defiant voice interrupted Gael:

- And you think you are one of the rich people?

Gael was pinned in his place, instantly. All the students, including Dalya and Amira, they immediately turned around. A few steps away from the queue, there stood a beautiful girl, little size, thin, with a clear face, beautiful platinum blonde wavy hair and clear brown eyes.

Dalya whispered immediately to Amira:

- Who is she?

Amira murmured:

- Assami Eyelord ... the younger sister of Eriem!

Dalya remembered to have met this girl, a couple of times in the College Library. Assami Eyelord served herself Corn bread, and she continued in a natural but daring voice:

- The one you have been mocking, since earlier ... she is richer than all the students gathered in this canteen.

Gael let out a mocking and arrogant laugh:

- She is not rich ...
- And you think you are? Assami stared at him.

Gael held himself, with difficulty, trying not to answer Assami's provocative words. His cheeks became red, his mouth went pale, and he clenched his hands' fists in a strong move. It was at this moment, that Eriem intervened between her sister and her friend.

- Assami!! That's enough!! Eriem exclaimed while giving her sister an angry look, which had no effect on Assami.

The younger sister of Eriem served herself a large bowl of fresh fruits, letting out an amused and innocent laugh:

- All I am saying is ... before pretending to be rich, one needs to make sure to really be rich ... that's all!

Dalya followed the scene with all her attention, trying to understand Assami Eyelord's words. Amira grabbed Dalya by her arm and she whispered:

- It's better to leave ... now!

Dalya and Amira took their lunch trays, and they went away to settle in a table, at the other end of the canteen room.

- I didn't know Eriem had a sister in this college! Dalya exclaimed as soon as she sat down.

- And fortunately they are not alike. Assami is far away from her sister Eriem's character. Said Amira, while starting her soup. She continued:
- Assami even complimented me on my hair once. She is calm and polite.
- And mostly audacious!! Dalya laughed. To stop Gael and make him lose his words!
- Yes, I admit that it was a beautiful scene to watch!! Amira choked on her soup and her laugh.

Dalya and Amira finished their lunch quickly. Then, they both made their way to the Library. The History course was starting in an hour, they had plenty of time. As soon as they entered the Library, Miss Guendolyn welcomed them joyfully:

- Happy to see you Mesdemoiselles!! Well rested during the holidays, I hope?
- A little, yes. We had a lot of homework to do. Dalya replied.
- I would have not refused one more holiday month! Amira sighed.
- Hold on strong, Miss Amira. You only have a few months before the long summer vacation. Miss Guendolyn could not retain her innocent laugh.

The two students greeted Miss Guendolyn and then they entered the immense Library. Amira placed her bag on a study table, and then she walked toward the books' shelves, thinking aloud:

- There are … 2 very well-written books, that summarize the essential of the Physics course … with exercises and even solutions in the last pages … I remember their locations …

Dalya followed her friend through the shelves:

- You think 2 books will be enough for me, to catch up in the Physics class?

Amira took a book and she handed it to Dalya:

- Yes, because I will also give you my last year's notebook … it will be more than enough … I can work the lessons with you … and if you have any questions, I'm here for it …

Amira turned right into another wing and she continued her search for the second book:

- I hope it's still there … if Miss Guendolyn haven't changed its location …

While following her friend, Dalya's head was occupied by another question, but it was not about the Physics class. After a few seconds of hesitation, Dalya asked her friend:

- Amira …
- Hmm … yes? …
- I didn't understand what Assami Eyelord meant … earlier … in the canteen.

Amira stretched out with all her strength to catch up a book from the 5th shelf, and she gave it to Dalya:

- And here's the second book! It is very compact and convenient ... but very useful! ... What haven't you understood from Assami Eyelord?

Dalya approached Amira and she whispered:

- When she said that I'm richer than all the students gathered in the canteen. What did she mean by that?

Amira was surprised and astonished by her friend's question:

- Dalya ... do you have any idea about the fortune of the Late Mr. Governor?
- I know he is rich. Dalya murmured.

To correct her friend, Amira exclaimed:

- Dalya ... he is more than rich!! His fortune is colossal. The Late Mr. Governor is the 2nd richest person in the Country. The Continent even. The grand Mansion where you live is only a grain of sand. He has companies, factories, businesses, properties, houses and lands, across the entire Country.

Dalya froze in her place. Amira continued:

- And he left his entire fortune to you, Dalya! You have no idea what you're going to inherit! You are not just richer than all the students gathered in the canteen, like Assami Eyelord said ... you will become the 2nd richest person in the Country!

What Amira had just told her, was way far from what Dalya imagined. She never thought to ask how rich the Late Mr. Governor was. At that moment, Dalya thought aloud:

- So ... that's why his nephew Mr. Ferdinand Edelmen and the Lawyer Mr. Ernest Laszlo hate me ...

Amira chuckled discreetly:

- And it's perfectly normal they hate you and wish you would fail, Dalya! You're going to make them lose not just a small amount of money, but a colossal fortune!!

Some things started to be clearer now. Yet, Dalya had another question in her mind:

- And ... why did Assami said that Gael was not rich?
- Because he is not! Amira replied immediately.
- But he is part of the Nobility. Said Dalya.
- So what?
- He comes from a Noble family ... so he's rich! Dalya affirmed

Amira held her laugh, with difficulty:

- Oh!! But where did you come up with such an idea?

Dalya was surprised by this question:

- This is what usually happens ... I think ... Noble people are always rich ...

Both students returned to their study desks, holding books in their hands. Amira Mounier sat on the chair, and then she looked at Dalya with an amused smile:

- Well, I am delighted to correct your informations. The Noble people are not rich!
- How? Dalya was curious to understand.

Amira explained:

- For example ... Gael Benoble ... his grandfather was a Minister in the Government once; a very long time ago, only once. And since then, Gael's father has been trying by all means to be part of the Government. Currently, Gael's father has a job in a Ministry office ... but it is a position of no value. And yet, he acts like he is ruling the entire Government, all by himself. Gael's father only lives in the former glory of the grandfather. But he has no power, and even less money.

Dalya didn't believe her ears. She remained shocked by the news. Amira continued:

- Another example ... Lakita Fleuritel!
- The student who reported me to Eriem and her court, because I helped the school concierge?

Amira relaxed in her chair:

- Yes ... well guess why this girl reports everything that happens in this college? ... Her family owns newspapers specialized in the tabloid press. She has this character defect in her genes and blood. They report and sell people's scandals and falls, in order to make money ... but all their newspapers are bankrupted ...

Dalya also lay back on her chair, shocked and surprised at what Amira was telling her. Her friend went on to explain:

- And Salman Elpacha ...
- The one who participated in the essay contest in December? Dalya asked.
- Himself!! ... His family includes notaries of many generations ... except that they are penniless.

Dalya straightened up:

- But ... Salman Elpacha?! ... There are always luxurious cars waiting for him, at the school exit ... at the end of classes!

Amira opened a book, sighing:

- Appearances only, Dalya ... just appearances. My father refused to work in their accounting department. One, because their business are often doubtful. Two, because they are a family of notaries who use their clients' money for their own needs ... and it's illegal.

A few seconds of silence later, Amira continued:

- And the icing on the cake ... her highness Eriem Eyelord ... her father is an entrepreneur in the construction field. Although he is known to be a man without scruples and very stingy, his business is doing well. Except that ... the Eyelord family is imprinted with scandals; cheatings, extramarital affairs, drugs' addiction, violence ...
- Eriem Eyelord! Dalya exclaimed in shock.
- And despite all that, she acts arrogant and rude! And to think that I wanted to be her friend and join her group! I would have been better alone instead of chasing after these arrogants!

Amira got angry for an instant, before continuing in a calmer voice:

- Assami Eyelord seems to be the only normal person in this sick family.
- Yes, she is very polite and nice. Dalya confirmed.

Amira looked at her friend:

- So ... are you convinced now that Nobility does not necessarily mean rich?
- It's just ... it's hard to believe that ...

Amira answered with an angry tone:

- Yes, I understand you, especially when all these morons act like kings of the world! ... But Nobility is only a title Dalya, a middle name. All these Noble families are poor ...

Dalya flipped through the pages of an open book in front of her, without really noticing what was written. Her mind was occupied by news a bit hard to believe. Dalya murmured in a confused voice:

- A poor Nobility ...

Amira confirmed:

- Yes, a poor Nobility ...

Chapter 13

Detention

Monday, January 11th, 1892. At the Royal Georgetown College. In the Music classroom. 20 minutes before the beginning of class.

- It's a beautiful violin. Dalya affirmed while observing her friend Amira adjusting the violin cords.
- Yes ... it's a wonder. Amira said. I wish I can buy a violin like this, one day.

Dalya sat on a chair near her friend:

- You play very well. I've heard you several times before, the last semester. During rehearsals ...
- Thank you! Amira blushed a little. I must admit that it takes a lot of practice. It took me months to master only the cords.

While Amira was cleaning her violin, Dalya thought aloud:

- Do ... do you think Professor Haîyang will teach me how to play an instrument this semester?
- Certainly!! Exclaimed Amira. And besides, I could never understand why she ordered you to clean the classroom windows, during the previous class. Professor Haîyang is known to be firm, certainly, but she is nice nonetheless.
- I really hope I can have an instrument to learn, this time!! Dalya wished.
- Here... try on my violin. Just to see if it suits you. Amira proposed to her.

When Dalya took Amira's violin, she was surprised:

- It is well light!!
- And fortunately ... imagine having a heavy instrument to lay on your sho...

Amira was interrupted by an arrogant voice:

- And you hope to learn Music too?

Eriem and her court made their entry into the classroom. And as usual, Gael enjoyed diminishing Dalya and mocking her, in front of all the other students:

- How can Music be useful for a girl like you?

This time, Dalya lost her cool temper. She was tired of being teased each day at school. Dalya replied in a defiant voice:

- And why shouldn't I have the right to learn Music? What makes me different from all of you?

All the students went silent and froze in their places. Everyone was surprised that Dalya answered. They all got used to her silence. Amira whispered to Dalya:

- Ignore them ... don't bother to answer them ...

Except Dalya could not and would not be silenced up, anymore. She spoke to all the students with a defiant voice:

- I follow the same classes as you all ... I passed the same exams as you all ... and if the Music class is useful for you, it is useful for me too, as well!

Except that Eriem and her court didn't share the same opinion as Dalya. Eriem came close to Dalya, with slow steps:

- Oh ... but don't fool yourself ... you're just a poor little veggy sel...

Dalya interrupted Eriem with a strong voice:

- I am poor, yes! But at least I don't pretend to be rich!

A wave of exclamation arose throughout the Music classroom. Amira came close to Dalya and she tried to calm her:

- Dalya ... we'd better review Professor Haîyang's homewo...

But before Amira could finish her sentence, Eriem's hand seized the violin that Dalya was holding, and she crushed it to the floor with a loud bang. The screams of several students filled the classroom. The violin broke into several pieces. Dalya jumped at this unpredictable move. Amira exclaimed:

- But ... what ... look at what you've done?!! ... It is ... but ... Eriem ... are you insane?!

Eriem ignored Amira and she addressed Dalya with a threatening voice:

- Speak to us again in that tone, and I promise you that you will no longer follow any class in this school!!

Before Dalya could answer to this threat, a mature voice was heard:

- What is happening here?

All the students, including Dalya and Amira, froze in their places. Professor Haîyang took a step toward the gathering of students. While observing the violin broken into many pieces on the floor, Professor Haîyang asked in a firm tone:

- Who did this?
- Dalya Bouvard, Professor. Gael replied without a second late.

Immediately, Dalya jumped and exclaimed:

- It's not true! It's not me! It's Eri...
- Silence! Professor Haîyang ordered, before saying in a calmer voice:
- Dalya Bouvard ... follow me to the Principal's office.
- But ... Professor ... I didn't break it!! ... She did it ... Eri...
- Immediately, Dalya!!

All the students displayed joyful smiles. Gael was very proud of his achievement. Eriem didn't hold her arrogant smile. Before Dalya would turn around to leave the classroom, Professor Haîyang ordered in a firm tone:

- And you too, Amira Mounier. To the Principal's office!

Amira looked like slapped by that order. The other students couldn't believe their ears, and more laughs were heard from them. Only Dalya dared to react:

- But ... Professor ... Amira didn't touch anything, either! ... She didn't brea...
- To the Principal's office ... both of you ... now!

Professor Haîyang seemed calm but authoritative. She opened the door of the classroom, motioning to Dalya and Amira, to move forward. Both students had no other choice but to obey and leave the classroom, under the laughs and applauses of the other students.

The trip to the principal's office Mr. Darkfett went by in a heavy silence. Dalya blamed herself for having caused troubles to her friend, and not keeping her silence in front of Eriem's provocations. Amira walked in silence too, her cheeks were red and she feared her meeting with Director Darkfett.

When they arrived at the Director's secretary desk, Professor Haîyang asked in a calmer tone:

- Can we meet Director Darkfett, please?

Miss Uplerine stared at Dalya and Amira, who followed the Professor. She wondered why the two students were looking down. Miss Uplerine got up and opened the door of the Office. An icy voice replied to Miss Uplerine:

- Let them come in.

Immediately, Professor Haîyang stepped into the big office of Director Darkfett. You may think that with time, the severe and cold attitude of the Director would have changed, but no. He was a small little man, a white snow hair and little piercing black eyes. He wore a dark and elegant suit. Director Darkfett raised his eyes from the folder he was holding in his hand, and asked in a curious tone:

- Good morning Professor Haîyang ... what is happening?

Professor Haîyang explained in a soft and calm voice:

- I am sorry to disturb you, Director Darkfett ... it happens that I have discovered a completely destroyed Music instrument.

The folder in the Director's hands fell suddenly on his desk:

- How? ... A Music instrument ... destroyed? ... That is the first time that something like this happens in my school!

Professor Haîyang stepped toward the Director's desk and she told him in a calm voice:

- Both these students have destroyed a violin.

At this announcement, Dalya and Amira couldn't believe their ears. They fought back immediately:

- We didn't do anything!!
- They provoked me!!
- It's Eriem who broke the violin!!
- I was holding the violin in my hand ...
- And she took it from her hand and destroyed it!!
- It's Eriem that should be here, not us!!
- Silence you two!! Ordered the director.

Dalya and Amira went silent at once. Director Darkfett seemed surprised and pleased to have a good reason to reprimand these two students. Professor Haîyang continued with a cold calm:

- When I entered my classroom, there was nobody else, except Dalya Bouvard, Amira Mounier, and ... the violin destroyed on the ground.

Dalya and Amira exchanged a confused and puzzled look. They never have thought that Professor Haîyang would lie and accuse them wrongly!

Director Darkfett stood up from his chair and walked toward the two students. He examined them, as if they were two insects he wished to crush:

- Well ... well ... it seems that I have undisciplined students in my school ...

The Director spoke to Dalya, with a mean and devilish smile:

- I have already warned you, little veggy seller ... they've forced your admission in my school, that doesn't necessarily mean that you'll stay here ... I will not accept that a veggy seller neglects the order and discipline in this school!

Dalya's throat tightened. Director Darkfett then addressed Amira:

- And you, little stuttering girl ... you enjoy making troubles now? ... Have I not been clear enough with you? ... Haven't I enough explained to you that you are a disgrace to this school?

Dalya and Amira didn't dare to speak a word, let alone raise their heads. They remained motionless standing. When the Director went back to sit on his chair, Professor Haîyang said:

- Both students deserve a detention, Director Darkfett.

The Director was pleased with this idea; he displayed a wide happy smile:

- Certainly!!

Professor Haîyang continued:

- I suggest that these students spend 2 hours of work, 2 times a week ... in the College kitchen.

Director Darkfett was somewhat surprised by the originality of this idea. Most detentions were detention hours in a classroom under the supervision of a teacher, and the student had to write hundreds of times the same sentence. But as the Director hated these two students above all, he rejoiced in advance of the humiliation they will get:

- It is a great idea, Professor Haîyang!! ... A detention in the College kitchen!! ... During their free time ... for 1 month!!
- I suggest 3 months, Director Darkfett.

Dalya and Amira jumped. Did they hear correctly? 3 months of detention in the College kitchen? But this is insane!! Never such a detention has existed before, either in this school or in another elsewhere.

Director Darkfett himself was surprised by this idea. And He who thought being the meanest and cruelest, he was astonished to discover that Professor Haîyang was even more cruel than he was. Director Darkfett thought aloud:

- 3 months detention ... in the College kitchen ...

Professor Haîyang stepped forward and she defended her idea, with a strong voice:

- It is a valuable Music instrument, Director. Their act is unforgivable. If you punish them for only 1 month, discipline in this school will be ignored by other students, and the order will collapse. I insist, Director, 3 months of detention in the College kitchen, at a rate of 2 hours 2 times a week!

Director Darkfett replied immediately, displaying a cheerful smile:

- Alright then ... I will leave you in charge of it, Professor Haîyang!

He addressed the two students with an arrogant tone:

- The fooleries will be paid very costly, in this school! ... You will learn the discipline, by fair means or foul!

Professor Haîyang went back to the classroom, followed by Dalya and Amira. Both students were silent, still shocked from their detention. The other students were all gathered around Eriem and Gael. And at the sight of Dalya's defeated face, Eriem and Gael exchanged a proud and triumphant look.

- Let's start this semester's course ... take your seats.

Instantly, all the students, including Dalya and Amira, settled in their chairs. Professor Haîyang took out some papers from her briefcase, and she announced:

- During this class, we will correct the questions that you have worked on during the Christmas holidays ... let's start with the first question ...

Dalya didn't listen to a single word for the rest of the class. She had a severe headache, her throat was tight, her forehead was sweaty, her cheeks were red ... Dalya still couldn't believe what had happened, just a few minutes earlier. She was lost in her thoughts:

- *3 months of detention ... for doing nothing ... but why did Professor Haîyang lied about me and Amira? ... She perfectly noticed all the students present in the classroom ... why did she insist on 3 months of detention? ... the school kitchen ... Amira has done nothing ... why ... it's not fair ... we did nothing ...*

All through the Music class, Dalya Bouvard tried to find answers to her many questions. She failed to understand the attitude of Professor Haîyang. Her classmate Amira was sitting a few chairs away from her. Dalya didn't dare to look at her. Just as Dalya succeeded to have a friend since her arrival at the school, Amira was in detention because of Dalya ... and for 3 months!!

Without noticing the time passing, the end of classes' bell rang. All the students put away their books and left the classroom. Professor Haîyang stepped toward Dalya and Amira:

- Your detention starts next week ... at your next free hour, wait for me in front of the teachers' room.

When the Professor left the classroom, Dalya remained motionless in her chair. Amira approached her without saying a word. Dalya gathered all her courage; she raised her eyes toward Amira and dared to say:

- I ... I'm really ... really sorry ... I never thought we would get here ... I should have taken your advice and not answered their provocations ... I shouldn't have talked ... I am sincerely sorr...

At this moment, Amira did an unpredictable gesture. She hugged Dalya in her arms with all her strength, and she reassured her as best as she could:

- It's not your fault ... I was there, you have done nothing wrong ...
- But that's unfair, Amira! Spending 3 months in detention, we didn't do anything!
- It will go on soon, don't worry about that Dalya!

When they came out the College exit door, Dalya turned toward her friend and she asked:

- Your father would be very upset to know that you're in detention, would he?

Amira hesitated for a few seconds:

- I have no idea about his reaction ... this is the first time I am punished at school.
- I will go home with you, Amira ... to explain to your father what really happened!

The two students walked toward Amira's house. Winter had lost his celebration and merry air. The cold wind was blowing freely. The trees were hardened and frightening. The sky got even darker.

The Mounier house was well distinct. Of all the houses in the street, it was the only wood house in blue. A small house of 2 floors, large windows and a small entrance door.

When Amira opened the front door of her house, Dalya followed her inside. The house was tidy. A small hall in the middle, a staircase in front, a little kitchen on the left, and a little living room on the right. And despite the house seemed tiny, Dalya found it very warm and welcoming. Immediately, Mr. Jacob Mounier came up from the living room on the right:

- Good evening champion!!
- Good evening, papa. Amira answered in a low voice.

Mr. Jacob Mounier had not lost his chubby belly and filled cheeks. He was wearing a brown suit and a blue tie, indicating that he had just returned from his job, as well. When he noticed Dalya, Mr. Jacob Mounier rushed to greet her:

- And good evening to you, Mademoiselle!! It is a great pleasure to welcome you in my house!! Come in!! Please!!

Dalya smiled with difficulty:

- Thank you, Mr. Mounier.
- I am glad Amira have brought you home today!! ... You should definitely join us for dinner tonight!!

Amira and Dalya exchanged a confused look; none of them knew how to tell him the news. Finally, and in front of the silence of the two girls, Mr. Jacob Mounier felt that something was bothering them:

- Is everything alright, Mesdemoiselles? What is going on?

Amira ventured the first:

- It's ... it's ... nothing serious ... it's a little incident ... at school ... this afternoon ... there has been a misunderstanding ... with a teacher ... in the Music class ...

Mr. Jacob Mounier sat on his chair, and he stared at Amira with all his attention, trying to decipher what his daughter was telling him. After several minutes, Amira was still unable to tell him the news. She was breathless, her cheeks turned red puffy and her throat tightened.

Dalya decided to intervene. She took a deep breath, and then she explained:

- Mr. Jacob Mounier ... me and Amira, we are in detention at the college kitchen, for 3 months ... we have been wrongly accused of breaking a violin, before the start of the Music class, this afternoon ... and no matter how much we protested and tried to explain to the Professor and the Director that we didn't break it, no one wanted to hear us.

Mr. Jacob Mounier was shocked by what he has just heard; he lay back on his chair:

- How? ... Detention? ... The school kitchen?

Dalya continued:

- I'm so sorry, Mr. Mounier. Everything is my fault. Amira asked me to stay silent, but Eriem Eyelord provoked me. Amira did nothing at all. It's my entire fault. I'm really sorr...

Mr. Jacob Mounier jumped out of his chair, and he yelled so loudly, that his voice echoed throughout the tiny house:

- BUT IT'S GREAT!! THIS IS GREAT NEWS!!

Mr. Jacob Mounier hugged the two girls in his arms, simultaneously and tight. Dalya and Amira exchanged a confused look. This was the last reaction they thought they would see. Mounier Jacob sat back on his chair and he appeared to be the happiest of fathers. Dalya dared to say:

- You have not heard me right, I believe, Monsieur. We are in detention ... 3 months of detention ...
- Yes, yes, I heard you well! Mr. Jacob Mounier repeated, before turning toward his daughter:
- Congratulations Champion!! I'm proud of you!!

Amira stuttered in confusion:

- But ... I ... aren't you upset? ... of me?
- This is your first detention since ever!! ... Quite the opposite!! I am very proud of you!! ... Your first foolery and you have 3 months of detention!! ... If someone had told me this before, I would have not believed it!! Congratulations Champion!!

The two girls understood nothing at Mr. Jacob Mounier's reaction. Amira asked:

- You're proud of me ... because I'm in detention?
- Of course!! Jacob Mounier laughed. Since your mother passed away, I always feared you would be too nice, too quiet, even too pacifist. Now that you do fooleries, it reassures me

that you're normal, just like the other kids of your age. It proves to me that you dare, you take risks and you have fun too!!

Dalya and Amira didn't believe their ears; they were relieved that Mr. Jacob Mounier wasn't so upset by this news. The father went on a joking tone:

- Sure ... I do not expect that the detentions multiply, Mesdemoiselles ... you must focus on your classes and studies!!
- Yes, papa!
- Yes, Monsieur.

Mr. Jacob Mounier addressed Dalya in a kind voice:

- I am glad that my daughter finally have a true friend at school ... and I admit, since Amira have met you, her elocution and her confidence, they have greatly improved. So thank you Mademoiselle, for being a beneficial friendship for my daughter ... and thank you for bringing her in detention!!

Since their first meeting, Dalya appreciated the kindness and politeness of Mr. Jacob Mounier. He was very nice, attentive and very courteous. But since now, Dalya esteemed him even more. With great difficulty, Dalya held her laugh and her surprise:

- My pleasure, Monsieur.

Moments later, when Dalya was escorted to the exit door, Amira hugged her warmly:

- Thank you for coming with me ... to tell my father the news.
- I am relieved that your father has well accepted it. After all, it's the least I can do for bringing you in detention with me!

Before Dalya closed the door, she heard Mr. Jacob Mounier ask in an amused way:

- Well ... for once, champion, you are the one who brings a story to tell for dinner, tonight!! ... I want to know all the details ... what exactly happened? ... 3 months, I admit it's a bit heavy as a punishment ... in the college kitchen, you said? ... I never heard of such a detention? ... But what will you do in the kitchen?

Dalya Bouvard left toward the grand Mansion, displaying a relieved smile ... despite the 3 months of detention!

Chapter 14

New courses

Wednesday, January 13th, 1892. The new Physics course.

The Physics course was held in a large classroom. When Dalya walked in it for the first time, something reminded Dalya of her Uncle Giorgi Bouvard's workshop. Many kinds of weird gadgets and equipment were placed on a long counter, occupying nearly half of the classroom. Several chairs and small desks were arranged symmetrically. A long blackboard stood along a wall. The large classroom was lit by big windows, extending up to the ceiling.

Dalya put down her bag on a chair, and she walked to the counter full of odd objects. Dalya recognized only a few tools, but she didn't know what most of these items could be used for.

- Impressive, isn't it? asked Amira
- Yes!! Dalya replied in a surprised voice

Amira explained to her friend:

- We studied electricity in the previous months ... the tool you see there is a model of a simple electric circuit ... and those over there, those are several types of batteries ... and here are switches … right there, these are bulbs....

While listening to Amira's explanations, Dalya was fascinated by the strange items placed on the long counter. Physics was a new subject to study, and it seemed like a fun course. Amira continued:

- The course is simple ... it will take you a few hours to catch up ... I brought you my notebook of the previous semester ... keep it as much as you need it.
- Thank you so much!

While the two students continued to explore the items of the Physics course, a silhouette entered the classroom. He was a young man in his early thirties, wearing a nice suit and tie, and holding a large briefcase.

- Good morning Mesdemoiselles!! He said with an enthusiastic voice.

Dalya turned around to find her new Professor of Physics, Mr. Roger. He was the youngest of all her other teachers. Professor Roger exchanged his jacket with a long white blouse. He approached the two students:

- I was informed of a new student in my class this semester ... I presume you are Mademoiselle Dalya Bouvard?
- Yes, Monsieur.

And just as Amira assured her, Professor Roger was nice and friendly. He smiled:

- I am honored that Professor Canfield chose to include my course in your training ... he informed me that you would be happy to take a practical course!

Dalya politely replied:

- Yes, Professor. Physics seems to be an interesting course to study.

Amira whispered:

- And mostly more fun!

The young Professor Roger answered in an amused tone:

- I'm flattered Miss Amira! I am convinced that there is nothing better than practice to learn well and understand the lessons faster.

Dalya remembered one thing:

- It is true! In the workshop of my uncle Giorgi, he often explained to me how some items and machines worked. It was fun, and I still remember it all!
- Well then ... you will be well served in my class, Mademoiselle! ... I will provide you with the previous semester's files ... read them carefully, do the exercises at the end of each lesson ... and feel free to ask me any question that crosses your mind!
- Thank you, Professor.
- And Miss Amira ... in the uniform closet, please provide our new student with gloves, protective glasses and a white blouse ... before the beginning of our practical part of the course.
- Right away, Professor! Amira said.

The day's course started when the other student entered the classroom. When all the students took their places, the young Professor Roger announced the schedule of the next courses:

- As usual, my Physics class is divided into 2 areas: electricity and light ... This semester we will study in more details the current and voltage ... and in terms of light, we will finish the chapters about the shadows and moon phases ... before starting the chapter of the colored lights!

Thursday, January 14th, 1892. The new Chemistry course.

- The entire Periodic Table?! To learn by heart?!

Dalya was surprised when reading a paper that her friend Amira gave her. The two students were walking to the Chemistry course classroom, after spending a few minutes in the Library. Amira explained:

- Yes! This Periodic Table of the elements is the basis of Chemistry ... all the equations and the next lessons will be easier for you, when you have learned by heart this list ... I will explain it to you in more details, after our course ...

Dalya held the paper, trying to decipher it. Different symbols and details were very new and strange to Dalya:

- It seems hard!!

Amira reassured her:

- Only at the beginning ... you just need a little practice for Chemistry ...

When suddenly, Dalya stopped walking in the middle of the corridor:

- Practice for Chemistry ... practice for Chemistry ... Uncle Giorgi!! He was the one who discovered the Excelbox's metal!! ... He will not refuse to help me in the practice for Chemistry!! ... His workshop is designed specifically only for that!!

Amira turned toward her friend:

- A workshop?! .... It's an excellent idea!! ... Can I accompany you to your uncle's?
- If you don't mind a full workshop bursting with items and bizarre tools... you're welcomed to come!

When they arrived at the classroom, Dalya and Amira discovered that the room was almost full. The chairs were full of students preparing to start the course. The Chemistry classroom was similar to the one in which the Physics course was held. In addition to the chairs and tables installed in symmetry, and the long blackboard that stood along a wall, the Chemistry classroom also had a long counter occupying half the room. Hundreds of transparent glass jars of several bizarre forms and types, were set up. A multitude of liquids of different colors filled some glass jars. Dalya has never seen glass jars in such forms and so many.

When weaving between the tables to take their places, Dalya noticed the presence of someone writing on the large blackboard.

- It's Miss Gallet!! Our Chemistry Teacher!! Amira whispered, sitting in a chair in front of Dalya.

Miss Gallet appeared to be a young woman very gentle and graceful, as Amira had already told Dalya. The woman was wearing a pretty pink dress with green motifs, a pink ribbon holding her long blond hair in a ponytail, bright pink pearls around her neck, bright pink shoes, and even pink round glasses frame. Miss Gallet was a pretty young woman in her early thirties. She was busy writing on the blackboard.

When all the students settled, Miss Gallet turned around and she greeted them with a delighted smile and a soft voice:

- Good morning everyone!! Welcome to the second semester of the Chemistry class!! ... Please open your notebooks and note down the titles I've written on the board. We will start this semester with the study of volume, pressure and mass air ... and then we will study the molecules and atoms...

Dalya leaned toward her friend Amira, and she whispered:

- How do you write the last two words that the Professor said?

Amira held an amused laugh, and she inclined her notebook for Dalya to copy the words over her shoulder. The Professor took out of her briefcase some papers; she distributed them herself, while walking slowly through the students' desks:

- I've prepared for you a little summary of the first chapter, regarding the atmosphere ... its characteristics and its different layers ... notice in the drawing that I have made, the atmospheric layers are different by the kilometers' amount ... the troposphere is the one that concentrates 90% of the air in the atmosphere ...

Dalya had a hard time to write a word that Miss Gallet recited. Dalya murmured:

- Traupo ... troppo ... troppeau ...

When suddenly, Miss Gallet who had arrived at Dalya's desk, she realized Dalya's difficulty. The Professor handed a paper to Dalya, and she pointed her finger to a written word, whispering:

- Troposphere ...

And right away, Dalya copied the right word. Miss Gallet asked, in a curious and gentle voice:

- You are Mademoiselle Dalya Bouvard, aren't you? ... The little girl who was chosen by the Late Mr. Governor?

Pens stopped writing, and eyes turned around toward Dalya. She timidly answered:

- Yes, Professor.

For a few seconds, Miss Gallet observed Dalya with a fascinated gaze:

- Professor Canfield told me about you ... I'm delighted to have you in my Chemistry class, Mademoiselle. And I would ensure that you catch up your delay, before the end of this semester. Wait for me at the end of the course, I will provide you of the previous lessons.
- Thank you, Professor.

When Miss Gallet continued her tour around the desks, distributing the course papers, Amira turned around to Dalya and she whispered:

- Miss Gallet is nice!! Told you so!!

Friday, January 15th, 1892. The new Latin course.

At the entry door of the immense garden in the grand Mansion, a white silhouette with sapphire piercing eyes, was waiting for Dalya's return from school. And as usual, the snow Panther got up quickly, whenever she noticed the little girl crossing the grand Mansion's entrance gate.

- Good evening Séraphine ... did you had a good day?

Dalya got used to talking to the snow Panther, as a true friend. And as strange as it may seem, Séraphine always answered Dalya's conversation, either by a smile or with a meow according to the mood. Since her first night in the grand Mansion, Séraphine followed the little girl like a shadow, and it was as if she kept an eye on Dalya. The snow Panther was a very strange animal.

When she arrived in her bedroom, Dalya relaxed on one of the chairs and she let out a long sigh. She remained motionless for several seconds, thinking. While the snow Panther sat on the chair in front of her and stared at the little girl with all her full attention.

- It was a long day for me ...

Séraphine put her head down on the edge of the chair, observing and listening to Dalya.

- Guess what class I had today? ... Latin!

While Dalya was speaking about her day, Séraphine's eyes were wide open, fascinated and attentive, as if Dalya was telling her a story.

- And guess how many Latin words I understood in this course?

Séraphine let out a little meow. Dalya continued:

- Not a single word!! None!! Nothing at all!!

Dalya stood up from her chair:

- I didn't understand a single word of what the Professor was saying. For several hours, the Professor spoke in Latin, and I didn't understood anything after her "Good morning dear students" ...

Séraphine displayed a smile. Dalya sighed:

- You wonder how will I pass this class, don't you? ... I was asking myself the same exact question!

At that moment, Dalya giggled, under the amused eyes of the snow Panther.

- Yes, I admit that my situation is pretty funny!! ... the Professor spoke only Latin ... everyone seemed to follow her, except me ... I haven't written anything on my notebook ...

not a single word ... and I will have to take the course for the next 6 months ... I don't even know how to start learning it!!

Séraphine got up from the chair, and she went to a fruit plate that the maid Cristelle always took care to fill in Dalya's bedroom. The snow Panther came back toward Dalya with two bananas hanging from its jaw.

- Thank you Séraphine... it's always a pleasure to talk to you!

Dalya peeled a banana for the Panther, and she peeled another banana for her. The little girl and the snow Panther enjoyed their fruit, while continuing their conversation.

Chapter 15

A simple little flute

Monday, January 18th, 1892. The Music course.

Upon entering the Music classroom, Dalya was anxious. It was the day of the Music instruments practice. In the previous semester, Professor Haîyang had ordered Dalya to clean the classroom windows. It was another opportunity for Eriem and her court to laugh and humiliate Dalya.

- Professor Haîyang has always been nice and fair ... I admit it was very strange that she asked you to clean the windows ... I could never understand why she asked you to do that!

Amira was thinking aloud, putting her bag on the chair. When she turned toward her friend, Amira noticed Dalya's concern. She tried to reassure her:

- Everything will be alright this semester!! ... You will see!!
- Do you think after she has given us 3 months detention, Professor Haîyang would be more indulgent with me? Dalya asked, looking anxious.
- Don't worry! ... She has no reason to give you more chores!!
- I hope so. Sighed Dalya.

When all the students took their places, Professor Haîyang announced the beginning of class, in her usual calm strong voice:

- Welcome to this Music course!! ... at the beginning of this semester, all of you will study the same Music song ... the Philosopher's Stone ... on the papers that I will hand you right now, you will write the details of the Music notes ... and then you will practice on your instrument ...

Professor Haîyang walked between students' desks, distributing papers of the Music song:

- In a year from now, your presentation of this Music song will be your final exam ... so, repeat as much as possible ... learn by heart your notes ... and practice as often as you can!

Arriving at Dalya's desk, Professor Haîyang paused for a moment. The young woman observed Dalya with an intense and serious look. Dalya didn't dare to move or make a sound. And with an unpredictable move, Professor Haîyang put a paper of the Music song on Dalya's desk, and she said with an encouraging tone:

- Good luck, Dalya Bouvard ... Good luck!

The young woman continued her tour between the desks. Amira and Dalya exchanged a happy look and excited whispers:

- I cannot believe it!
- I told you not to worry about it!!
- Do you think I will have an instrument like all of you?
- Certainly!! ... If she gave you the melody paper, it's not for nothing!

Amira was well right. Several minutes later, the students moved to another section of the classroom, and they each held their Music instruments. Professor Haîyang walked around the chairs, to correct the postures and moves of her students. Amira adjusted the cords of her violin, while Dalya was sitting near her, watching in silence.

- And here is your instrument ... Mademoiselle Dalya Bouvard!

Dalya jumped out of her chair and she took the flute that Professor Haîyang gave her. Fascinated by the instrument, Dalya observed it for some long seconds. It was a long wood flute, beautifully carved with symmetrical holes, and a small ring on one side. It was a beautiful Music tool. And Dalya was happy to learn playing an instrument ... like all the other students. Professor Haîyang explained to her:

- Since you have a lot of catching up to do, you will keep this flute with you, at home ... it is imperative that you practice on it, as much as possible; in your home ... you will give me back the flute at the end of your presentation ... and in one piece, please!

Dalya answered with a happy tone:

- Thank you Professor!! Understood Professor!! I'll take care of this flute!!

And it looked like a smile appeared on the corner lips of Professor Haîyang. But the young woman pulled herself together quickly, and she continued to explain to Dalya, in a formal voice:

- First, you will learn by heart the melody notes ... then, you will practice on the flute in silence ... each hole corresponds to a note ... memorize the notes on the flute ... just like that ...

For a few minutes, Dalya listened attentively to the Professor's explanations regarding the use of the flute. The young woman took out of her pocket an item, and she gave it to Dalya:

- Here is an elastic ... hold it like this... and make that move with your fingers, as much as you can ... this exercise aims to reinforce and strengthen your fingers ... and you can easily and rapidly play the notes on the flute ... is that clear enough?
- Yes, Professor!

Dalya Bouvard playing a Music instrument! She never thought about it, not even in her dreams. Dalya was happy to learn a new thing in the Music class. When the Professor went away, Amira came near her friend:

-   It's a beautiful flute!! … It's pretty easy, you'll see!! I will help you practice on it!!

With difficulty, Dalya held her joy and she whispered all excited:

-   I am playing a Music instrument!! It's incredible!!

The two students exchanged a discreet laugh, innocent and accomplice.

Several steps away from them, the stares of Professor Haîyang were focused on Dalya. A serious and worried look. Miss Haîyang had received very clear orders from the great Master. And she had to follow them!

Chapter 16

Cutting the rice

Tuesday, January 19th, 1892. At the Royal Georgetown College.

While all the other students enjoyed their free time, Dalya and Amira waited for Professor Haîyang in the corridor, outside the teachers' room.

- What will we have as detention work, in your opinion? Dalya asked.
- Washing dishes ... folding towels ... sponging cutlery. Amira thought aloud.
- We will be busy for the next 3 months ... with my extra classes and my catching up to do ... I wonder how will I succeed this semester? exclaimed Dalya
- Don't worry, we will come out fine! Amira reassured her.

When Professor Haîyang came out of the teachers' room, she spoke to two students with a joyful smile:

- Good morning Mesdemoiselles ... follow me, please.

Dalya and Amira exchanged a worried look. Only a few days earlier, Professor Haîyang insisted to inflict on them a 3 months detention while lying, and now she smiled at them. None of the two students could understand the strange behavior of Miss Haîyang.

When the Professor and the two students entered the school kitchen, the interior was noisy and active. It was a huge kitchen, several light gray marble tables were placed in parallel, large windows illuminated the room, stoves and cookers in shiny steel were installed in each corner. All the kitchen staff was dressed in white uniforms impeccable and ironed.

A man stood out among all the other employees in the kitchen. A big size, muscular arms, straight black hair, a fair light skin, approaching his mid-thirties. The young man was the only one to wear a black kitchen uniform. His walk was slow, and his eyes scanned the work of the employees, in a serious stare.

Professor Haîyang approached him, motioning to her two students to follow her.

- Good morning Mr. Shang.

With a foreign accent, the man bowed respectfully:

- Professor Haîyang.

His allure was intimidating, but his authoritative voice was even more. Professor Haîyang spoke to him:

- I present to you Mademoiselle Dalya Bouvard ... the student who will follow her detention here, in the school kitchen ... as of 2 hours, 2 times a week, during her free hours ... for the next 3 months! ... I will give you her time schedule for you to arrange the detention work!

The man observed Dalya for a long second, with a curious and interested look. Dalya froze motionless in her place, she had the strange feeling that the man was examining and evaluating her, with only a glance of eyes. After a few seconds that seemed an eternity to Dalya, the man displayed a pleased and determined smile:

- 3 months ... 2 hours ... 2 times a week ... perfect! ... we need help in the kitchen!

Professor Haîyang presented the second student, with a curiously innocent voice:

- And here is ... Miss Amira Mounier. She will follow the same detention as Dalya Bouvard.

The man seemed surprised and confused. Apparently, he thought of receiving one student and not two. Professor Haîyang showed off an amused and provocative smile:

- 2 students in detention … since you think you are that talented!

Dalya and Amira exchanged a puzzled look. They had the same question in mind, at this instant: what did Professor Haîyang mean by her comment?

The man glared a cold look at Professor Haîyang, and he tried to appear courteous:

- Understood ... I will take care of the 2 students, then!

When Professor Haîyang left the kitchen, the man ordered Dalya and Amira to follow him. Passing through the various tables of working and cooking, Dalya noticed that the employees were watching them, with a curious and silent stare.

When they arrived at the other corner of the kitchen, the man turned around and he spoke to the two girls, with a firm authoritative voice:

- I am Chef Shang, the Cook of this school kitchen. I will personally manage your detention during the next 3 months.

He pointed at Amira to sit on a chair, near a huge basket of potatoes. He handed her plastic gloves:

- You will have to peel these potatoes.

Amira murmured in a shy voice:

- How many ... Chef?
- The entire basket! He replied in a firm voice.

Amira complied with slow moves. She put on the gloves, took the knife that Chef Shang gave her, then she observed for a few seconds, with fright, the huge potatoes basket waiting for her.

Chef Shang then turned to Dalya:

- Sit in front of that table.

Dalya did so, too. The kitchen table was near Amira's place, which delighted the two students.

- Put on these gloves. Ordered Chef Shang.

Dalya watched Chef Shang make a hand signal to one of the kitchen staff. Immediately, the employee put on the table before Dalya a big bowl of white rice, half-cooked. Chef Shang handed a knife to Dalya and he ordered her:

- Cut the rice into two.

Dalya took the knife from his hands, but she froze for a moment:

- But ... I ... what? ... The rice can't be cut, Chef ...

With a slow move, Chef Shang took the knife from Dalya's hands, he took one single rice seed, he placed it on a small wood board on the table, and then he cut the tiny seed of rice in two identical pieces with a firm and quick movement. Dalya froze open-mouthed. Chef Shang handed her the knife back and he ordered her for the 2nd time:

- Cut the rice into two.

Dalya didn't believe her ears. Peeling hundreds of potatoes, that was a normal detention. But cutting thousands of tiny half-cooked rice seeds ... one must admit that it was an unusual task. Yet, Dalya had to obey. She took the knife and she cut a tiny seed into two.

- Do not bend ... keep your back straight ... pass the knife with a single firm move! The Cook Chef corrected her, few times.

After a couple of minutes, the Cook Chef left the two girls alone, and he returned to supervise his other kitchen staff. Immediately as he was gone, Amira stated in a serious voice:

- I have a new theory!

Dalya turned around to her friend:

- Which is?

Amira Mounier took on her 5th potato to peel, and she announced:

- This is a school that gathers only fools!

Both students giggled discreetly, so as not to attract the Chef's anger, on their first day of detention. Except that, while the little girls were busy each in their detention work, the eyes of General Shang followed them from afar. His goal was very clear!

Chapter 17

A secretary

Wednesday, January 20th, 1892. In a streets' crossing, in Downtown of Georgetown.

- No no! At 10 AM, it is at Mr. Tudor's house, in the 35th street! Alfie got upset.
- And I am telling you that we have an appointment at 10 AM for snow removal at Mrs. Lance's boutique, in the 11th street! Maurice stated.
- Maurice, I'm sure! We have to be at Mr. Tudor at 10 AM!
- Maybe you got the wrong day, Alfie ... I'm sure it's the morning of Mrs. Lancel boutique today!

Alfie Jaq rubbed his cap all confused, and he sat on a bench:

- But I rarely make mistakes in appointments ... I'm sure I heard Mr. Tudor, today, at 10 AM!

Maurice Gus sat next to his friend on the bench:

- Well I've heard that we should clean the driveway of Mrs. Lancel, today at 10 AM ...

After a second of thinking, Alfie decided:

- We will wait for Tom then! He will correct us!

Alfie and Maurice didn't wait so long to see Tom Choux approach them. He was a small little boy, with blond hair, a permanently printed cheerful smile on his face. He wore a big man's coat that overflowed from the sleeves, gardening boots till his knee and a big blue cap on his head.

- Hello Maurice! Hello Alfie! it looks like a lovely day ...

Maurice stood up:

- Hello Tom ... we were waiting for you ... Alfie and I have an appointment conflict...

Alfie asked:

- Don't we have an appointment for snow removal at 10 AM at Mr. Tudor today?

Tom Choux replied cheerfully:

- Yes Yes!! Mr. Tudor, today at 10 AM!!

Instantly, Alfie jumped:

- I knew it! See Maurice, I didn't get the wrong date! It is at Mr. Tudor's house today!

Maurice was confused:

- But ... It's that ... but Tom, yesterday you told me we should start at Mrs. Lancel today ... at 10 AM...

Tom Choux smiled joyfully back at Maurice:

- But of course, yes!! Mrs. Lancel also today at 10 AM!!

Maurice and Alfie exchanged a confused look. None of them understood what was happening. Maurice tried to understand the situation:

- Tom ... we have 2 appointments for snow removal, at the same time, in two different places ... how is that possible?

Tom explained to them in a cheerful voice:

- Not just 2 appointments ... there is also a 3rd appointment with the Florian house in the 17th Street ... and a 4th appointment in front of the herbalist close to here.

Alfie couldn't believe his ears:

- 4 appointments ... at the same time?

Tom Choux proudly replied:

- Exactly yes! I took all the appointments at 10 AM!

Maurice and Alfie were paralyzed by what they have just learned. They had hired Tom Choux to take their appointments for snow removals and organize their agenda. But they never thought they would face such a situation. Maurice pulled himself together:

- But ... Tom ... why did you get all these appointments at the same hour?

With a constant smile on his face, Tom answered:

- You told me to note any appointment starting from 10 AM...

Alfie got angry:

- And you didn't think to set intervals between the appointments? How are we supposed to clear the snow of 4 houses at the same time?

Tom rubbed his hat for a moment; he didn't seem to understand the problem he had created:

- Should I have taken all the appointments at 11 AM?

At this moment, Alfie failed to contain his anger; he turned red and he walked toward Tom to give him a blow to the head:

- YOUR BRAIN IS OFFSET!! I'LL PUT IT BACK TO ITS PLACE!!

Maurice stopped Alfie and prevented him from advancing any further toward Tom Choux:

- No no!! Alfie calm down!! I have an idea!! Calm down!!

Alfie controlled his anger with difficulty. Maurice explained:

- I will take care of Mrs. Lancel's boutique ... and you'll take care of Mr. Tudor's house ...

A few seconds of thinking later, Alfie replied:

- We need a helping hand ... I will ask the other newspaper boys to help us ...

Maurice approved of his friend's idea:

- That would be great! We can hire them with us!!
- Yes ... 40% commission on every snow removal ... I will ask Heins to join you ... and Theo will help me to quickly finish the house of Mr. Tudor ...
- You think we can ask the twins Kiel and Bay, to take care of the Florian's house and the herbalist?
- Certainly!! Kiel and Bay won't refuse a paid job!!

Alfie took his tools' bag:

- We must rally the troops! ... I'll call Heins and Theo ... they must be near here somewhere!

Maurice completed Alfie's idea :

- And I'll bring Kiel and Bay ... we gather here in 15 minutes!

Tom Choux jumped, all excited and motivated:

- And I will take care of all the appointments, one hour afterward!! All the appointments will be noted for 12 AM!!

This time, Maurice handed a large snow shovel to Alfie:

- I changed my mind. Put his brain back to its place!

Chapter 18

Pastry

Saturday 23rd January 1892. At the grand Mansion.

Igor filled the big bucket of firewood logs. He had to load chimneys in the employees' rooms, in the Library, and in Dalya Bouvard's bedroom. He decided to start with the closest place; the employees' rooms.

After several minutes and several wood resupply paths, Igor headed toward the Library. Opening the door, Igor noticed the snow Panther lying down on a carpet in front of the fireplace. Igor exclaimed:

- You are living the good life in this place, Séraphine! ... Eating and napping, all day!

Igor stopped and froze in front of the Library's fireplace. The chimney was well lit; the wood logs place was already filled. Igor thought aloud:

- Someone loaded the fireplace without telling me?!

Still, Igor was happy to have one less chore to do. He left the Library and walked toward Dalya Bouvard's bedroom. The long big stairs made it painful and difficult to transport wood logs. Igor complained of his work, while opening the bedroom door:

- If only these many stairs didn't exist, I could have loaded the chimneys in fifteen minu...

Igor was paralyzed standing, facing the bedroom fireplace:

- Again?! ...

When Igor entered the kitchen, he was furious:

- When one of you loads the chimneys, at least let me know! ... It will save me from having to go up and down the stairs, for nothing!

Cristelle was preparing Dalya's dinner tray, while Océanie was arranging the employees' dining table. Océanie exclaimed:

- What are you talking about?

Igor asked:

- Are you the one who loaded the Library chimney?

Océanie laughed aloud:

- Loading the wood is the only task that I have always refused to do! It is out of question that I damage my nails and my fingers!

Igor turned around:

- Cristelle ... did you load the fireplace of Demoiselle's bedroom?
- No ... I've only arranged her room.

Igor then asked himself:

- The Cook never touch the firewood logs ... the Gardener spent all day in the garden ... but then, who loaded the chimney in the Library and the Demoiselle's bedroom?

At that precise moment, a little voice answered:

- Me!

The surprised looks of Cristelle, Igor and Océanie, turned around to notice Dalya Bouvard on the kitchen's door. The little girl continued in a natural voice:

- I had some free time, and I took care of reloading the chimney in my bedroom and in the Library ...

Océanie and Igor exchanged a confused look. They had never expected to hear such a thing. Igor asked again hesitantly:

- You ... you've loaded the fireplace, yourself? ... You recharged the chimney of your own bedroom?

Dalya naturally replied with a proud smile:

- Yes, I did it myself!

At this instant, Océanie and Igor struggled to hold their astonishment and laughs. Océanie asked Igor:

- Can she also recharge the employee's bedrooms' fireplaces?

Dalya replied cheerfully and without hesitation:

- Yes, I can do that too! I will be happy to help in the housewor...

Except that before Dalya could finish her sentence, Cristelle took Dalya's hand and she quickly drove her out of the kitchen:

- Where would you like to be served dinner Mademoiselle? In your bedroom or the dining room?

Before leaving the kitchen, Cristelle gave a threatening toward Océanie and Igor:

- I will take care of you later! You just wait, both of you!

Océanie and Igor laughed so loud and hard, they had tears in their eyes:

- She recharges the fireplaces now! Mr. Bûchebois will have a heart attack when he discovers that!
- She seriously answered me!! She wants to recharge the employees' chimneys!!
- I have never laughed so much in my life! An Heiress who recharge fireplaces!

When they arrived at the hall of the grand Mansion, Dalya didn't understand Cristelle's reaction, nor Océanie and Igor's laugh. Dalya repeated to Cristelle with a sure tone:

- I will be pleased to help you in the housework, Cristelle ... I have free time ...

Cristelle retained with difficulty her anger against Océanie and Igor, and she tried to explain to the little girl in a calm and caring voice:

- It's nice and generous of you, Mademoiselle ... but you cannot help us with housework, here at the grand Mansion!

Dalya protested:

- But ... at the annex house, I always helped my parents in the housework ... I used to help my father in the garage, and mother in the house ... why can I work at the annex house, and not the grand Mansion?

The logic of the little Dalya Bouvard was so simple. She could do housework everywhere, in all places. Cristelle smiled:

- Yes, Mademoiselle ... and I understand that doing housework makes you happy ... except that, in the grand Mansion, you cannot work ... you're an Heiress!

A few seconds of thinking, Dalya didn't seem convinced:

- So the Heirs don't do any housework? ... But then, what do they spend their days at?

The maid Cristelle wasn't expecting this question. She hesitated in finding her words:

- Well ... I think they ... you have to take care only of your courses at school ... and do what pleases you!

And before Dalya could answer Cristelle, the maid of the grand Mansion affirmed in a cheerful voice:

- For your dinner tonight, I will make you a good cup of fresh fruits for dessert ... with yogurt and honey on top of it ... you'll love it!

The maid Cristelle turned around and she walked with a firm step toward the kitchen. And instantly, Dalya heard Cristelle scream furiously with all her strength:

- BUT WHAT IS WRONG WITH BOTH OF YOU!! AREN'T YOU NOT ASHAMED OF YOUR ATTITUDE!! IGOR DON'T YOU REALIZE SHE IS OUR EMPLOYER!! OCÉANIE AREN'T YOU NOT ASHAMED TO ASK HER TO RELOAD THE ROOMS' CHIMNEY!!!

Amidst the laughs, Océanie and Igor defended themselves as best as they could, with difficulty, trying to stop laughing:

- But she is the one who have decided to reload the chimneys!
- I've only proposed the idea!! How could I know she would take me seriously!!
- Anyway, as of now, I should ask her if she had already reloaded her bedroom's fireplace, before carrying the wood all upstairs ...
- IGOOOOORRRR!!! Cristelle roared in a loud voice.

Dalya decided to return to the Library. She took a book and sat down between the cushions, in front of the fireplace greatly lit. The snow Panther was lying down near her, warming her fur from the fireplace heat.

While thinking for several minutes, Dalya was still confused. At the time when she lived with her parents, Dalya rarely had free time to herself; at times she would help her mother in the kitchen, at other times she carry out the work as ordered by her father. And here it was, for the first time in her life, being away from her parents, Dalya had free time. She repeated to herself some words that Cristelle said a few minutes ago:

- Do what pleases me ... do what pleases me!

Sunday, January 24th, 1892. In the French neighbors' house, Les Poirier.

It was an ordinary winter day for Richard Poirier. It was his day off; he was reading his newspaper in the living room of the house, sitting in front of the fireplace while sipping his hot ginger tea. The large windows of the living room offered a beautiful view of the garden covered with a layer of snow. The sky was filled with gray clouds.

At one moment, the calm of the living room was interrupted by the noise of discrete but well heard steps. Thinking it was Mrs. Glorina who was walking, Richard didn't take off his eyes from his newspaper.

When a little silhouette walked toward the big staircase of the house, heading to the upper floor. Her hair was covered in white powder, she wore white apron too big for her, her fingers and hands were covered to the elbows, with a white and yellow liquid. This little silhouette captured Richard Poirier's attention. He observed her, while she was walking up the stairs, and she was talking to herself in a small voice:

- The butter always melted ... dry ingredients mixed separately than liquid ones ... and the jam at the end ...

The little silhouette continued her way up the stairs, to the upper floor without noticing the presence of Richard Poirier in the living room.

The young man sipped his tea, wondering what that silhouette was doing and why was she covered in white powder. Richard Poirier continued to read his newspaper. When a few minutes later, the same silhouette came down the stairs, murmuring in a low voice:

- The fruit to be caramelized before ... and butter in the cake pan so it does not stick ... then the brown sugar to give color to the fr...

Dalya Bouvard stood still on the last step of the stairs. It was only at that moment that she realized the presence of Madame's son, Richard Poirier. The young man was sitting on a lounge chair, the newspaper in one hand and a cup of tea in the other. He watched Dalya for a moment, he was curious to know what was she doing. Before he asked, Dalya approached the living room, some steps, and she greeted him with a hesitant smile:

- Good morning.

Richard replied instantly, putting down his cup of tea:

- Good morning.

Dalya was always embarrassed at the presence of Richard Poirier. Although most of the time, the young man was quiet and courteous, Dalya thought he was intimidating. She guessed immediately that Richard wanted an explanation for her comings and goings. So Dalya informed him in an intimidated voice:

- I ... I was ... Mrs. Glorina instructed me to ask Madame ... upstairs in her bedroom ... if she wants pears or apples for the pie.

Richard Poirier folded his paper in two, to better observe her:

- You are making a pie in the kitchen?
- Yes, with Mrs. Glorina.

Richard understood the flour on Dalya's hair, and her hands covered with butter and sugar. Feeling increasingly embarrassed and uncomfortable, Dalya quickly turned around to the corridor leading to the kitchen. And Richard continued reading his newspaper.

Except that this time ... Richard became all confused, he simply couldn't remember what he was reading.

As soon as she entered the kitchen, Mrs. Glorina greeted her with a large smile:

- So? Pears or apples?
- Madame would like pears. Dalya answered, while returning to her place around the large kitchen table.
- Excellent choice!! Mrs. Glorina laughed. I admit that the caramelized pears are delicious!

Dalya started washing some pears and peeling them, while Mrs. Glorina put a cake mold on the kitchen table.

- I am happy to have you as a company, Mademoiselle!!
- I had no homework this weekend ... and there was not much to do in the grand Mansion ... I wanted to help with the housework there, but the employees prevented me from participating ... I was bored a little ...
- And you have done well to come visit us today, Mademoiselle. Better than being alone in this huge Mansion.

Dalya greatly enjoyed Mrs. Glorina's company, she was a very nice woman, caring, and mostly dynamic. While Dalya was peeling the 2nd pear, Mrs. Glorina finished mixing all the pie's ingredients, stirring them with a long wood spoon, in a quick movement.

- And I admit ... Mademoiselle ... I'm flattered that you are interested in my pastry ... do you enjoy cooking?

Dalya took a 3rd pear, and naturally replied:

- I would be happy to learn to cook. Previously, Mother would order me to warm up milk or bread in the morning, wash or cut fruits and vegetables sometimes ... I never cooked alone before ... but since I am in detention in the school kitchen, I like watching Chef Shang and the other employees, cook the midday meals to serve at the can...
- You are in detention? Exclaimed Mrs. Glorina, frozen in her place, her face was confused and surprised.

Dalya hesitated a few seconds, and then she explained to the woman:

- Yes ... I'm in detention ... me and my friend Amira ... in the school kitchen ...
- You don't look like a girl who would do silly things. For how long? Mrs. Glorina continued to stir her mixture in a slower movement, shocked by what she learned.
- For 3 months.
- 3 months?! Exclaimed Mrs. Glorina. But why is that? ... What happened?

Dalya explained the scene that happened in the Music classroom. Mrs. Glorina didn't waste a crumb of this story. At the end, Mrs. Glorina sighed:

- That's unfair, Mademoiselle. I'm so sorry for you and your friend.
- 3 months will pass quickly ... and besides, I have company. Dalya reassured her.

Mrs. Glorina retained her laugh. Then, she asked Dalya all curious:

- But then ... what do you do in the school kitchen? ... what is your detention work?
- My friend Amira peels potatoes. She have a huge basket to peel, each time. And I cut the half-cooked rice in half.

This time, Mrs. Glorina stopped:

- You cut ... what?
- The Cook Chef ordered me to cut the half-cooked rice in half.

Mrs. Glorina lost her words for a few seconds:

- It is not possible, Mademoiselle. Perhaps you misunderstood ... Are you sure this is what you are asked to do?
- Yes, Mrs. Glorina. The Cook Chef even corrected me 2-3 times. Dalya answered by taking a 5th pear to peel.

Mrs. Glorina continued her task; she buttered the pan pie with slow movements. Suddenly, the woman paused for a few seconds and she thought aloud:

- But ... cutting the rice ... this is strange ... very strange ...

Dalya didn't understand Mrs. Glorina's reaction, she dared to ask her:

- Why is it strange to cut rice in half?

Mrs. Glorina turned to the little girl:

- Well ... I've seen all kinds of recipes, Mademoiselle ... different cultures and origins ... but I never heard anything like this before. Rice cut in half? ... That's weird.

Dalya didn't know much about cooking. Except that the confused reaction of Mrs. Glorina about her detention's task, aroused Dalya's curiosity. If the rice shouldn't be cut into two, so why did the Cook Chef ordered her so?

The voice of Mrs. Glorina interrupted Dalya in her thoughts:

- But anyway ... I am delighted to teach you pastry, Mademoiselle!! You can come whenever you want!! I will make you, the best pastry Cook in Georgetown City!!
- Thank you very much, Mrs. Glorina!

Dalya Bouvard's day ended with a delicious pears cake and a cup of hot tea, shared with Mrs. Marianne Poirier in her bedroom. After finishing her cake, Dalya greeted Mrs. Glorina and she went back to the grand Mansion.

Chapter 19

A first clue

That night. In the grand Mansion.

In her bedroom at the grand Mansion, while Dalya was about to go to bed, she dared to ask Cristelle a question that worried her for the past few hours:

- Cristelle ... why should rice be cut in half?

The maid put a second piece of wood log in the fireplace, and she turned around surprised by this question:

- What Mademoiselle?... nobody cut the rice in half ... Who told you such a thing?

While wrapping herself with the soft cover under the bed, Dalya hesitated for a moment. She didn't dare to confess to Cristelle that she had a detention at school. So Dalya avoided Cristelle's question, by asking another:

- Are you sure Cristelle? ... Have you never seen the Cook cut the rice in half?

Cristelle approached the little girl, she adjusted the blanket on the bed, and she could not hold an amused giggle:

- No Mademoiselle, very sure of it! ... And besides, the rice seeds are so tiny, why should we cut them? ... It's a strange idea you have there!

When the maid Cristelle wished her a good night and closed the bedroom's door, Dalya sat on her bed, and she opened a book to read before sleep. Except that after several minutes of reading, Dalya dropped her book on her lap, and she sighed:

- So why the Cook Chef ordered me to cut the rice seeds in half?!

The reaction of Mrs. Glorina and Cristelle on this issue was strange. The two women were surprised by this task. So it is only natural that Dalya's curiosity increased. Sitting on her bed, she thought for several long minutes about this question. But failing to find an answer, Dalya got up from her bed and she walked to the living room where there was a small desk.

Dalya sat in front of the office desk. She watched a little box in shiny and indestructible metal. A small rectangular opening on the edge, was still opened. The top side of the box was opened on a transparent and light glass cage, of oval shape. Welded by four yellow gold cylinders, forged in a shape of vine plant, the cage was recharging on the night's light. A little round clock inside the cage, included two needles. The small needle indicated the date of 12th December 1892. And the big needle flickered between the nights of January 24th to 25th, 1892.

That strange box, as Dalya called it the Excelbox, never ceased to surprise not only the little girl, but all those who knew it. And in terms of answers, the strange box always provided ones...

Dalya Bouvard took out a little paper from a drawer, and she wrote on it:

What is the 1ˢᵗ clue?

Once Dalya placed the paper in the rectangular opening, the strange box was reawakened instantly. A blinding and brilliant light pierced the entire bedroom for a few seconds. A little paper appeared on the rectangular opening. And like many times before, Dalya took the answer from the Excelbox, hoping to find a clear and easy clue.

How long before a heart will be born?

16, 1

Dalya reread the paper several times. After a few minutes she lay back on her chair and sighed:

- A riddle again!

Well, yes. Because the Excelbox has decided to answer not only to the question of the rice cut in half ... the Excelbox decided to answer many other upcoming doubts ...

The next day, in the afternoon. At the end of classes. In the workshop of her uncle Giorgi Bouvard.

When Amira stopped in front of Giorgi Bouvard's workshop, she watched the strange house with a fascinated look. It was a funny little house, built only on one floor, with small windows.

- It looks like an experimentations laboratory!

Dalya replied in an amused voice:

- And yet ... you have not seen the inside of it!

At her first steps, Amira let out a surprised and amazed laugh:

- It's ... It's beautiful!!

The workshop was a big bazaar. Items piled everywhere, gadgets hung up abundantly; the furniture of the house sank into chaos. Disorder reigned as master. Immediately, a long silhouette welcomed the two students.

- Welcome Mesdemoiselles!! I'm delighted of your visit!!

Uncle Giorgi wore his usual work outfit; a long apron with multiple pockets filled with objects, and on his head large round glasses of a magnifying effect.

- Good morning Uncle Giorgi ... Thank you for having me and my friend, and for helping me practice my Chemistry class. I've learned the Periodic elements table, by heart ... and I'm ready to practice now!

The old man invited the two students to sit on chairs around a table in the middle of the workshop.

- You are welcomed at any time!! ... And I am happy to help you, Biggo!! ... Chemistry is the finest of all sciences!! ...

Dalya greatly appreciated her uncle Giorgi Bouvard. He was always considerate and attentive toward her. And for having consulted him a thousand times before, uncle Giorgi always helped Dalya to find solutions and answers.

Uncle Giorgi put on the table many jars in transparent glass, just like the ones in the Chemistry course, at school.

- I have prepared for you several elements to mix ... it's all about dosing ... and you can observe the immediate chemical reaction when mixing specific elements ...

While uncle Giorgi was searching for a jar in a corner of the workshop, Dalya and Amira wore their gloves and large protection eyeglasses. Dalya remembered something:

- I received the first clue!

Amira jumped out of her chair, as soon as she read the paper that her friend Dalya gave her:

- It's easy!! ... It's 9 month!!

Since several months now, whenever the Excelbox provided her with riddles to solve, Dalya's brain was anxious to find answers and understand the clues. And Dalya used all the help she could find:

- How? ... Why 9 months?

Amira turned around to face Dalya, and she explained to her:

- How long before a heart is born ... it is a matter of biology ... it's a new course that we started last year ... biology is a class where we study human anatomy, the human body and organ functions ... and the question of the clue is: how long before a heart is born ... we're all born at 9 months ...
- A question in biology? Exclaimed Dalya even more confused now. But ... I ... I wanted to understand why the Cook Chef ordered me to cut the rice in half ... I get a biology riddle?

Amira thought for a few seconds:

- I must confess that it is a strange clue ... and even the question is not specific enough ... we are all born at 9 months, but there are premature births at 8 months ...

Dalya was confused about the biology question. And even Amira began to doubt her answer. When finally, Amira decided firmly:

- I think 9 months would be the ideal answer. Yes. As long as there are no specificities, let's keep 9 months as a main response.
- Yes, you're right. Dalya confirmed, nodding her head.
- And about the number down? 16.1? ... Do you have any idea what it is? Asked Amira.

Dalya shared her thoughts aloud:

- For the Second Challenge, I had to find books' locations. Except that I had 3 numbers; the aisle, the row and the shelf. This time, I only have 2 numbers ... 16 and 1!

Amira exclaimed:

- So then, we will search in all the rows and aisles which have these numbers!

Dalya replied in a worried tone:

- There will be hundreds, if not thousands of books in a single row!! ... How will I find the specific book that the clue indicates me?

Her friend answered in a sure voice:

- Don't worry about that! You still have 11 months before the next Challenge. And I will help you find this book! ... Where should we start from? ... The school Library? Or the Grand Mansion's Library?

A few seconds of thinking sufficed, and Dalya answered, with a convinced tone:

- The place where I have found the other books ... it was at the National Georgetown Library!

Amira smiled and exclaimed happily:

- This will be a fun search!!

Suddenly, the deafening sound of an explosion shocked the entire workshop. Uncle Giorgi landed underneath a stack of objects and tools. A large cloud of dust invaded the workshop. By opening a small window to let some air, Dalya replied to her friend:

- A fun search ... provided we get out alive and in one piece, from uncle Giorgi's workshop!

Despite her doubts about the strange experiments of her uncle Giorgi, an uncontrollable laugh conquered Dalya and her friend.

Chapter 20

Lyor's refusal

Monday, February 01ˢᵗ, 1892. In the Law Firm.

It seemed like a beautiful winter day. The ground was covered with a beautiful snow layer. The sun was present in a blue sky. And the people of Georgetown city got used to the cold winter.

Dalya opened the door of the Law Firm. The only person she enjoyed meeting of this entire office was Mr. Sloan Wilfrid. She was touched by his politeness and kindness toward her. But other than Mr. Wilfrid, Dalya didn't like anybody else in this place.

Dalya walked through the offices in slow and hesitant steps. She was forced to notify the Lawyer Mr. Ernest Laszlo, about all the clues emitted by the Excelbox.

- Good morning. May I see Mr. Ernest Laszlo, please? Dalya asked, displaying a nice smile to the Lawyer's secretary.

The young woman didn't like Dalya, since the first day the little girl appeared in the Law Firm. The secretary stared at Dalya with an arrogant look, from head to toe. After a few seconds of silence where Dalya was forced to be polite, the woman ordered Dalya haughtily:

- Go in!

When Dalya entered the big office of the Lawyer, and stepped forward, she noticed several familiar faces; the Lawyer Mr. Ernest Laszlo was sitting behind his desk. Mr. Sloan Wilfrid and Lyor Laszlo sat on chairs in front of their employer's office. Dalya felt there was tension in the air. And she was right. She remained still standing near the office entrance door, while the three men ended their conversation.

Mr. Ernest Laszlo dropped a folder on his desk with an upset move:

- When I ask that a report is completed, it must be!

His son Lyor replied in a sure voice:

- We have collected all the informations and sales numbers, of the Concrete factory owned by BalthEnterprise. In order to allow better decisions on the future of this facto...
- The report is incomplete!! Mr. Ernest Laszlo replied in a high tone.

Sloan Wilfrid was always in a quieter and moderated attitude:

- It is an audit report, Mr. Ernest Laszlo. But we may have wrongly understood your request. Is there any other information that you wanted to read in this report?

Mr. Ernest Laszlo took the document in his hands, and he addressed his two employees in an irritated tone:

- This is a report that shows me that the factory is in progress!! In the last pages, there are even solutions to speed up the sales numbers and improve the performance of its machines!! This is a report that tells me that this Concrete factory can be saved!!
- Because this is the case!! Lyor exclaimed with an enthusiastic tone. The factory only needs more time to catch up on its production delays. There was a time when this factory was the most efficient of all the othe...
- I don't care at all about this factory!! Mr. Ernest raised his voice. I want to read a report confirming me of selling this factory!! And that's all!! A simple report!! But it seems that even at this simple task, you fail Lyor!!

Mr. Wilfrid tried to intervene, but he was unable to place a word. He was interrupted by Lyor who wanted to defend his work:

- The report you hold in your hands, Monsieur, reflect the exact numbers and the real situation of this factory. The collected data indicate that the Concrete factory should not be sold but renova...
- I didn't ask your opinion on the subject! Mr. Ernest announced in an arrogant tone.

To calm the conversation between the father and the son, Wilfrid opened his mouth to speak. Except that a strange little object caught Wilfrid's attention and made him turn mute. Sloan Wilfrid noticed on the desk of the Lawyer Mr. Ernest Laszlo, a little paper, which appeared to be a list of people. Lengthening discreetly his neck, Sloan Wilfrid was able to read familiar names: Mr. Strauss ... Mr. Jean-Pierre ... Mr. Marius ... Mr. Quentin ... Mr. Eliott...

As the right hand of the Lawyer Ernest Laszlo, Sloan Wilfrid was aware of the entire Firm's business. Except that this little list aroused Wilfrid's curiosity. Wilfrid knew all the men on this list, but he didn't know why they were all gathered in a list...

The conversation between Ernest and Lyor Laszlo had to be calmed down before it escalates. Sloan Wilfrid pulled himself together and he tried to intervene:

- What Lyor is trying to say, is that the factory will be more profitable to us than sellin...
- This is not my opinion!! It is the result of this report and these numbers!! Lyor defended himself in a tone slightly more elevated than usual. If the report reaches the managers, the Directors' board may decide the fate of this facto...
- I AM THE DIRECTORS' BOARD!! Mr. Ernest exclaimed, giving a strong punch on his desk.

A heavy silence settled for a few seconds before Mr. Ernest Laszlo addressed his son Lyor with an icy and menacing tone:

- You seem to forget that you're still an apprentice, Lyor ... you are far away from becoming a skilled Lawyer ... get that into your head, Lyor ... and I will remind you for the last time, that I am the sole responsible of BalthEnterprise ... I am not asking your opinion ... I simply demand a complete and well done work ... every day, you prove to me that you're even more incapable and incompetent than I thought!

At this moment, Mr. Ernest Laszlo raised up his eyes to notice a little silhouette standing at the door of his office. For several minutes, Dalya stood there, not daring to move or interrupt the conversation of the three men. Mr. Ernest Laszlo spoke to Wilfrid in a calmer tone:

- Redo this report for me ... I want it by tomorrow morning!
- Understood, Monsieur.

While Mr. Wilfrid and Lyor turned around and left Mr. Ernest's office, the Lawyer ordered Dalya to step forward. Halfway, Mr. Wilfrid greeted Dalya with a nice smile, while Lyor didn't even look at her and he walked out retaining with difficulty his anger.

- What is it? Mr. Ernest Laszlo asked coldly.
- Good morning, Monsieur. Dalya whispered. I ... I came to inform you of the 1st clue ... of the Third Question ...

While handing him a small paper, Dalya was uncomfortable under the scrutinizing looks of the Lawyer. He took the paper, and put it on his desk, without even reading it. His icy stare contained such anger that he had trouble retaining. Ernest Laszlo stared at the little girl, several long seconds, before asking with an authoritative voice:

- Is that all?
- Yes, Monsieur.

Dalya greeted him with a forced smile, and she turned around to leave his office, with rushed steps. She hated being in the presence of the Lawyer. He inspired her no trust or kindness. Before closing the office door, Dalya turned around discreetly, and she could see from the corner of her eye that the Lawyer lay back on his chair and continued to observe her with a strangely aggressive look...

In the corridors of the Law Firm, Dalya slipped between the other employees to find a specific office. She knocked 2 times on a closed door.

- Come in.
- Good morning, Monsieur Wilfrid.

The young Lawyer put down off what appeared to be Lyor's report, and he stood up to greet the little girl with a big cheerful smile:

- It's always a pleasure to receive you in my office, Mademoiselle!! How are your classes? The back to school went on well, I hope?
- Very good, Monsieur. I had some extra courses than the previous semester; Professor Canfield thought I could take some more classes.

Dalya decided that in addition to her new courses, she wouldn't speak about her detention in the school kitchen. She didn't wish Mr. Wilfrid to have a low opinion of her. She chose not to mention it.

- This is excellent, Mademoiselle!! Continue on!!
- Yes, Monsieur. Dalya blushed.
- And what brings you to my office today? Is there something you need?

After a few moments of hesitation, Dalya decided:

- I was wondering if you can help me register in the National Georgetown Library. The secretary of the Library said that minor children must be registered by their ... their ...
- Parents ... or legal guardian.

M. Wilfrid finished Dalya's sentence. Without further explanation, he understood that Dalya's parents would refuse to help her in anything; the Bouvard parents didn't speak a word to their own daughter since some time now. Dalya had no choice but to ask Lyor Laszlo, her legal guardian, to register her in the National Library. And given that all the previous interactions between her and Lyor turned into a confrontation, Dalya decided to seek the help and mediation of Mr. Wilfrid. He smiled happily:

- Certainly, Mademoiselle!! You will be signed in!! With pleasure!!

A few seconds later.

- Out of the question!! No!!

Lyor didn't even look at Dalya who stood at the entrance to his office; he was searching for a paper in a sea of documents, removing files with a brusque move. And as usual, Lyor seemed upset and in an angry mood. Wilfrid got used to the stubbornness of his pupil:

- Lyor ... she needs her legal guardian to register her himself in the National Library. It is a simple procedure. I would have done it gladly, but you know the legal paperwork.
- I don't have time for her!!
- It will require only 10 minutes ... and she will have access to all the books in the Library.

Lyor let out a furious look toward Wilfrid:

- I don't care at all!! It's a no!!

Wilfrid stepped closer to Lyor's desk and he whispered softly:

- She never asked for anything ... she doesn't deserve being denied this registration in the Libra...

In an instant, Lyor stood up from his chair with a rapid move:

- I don't deserve to be treated as an incapable because of her!!

Dalya walked a few steps inside the office:

- I didn't call you an incapable ... at least, not today!

Wilfrid retained a laugh with difficulty. He turned toward Lyor, having well guessed the reason of his pupil's anger:

- The Concrete factory will be sold Lyor ... Mr. Ernest's decision was taken before your report by the way ... you did a great job, the report was well written and detai...
- This is not what he thinks, Wilfrid!!
- And I understand your anger, Lyor, believe me. But don't punish her for something she didn't do. She has nothing to do with it.

At this moment, Lyor screamed while pointing out at Dalya:

- SHE IS THE SOURCE OF ALL MY PROBLEMS!! YEARS OF HARD WORK AND SLEEPLESS NIGHTS TO GAIN HIS ESTEEM!! SHE TAKES IT ALL IN ONE SECOND!! IF SHE HAD NOT BEEN HEIRESS, HE WOULDN'T HAVE TREATED ME AS INCAPABLE!!

Dalya didn't understand all of Lyor's words, but she insisted to correct a sentence:

- I didn't choose to be Heiress!! It is the Governor who wrote my name in his Wi...
- GET OUT!! Lyor yelled.
- Lyor!! Mr. Wilfrid tried to calm him down, being surprised by Lyor's anger.
- But I didn't do anything to you!! Dalya protested.
- I SAID GET OUT!! Lyor seemed enraged.

Wilfrid turned toward Dalya, and he forced himself to smile:

- I am sorry, Mademoiselle ... but I think it would be better to come back another day ... we will discuss your registration later ...
- GET OUT!! Yelled Lyor for the 3rd time.

When pushing the exit door, Dalya found Amira at the exit of the Law Firm.

- So then? Amira stood up from a step on the stair.
- He refused to help me. He doesn't want to sign me up in the National Library.

Dalya replied with an upset voice. She didn't dare to tell her friend about the incomprehensible and unpredictable anger of her legal guardian Lyor. Amira exclaimed, putting her schoolbag on her back:

- Too bad for him, then. I will ask my father for help. He will sign me up at the National Library, and we will look together for this book!
- Sorry to bother you with that. Dalya followed her friend down the street.

Amira stopped in front of Dalya:

- Are you kidding?! This is the most beautiful adventure that happened to me since ... ever!

Dalya couldn't hold her laugh:

- A 3 months detention in the school kitchen and a book to search for like a needle in the sand ... you call this a beautiful adventure?

The two little girls continued on their usual way to their homes, laughing aloud, despite the denials, the doubts and the riddles waiting for them. The end of the day promised to be more calm and serene.

Chapter 21

The Cold

Thursday, February 04th, 1892. At the Royal Georgetown College.

The winter this year was very cold and long. The snow was falling frequently during the recent days. The trees seemed murdered forever by the cold; the sun was often hidden by gray and filled clouds. The entire city of Georgetown was sprinkled with a white snow layer.

Alfie Jaq and Maurice Gus had an appointment for snow removal in front of Mr. Weggman's house. It was a beautiful mansion, luxurious and refined.

- He has big stairs! Alfie sighed, in front of all the snow which covered several steps of the entrance.
- The bigger the stairs, the bigger the payment!! exclaimed Maurice with trembling teeth, he continued in a low voice:
- I feel that this winter will kill me ... I hope the spring is close!

As always, Alfie felt so little of the winter's cold. He wore his usual red bow tie, a cotton sweater, black pants, a big waterproof coat, and large snow boots. Maurice, unlike his friend, felt very well the winter's cold up to the bones. And being chilly, one would have thought that Maurice was wearing all the clothes he could find in his house, on that day. Several sweaters and several pants, a green cap hiding his tiny ears, large black boots, and a coat that hardly closed on him. Maurice was still shivering from cold.

- So I'll start cleaning the entrance and ... Alfie asked.
- And ... I sweep after you! Maurice answered by taking a large broom.
- Let's go. Come on! Come on! Alfie encouraged himself aloud.

Both boys were active in their snow removal work. And a long day was waiting for them.

In the opposite street, there was a huge building in front of the house that Alfie and Maurice were clearing out of snow. The huge building was of red bricks, black fence around the entire place, hundreds of windows and a large garden. The huge building looked magnificent and intimidating.

At a moment, at one of the building's window, a little silhouette noticed Alfie and Maurice being busy in their snow removal. She immediately took her coat and she ran to the exit door of the Royal Georgetown College.

- Good morning Alfie!! Good morning Maurice!!

Both boys turned around to see their friend Dalya Bouvard standing in front of them. Alfie smiled at her:

- Hello Dalya!! It's nice to see you!!

Maurice came down the steps and he nearly lost his balance:

- Hi!! Is it really there where you follow your classes?
- Yes, that's the college, over there. The Latin course hasn't begun yet, and I noticed you through the windows.

Alfie and Maurice remained amazed at the enormity of the red brick building.

- It's ... very big!! Exclaimed Maurice. I will get lost inside, if I step in.
- Me, they would have to pay me to step inside of it!! Alfie laughed.

Maurice corrected his friend:

- What?! ... They don't pay you to study!! You have to study to get paid!!

Dalya laughed at her friends' arguing, before asking them:

- So ... how is your business going on?
- Perfectly well!! Alfie screamed with a cheerful voice. We have had a good unpredictable snow during the recent days; we are picking up a fortune!!

Before Maurice could place a word, a little silhouette approached Dalya and her 2 friends.

- What are you doing outside? Amira whispered timidly.

Dalya smiled back at her:

- These are my friends ... I present to you Alfie Jaq and Maurice Gus. They clear the snow out of the house entries, at this time of the year.

Amira Mounier smiled at the two boys and she observed them curiously. Dalya continued the presentations:

- And this is Amira Mounier ... she is my classmate and my only friend in this school.
- Nice to meet you! Said Maurice.

Alfie who was usually very talkative and not measuring his words, he became all silent for once. He stuttered some incomprehensible words:

- I ... yes ... well ...

Maurice took the big discharge bag in his hand and he asked:

- And you study all the classes together?
- Almost, I have only 2 more classes than Dalya. But we work all our homework together. Amira replied in a joyful voice.
- And luckily she helps me with my homework!! With all the delay I have to catch up, I can never pass the exams. Dalya laughed.

Amira dared to ask:

- Do you know each other since a long time?

Alfie seemed to have lost the use of speech. He was pale and he looked lost in his thoughts. Maurice replied while watching with a confused look his friend:

- Long enough, yes ... Alfie sells newspapers ... I wax shoes ...
- When I worked at the market in front of the Toscana restaurant, we met very often. Dalya explained.
- And this winter, we have decided to clean the snow house entries! Continued Maurice. All ways are good to earn more money, isn't it right Alfie?

Dalya and Maurice exchanged a confused and worried look. Since ever, nothing could mute Alfie. And for the first time since they knew him, Alfie was still standing, his eyes lost and absent.

- And ... how many houses you still have left to do? Asked Amira, who also didn't understand Alfie's attitude.
- Only 2 more for today. Replied Maurice, when he picked up his broom. I admit that the mornings are easier than the afternoons. At least the midday sun warms me! Provided that the winter ends soon! I am wearing all the clothes in my closet and I still feel the cold!! But where does it come in?

Dalya and Amira exchanged an amused giggle. Dalya removed her blue scarf and she wrapped it around Maurice's neck:

- Here you are ... maybe with a 4th scarf, you will get warmer! I am offering it to you!

Maurice thanked her with a happy smile. He looked like a polar bear with the entire pile of clothes he was wearing. And yet, Maurice had blue lips and he was shivering from cold.

At this moment, Amira Mounier removed her scarf too, and she gave it to Alfie, with a nice smile:

- Here, my scarf can be more useful for you; there is still work for you outside.

Alfie took the light pink scarf and he observed it with an amazed look, like it was the most wonderful thing that he had ever received. Alfie looked at Amira, but he remained speechless. One would have thought that Alfie's brain stopped working. Dalya and Maurice exchanged a worried and a confused look, and they whispered:

- What is happening to him?
- I don't have the faintest idea. He seems to be lost somewhere in his mind.
- Yet it has never happened to him before.
- Yes, I know. It's really weird.

Facing the motionless attitude of Alfie, Amira took her pink scarf out of Alfie's hands and she wrapped it on the neck of the boy. Alfie displayed a wide smile, while watching Amira Mounier.

When a distant voice reached them in the street. It was Salman Elpacha who was perched on one of the large windows of the school classroom. Several students were watching through the windows of the classroom and they were laughing. Salman Elpacha screamed in a mocking tone, while addressing Alfie:

- Hey ... you with the pink scarf ... isn't it a female scarf?

Instantly, Alfie awoke from his daydream, and he yelled with all the strength of his lungs:

- Hey ... you ... the cold is male or female? ... Huh? ... So shut up! ... Go back to your class, before I decide to teach you a lesson, myself!!

Instantly, Salman Elpacha froze up straight and he lost his smirk. He immediately closed the window of the classroom, and he walked away with the other students. Maurice whispered to Dalya, in an amused and reassuring tone:

- Alfie was lost for a while. But now, he is found.

Dalya and Amira choked on laughing. They greeted the two boys, and then they went back inside the school. Instantly, Maurice approached Alfie who was watching Dalya and Amira crossing the street.

- By the way ... what happened to you, earlier?

Alfie smiled as if he had found a diamond:

- If I tell you, you will not believe me!
- Try me anyway, I may believe you. Maurice replied to him; he was worried about his friend's attitude.

A few whispers later, Maurice stared at Alfie with a surprised look, before exclaiming:

- That is not possible! You are insane! All of that in one minute?! You're officially crazy!

Alfie gave him an upset look:

- You just said a second ago ... try me anyway, I may believe you!

Maurice sighed for a moment:

- Sorry Alfie ... it's just that ... what you just told me is ...
- Crazy, isn't it?
- Yes, a bit. But, if you're sure ...
- I'm a thousand percent sure Maurice!

Alfie and Maurice watched for a long moment the two little girls walking up the steps of the Royal Georgetown College. The idea that Alfie shared with his friend, was impossible and insane. After a few seconds of thinking, Maurice affirmed to his friend in a decided tone:

- If you're sure about it, Alfie ... then I will help you!

Chapter 22

Unusual

Saturday, February 13th, 1892. In the neighbors' house, les Poirier.

On this weekend, in the house of the French family, les Poirier, everything went as usual. Mrs. Marianne Poirier spent her day lying in bed in her bedroom, reading a book. Mrs. Glorina was busy in the kitchen preparing meals. Richard Poirier was in his office, working on his reports. Everything was as usual. Well ... almost everything.

After spending all morning sitting at his office's desk, Richard Poirier relaxed for some minutes on his chair. The report was almost done; it only needed a quick editing and some notes to add. Having a reference in his report to recheck, Richard thought to stretch their legs a bit. He left his office and headed to the Library in the living room downstairs.

Seconds later, a little silhouette appeared in the corridor of the upper floor. She walked in discreet and slow steps toward Mrs. Marianne's bedroom. This little silhouette was holding a large silver tray in her hands. At a moment, this silhouette stopped and walked several steps back. She hesitated for a second before deciding to enter a specific room. Richard Poirier's office.

The little silhouette discovered Richard Poirier's office for the first time. And she was fascinated by what she has found. Never an office appeared so neat and impeccably organized. A big desk table of precious wood, occupied the place, well comfy chairs and divans, a bright chandelier adorned the ceiling, a golden fireplace lit up the room, a large Library where books and files were perfectly arranged there. It was an elegant office, reflecting the calm and the ordered mind of its user, Richard Poirier.

Approaching the desk table, the little silhouette smiled while discovering several notes and pages written in a beautiful elegant and clear handwriting. The little silhouette didn't dare to stay longer in this room, at the risk of being discovered. She put down a small plate on the office table, and she left the room. As quietly as she came in.

Richard had confirmed his reference. When he returned to his office, Richard stood still, while facing a strange item placed on his office table. A plate of a strawberry tart, a small silver fork wrapped in a little napkin. Richard Poirier was confused:

- It's unusual ... Mrs. Glorina never brings me cakes to my office ...

Richard took the fork anyway, and he tasted a bite of the cake. Instantly, Richard exclaimed in a curious tone:

- Strange ... very strange ... this cake lacks of sugar ... Mrs. Glorina never missed her cakes before ... that's unusual!

Chapter 23

Counting lentils

Tuesday, March 01st, 1892. At the Royal Georgetown College.

At the end of their classes, Dalya and Amira went to the school kitchen. The day was busy and full with classes and studies. Walking through a corridor, Amira sighed:

- My head is heavy ...
- I admit me too. Both History and Geography courses were too long ... I thought this day would last forever! Dalya exclaimed.
- And yet, we are at the beginning of the semester. We didn't even get yet to the most difficult chapters. Amira said.
- Did you see Eriem Eyelord sleeping earlier on? ... It was hard to keep an eye opened! Yet the History Professor gently woke her up ... his favorite student ... if someone else dared to sleep in his course, Professor Ajanar would have yelled and screamed and made a sce..

When suddenly, Amira interrupted her friend:

- Didn't you notice that the History Professor ignored you the entire class? He didn't even say your name when he made the call!! He acted as if you did not exist!!

Dalya laughed happily:

- And that's fine with me! ... Being ignored is better than hearing the mean comments and critics of Professor Ajanar ... I can finally study the History lessons and better focus!

Amira struggled to hold an amused laugh:

- Well anyway, the Geography teacher, Mr. Felozi seemed forced to endure your presence ... he appeared to make a huge effort to avoid you and ignore you!!

Dalya looked up and prayed:

- And I hope with all my heart that both History and Geography teachers ignore me for the rest of the semester!! Please!! Please!! Please!!

Both students laughed, while crossing a school corridor. Amira thought aloud:

- I wonder if the behavior of the History and Geography Teachers has changed because of Professor Canfield?

Dalya didn't need a second to find the answer to this question:

- Certainly, yes! Since Professor Canfield recorrected my exam papers and changed my grades!

Amira was curious:

- What do you think happened between Professor Canfield and these two Teachers?
- I don't have the faintest idea …

When Dalya received her new grades in these two subjects, she was delighted to have been right. To have correctly answered several questions, Dalya thought she deserved more than a zero. She remembered that Professor Canfield handed her the grade's report, insisting that she consults him at the slightest worry. She didn't dare to ask him how or why her grades have changed. But Dalya was grateful to Professor Canfield, for watching over her and her education, just as the Late Mr. Governor had trusted him to do.

When they arrived at the school kitchen, Dalya and Amira noticed that the Cooking work was well advanced. All the kitchen employees were busy in their tasks. The stoves were all lit, and many foods were already cooked.

When Amira and Dalya walked to their usual place, a silhouette approached them. The Cook Chef was as always dressed in his black apron, impeccably ironed, an intimidating and a serious air. The Cook Chef Shang spoke to Amira first:

- You will have the zucchini to peel this month. We use the zucchini flowers in meals; you will then put them here in this container. Dadès the school concierge will pick the zucchini peels when you are done. He uses them to fertilize the garden soil. Here are some new gloves to use.

Amira sat on a chair, and she started her work, delighted to have a new vegetable to peel other than potatoes. The Cook Chef approached Dalya and he pointed at a big jar:

- This month, you will have to count the red lentils.

Dalya thought he had misheard. She repeated:

- I will have to cook the red lentils?

The Cook Chef took the jar and he emptied its contents on a big white tray. Then, he answered Dalya in a natural and calm voice:

- No, Mademoiselle … you will have to count the red lentils.

Dalya observed the large tray. There must have been millions of tiny red lentils. Dalya never had to do such a task. She was confused:

- Counting lentils? … But why? … we can measure with a scale to know how many grams there are … I never heard anyone counting the lentils …

The Cook Chef was not a man to give explanations for his orders. Chef Shang was an intimidating and strange man. And yet, he answered Dalya's confusion with a serene polite voice:

- Each task has its uses, Mademoiselle Dalya.

Dalya didn't knew what Chef Shang meant by those words. She decided to sit at the counter and she began to count the red lentils. When the Cook Chef went back to work in the kitchen, Amira exclaimed:

- Did you know that red lentils are much more delicious than the brown lentils ... in a soup with garlic, pumpkin and carrots ... a delight!

Dalya replied:

- I never tasted these red lentils before ... I didn't even know it existed!
- I'll cook them for you; next weekend ... my father loves this soup! And I'm sure you'd enjoy it too!

Dalya held a confused laugh:

- Yes, for sure ... I'd like to eat them, but not count them!

Amira peeled her 5th zucchini:

- It is strange that the Cook Chef ordered you to count them ... I wonder what's the point of counting the lentils ... It would be much simpler to weigh them.

Dalya sighed:

- It will take me forever to count these lentils, there are many millions! I think the Cook Chef just wants to inflict a difficult punishment ... counting lentils, with no valid reason.

Several minutes later, Dalya's eyes were dizzy. By focusing too hard on counting the identical lentils, her sight became blurred and her eyes hurt. It was not a simple detention as she thought. Counting lentils demanded focus and perfect vision!

Sitting in her chair, Dalya decided to count aloud:

- 145 ... 146 ... 147 ... 148 ...

And to make her friend smile and lighten up, from her heavy detention, Amira thought aloud:

- 69 ... 70 ... 71 ... 72 ...

Dalya turned around toward her friend, and she giggled:

- What are you doing?! ... You are misleading me! ... 149 ... 150 ... 151 ... 152 ...

While peeling zucchinis, Amira spoke aloud:

- Exactly, that's my goal! ... 83 ... 84 ... 85 ...

Chapter 24

A tense throat

Saturday, March 05th, 1892. In the house of the French neighbors, les Poirier.

Richard Poirier had an important appointment this afternoon. He greeted his mother in her bedroom, and then he took on his coat and gloves. Before leaving the house, Richard headed toward the kitchen. Opening the door, he announced in a natural voice:

- Mrs. Glorina ... I came to inform you that I won't be lat...

Richard Poirier froze for a moment, at the kitchen's doorway. Mrs. Glorina was preparing a tea tray of two cups and a teapot. And a little silhouette was standing in front of the kitchen table. It was Dalya Bouvard. In front of a large basket full of eggs, Dalya was busy separating the yellow and white of an egg. Stressed and focused on this difficult move, Dalya didn't look up to the young man.

- Yes Monsieur Richard? You were saying? Asked Mrs. Glorina, with her usual kind smile.

The tone of Richard's voice changed dramatically, becoming more tense and serious. Richard decided to continue anyway:

- I ... I won't be late this evening. I will join Mother for dinner tonight.
- Understood Mr. Richard, I will prepare the dinner table for two, then. Said Mrs. Glorina while filling the teapot of boiling water.

Dalya froze her hands a few seconds to slowly swing the egg white into a container, while retaining the egg yellow with a spoon. Richard watched her for a minute without daring to interrupt her. He continued to speak to Mrs. Glorina:

- And I wanted to inform you that I will have guests for dinner ... next Wednesday.
- How many people, Monsieur?

Richard took a few steps toward the kitchen table:

- 4 people. I will make at your disposal the driver, for necessary shoppi...

When a little upset voice, interrupted Richard:

- And here's the 5th egg that I miss!!

The egg yolk had slipped from Dalya's fingers and landed in the already full container of yellow and white eggs. It was only then that Dalya realized the presence of Richard Poirier in front of her; Dalya greeted him with a discreet smile. Mrs. Glorina could hardly hold her laugh while speaking to Dalya:

- Separating the yolk from the egg white, it will require some practice and more time, Mademoiselle. Try without the spoon, only with your fingers.

Immediately, Dalya took a new egg and she broke it in two. Mrs. Glorina turned to Richard:

- And what would you like for the dinner menu, Monsieur?

Richard detached his attention from Dalya, who was moving her fingers slowly and firmly holding the egg shell. The young man replied to Mrs. Glorina:

- It is an ordinary dinner. A soup, fried vegetables, roasted meat ... and for dessert, I let y...
- No no no no!!

Despite her fingers moved so slowly, the egg yolk slid quickly to the container, leaving Dalya speechless and shocked. Apparently, separating the yolk from the egg white was not as simple as she had planned. Dalya thought aloud:

- But ... what ... it slips before I could even touch it ... yet I move so slowly ... separating them is impossible ... it is the 6th egg!!

Suddenly, something interrupted Dalya in her thoughts. Approaching her, with slow steps, Richard took a new egg from the basket, and he gave it to Dalya, displaying an amused smile:

- Perseverance, Mademoiselle. Perseverance.

Dalya took the new egg from Richard, in a shy hand gesture. Despite the intimidating presence of Richard Poirier; he was always courteous with Dalya. But on that day, Richard's words seemed strange. Perseverance was the answer to the 2nd Challenge. Could it be that Richard Poirier followed closely and was interested in Dalya's Challenges? It was a question that surprised the little girl's heart. However, Dalya just smiled timidly. Richard finished his conversation with Mrs. Glorina:

- For dessert, I let you chose. I will notify the driver to wait for you, tomorrow.
- Understood, Mr. Richard.

When leaving the kitchen, Richard Poirier turned around for a minute, before closing the kitchen's door. He was aware that Mrs. Glorina was teaching Dalya the art of pastry, since many weeks now. He should have got used to the frequent visits of Dalya in his house ... Nonetheless ... it was not that simple. Richard Poirier was still always uncomfortable at the presence of Dalya Bouvard.

For a few minutes, Richard stared at the little girl through the narrow opening of the kitchen door. Dalya tried for the 7th time, and she had decided to act quickly. When she broke the egg, Dalya threw the egg white with a quick movement in a new container, and then she rose up the egg yolk in a sharp move.

- It's ... it's ... it's separated!! ... Finally!! Dalya jumped in her place, exclaiming in a proud and joyful voice.

Mrs. Glorina put down a cookie plate on Madame's tea tray. She stepped close to check the container in front of Dalya and then she laughed joyfully:

- Congratulations Mademoiselle!! You have succeeded!!
- 7 eggs to get there, still!! Dalya cleaned her hands with a towel.
- It's called practice. Mrs. Glorina laughed. And don't worry about the eggs; I'll need them for the dessert of Mr. Richard's dinner.
- It's thanks to the egg that he gave me. It is the only one I could separate. Dalya laughed.
- One lucky egg!

While Mrs. Glorina and Dalya laughed aloud, the young man was still standing, watching through the narrow opening of the kitchen door. Richard Poirier felt his throat tightened up and tense. And it was a very rare and an unusual sensation, that Richard Poirier felt ... only whenever he is meeting this strange little girl.

Chapter 25

An unappreciated intelligence

Tuesday, March 08th, 1892. In Ord Wood factory.

The immense Ord factory was just outside Georgetown city, near the town port. The Ord factory was specialized in transforming wood into doors, windows, and other useful furniture.

The Lawyer Mr. Ernest Laszlo walked as master of the place. He examined the factory in a scrutinizing look. Walking to his right and his left, the managers provided him with the necessary explanations in turns.

- In this section, the manufacturing of house doors...
- We first address the shape of the door, and then the coating and the color. It's a process that takes few days ...
- And on this side, the making of windows, several types and kinds of shutters ...

From time to time, Mr. Ernest Laszlo expressed his remarks:

- The turnover is significantly lower than the previous year ... why is that?
- This is due to the delay of our Canadian supplier to deliver the wood this year ... the fires that ravaged the Eastern region, have unfortunately affected the wood industry, and we had some delays in the delivery ...

Lyor was walking behind the men. He observed with a discreet look the works and machines. For all the visits to the factories and companies held by BalthEnterprise, Lyor was forced to attend with his father's presence. Although, it was Mr. Ernest Laszlo who was entirely and unquestionably in charge of all the decisions...

After several minutes of walks and inspections, Mr. Ernest stopped in front of a big cutting wood machine, at the back of the factory:

- And ... what about these machines?

A manager walked forward:

- These are engines that require maintenance ... we store them in this part of the factory, while waiting to find a solution to repair the...

Mr. Ernest interrupted him with a firm order:

- These machines are to throw away ... we will buy new ones! ... On my next visit, I would like to see this corner of the factory empty!

The managers were astonished by this radical order, they exchanged a hesitant look. One of the managers dared to protest:

- But, Monsieur Ernest ... these machines are still useful and working ... they just need maintenance ... new machines are not available in the market ... it will take us 10 months to buy new ones ... and production could reduce significantly, or even stop!

At this moment, Lyor noticed a brief smile on the corner of his father's lips. And instantly, Lyor Laszlo understood his father's purpose; Mr. Ernest wanted to delay and even stop the production, in order to sell the factory!

With a fiery and impulsive temper, Lyor didn't hesitate to intervene, so as to break his father's plan. Lyor Laszlo exclaimed with a determined voice:

- The machines will cost less to repair rather than to buy new ones! We can contact the company that manufactures them in Canada, and a maintenance worker can come to Georgetown to fix them!

The managers turned toward Lyor. Their faces lit up with this idea:

- Yes! For sure! It will cost much less money and less time!
- And we can even ask to train our workers for maintenance, so as to prevent any further breakdowns!
- It is an excellent idea!! It will significantly increase our production!!

Since always, Mr. Ernest Laszlo underestimated the intelligence of his son Lyor. But as of now, Mr. Ernest didn't appreciate his son's intelligence at all. And certainly not when Lyor is getting more and more interested in the affairs of BalthEnterprise...

Chapter 26

A 2nd detention

Friday, April 01st, 1892. At the Royal Georgetown College.

- I am glad that our 3 months detention is finally over!! Amira laughed, picking up her notebooks of the Latin course.
- Fortunately yes! Dalya sighed, heading out of the classroom.

Amira could not resist teasing her friend:

- I believe that if you had one extra hour to count lentils, you would have had migraines for life!
- I could barely see the steps of the stairs after the detentions. Cristelle couldn't understand why I often tripped on the stairs of the grand Mansion.

Dalya and Amira were heading to the school canteen. And for the first time since 3 months, they were thrilled not to head toward the school kitchen for their detention.

Having served themselves lunch, Amira and Dalya settled into their usual table.

- Do you think we'll have a lot of homework for the long weekend? Dalya asked while eating her salad.
- Of course yes! Don't even ask this question!! Amira replied with an amused tone.

Dalya relaxed on her chair and she sighed:

- Too bad ... I would have liked a free long weekend to move forward in the Latin course ... I'm 4 lessons late...

Amira put a banana on her friend Dalya's tray:

- Here, I offer you my banana, I know you love this fruit ... and I'll take your apple!!

Dalya watched the exchange that her friend Amira was doing, without opposing it, and having her mind busy elsewhere:

- And what if I start the homework on Friday night, staying late at night? ... I will have at least one day free, to study for Latin!!

Amira tasted her vegetables dish, and despite her mouth full, she said to Dalya:

- If ... the ... Cook ... makes ... his chocolate ... cake ... I would come and help you ... to finish the long weekend homework ... as quickly as possible ...

Dalya observed her friend for a long minute with a curious look, and she dared to ask her:

- Would you have helped me in homework, if there wasn't any chocolate cake?

Without a second to think, Amira replied instantly:

- Certainly not!

Dalya and Amira giggled. When suddenly, a loud laughter noise frightened the two students. Dalya turned back to the origin of the noise, and she was surprised to discover a scene, a few steps away from her!!

Eriem and her court sat around their usual table. And they were all having fun and laughing, while watching Gael pouring juice on top of a student's head!

Dalya recognized the student. He spent several hours studying in the Library, near the study desk of Dalya and Amira. His name was Esteban, and he was known to wear the biggest eyeglasses of the entire college. A little size shape, thin and chilly, Esteban was quiet and timid.

While Gael was pouring his second glass of juice on the head of the student, Eriem and her court burst out laughing, the poor Esteban didn't dare to move or make a sound, not even defend himself.

Dalya had witnessed this scene before. And having lived it previously, Amira remembered better than anyone how this humiliation felt. At the sight of the student who trembled under the juice poured on top of his head, the smiles faded from Dalya and Amira's faces.

On the 3rd poured glass of juice, Dalya could no longer be silent. She pushed her chair to get up, and immediately Amira retained her by the hand:

- Don't intervene! ... You'll get into troubles!!

Except that Dalya was determined to act:

- I didn't stop them when they did it to you ... and I regret it!! ... It's out of the question that I let them do it for the 2nd time!!

Before Amira could speak another word, Dalya grabbed a thing from her lunch tray, and she rushed to the scene with decided steps. Gael was talking to his friend Eriem and her court in an amused tone:

- Carrot juice is beneficial for the hair ... that's why I recommend it very often ... not to drink, but to pour it on the head!!

A voice behind Gael replied in a defiant tone:

- So why don't you try it on yourself, instead of others' heads!

The student's laughs stopped instantly. And all eyes turned toward the new voice. Gael was surprised to discover who it was, as much as the other students.

-   Dalya Bouvard who dares to interrupt me!

Dalya stepped forward; she looked Gael in the eye and she asked him with a calm but threatening tone:

-   Why don't you go sit back to enjoy your lunch, and leave the student alone? ... Today's cooked vegetables look delicious!

Gael said in an amused tone:

-   Why should I? ... Would you like to have the cooked vegetables on your head?

Eriem and all the students around her, let out a wicked laugh. The poor Esteban still had his head down, and he didn't dare to look up or move. Yet, he listened to the scene between Dalya and Gael with all of his attention.

-   Gael ... sit down ... and leave him alone ...

Although Dalya spoke these words calmly, except that her eyes were defiant. Suddenly Eriem and her court went silent. The scene became intense. Gael was not a boy to easily accept threats. And even less from a person he hated.

-   Or else what? ... Don't forget who you are Dalya!! ... a little veggy seller at the marke...

Dalya interrupted him with an angry voice:

-   At least I assume what I am ... I don't live in the past glory of my grandfather!

Eriem let out a shocked scream. All the students had their eyes wide open, stunned by what Dalya had just said. Gael couldn't believe his ears; he was paralyzed for a long second. Dalya didn't believe her own words either; she never thought to be capable of answering that way. Even Esteban all soaked up in juice, he looked up at Dalya. He seemed as surprised as anyone by the audacity of Dalya Bouvard.

Gael couldn't swallow this humiliation, certainly not in front of Eriem and her court. And in lack of words for once, Gael had in mind only one thing to do: punching Dalya. He walked straight toward her with furious steps. And as she had predicted, Dalya retreated several steps back. And with a quick movement, Dalya threw a small item on the floor. In a second, Gael slipped and he landed on the floor ... because of a banana skin that Dalya put in front of him!

Eriem and her court froze in their chairs, not daring to make a move or say a word. Gael didn't understand what could have possibly dragged him to the floor. Amira let out a surprised scream, and she jumped out of her chair to come near her friend Dalya. Students in the other canteen tables exchanged discreet laughs. Esteban observed Gael lying on the floor, not believing his eyes.

Being aware that she wasn't of the same size to confront him, Dalya used the banana skin to prevent Gael to move a step closer to her.

- You should have sat down Gael ... I've warned you!

Amira pulled Dalya's arm and she whispered in a worried tone:

- Let's return to our table...

But before Gael could reply, a new voice has invited itself into the scene.

- It seems that you are enjoying more troubles, lately ... Mademoiselle Dalya Bouvard!

Dalya turned around to be in front of Professor Haîyang. The young woman displayed a strangely delighted smile. Dalya replied in a calm tone:

- Gael is the one looking for trouble, Professor Haîyang. He was pouring juice on Esteban's head ...

Without taking her eyes off Dalya, Professor Haîyang stated in a firm tone:

- You are in detention!

These words whipped Dalya right in the face. She retorted angrily:

- I didn't do anything!! Gael is the one who has been harassing the student, pouring juice on his head!! Look at him Professor!!

Amira defended her friend the best that she could:

- It's Gael who started it!! ... Gael always does this joke to make his friends laugh!! ... He did it to me too!!

Professor Haîyang replied calmly:

- You are both in detention ... for 4 months ... in the school kitchen!

Dalya and Amira exchanged a confused look. Amira was outraged:

- But we've just finished our detention! We haven't done anything, I swear!!

In front of the strange smile of Professor Haîyang, Dalya affirmed:

- I didn't even touch Gael!! ... He slipped alone!!

At this moment, Professor Haîyang turned her eyes toward the banana skin that was still on the floor:

- He slipped alone? ... Just that?

Gael was helped by a student to get up. He claimed to have backache, emitting cries of pain. Eriem was very pleased that the situation turned against Dalya. All the students who surrounded him hardly retained their wicked laughs.

126

Barely a minute ago, the banana peel seemed to be a good idea for Dalya to avoid the attack coming from Gael. Except that after Professor Haîyang's presence, Dalya changed her mind. Yet, Amira and Dalya tried with all their strength and energy to explain to Professor Haîyang.

- I only stopped Gael from harassing Esteban!! I asked him to go sit back at the table!! I didn't touch him!! He was the one coming to attack me!!
- It's not our fault!! Gael is the one who started it!! He acts as a clown by humiliating others!!
- Look at the student!! He is soaked in juice!!
- We don't deserve a detention!! Gael is the one who should be in detention!!

Professor Haîyang was oddly calm. Dalya and Amira didn't understand what made the young woman smile. A satisfied and a determined smile. And yet, Professor Haîyang spoke to the two students one last time before leaving the canteen, in a decided voice:

- I will notify the Cook Chef of your detention ... 4 months!

A few hours later, in the grand Mansion.

Since a while now, the snow Panther has been waiting patiently for Dalya's arrival, at the end of each school day. At the grand Mansion's entrance, Séraphine was lying down almost asleep. This April day was a gentle and peaceful air. Spring had embellished the gardens with a green and colorful cover. The birds adorned the silence with singing and tweeting, and squirrels were cleaning their homes in the trees of the grand Mansion. Spring in the city of Georgetown promised to be joyful for everyone ... almost everyone.

When suddenly, a little silhouette appeared, walking hurried steps toward the entrance of the grand Mansion. Immediately, the snow Panther straightened up, and she went down to the ground.

- It's unfair!! We don't deserve this detention!! 4 more months in the kitchen! But this is insane!! We will spend our entire summer vacation in this detention!! Professor Haîyang has seen Esteban soaked in juice from head to toe!! And Amira telling me that Professor Haîyang was nice! No but it's unfair!! So unfair!!

Dalya Bouvard surpassed the entrance of the grand Mansion, with upset footsteps. And for the first time, the little girl didn't greet the snow Panther as usual. Anger invaded Dalya, without her being able to calm down or control herself. Followed by the snow Panther like a shadow, Dalya walked up the stairs of the hall toward her bedroom. Coming out of the living room, Cristelle said with a joyful tone:

- Good evening Mademoiselle ... how was your da...

Dalya went up the stairs, while thinking in a loud and angry voice:

- She is mean and unfair!! Professor Haîyang knew very well that it was Gael's fault!! And for stopping him from doing his joke, what do I deserve?! A 4 months detention!! I should be studying during these 4 months to catch up in my classes!! But does Professor Haîyang cares about this? Not at all!! It's really unfair!!

Cristelle was standing in the hall; she has never seen Dalya Bouvard so upset. With a curious look, the maid watched the little girl followed by the snow Panther; both walking to the upper floor.

When she entered her bedroom, Dalya threw her briefcase on the bed, and she paced up and down. The snow Panther sat on a chair near the window, and she stared at Dalya, not daring to make a sound. For a long time now, and without any logical explanation, Séraphine would feel all the little girl's emotions; joy, fear, anxiety, boredom, happiness ... and on that day, anger!

- And Amira did nothing! She didn't even talk! Why did she have a detention too? This is insane! It is unfair! 4 months detention for doing nothing!! Eriem and Gael should be well satisfied now!! I imagine they will even celebrate it tonight!! It's mean!! It's unfair!!

A silhouette quietly entered the bedroom, and asked in a small voice:

- Everything is alright, Mademoiselle?

When Cristelle appeared, Dalya stopped walking, and she collapsed on the bed. Cristelle joined Dalya, and she sat next to her:

- You looked upset when you arrived ... did something went wrong at school?

For a few minutes, Dalya told her what had happened in the canteen, a few hours earlier. Cristelle was surprised and shocked by what she heard:

- That's unfair!! I understand your anger, Mademoiselle!! 4 months of detention is way too much!! And your poor friend did nothing anyway! It's unfair!!

Dalya sighed:

- Yes ... and yet, I have no idea what our next detention will be like ... the Cook Chef gives me strange work to do ... I was happy to have finished my 3 months detention... now I have 4 more months to endure!!

Cristelle tried to relieve the little girl:

- Don't worry, Mademoiselle!! 4 months will pass quickly!! ... And you will not be alone; you will have your friend along with you!!

As unexpected as it was, a little giggle escaped out of Dalya at this moment:

- About that, you are right Cristelle!! The detention hours go on quickly and pleasantly with Amira ... she makes me recite the lessons during our detention work ... and we often finish our homework in the school kitchen!!

While standing up, Cristelle exclaimed in a reassuring tone:

- Well you see now, Mademoiselle!! ... Even if it's an unfair detention, you can come up with something good out of it!!

Before leaving the bedroom, Cristelle asked in a thoughtful tone:

- Do you want tea before dinner, Mademoiselle?
- Thank you, Cristelle!! ... I will change my clothes, and be in the Library to do my homework.
- Perfect then!!

Dalya was very grateful to the maid Cristelle for having cheered her up. The little girl's anger calmed down a bit. Yet, many questions remained in her mind:

- Why did Professor Haîyang put us on detention, without even knowing the facts? ... And yet, everyone tells me Miss Haîyang is always kind and fair ... she is a very strange woman ... 4 months of detention and I don't even know why!!

Heading toward the dressing room to change from her school uniform, Dalya stopped because of a weird sound. The snow Panther was standing near the little desk, and she was emitting a strange and insistent meow. Dalya approached the snow Panther:

- What is it Séraphine?

At this precise moment, and after having the full attention of the little girl, the snow Panther made an unusual move. Séraphine lifted her paw and caressed with an insistent gesture, a small box placed on the desk table. And as incoherent as it may seem, Dalya Bouvard instantly understood what the Panther wanted:

- You want me to request a clue ... now ...

One would think that the snow Panther smiled at Dalya. Séraphine was a mysterious animal in all ways.

Despite a few seconds of hesitation, Dalya complied. The events unfolding around her, were unusual and unfair, Dalya needed some clear answers. And the Excelbox always provided some...

Dalya approached the Excelbox, and she wrote a question on a small paper:

What is the 2nd clue?

When the paper disappeared inside the box, a light awoke and the Excelbox revived. The snow Panther gave a strong happy meow, her long tail straightened up in the air, and her sapphire blue eyes shone with a thousand lights. One second was sufficient, and a small paper appeared on the verge of the Excelbox. Dalya read:

How long before a heart will dare?

20, 9

Dalya looked at the snow Panther and she sighed:

- Another riddle ... a strange question, and strange numbers ... do you have any idea what this clue means, Séraphine?

The snow Panther raised her sapphire eyes toward the little girl and smiled tenderly. Dalya put down the clue on the desk, and she went toward the dressing room with tired steps. The day was very long and difficult, and the little energy she still had, Dalya preferred to use it in completing her homework. The 2nd clue was even more mysterious than the first one. Tonight, Dalya didn't have the strength or energy to try and understand the 2nd clue...

Except that, Dalya didn't notice a tiny little detail. Several hours earlier ... in the school canteen ... a few tables away ... while Dalya and Amira were confused and shocked by their new 4 months detention ... while Gael and Eriem were happy and laughing amused ... while the poor student Esteban was drying his hair of the juice poured over his head ... while the canteen returned to its normal mood ... a little silhouette sitting nearby, had followed the entire scene from its beginning. Eriem's little sister, Assami Eyelord was smiling. It seems that unintentionally, Dalya Bouvard, the little veggy seller at the market, was about to have an ally well soon. It was clearly decided ... Assami Eyelord seemed to have changed sides. And when a heart dares, nothing can stop it...

Monday, April 04th, 1892. In the kitchen of the Royal Georgetown College.

This time, Amira was ordered to peel carrots. Dalya was sitting on the opposite side, watching her friend, and waiting to know her own detention work. Amira was thinking aloud:

- A heart is only an organ ... how can a heart dare? ... the sentence of the 2nd clue is not consistent ...

Dalya sighed:

- And the same question is repeated ... how long before ... am I supposed to find a period of time?

Peeling her 3rd carrot, Amira thought:

- A period of time for a heart to dare! ... even in grammar, this question is incorrect ...

Dalya used all the help and advice of her friend to understand the clues:

- And the numbers? ... 16,1 ... 20,9 ... we looked everywhere, at the National Library, the grand Mansion Library ... even the school Library ... this book cannot be found!!

Amira replied with a confused tone:

- I am beginning to doubt that it's not a book you should be searching for ... the book's location is not complete ... maybe these numbers indicate something else ...

Dalya let out a long sigh. Amira peeled a 5th carrot, and she encouraged her friend:

- Come on!! Courage!! Courage!!... You still have 9 months and 3 other clues to have ... we will find the answer!!

Within minutes later, the Cook Chef appeared before Dalya, and he gave her 15 cents:

- We are short of salt ... I need you go to the grocery store in rue de la Bastide, and bring me 100 mg of fine seeds salt.

Dalya rejoiced at her easy task, it was a simple thing to do. The Cook Chef ordered her:

- The trip is short ... it should take you 20 minutes back and forth ... don't be late!

Dalya answered, very pleased at her easy detention work:

- Yes Chef ... immediately Chef!

The sooner said, Dalya left the kitchen, and she ran to the grocery store at rue la Bastide.

Several minutes later, Dalya returned to the school kitchen, breathless and holding the package in her hand. When the Cook Chef took it, he examined the salt and he asked Dalya calmly:

- You made 35 minutes ...

Dalya replied breathlessly:

- It's just ... the trip … was a bit long ... Chef ...

For a few long seconds, Chef Shang examined Dalya with a focused look, as she tried to catch up her breath. When the Cook Chef returned to his employees, Dalya sat on a chair near Amira, who had peeled several carrots. Amira was humming a cheerful voice:

- Carrots ... carrots ... lovely little carrots ... carrots ... carrots … lovely little carrots …

When Dalya's breath became normal, she asked Amira in a seriously curious voice:

- You are in a 4 months detention, in the school kitchen, with a large basket of carrots to peel ... and you're in a good mood?!

Amira giggled:

- Carrots ... carrots ... lovely little carrots ...

Despite all the worries and the unanswered questions, Dalya couldn't help laughing. Amira's good mood was contagious.

Barely 10 minutes passed, the Cook Chef came back to Dalya, and he asked her:

- I need 100 mg of pepper seeds ... from the same grocery store ... only this time, hurry up!

Although Dalya was surprised that the Cook Chef didn't ask her to bring pepper with the salt earlier on, yet Dalya instantly obeyed:

- Yes, Chef!

The trip to the grocery store for the 2nd time went faster. Dalya returned several minutes later to the school kitchen, bringing the requested package.

- Good ... good. The Cook Chef thought aloud, while examining the pepper seeds.

Dalya sat down to catch her breath. The Cook Chef spoke with one of his aides. Amira asked:

- Are you alright? Not too tired of these trips?

Dalya giggled nervously:

- My legs hurt ... my toes are swollen ...

At this moment, Amira whispered with a serious air:

- Luckily I only got carrots to peel ... if the Cook Chef had charged me of these shopping trips; he would have waited until next week for his salt!!

Dalya held back her laugh by covering her mouth with her hands. Amira giggled:

- And when I would have brought salt to the Cook Chef, he shouldn't even think to ask me for a second trip!! ... I hate the word and the movement of "running" ... it takes me an entire day for the purchases at home!! ... And yet! me and my father, we split the grocery shopping list ...

Dalya hardly recovered from her giggles, she asked curious:

- Your father does the grocery shopping?

Amira said in an amused tone:

- Yes! My father loves to buy fruits and vegetables ... he always gets back home, having eaten half of the purchases ... 1 kg of apples purchased, only half a kilos arrives at home ...

Before Dalya could answer her friend, a voice interrupted them. The Cook Chef came close to Dalya and he asked:

- I will need 100 mg of paprika ... make sure the seller mold it well, I want it in powder.

Dalya observed the Cook Chef for a long second, and she asked in a confused voice:

- The ... the paprika? ... From the same grocery store? ... In rue de la Bastide?

The Cook Chef realized Dalya's doubt and confusion. And yet, he replied by displaying a calm attitude:

- Yes, Mademoiselle Dalya ... paprika ... 100 mg powder ... the same grocery store from where you have brought me salt and pepper, earlier.

Dalya and Amira exchanged a perplexed look. To do the same shopping trip and the same route, for several times and repeatedly... the Cook Chef's demands were odd.

Hesitantly, Dalya stood up and she was about to leave the kitchen. When suddenly, she stopped and asked the Cook Chef:

- Chef Shang, do you want something else of the same grocery store? Besides paprika?

The Cook Chef replied with an innocent smile:

- No ... only paprika ...

Dalya observed the Cook Chef for a long second. She was not convinced by his answer.

After several minutes, Dalya returned back from her 3rd trip, and she handed the powder paprika to the Cook Chef. Dalya sat on a chair, breathless and feeling a sharp pain in her legs. Amira had almost finished peeling the carrots in the basket, she whispered:

- I wonder why he asks you to do different shopping trips, to the same grocery store, every 10 minutes!

Dalya replied to her friend in a whisper:

- I know, it's very strange! ... The Cook Chef should give me the entire list of shopping to do in one trip instead of making several ones. I can't feel my legs.

Amira got upset, munching half a carrot:

- This is all Gael's fault!! 4 months detention because of him!

While her friend Amira got angry against this unfair detention, a strange idea invaded Dalya's mind. She stared at the Cook Chef, while he was teaching an employee, how to cut a white fish fillet. The hand moves of the Cook Chef were firm, fast and precise. Within seconds, the fish fillet was cut into small identical cubes.

Since the beginning of their detention, the Cook Chef's punishments were incomprehensible to Dalya Bouvard. Except that this time, Dalya had in her mind the shadow of an insane idea. The Chef Shang seemed to be something other than ... only a Cook Chef!

Chapter 27

A laugh

Saturday, May 07th, 1892. In the house of the French neighbors, les Poirier.

At the end of the afternoon, Richard Poirier went back home. It was a long and busy day at the Government headquarters. Dark circles under the eyes and a pale face, Richard looked tired and exhausted after the accumulation of several sleepless nights.

- Do you wish something else, Monsieur Richard? The driver asked, opening the car door.
- No, thank you. I have no more appointments for today. You can leave. Richard answered, while heading toward the house entrance.

After putting his files and coat in his office, Richard immediately headed toward his mother's bedroom to greet her.

- Good morning Moth...

Except that, after a brief look in the bedroom, Richard realized that his mother was not there. He went down straightaway to the living room. Sometimes, his mother would sit near the fireplace, reading a book or having her tea. Except that the living room was empty and quiet. Richard approached the large windows of the living room, and he looked for his mother. Mrs. Marianne Poirier would sometimes take a walk in the garden, especially in warm season, when the wind was almost nonexistent. But Richard's mother was missing.

At this moment, Richard panicked:

- Mother never leaves the house ... she is neither in her bedroom nor in the living room, not even in the garden ... but where could she be?

Richard checked some rooms and other places in the house, thinking:

- *If Mother's health condition worsened while I was away at work, they would have warned me about it ... was she unwell while I was busy? ... But ... no one informed me ... was she taken to the hospital?*

After several minutes of searching, there was no trace of Mrs. Marianne Poirier, Richard became increasingly worried. He had only one more idea to do; and it was to find the housekeeper of the house Mrs. Glorina, to ask her where his mother was. And Mrs. Glorina was almost always in the kitchen; Richard walked toward it with hurried steps. Opening the kitchen door, Richard asked:

- Mrs. Glorina, where's is Moth...

At the kitchen's door, Richard was stunned and surprised by what he found. His brain was slow to understand what was happening.

The small kitchen of the Poirier house was a beautiful place. A large wood table set in the middle, several windows around the kitchen inviting natural light, a large oven and a beautiful stove occupied an entire part of the room, a huge cupboard with several shelves, gathered the luxurious table silverware. Gentle warmth and a delicious smell came out of the kitchen.

Mrs. Glorina was drying cutlery with a cloth and putting them away in their usual places ... And to his big surprise, Richard found his mother in the kitchen.

When Richard appeared, Mrs. Glorina and Mrs. Marianne Poirier smiled at him joyfully. Richard had some troubles to understand:

- Mother ... but ... what ... I looked for you everywhere ...

Mrs. Glorina exclaimed:

- Sorry to have scared you, Mr. Richard! ... The kitchen was warm because of the oven's heat; Mrs. Marianne didn't mind to stay in. I even brought her the living room chair, so that she would remain comfortably seated.

Of all the places that Richard had thought to find his mother, the kitchen of the house didn't come to his mind. His mother never stayed and sat in the kitchen. And the most surprising thing wasn't that Mrs. Marianne Poirier was in this place, but what she was doing there.

Richard approached the big kitchen's table to see what his mother was doing. Well ... Mrs. Marianne Poirier was comfortably seated on an armchair, and she was spreading apricot jam on top of many little cakes, using a small brush. Her hands trembled a little, and it was the perfect move to better spread the jam on all the cakes.

And while his mother's moves were as clear and simple, yet Richard had never seen his mother cook or participate in a meals' preparation before. Richard couldn't help being curious about the unusual attitude of his mother:

- Mother ... what are you doing?

Mrs. Glorina answered right away, before storing several plates:

- Mrs. Marianne didn't mind joining us in the kitchen to make cakes for the military hospital feast ... we had to spread jam on the cakes before they cool down. Mrs. Marianne agreed to participate in it.

Richard looked confused and puzzled by this strange scene. When a little voice interrupted Richard's thoughts.

- It was my idea!

A 3rd person was at the other end of the kitchen table. Richard was so concerned about his mother; he hasn't seen this 3rd person. But when she spoke, Richard understood everything in an instant.

Because if there was a person who didn't hesitate to shake the boring routine of the Poirier house, if there was a person who dared to challenge the habits of the Poirier family ... it was Dalya Bouvard.

When he turned toward her, Dalya felt her cheeks blushing. Her hands were within a mixture of bread dough in a large bowl. Dalya explained to Richard, in a little voice:

- I thought that Madame will be pleased to prepare cakes, here in the kitchen ... with me and Mrs. Glorina ... and it would be a change of her usual bedroom and the living room ...

Richard Poirier had to admit, he was fascinated by the unexpected ideas of this new neighbor, and also by the simplicity of her actions. With difficulty, Richard Poirier held an amused laugh, and he asked in a calm tone:

- And have you finished?
- Almost, Monsieur. Mrs. Glorina replied. We still have only the bread to bake. I can make you a tea now, if you wish?

Richard observed the slow and frequent hand moves of his mother. Mrs. Marianne wasn't even listening to the conversation that took place in front of her, being busy spreading gently the jam on the many cakes. Richard Poirier smiled at his mother, in a caring look. Because there was a time when he believed that his mother will no longer enjoy life again. Richard answered:

- Needless to bother you, to prepare tea for me. I will wait for dinner tonight.
- Understood, Monsieur. Mrs. Glorina finished storing all the dried plates.

Richard took a quick look at Dalya who was struggling with the big dough, and he asked with a tense throat:

- Maybe if ... if there is any extra cake ... I would like to taste one.

Dalya froze in her place, raising her head to see Richard Poirier smiling at her. At that moment, she didn't understand what heated up the most her cheeks; Richard Poirier's smile or the dough that imprisoned her hands since several minutes now.

Immediately, Mrs. Glorina replied cheerfully:

- But certainly, Monsieur!! We prepared many extra cakes ... I will serve you one in the living room with Mrs. Marianne, with a good te... but ... what on earth is that?

Mrs. Glorina stopped and she approached Dalya. The woman's eyes were focused on the large bowl in front of Dalya. This aroused the curiosity of Richard and even Mr. Marianne who stopped and bent over to see what was happening at the other side of the table. Mrs. Glorina thought aloud:

- What is this dough?

Dalya tried to remove her hands from the dough, but the more she tried, and the more dough was holding her hands prisoners. Mrs. Glorina exclaimed:

- But ... what happened?

Dalya hesitated a moment before answering:

- It's just ... for a while now ... this dough sticks to my hands ... I ... I am unable to remove my hands off this dough ...

Mrs. Glorina touched the surface of the dough with a finger only, to know what was wrong:

- How much baking powder did you put in it, Mademoiselle?

Given the curious looks of Mrs. Glorina, Richard and Mrs. Marianne, Dalya answered hesitantly:

- The ... the entire baking powder that was ... in the container ...

On that moment, Mrs. Glorina burst out laughing:

- The entire baking powder?! ... you had to put on a little spoon only ... I was about to keep the rest of the baking powder for the upcoming months ... you used the banking powder of several months in one dough?!

Mrs. Marianne laughed silently, until tears came out of her eyes. Mrs. Glorina sat on a chair; her legs couldn't hold her standing, her laugh echoed throughout the kitchen, she was unable to abstain herself in front of Richard. The two women had a crazy uncontrollable laugh.

Dalya herself couldn't help but laugh at her incident, she exclaimed:

- Well then ... the pastry seems to be more dangerous than I thought.

Richard Poirier gently closed the kitchen door, and he went up to his room. Within minutes, he no longer felt tired and exhausted from the long day of work. An unpredictable scene made him forget all his fatigue. Or maybe was it an unpredictable person ... in any case, Richard Poirier went up the stairs with a light and amused smile.

Chapter 28

A nice help

Wednesday, May 11th, 1892. Latin class.

At the end of the Latin course, all the students closed their books and prepared to leave. Amira came close to her friend:

- The exams are approaching ... we need to start studying for them ...

Dalya finished packing her bag, and she said with an anxious voice:

- I have a bad feeling that I will fail the Latin exam ... I understand nothing of what the Professor is speaking about ... I learned by heart, made summaries and tried to understand ... but I am failing at it!

Amira tried to reassure her:

- Don't worry! we will study together ... and the worst case scenario, you will have catch-ups hours or exams to take again next semester ...

Despite Amira's encouragement, Dalya didn't appear so reassured. The Latin seemed an indecipherable language. All the students have learned it for years. And for Dalya to learn it in a few months, it seemed impossible.

The two students separated at the Latin classroom door. Amira walked toward the Library to give back her borrowed books, and Dalya took the opposite corridor.

Heading to the school exit, Dalya met a familiar silhouette in a corridor.

- It's always a pleasure to meet you Mademoiselle Dalya Bouvard!

Professor Canfield could be easily distinct among a hundred people. His obsession with checked suits looked very good on him. He was always very elegant and in a cheerful mood.

- It's perfect that I meet you now. I thought to ask about you. Are you getting ready for your exams, Mademoiselle?

Dalya appreciated Professor Canfield for his kindness and the attention he had for her education. The training of Dalya Bouvard was a responsibility entrusted to him, and Professor Canfield took it very seriously. He followed assiduously all Dalya's classes and exams.

- Yes, Professor. The Chemistry and Physics courses are completed; the teachers are currently giving us exercises for the exams. The Mathematics course was of a higher level than the previous semester. I will try to get a good grade on the final exam. And the Music teacher Miss Haîyang reviewed with us the entire theoretical course.

Professor Canfield smiled:

- Excellent ... excellent ... and about the History and Geography courses ... everything went well this semester, I presume?

In fact, both these classes went great. The History and Geography teachers completely ignored Dalya and her existence in the classroom. They didn't even speak her name at the calling. Which didn't bother Dalya at all; she was focused copying her lessons and exercises.

- Yes, Professor. The courses went very well. The History and Geography teachers promised us hard and complicated exams ...

At Dalya's remark, Professor Canfield let out an amused laugh:

- I have no doubt that you will succeed these classes, Mademoiselle!!

At this moment, Professor Canfield was happy to have corrected and threatened both the History and Geography Teachers. Professor Canfield continued to ask Dalya:

- And your Latin course? How do you feel about it?
- Honestly ... the Latin is a new class for me ... I'm not sure I ca...

When suddenly, Professor Canfield called out a man in the corridor:

- Professor Wyatt!! There you are!! I looked for you everywhere during these two days!! I need a minute of your time, please.

Professor Canfield spoke to Dalya:

- Sorry Mademoiselle, but I have to leave. I am delighted to hear of your progress. Keep going! I have no doubt that you will succeed just like any other student of this school. And ... I remind you that my office is always opened to you, for the slightest concern.
- Thank you, Professor!

Dalya continued on her way out of the school. While turning a corridor, Dalya walked with a busy mind:

- *I should have confessed to Professor Canfield that Latin was not a simple class ... even Amira's previous notes didn't serve me much to understand the course ... I'm already late by 6 lessons and the exams begin in a few weeks ... I cannot pass the exam, without knowing the lessons ... it's insane ... I think I'll review the course over tonight, one last time ... and if I don't understand it, I will meet with Professor Canfield in his office tomorrow morni...*

When suddenly, before coming down the big stairs of the school hall, Dalya was shaken by an abrupt and unexpected incident ... someone from behind, poured water on Dalya's hair!

Not believing what was happening to her, Dalya was paralyzed standing for some long seconds. Her hair wet, Dalya felt the water running down her neck.

When she turned around, Dalya was stunned and surprised. Several students were crossing the corridor with fast and busy steps, without giving any attention to Dalya and her wet hair. 3 students from a preceding class were gathered near a big window, they were pointing out at buildings and institutions, naming them, laughing and having fun. They didn't even notice Dalya's presence.

- But ... who threw water on me? ... That's mean! ... who dared? ...

There was no trace of Eriem or Gael and their court. Dalya remained speechless, her hair all wet, standing in the middle of the corridor. After some long seconds, Dalya decided to move, and dry her hair in the girls' bathroom. And one had to admit that luckily the bathroom was empty, Dalya pulled a towel and she dried her hair, exploding in anger:

- No, but it's really a school filled with crazy people!! ... It's probably Eriem and Gael who did this!! ... Gael would do anything to amuse Eriem and her court!! ... I don't have time for this nonsense, and they enjoy playing these little games!! ... I am so busy preparing for the exams, and they are having fun, wasting my time!! ... Gael is going to pay for th...

Suddenly, a little noise interrupted Dalya's anger. She stopped drying her hair, and she noticed a strange thing ... someone slipped a folder under the girls' bathroom door. The folder reached Dalya's feet, in a fast launch. Immediately, Dalya took it. And Instantly, Dalya opened the bathroom door. Except that the corridor was ... completely empty.

- What is this game? ... First they throw water on me, and then they slide this folder from under the bathroom door! ... But what is going on?! ... What is this nonsense?!

Dalya couldn't understand what was happening.

And curious as she was; Dalya opened the file that was given to her. It seemed to be filled with several little papers. By reading the content, Dalya needed some time to understand what she was holding. She remained frozen, standing in her place, for several long seconds. Dalya couldn't believe what she was holding in her hands. She was so shocked, that she didn't even hear the coming of a student into the bathroom.

Amira smiled with amusement:

- I thought you were already out of schoo...

Noticing Dalya's hair, Amira exclaimed:

- Why is your hair all wet?! ... What happened to you?! ... What's going on?

Dalya remained motionless, still reading the papers she held in her hands. In front of Dalya's strange attitude, Amira approached her:

- What are you reading? ... Wait a second ... but ... how ... where did you get these papers from?

Dalya recovered with great difficulty. She looked at Amira in a surprised and happy look:

140

- These are ... detailed vocabulary Latin cards!

The cards were in a clear handwriting, distinct colors, well detailed by definition and even the pronunciation of words. Amira's eyes became wide open:

- I have never seen such cards ... not in the manual nor at the Library ... and even the Latin Professor never mentioned such a method!! ... How did you get them?
- I don't know who gave them to me!

Dalya told her friend that a stranger poured water on her from behind, and that she received these files from under the bathroom door, when she came in to dry her hair. After a long second of silence, Amira jumped joyfully:

- With these cards, you will quickly catch up in Latin!! Or even exceed all of us!! ... It's awesome!!
- Certainly, yes!! A minute ago, I thought to ask Professor Canfield to give up the Latin class ... I think with these cards, I may at least reach the average of 10/20 ...

Amira exclaimed delighted:

- And even more than 10/20!! ... Will you lend me these cards for a weekend, to copy them? It will help me to study for the exams, too!!
- Yes of course!! ... We will both study on them!!

When Amira came out of the girls' bathroom, she thought aloud:

- It really is a nice help!!

And a few minutes later, while leaving School, Dalya murmured in a happy voice:

- Yes ... a nice help!

Meanwhile, through the large windows of the Royal Georgetown College, 3 students were observing Dalya and Amira, leaving toward their homes, laughing aloud about this nice help. Hélène Lagénéreuse asked in a soft voice:

- Do you think it will be enough for her to succeed the Latin exam?

Esteban Warner replied in a calm confident voice:

- Certainly. These are full and detailed summaries.

Assami Eyelord, Esteban Warner and Hélène Lagénéreuse, exchanged an accomplice and determined smile. While walking back home, Dalya Bouvard, the little veggy seller at the market, had no idea that she was gathering allies by her side. And for Assami Eyelord, Esteban Warner and Hélène Lagénéreuse ... it was only but the beginning.

A strange little box wasn't that innocent ... The Excelbox was cooking something ... when a heart dares ... be assured, nothing can stop it!

141

Chapter 29

You don't want to know

Wednesday, June 01st, 1892. At the Royal Georgetown College.

The last days of the school year, were well busy for teachers and students. All the exams were completed, for all levels, in all subjects and classes. The teachers were busy correcting the last exams papers, and the students were unwillingly busy writing down their summer homework.

Professor Canfield passed in the corridor, and he stopped in front of a meticulously organized office.

- Good morning Miss Uplerine!

The young woman seemed focus while reading a document. And it is only when Professor Canfield repeated his greeting for the 2nd time that Miss Uplerine raised up her eyes and she noticed his presence:

- Good morning Professor Canfield ... what can I do for you?

Professor Canfield answered with a courteous tone:

- I am sorry to bother you, Miss Uplerine ... I wish to know the exams' results of a student, please.

Instantly, Miss Uplerine pulled out a paper out of an index folder, and she handed it to him with an amused smile:

- Mademoiselle Dalya Bouvard ... I presume?

Professor Canfield was surprised that Miss Uplerine read directly through his mind:

- Exactly! Right on target!

When the Professor took on Dalya's tests results, he read it carefully, with a serious and focused look. After a few seconds he thought aloud:

- She has well succeeded her semester ... Mathematics is her strength... I knew I could count on Professor Roger and Professor Gallet to help her catch up on Physics and Chemistry ... History and Geography ... well ... well ... the Music, It's not bad either ... Latin? ... In Latin, she got the average grade! ... It's amazing! and I thought she wouldn't make it ... very well ... very well ...

Miss Uplerine dared to interrupt the Professor in his thoughts:

- How is this student's level?

With a proud smile, Professor Canfield replied:

- For a girl who has never been to school before ... she had to work considerably harder to catch up on her delays ... her level is quite good ... 2 or 3 more semesters, she will be at the same level as our students!

Miss Uplerine smiled kindly:

- She a brave little one. She works assiduously.

Professor Canfield confirmed:

- Certainly, yes! She is very smart and studious ... it seems that the school's Library is her favorite place ... I never search for her elsewhere than in the Library!

Before leaving the Secretary's office, Professor Canfield looked at Dalya's tests results paper, and he thought aloud:

- And for this summer, I have to prepare for her more catch up courses in Latin ... and maybe introduce her to the civilizations' class, so that she can start it in September ... she doesn't need any more catch up in History and Geogr...

When suddenly, Miss Uplerine interrupted him:

- Professor Canfield ... I believe you would be interest to read this document.

When he looked toward the young woman, Professor Canfield noticed that Miss Uplerine displayed a serious and grave face. And when he took the paper from her hands, Professor Canfield was struck by what he read:

Request to the Courthouse

City of Georgetown, Washington

Hereby, I, Director of the Royal Georgetown College, Sylvere Darkfett, submit an application to withdraw the student Dalya Bouvard off this school, canceling the order given in the Will of Late Iskander Balthazar. This is due to her poor grades, and her inability to keep pace with the courses' progress. Her catch-up sessions and her low level, delay the classes, and disrupt the education of other students in her class...

In a second, anger conquered the Professor. Always calm and serene, at this instant, Professor Canfield lost his calm temper. His eyes were shocked, his lips trembled and his cheeks blushed:

- But how dare he?! She has an average grade in all her courses!! She succeeded better than our own students in Mathematics!! She caught up on her delays in a record time!! This is despicable!! This is low!! This is pure stupidity!!

Miss Uplerine got up from her chair and she approached the Professor:

- Director Darkfett asked me to send this letter yesterday afternoon ... before sending it, I thought that the contents of the letter would interest you, since you are the tutor of this little girl ...

Professor Canfield pulled himself together with great difficulty:

- You ... you have done well to inform me ... thank you Miss Uplerine! ... I will notify the Law Firm and her legal guardian Lyor Laszlo ... immediately!! ... he must absolutely stop this masquerade ... the Court should be informed of the good results of Dalya Bouvard ... the Lawyers will defend Dalya Bouvard's right to study here in this College !!

With a calm and polite voice, Miss Uplerine asked:

- Professor Canfield ... I'm a simple executive secretary in this school, however ... may I give you my opinion, about it?
- Of course, Miss Uplerine, certainly!!

At this instant, Miss Uplerine displayed a confident smile:

- I would like to handle this matter myself ... with your permission, Professor.

For a few long seconds, Professor Canfield observed the young woman with a confused and perplexed look. He tried in vain to understand what Miss Uplerine asked him. And without losing her confident smile, Miss Uplerine explained:

- If this letter reaches the Court and the Lawyers, the Court proceedings may take several months ... and the little girl can miss the back to school in September ... that is the reason why I propose to resolve this matter ... myself!

Professor Canfield read the letter in his hands, and he thought aloud for a moment:

- These are the last wishes of Iskander Balthazar ... he trusted me with her training and her education ... she succeeded well all her courses, despite her delay ... she deserves to stay in this College ... I can try to convince Director Darkfett ... but he seems to hold a grudge against Dalya, from the first day she came here ... I can talk to the other members of the board ... but the board has no authority over the Director's decisions ... and it's true, the Court may rule after months or even a year ...

144

After several seconds of thinking and debate in his mind, Professor Canfield looked at Miss Uplerine:

- Do you really think you would be able to prevent Director Darkfett's decision? All by yourself?

Miss Uplerine answered with a confident and determined voice:

- Oh yes! ... and I guarantee you that no other dirty maneuver will be attempted toward this little girl ... never again, throughout her entire schooling in this College ... you have my word ... the word of a woman!

Professor Canfield had a duty to tutor and protect Dalya Bouvard. He made his decision in one minute:

- So then ... do what is right, Miss Uplerine! You have my approval and my support. Iskander Balthazar and I, we would be eternally grateful to you for your help. You will save the future and the education of a studious and innocent little girl!

Miss Uplerine went back to her desk, and she sat in her chair, displaying a defiant firm smile:

- Straightening out Director Darkfett, it would be with great pleasure, Professor Canfield ... very great pleasure!

Professor Canfield greeted Miss Uplerine by bowing his head, and smiling gratefully. And before leaving the office, Professor Canfield asked in a curious tone:

- But ... tell me ... how will you handle this matter?

Miss Uplerine let out a little amused laugh:

- Oh sorry Professor ... but you don't want to know ...

And even you, dear reader ... you don't want to know how Miss Uplerine prevented the malice of Director Darkfett ... All I can assure you, is that Dalya Bouvard continued to follow her classes at the Royal Georgetown College ... and that Director Darkfett needed a long moment for recovery ... the summer holidays seemed busy, for everyone ...

Chapter 30

The Pantry

Friday, June 03rd, 1892. In downtown.

- Here we are!

Dalya and Amira arrived at the door of the Toscana restaurant. And for a few seconds, Dalya observed the outside of the restaurant. The very distinguished place has not changed its looks. The Toscana restaurant remained the same luxurious place as it was, since Dalya worked in the Saturday market, right in front of it.

The canteen of the Royal Georgetown College was closed during the summer holidays. The Cook Chef; Mr. Shang has ordered Dalya and Amira to join him in the kitchen of the Toscana restaurant, to continue their detention.

The kitchen of the Toscana restaurant was most professional and sophisticated than the one at school. The counters were in gray marble, kitchen utensils and pans were of copper and ceramic. Several top windows were opened to clear off cooking odors. All employees were dressed in clean and perfectly ironed uniforms, white and black, depending on their rank and function. They all worked in a focused silence, each one of them busy cutting and preparing the ingredients to be cooked.

In a corner of the kitchen, near the exit door toward the back of the restaurant, Dalya noticed the presence of a familiar silhouette, her father Antman Bouvard. He was reading carefully a list in his hand, while two of his aides were carrying empty boxes outside of the kitchen.

Since several months now, Dalya knew that the Toscana restaurant had employed two transporters aids under her father's responsibility. Every day, Antman received a shopping list to get, and he took care to assign the trips to his 2 assistants.

Dalya was pleased to meet her father at his workplace. In the grand Mansion, he didn't speak to her since many months. Dalya hoped that at the Toscana restaurant, her father would be more tolerant and less upset at her. Dalya had finally an opportunity to reconcile with her father and approach him. As soon as she would finish her detention work...

When Dalya and Amira appeared in the kitchen, Chef Shang abandoned his employee and he walked toward them, with a courteous and intimidating allure:

- Good morning, Mesdemoiselles.

Dalya and Amira exchanged a worried look. They didn't know what the Cook Chef would assign to them as detention work, this month. Chef Shang addressed Amira first:

- We are making a tomato soup with herbs ... I need you to peel the tomatoes in the basket ... residues will be recovered by a cook aid later ...
- Yes, Chef! Amira said, before walking to the work place that he pointed out.

The tomatoes were somewhat complicated to peel. But Amira's detention was much less difficult than the one awaiting Dalya Bouvard.

The Cook Chef asked Dalya to follow him. Moments later, they stopped in front of a large room. Chef Shang explained to Dalya:

- Here is the supplies room. It is called the Pantry. You have to clean this room. Take out the empty containers, clean the dust, arrange the jars, and reorganize provisions in their corner.

At this instant, Dalya rejoiced; it seemed to be an easy task. Especially as Dalya loved to clean and organize closets and shelves. She answered without hesitation:

- Yes Chef! Right away!

When Dalya walked only 2 step inside the room, her legs lost their balance, she slipped and fell on her back abruptly. It took Dalya few minutes to understand what made her fall. When she realized a strange thing:

- What is … why ... the ground is slippery!

And it was true. The floor of the Pantry was overwhelmed with transparent oil, which made the slightest step and move impossible. With difficulty, Dalya tried to stand up, while holding on to a shelf, and thinking aloud:

- I will clean this oil first and then I will reorganize the entire Pantry!

Still standing near the Pantry door, the Cook Chef corrected Dalya:

- It will not be necessary, Mademoiselle. You will organize the Pantry, walking on the slippery ground.

When Dalya was able to stand up, firmly holding on to a shelf, she observed the Cook Chef with a confused look. She was surprised to what her ears have heard:

- But Chef ... that's impossible!

Instantly, the Cook Chef stepped inside the Pantry. He took a bag of flour, and he removed it to the opposite side of the Pantry near other bags of pasta and wheat. The Cook Chef easily moved around, without the slightest imbalance in his legs. He smiled at Dalya:

- If I can do it ... then it is not as impossible as it may seem!

Dalya was surprised by the ease and balance of the Cook Chef. After a few seconds of hesitation, Dalya released her hands holding firmly the shelf, and she stepped forward, imitating the Cook Chef. But before making a third step, Dalya lost her balance, she slipped and landed on the ground. Her back hurt, Dalya murmured:

- I ... I can't, Chef. It's difficult. I can organize the Pantry faster if I clean the floor ...

The Cook Chef knelt in front of Dalya, and he replied with his usual calm:

- Sorry, Mademoiselle ... but it's not up to you, to dictate the rules of your detention. Organize the Pantry, walking on the slippery ground.

Chapter 31

8:30 every morning

A week later. Friday, June 10th, 1892. In the Toscana restaurant.

That morning, Dalya and Amira decided to go early to the Toscana restaurant, to start their detention work. The school teachers gave the students mountains of holiday homework. And the sooner the two girls can finish their detention, the sooner they can start on their homework. Opening the restaurant door, Amira thought aloud:

- We should begin with the Mathematics homework ... it's the easiest one, it will take us only 2-3 days ...

Following her inside, Dalya agreed with her friend's plan:

- You're right ... it's better to get rid of the simplest homework first ... and we can work on Physics and Chemistry lessons afterward ... we have a list of words to search for ...

Amira jumped:

- Can we work the History and Geography courses in the grand Mansion Library? If you don't mind ... Mr. Ferrero, the Cook Chef prepares the best cheesecakes that I've ever tasted!! ... that pastry helps me work better ...

Dalya laughed at her friend's request:

- With pleasure, yes!! ... The Cook Chef Mr. Ferrero will be happy to make the cake for you!

Amira opened the kitchen door of the restaurant, and she continued to plan her homework strategy aloud:

- And the Latin course ... I know it's hard ... but if we both work on it, we can advance quickly ... we will learn by heart for 15 minutes and then we will recite to eac...

Heading toward their usual place at the end of the kitchen, Dalya and Amira were interrupted by an abnormal scene. Near the door leading to the outside of the kitchen, Dalya's father was speaking to his 2 assistants. Antman appeared very angry at his two aides, he screamed:

- IDIOTS!! MORONS!! HOW MANY TIMES DO I HAVE TO REPEAT IT TO YOU!! YOU ARE INCOMPETENT!! IMBECILES!!

Dalya was paralyzed in her place, shocked by her father's attitude. Dalya was used to her mother's violence. And she was well aware of the angry character of her father, but she never thought to attend it, one day. Antman screamed in an enraged tone toward one of the aides, and he insulted him with vulgar language:

- YOU'RE AS STUPID AS A PIG!! YOU SHOULD USE YOUR BRAIN, YOU FILTHY CON!! DUMB!! IDIOT!!

The aide remained calm and silent while Antman reprimanded him with horrible insults. Only a few days before, Dalya was happy to work with her father at the Toscana restaurant. Dalya thought to get a bit closer to her father and reconcile with him. But at this instant, Dalya couldn't believe her ears...

- AND YOU RAT FACE!! YOU NEVER LEARN ANYTHING!! IMBECILE!! I TOLD YOU TO EMPTY THESE BOXES FIRST!! JERK!! DUMBASS!! A NOBODY!! PIECE OF TRASH!!

By noticing the pale face and shocked expression of Dalya, Amira felt the embarrassment and discomfort of her friend. Although Amira and Dalya were close since several months now, Amira never dared to ask Dalya any questions about her parents. Amira suspected that the Bouvard parents were hard and tough people, but she was far from imagining their aggressive and cruel character.

Suddenly, Amira took her friend by the arm and she forced her to move forward to their usual place of their detention tasks:

- Come on! We have to start our work!

Dalya didn't dare to look her friend in the eye. She didn't expect to find her father in such an aggressive and violent state ... insulting and vulgar at 8:30 am!

And as a good friend, Amira was sad for Dalya. So then, Amira pretended not to hear the insults and abuses of her friend's father. When they settled in the end side of the kitchen, Amira continued:

- So like I said ... for the Latin course, we will move faster if we work on it together... we will learn by heart for 15 minutes and then we recite and correct each other... with the cards you have received, we can even write the new les...

Except that, Antman Bouvard's voice was much stronger than Amira's voice:

- SHITHEAD!! CON!! IMBECILE!! INCAPABLE!! PIECE OF TRASH!!

Dalya was sitting in her chair, waiting for an employee to open the Pantry. She was paralyzed on her chair, silent and motionless, shaken by the insults and screams of her father. Unaware on what to do or say, Dalya couldn't dare to raise her eyes toward her friend. She never thought she would face such a situation. And determined to relieve Dalya from her embarrassment, Amira raised the tone of her own voice:

- And for the Music class, you have to practice more on your flute ... you will need a lot of practice ... try to play 2 or 3 hours a day ... you've made good progress on the flute lately ... you already master th....
- MORONS!! IDIOTS!! RATS FACE!! CON!!

150

Amira wore her gloves; she took a tomato and peeled it, ignoring the screams of Antman Bouvard. And although her throat was tight and her cheeks breathless, Amira tried to rise up more her voice:

- I think after this long detention, I will be the best and fastest Georgetown peeler!! It's true, Dalya!! At home, my father timed me to know how fast I am ... in 35 seconds I can p...
- MORONS!! VERMIN!! NOBODY!! STUPID LIKE A PIG!! IMBECILE!! IDIOTS!!

Despite all of her attempts, Amira failed to distract Dalya from the screams and insults of her father. Antman Bouvard's voice was much stronger and violent, shaking the plates and glasses. And his insults were increasingly dirty and vulgar.

Dalya lowered her head, didn't dare to look up or speak or move. Breathless and red cheeks, Amira lost her words and became silent, not knowing what to say or do to relieve her friend.

And for the first time since they have met, Amira had pity on Dalya. She even wondered how could Dalya endure to live with such parents, aggressive and violent.

Dalya was ashamed of the vulgar insults and violent nature of her father. She wondered how she will succeed to have a good productive day ... when the day starts with violence and vulgarity, at 8:30 AM...

And in fact, the author of this book wondered, as well ... how can anyone succeed in his life, waking up to violence and vulgarity at 8:30 every morning ... for many long years...

Chapter 32

A bucket of water on the head

2 weeks later. Friday, July 01st, 1892. At the Toscana restaurant.

To stand on the slippery floor of the Pantry, Dalya tried many ways; she wore hooked sandals, she used crutches, she walked on her knees, she used ropes hanging on the shelves. Except that, despite Dalya's ingenuity, the Cook Chef corrected and prevented her from using all these tricks. He insisted that Dalya should walk on slippery floor without any tools or help.

That day, the Cook Chef finished cooking the meat in a pan. He ordered his aid to follow this same precise technique. Seconds later, the Cook Chef decided to inspect the two students in detention.

- Try to peel the tomatoes in a circular way, Miss Amira. It will be easier that way. And put the seeds out with the peelings.

Amira had almost finished her basket of tomatoes to peel. She hurried up to finish her detention as soon as possible.

Chef Shang checked Dalya's progress. When he stopped in front of the Pantry, the Cook Chef was surprised by what he discovered; Dalya Bouvard was standing on the slippery floor, her legs were shaking indeed, but she walked with very slow moves. After hundreds of attempts and painful falls, Dalya finally managed to stand on the slippery floor and clean the Pantry!

Coming close to her, the Cook Chef repressed a proud smile, and he displayed a serious formal face:

- You still have a lot of work to do, Mademoiselle. It has been 2 weeks now, and the Pantry is not yet organized.

The storage didn't greatly progress in this place; there was still a lot of work to do. Dalya turned around and she explained:

- It's just that ... Chef ... I've just succeeded to stand on my legs, without falling on the slippery floor ... I will try to speed up the cleaning, Chef ...

A discreet proud smile crossed the lips of the Cook Chef; he underestimated Dalya Bouvard's determination.

When the Cook Chef left the Pantry, and returned to his kitchen aides, Dalya continued her work, she removed empty jars on a shelf in the Pantry, while moving as slowly as possible.

A few minutes later, when Dalya was busy in her task, she felt a presence behind her. The Cook Chef had returned, carrying a small bucket of water in his hand. Instantly, Dalya rejoiced:

- Would you like me to clean the floor, Chef Shang?

Without a spoken word, the Cook Chef came close to Dalya, and ... he gently placed the little bucket of water on top of Dalya's head!

Stepping back, the Chef Shang smiled and he explained in a calm authoritative voice:

- Now that you can stand on the slippery floor ... you will arrange the Pantry, with a bucket of water on your head!

Dalya couldn't believe her ears. She has never been ordered to do such a task:

- But, Chef ... This is insane! ... Nobody can do it! ... It's impossible!

The Cook Chef asked curiously:

- You declare losing before even starting?

Dalya couldn't release the shelf she was holding on so firmly; she couldn't make the slightest move, without expecting a fall. Dalya affirmed:

- I cannot make it!

Crossing his arms, the Cook Chef answered, with a serene voice:

- How do you know you cannot do it ... when you haven't tried enough!

Anger invaded Dalya instantly. Was it because of the impossibility of the detention, or the calm of the Cook Chef, or the feeling that each of his detention was unfair and wrong. And as rare as it was, Dalya lost her cool, and she exclaimed in an angry tone:

- And when will it be enough?

The Cook Chef felt the anger of the little girl. And this anger, Chef Shang was determined to use it to his advantage. A proud and a defiant smile appeared on the young man's lips. He answered Dalya with a determined voice:

- It will be enough when you finally succeed!

Dalya felt that the Cook Chef enjoyed imposing on her the most impossible detentions. And she didn't know the reason why. In front of the insistent stares of the Cook Chef, waiting at the doorstep of the Pantry, Dalya decided with difficulty to move, and make one more step on the slippery floor. And as expected, in a split of a second, Dalya fell, and the water bucket on her head wet her clothes.

- It's impossible! This is insane!

Before returning to the kitchen, the Cook Chef smiled:

- You will fill the bucket with water, and you will continue to store the Pantry ... on a slippery floor ... and with the bucket of water on the head.

Chapter 33

Clumsy

Saturday, July 16th, 1892. In the house of the French family, les Poirier.

Although he had many files to deal with that day, Richard Poirier's office was impeccably ordered. All the folders were placed in order on the desk table. The pencils kept in a small jar. The papers were well adjusted. Books perfectly classified. Richard Poirier's office perfectly reflected his well-arranged character and his meticulous nature.

Richard had a short lunch break before continuing his work. The sky was clear, and the sun shone with all its might. A warm breeze of the summer months, passed from time to time. The day seemed quiet and peaceful, without any interruptions.

At a moment, Richard heard someone knocking on the door of his office.

- Come in.

And instantly, Richard straightened up on his chair, he was surprised to see Dalya Bouvard in his office. She had never dared to interrupt him while he was working. Dalya smiled shyly:

- Good evening.

Richard greeted her by bowing his head. His throat tightened as soon as Dalya appeared in front of him. And it was an impulse that Richard Poirier still couldn't understand.

Dalya wore as usual a large white apron; her chestnut hair was raised and hidden in her big cap. Some white hair filled with flour, escaped from her hat. Her hands were clean of any ingredients, but her tainted apron, reflected pretty well the working hours in the kitchen. Dalya came close to Richard's desk with slow steps:

- Mrs. Glorina prepared tea for you ... she asked me to bring it to you ... she is busy preparing Madame's dinner.

Dalya placed a small silver tray on an empty side on the desk table. A pretty teapot, a porcelain cup, and a cake plate. Richard closed up his file and he asked her:

- Is this today's cake?

Dalya poured tea into the cup with a slow movement, and she smiled:

- Yes, freshly prepared!

Putting the teacup in front of Richard, Dalya continued in a natural tone:

- It is a lemon meringue tart ... with a layer of pie crust and lemon cream ... I picked the lemons myself in your garden, they are delicious ... I will ask the Gardener if I too can plant lemons in the grand Mansion's garden ... and the meringue layer on the top was easy to make ...

Richard observed Dalya, drinking his tea while she explained to him the ingredients and the recipe. The young man was fascinated by the naturalness of this strange girl. It is true that she was chosen as the Heiress to the biggest fortune in this Country, but her tainted apron, her hair bleached by flour, her boy's shoes ... and especially her spontaneous behavior, nothing indicated that she was an Heiress.

While Richard was watching Dalya, wondering why the Governor chose this girl to succeed him, Richard forgot the cup of tea in his hand. When Dalya jumped:

- Your tea!! It's pouring!!

Richard straightened his hand, but it was too late, half of his tea had spread out on his desk table, a few papers were wet. Dalya quickly put away several folders before the tea could reach them. Richard placed down his cup of tea on the silver tray. Dalya pulled a cloth from her apron pocket, and she dried the liquid on the desk table:

- Sorry for this incident ...

And although his throat was tight, Richard replied calmly:

- It's nothing ... it's my fault ...

When Dalya dried Richard's desk table, and she placed back the files to their original place, she let go of an amused and intimidated laugh:

- I better leave and let you work, before causing another incident.

Richard sat back in his chair, and he smiled at her. When Dalya closed the door, Richard went back to his work.

Two minutes later, Richard took his cup of tea and had a few sips. Except that while putting down his teacup, Richard missed the plate, and in an instant, all the tea dispersed on his desk table ... for the 2nd time.

The young man froze in his chair, still holding his teacup that was emptied entirely on the desk table, he observed with a shocked look, the state of his papers all wet with tea.

Because Richard Poirier was rarely clumsy in his moves. He was a young man, always calm, always careful and cautious, always ordered and organized. His office was always tidy and spotless. And yet ... on that day ... something shook Richard Poirier and made him clumsy.

Chapter 34

The origin

The summer was painful for Amira Mounier. Despite the free days, summer was not Amira's favorite season. She was sweating all day, her cheeks were red, and she felt heavy all the time.

That day, Dalya and Amira were in the Library of the grand Mansion. Despite the cold drinks that Cristelle brought them, the heat was stifling and the air was heavy to breath. The two girls had finished their homework of the summer vacation, a few days earlier. Dalya and Amira spent their days reading books at the Library of the grand Mansion. The snow Panther was still following the two girls everywhere. Séraphine was lying down on the cold marble floor.

Silence reigned in the Library. Lying down each on a divan, Dalya and Amira were focused in their readings. When suddenly, Amira asked:

- Dalya ... this strange box that gives you clues ... you told me once, that it was made out of a powerful and rare metal ... titanium, wasn't it?

Dalya looked up from her book:

- The Excelbox? ... Yes, it's Uncle Giorgi who discovered it. It's a very complex metal and stronger than steel.

Amira was reading an encyclopedia of precious metals and stones. After a few seconds of silence, she asked again:

- Dalya ... what do you know of the origin of this strange box ... the Excelbox?

Dalya looked at her:

- Not much ... it was given to me by the Late Mr. Governor ... it offers clues every time I ask, and recharges on the night light.
- Have you tried to find out more about it, in the books of this Library?

Dalya let out an amused laugh:

- Of course! ... I spent nights here, searching for the origin of this box! but no book seems to answer this question ...

Amira relaxed back on her chair:

- It's too bad ... it would have been fascinating to know the origin of the Excelbox!

Exhausted long ago from trying, Dalya sighed:

- Yes, it would have been very helpful to understand why and how the Excelbox was given to me!

13 years ago. A summer of 1879. In the city of Bayannur, China.

Iskander Balthazar sat in the hotel's veranda, having breakfast. The view outside was very different from the one of Georgetown city, back in the United States of America. Bayannur City was 600 km West of the capital of China, and a few kilometers of Mongolian land. The small town of Bayannur was printed in a dense green landscape, huge trees; green foliage everywhere, a fresh earth smell was in the air, and everywhere smiling cheerful Asian faces.

Iskander Balthazar was on a business trip in this city, to meet many important people of different commerce.

At his last spoon of the traditional rice soup, Iskander stood up; he wore his jacket on and left the hotel to go to his appointment. Outside, two travel cars were parked, one for Mr. Balthazar, and a second car to a few soldiers accompanying him. A little silhouette standing leaning on a car, let out an amused laugh:

- It took you some time!

Iskander Balthazar couldn't believe his eyes. He walked toward his wife, unable to retain a surprised laugh:

- I haven't made any noise this morning, especially to let you sleep and not wake you up!

Irea Senderlson wore pants, a beige jacket over a white shirt, and a little green hat that covered her golden hair. She already had breakfast in the bedroom, and hurried to join her husband's car. And just like a little girl cheerful and excited by a new adventure, Irea jumped and smiled:

- Well, it didn't work!

Iskander sighed in a worried tone:

- Are you sure you want to accompany me, Irea? ... we will cross 1 hour of jungle to meet with the Dean of a village ... and my appointment could last an hour or so ... I don't want you to get tired ... don't you wish to enjoy your day by visiting the market pla...

Irea interrupted her husband with a dynamic voice, before entering the car:

- Come on! Come on! Otherwise we will be late!

Iskander smiled and murmured:

- She is so stubborn!

Irea stuck her head out the car window and smiled:

- I heard that!

On the way, Iskander and his wife watched the beautiful natural landscape. Giant trees, large green entangled leaves, wildflowers in scarlet colors. Some monkeys followed the two cars, swaying between tree branches. Irea marveled like a child, nose and eyes glued on the car window.

After several minutes of the trip, both cars stopped on the way. The driver turned around and announced:

- We will stop for 5 minutes Mr. Balthazar, to allow the car engine to cool down ...
- Alright. Iskander said. But we mustn't be late for our appointment at the village!
- We will not be, Mr. Balthazar.

And before Iskander could say a word, his wife Irea got out of the car, exclaiming joyfully:

- Come on! We should take a walk!

Iskander raised his eyes up and said:

- But why did I agree to take you with me on this trip?!

Irea let out a childlike laugh:

- One, because you cannot refuse anything to me! ... And two, because you would have been bored without me!

Iskander also got out of the car:

- I admit that on these 2 points, you're perfectly right, my light.

The soldiers also came out of the second car to stretch their legs. It was a beautiful sunny day, calm and peaceful.

Irea walked a few steps into the jungle, fascinated by the beautiful and strange plants and flowers. It was very different from the landscape of Georgetown city. Iskander leaned on the car door, talking to a soldier, while keeping an attentive eye on his wife Irea who was walking in the jungle.

A few steps further, Irea noticed several beautiful unique blue flowers. She came closer to get a nearby look. They were little flowers with blue violet petals, inside yellow orange, and fresh green leaves. Irea has never seen such splendor.

When suddenly ... a thunderous scream echoed through the forest. Irea fell on the floor and she froze in her movement. Iskander jumped and his heart stopped. All the guards instantly hold up their guns, and they pointed them ... toward Irea Senderlson!

The young woman didn't understand why the soldiers pointed their guns toward her. Iskander became pale, his lips trembled. He took a single step forward, and he ordered his wife with a whispered serious voice:

- Irea ... do ... not ... move ...

Except that the young woman felt a breath right behind her. And when she turned around slowly, Irea was shocked by what she discovered. Face to face, two steps away from her, a beautiful terrifying creature was standing. A great allure, gray fur with black tattooed lines, big scary legs, a long tail, and piercing sapphire blue eyes ... the Panther was fascinating and terrifying!!

The Panther let out a second roar. And the soldiers advanced a step further. Iskander retained them, ordering them in a trembling voice:

- Do not fire! ... Irea is too close ... if you open fire on the animal, Irea will be harmed too!

Then, Iskander turned around and he ordered in a calm voice:

- Irea ... step back ... slowly ... few steps ... slowly ...

As soon as Irea made a move and tried to stand up, the Panther let out a 3rd roar, as loud as the first ones. Irea was paralyzed on the ground, she trembled from head to toe, her face became pale, her lips turned all white. For the first time in his life, Iskander didn't know what to do. His wife was in real danger, facing a frightening Panther!

At an instant, Irea noticed some small silhouettes who appeared near the Panther's long legs; there were 5 little baby Panthers!

Despite the scare of the situation, Irea was fascinated by the 5 little babies. They observed the young woman with a curious eye, staying close to their mother Panther. The 5 little babies all had the same blue sapphire eyes of their mother Panther, but they were in different colors of fur; there were 2 babies black night, 2 babies light yellow and 1 baby clear gray.

For a moment, Irea forgot her fear, the young woman looked at the mother Panther, and she smiled at the creature. And as strange as it may seem, the Panther smiled back too. Iskander Balthazar and the soldiers noticed the smile shared between the young woman and the mother Panther. It looked like as if Irea and the mother Panther understood each other without any need for words.

And without looking away from the mother Panther, Irea ordered the guards, in a sure strong voice:

- Lower your weapons! Immediately!

Straightaway, the guards lowered their weapons with a hesitant move; they were all confused at what was happening in front of them. Iskander was not reassured however, his wife was still a few steps away from the dangerous animal:

- Irea ... you must step back ... slowl...

Except that a strange and unusual thing happened at this precise instant. The mother Panther held in her mouth one of her little babies, and she took a step toward the young woman. Irea, still sitting on the ground, she didn't dare to move. And when the mother Panther was close to Irea ... the mother Panther gently put down her gray fur baby on the lap of the young woman!

Instantly, the mother Panther stepped back, and ... the magnificent creature bowed in front of Irea Senderlson!

A silence of confusion and amazement invaded all those who witnessed this scene. And while the young woman was shocked at the gesture of the mother Panther, Irea smiled while hugging the baby Panther that was given to her.

And immediately, all the guards bowed in front of the young woman. Iskander Balthazar asked, in a confused and worried tone:

- What is going on? What is happening? Why is everyone bowing to my wife Irea?

One of the guards smiled at him in astonishment:

- Nature has chosen her designated one!

Seconds later, the mother Panther turned around and continued walking through the jungle, followed by her other 4 babies. Irea hugged firmly the little fur ball in her hands, while observing the mother Panther disappear into the jungle. Instantly, Iskander ran toward his wife, and he helped her stand up. Irea smiled at him nervously, still in shock from the scene:

- Look at what I have received!! ... She trusted me with her little baby!!

Many contradictory feelings invaded Iskander at that instant. The fear of having nearly lost his wife, the happiness she's still alive, remorse for agreeing that she can travel with him, anger that his wife was exposed to such danger, astonishment that they were given a baby Panther, confusion about the guards and the Panther bowing to Irea. Iskander finally exclaimed in an upset and trembling tone:

- This is the last time you will travel with me, Irea!

Under the surprised stares and shocked whispers of the soldiers, Irea walked toward the car, and she replied with an amused tone:

- I heard this sentence before! ... Look how pretty she is! It's a female! We have a baby Panther now!!

Iskander entered the car after his wife, and he locked the door very firmly:

- There is no way we'll keep this animal! ... We'll hand it over to the villagers in the next villag...

Irea jumped out of her car seat:

- Oh no! You perfectly watched the mother Panther; she trusted me with her baby! I will not leave the Country without this baby!

When the two cars continued their trip, Iskander sighed in relief that the dangerous situation was over. And he also sighed because of his wife stubbornness. The rest of the trip was a long argument between Iskander and his wife.

- Irea ... it's a Panther! ... we cannot have a Panther as a pet ...
- Why not? ... The Attorney General of Georgetown city, Mr. Bellini has parrots!
- It's not the same! ... When she grows up, this Panther will be a giant size! ...
- Look at these blue sapphire eyes! ... What a cutie!! ... Do you think she will be as beautiful as her mother Panther? ... I will take care of her myself!!
- Her place is in the jungle! This animal cannot live in a house!
- Why not?! We have a huge garden and enough rooms in the grand Mansion!!

The next morning. In the city of Bayannur.

Early in the morning, the market merchants opened their shops. The market place was held in several small streets and it gathered hundreds of shops, set up one next to each other. All the traditional crafts were sold there. It was the most popular market in the city. All visitors of Bayannur city would buy from this market.

The soldier walked in hurried steps, toward one specific store. When he entered, he found a man sitting on a chair, cleaning a piece of his merchandise. The soldier bowed greeting him, and he announced to the man:

- Tā xuǎnzéle, shīfu! *(She has chosen, Master!)*

The sitting man looked up toward the young soldier:

- Nǐ quèdìng ma? *(Are you sure of it?)*

The soldier approached him:

- Yes, Master! ... yesterday morning, we were on route to a village ... we stopped on the way, in the middle of the jungle ... and she appeared, with 5 little ones ... she offered one of her cubs to a young woman ...

Master Fong Ka-Ho asked:

- And did she bow in front of the young woman?

The soldier smiled:

- Yes, Master! ... with all her splendor, she bowed to the young woman ... and then she left with her 4 remaining little ones ...

161

Master Fong Ka-Ho was surprised by the news that the soldier reported to him. The two men became silent and surprised by the unusual gesture of the mother Panther. After a minute of thinking, Master Fong Ka-Ho asked the soldier:

- Zhège Nianqing nǚrén shì Shei? *(And who is this young woman?)*

The soldier answered, with a sure tone:

- She is the wife of an important statesman ... they come from a far land ... the young woman seems nice, the man is very well respected.

Master Fong Ka-Ho seemed confused, he thought aloud:

- It's strange ... Hen qíguài ... usually, she only chooses people of our Country ... this is the first time she favors a foreigner ...
- All the soldiers had their guns ready and pointing toward the mother Panther ... but the young woman ordered us to lower our weapons!

Master Fong Ka-Ho was curious:

- And will the young woman keep the baby Panther?
- Certainly Master! During the rest of the trip to the village, the young woman insisted upon her husband to keep the baby Panther and carry it with them ... to their Country.

Master Fong Ka-Ho smiled:

- Our work begins now!

The soldier approached the man:

- I heard from the hotel, that the young woman will visit the market today.

Master Fong Ka-Ho patted the shoulder of the young soldier:

- And we will wait for her!

A few hours later. In the popular market place.

- But why do you insist on following me like a shadow, since yesterday? Irea asked, unable to hold her amused laugh.

Iskander got out of the car after his wife, and he replied in a natural voice:

- I don't know ... maybe to prevent you from a deadly serious situation, for the 2nd time!

Iskander didn't sleep that night; although his wife came out alive, Iskander still couldn't believe she escaped an assured death. Irea insisted on keeping the baby animal in their hotel bedroom, while she would do some shopping in the popular market place, that day.

- Are we going to keep it for a long time? Iskander asked with an irritated tone.

162

Irea turned toward her husband and she smiled at him:

- For a very long time! You'll get used to this adorable cutie baby!

Iskander sighed:

- This adorable cutie baby slept on top of my head, and she bit my toes this morning!
- Yes, I heard your scream! Irea laughed. This little one seems to adore you!

Irea and Iskander entered the alley full of shops. The market was lively and full of activity, many customers were buying, and sellers invited passersby into their shops. It seemed to be a busy day for everyone.

Irea visited the shops, and Iskander followed her everywhere. He tried to convince his wife to drop the idea of keeping this baby animal:

- I will buy you a dozen kittens, if you let this baby animal here in this Country ... kittens, puppies, goats, chickens ... whatever you want!

Outraged by her husband's offer, Irea turned to him:

- Monsieur the Governor is trying to bribe me?

Iskander lost his words:

- Well ... it's not really a bribe ... it's just a ... how about a horse?

Irea continued to examine the merchandises, and she affirmed with a decided tone:

- It will be a baby Panther and nothing else!

Iskander sighed:

- I have to follow you everywhere, watch over you so that you won't be killed, and convince you to abandon a dangerous animal! I feel like I am babysitting a child!

Irea laughed at the remark of her husband. On the counter of a shop, the woman noticed among many merchandises, some pretty traditional Chinese shoes, red color, with several embroideries at the edges. Irea asked the seller:

- How much for these traditional shoes?

The merchant smiled at the young woman, pointing his finger toward a shop at the end of the street, with a soft voice:

- That shop over there sells the shoes at better prices than ours! Go there, young Lady! You will be well served!

Irea was a bit surprised and confused by this suggestion. After a few seconds of hesitation, Irea left the shop, and she went to another one. Iskander, still following her, he asked in a worried tone:

- But who can train this animal in Georgetown City? ... We certainly cannot keep it free in town ... do you imagine when this Panther will grow up? How will we manage to raise her?

Irea observed the shoes in a second shop:

- She is still a baby, Iskander ... we can train and educate her ... Mr. Rosenwald, the Gardener can help me raise her ...

Before Iskander could say another objection, Irea smiled to a merchant:

- I would like to know the sizes of these red shoes, please ...

The merchant replied politely, with a courteous smile:

- Sorry young Lady, but we have no more size in these shoes. However, that shop over there ... at the end of the street ... that shop has all the sizes that you need, young Lady!

Irea thanked him with a confused smile. And she left the shop, toward another one. Iskander thought aloud:

- And how can we have the permit to transport such a creature? ... They hardly accept dogs and cats in boats!

Irea examined the merchandises of a third shop:

- I asked this morning at the hotel reception, for travel permits ... it is already in the process of being validated ... It will be ready tomorrow afternoon!

Iskander was short of ideas to convince his wife. Irea looked at the merchandises for a moment, and she pointed out something, while asking a vender:

- May I have one of these red shoes, please?

The Merchant bowed to the young woman, and he replied with a polite and friendly smile:

- My apologies young Lady, we have no more red shoes ... but this shop has many, all to your taste ... at the end of that street ...

The counter of this merchant was filled with at least a hundred red shoes. Yet, it seemed to Irea that all the vendors refused to sell their merchandises to her. And she also had the impression that all the vendors were telling her about the same shop. The one at the end of the street, of the popular market.

A strange curiosity invaded Irea. And without listening to her husband's arguments, Irea walked toward the only and same shop that all the vendors pointed out to her.

When she entered the shop at the end of the street, Irea was submerged by a delicious white jasmine scent. It was a modest shop, tidy and warm. Beautiful handicrafts were exhibited.

As soon as Irea stepped inside, a man greeted her with a warm and gentle voice:

164

- Welcome young Lady ... Welcome Monsieur ... My name is Fong Ka-Ho ...

Irea smiled shyly. A strange air of assurance and calm filled the shop. The young woman felt strangely serene. Iskander who has been following her everywhere since this morning, he too was overwhelmed by the quiet of the place as soon as he entered the shop.

Master Fong Ka-Ho addressed the young woman:

- It seems to me that you are seeking a particular item?

Irea replied:

- Yes ... embroidered red shoes on the sides, like these ... small sizes, please.
- Certainly, young Lady ... right away!

Master Fong Ka-Ho disappeared in a corner of his shop. Taking advantage of the merchant's absence, Irea asked her husband who was looking at an odd item:

- Iskander ... don't you feel something strange is going on here?

Iskander said in an amused tone:

- The only strange thing I find here ... it's your obstinacy to keep this baby Panther! ... What should I do to convince you not to adopt it?

Irea laughed:

- Are you out of ideas already? ... I thought it would take you days to try and dissuade me to take her with us!!

Iskander approached his wife:

- I'm not as strong and stubborn as you, my light! ... But I admit this is not a reasonable idea ... raising a Panther, in Georgetown City!

Irea observed her husband for a few moments before answering:

- I don't know why this mother Panther gave me her baby, Iskander.
- It may be only a maternal instinct.
- No ... I don't think so, no ... it was something much more than that ... for a mother to trust you with her child ... it was more than just a simple maternal instinct!

Master Fong Ka-Ho came close to the young woman, and he gave her the shoes she asked for, displaying a warm smile:

- Here is the best of my products, young Lady!

Irea was amazed by the beautiful details of the traditional shoes. She asked the merchant:

- How much for these two pairs?
- 10 Yuan, young Lady ...

Irea paid the merchant, and she took her shoes:

- Thank you, Monsieur. Have a good day!

And before turning around to leave the shop, Master Fong Ka-Ho called out the woman, and he offered her a little smooth metal gray box:

- You will do me a great honor, young Lady ... to accept a gift of our Country!

When Irea took it in her hands, she examined the strange box in all directions. One little rectangular opening was on one side. All the other sides were closed. And as strange as it may seem, when touching the box, one could clearly feel that there was a powerful force inside of it. And although the young woman didn't know what the box contained, Irea appreciated the merchant's gesture, and she insisted:

- Well then, I will pay you for this box!

And before Irea could take out money from her wallet, Master Fong Ka-Ho approached her and he said in a serious and calm tone:

- Young Lady ... in our Country, the custom is to accept nature's gifts, with only a promise to take care of them.

Iskander and Irea exchanged a confused look. The words of the merchant were strange. Irea displayed a kind smile toward the merchant:

- Thank you for your gift ... I will take care of this box!

At this instant, Master Fong Ka-Ho bowed in front of Irea Senderlson, just like the soldiers and the mother Panther did, the day before, in the jungle. Master Fong Ka-Ho slowly straightened up and he smiled proudly:

- The honor will be ours, to serve nature's designated one.

Neither Irea nor Iskander could understand the attitude and strange words of the merchant. They left the shop, confused and puzzled. Irea recovered rapidly:

- When are we having lunch? ... I'm hungry!
- We just had breakfast at the hotel, barely an hour ago! exclaimed Iskander
- I digested quickly! Irea laughed
- You will drive me crazy. Iskander sighed with an annoyed tone.
- I thought it was already done! Exclaimed Irea all amused.

While Irea Senderlson and Iskander Balthazar continued their shopping, the merchant of the last shop, at the end of the market place, Master Fong Ka-Ho was observing them with a calm and focused look. The young couple had no idea that they were carrying ... much more than a little gray metal box ... much more than a gift from a modest merchant of the market.

Immediately, the merchant, Master Fong Ka-Ho, who was observing the young couple walking away, was joined by two silhouettes. Both girls wore traditional clothes of their city, long straight silk dresses. One of the girls had long black straight hair, waving gracefully with every move. And the other girl seemed to be a teenager, and she was wearing a pretty cherry blossom pin on her hair.

The young woman asked:

- Did she take the box, Master?... Maybe we should have explained to her what it really was.

Master Fong Ka-Ho replied:

- Everything in its time, Haîyang... everything in its time ...

The youngest girl was also curious:

- Is she really the designated one, Master? ... It's so unusual for a foreigner to be chosen ... why her?

Master Fong Ka-Ho smiled:

- Nature never justifies itself, Tudi ... and yet Nature's choices are always well right!

The two women were confused and perplexed. After a long minute of silence, and without taking his eyes off Irea and Iskander, Master Fong Ka-Ho ordered the young girls:

- Haîyang ...Tudi ... notify the others ... our responsibility is to follow the box and protect it ... we are leaving Bayannur.

The two women exchanged an accomplice and excited smile:

- Yes, Master! Right away!

Chapter 35

And a 3rd detention

Monday, September 05th, 1892. At the Royal Georgetown College.

Dalya Bouvard was eager to go back to school. Her friend Amira, who was waiting at the school entrance, was not of the same opinion:

- I won't refuse one more month of school break!!

Holding her laugh with difficulty, Dalya replied:

- We get bored during summer ... the days are long and empty ...

Amira stopped in the middle of the corridor, and she said with an angry tone:

- At the exam's time, when you will have to study until late at night, when your brain is dizzy and full, I will remind you of these words!!

Immediately, Dalya corrected her answer, and giggled:

- Yes, I admit that the exams are not a pleasant time ... I take back my words!

Amira sighed in a sad tone:

- Goodbye summer vacation ... Goodbye the warm sun and refreshing juices ... Goodbye long naps and rest ...

While laughing, the two students walked to the Physics classroom. At the door, Amira bowed to her friend:

- Entrez Mademoiselle ... Entrez ... you are the one eager of the long lesson hours, crazy teachers and never-ending homework!!

The Physics classroom was just as it was before the summer vacation. Nothing changed. The large room was conveniently arranged for the theory and practical needs of the course, several tables and chairs for students, a huge counter with many strange items and practice materials, a huge blackboard and a teacher's desk.

Upon entering the classroom, Dalya and Amira were greeted by a familiar face. Professor Roger was very elegant in a suit and bow tie. The young man was smiling and welcoming:

- Glad to see you in my class, Mesdemoiselles! I hope you had a good summer vacation!!

Both students answered shyly:

- Yes, Professor.

Dalya and Amira took their usual places. Right away, Amira turned toward Dalya, trying to hold her anger:

- He is happy to see us?! ... He gave us mountains of homework!! ... The list of physics exercises took us two weeks to finish!! And yet, we were both working on it!!

Dalya hid her face in her hands, so as not to explode with laugh, in front of Amira's anger. Her friend continued whispering in an angry tone:

- And despite the tons of homework we had, you are eager to get back to school?! Are you crazy!!

Hours after the Physics class.

Dalya and Amira went to the school Library. And as always, the Library assistant Miss Guendolyn welcomed them with a warm joyful smile:

- I am happy to see you in this new school year, Mesdemoiselles!! I hope you had a great summer vacation!!

Dalya and Amira exchanged amused glances. Dalya laughed:

- Somehow, yes!

Amira sighed:

- Besides the detention we had in the Toscana restaurant kitchens, and the mountains of homework ... the summer vacation was too short!

Miss Guendolyn seemed amused:

- Well, I am delighted that your detention is over! Now, it is the beginning of the school year, and therefore a new start!

Dalya and Amira pulled out their borrowed books from their bags, and they put them on the carriage of the returned books. Dalya hesitated a few moments to talk, and she finally decided:

- Miss Guendolyn ... I ... I had a little problem with a book ...

The young woman observed Dalya in a worried tone:

- What problem Mademoiselle?

Dalya had no choice but to tell the truth. While opening a borrowed book, Dalya explained to Miss Guendolyn:

- During the summer vacation ... my little sisters ... the pests ... they drew some doodles on one of the books that I borrowed! ... I didn't dare to touch it to avoid any more damage.

Miss Guendolyn wore her eyeglasses; she took the book from Dalya, and she examined it carefully. After a few seconds, the young woman laughed:

- This is not the worst I've seen, don't worry!! ... It's only 2 pages, they drew only in colored pencils and in empty sides ... I will erase the drawings with a product, and it will be just like before!
- I'm so sorry, Miss Guendolyn ... my little sisters are uncontrollable ...

Miss Guendolyn said in an amused tone:

- It is nothing serious!! It's a little incident!!

A voice behind the two students manifested:

- And the school rules are very clear, about it!

Miss Guendolyn blushed, Dalya jumped, and Amira dropped her book. Professor Haîyang displayed a strangely delighted smile. Professor Haîyang continued:

- Any damaged book is punishable by a detention!

Miss Guendolyn laughed in an intimidated tone:

- Yes, but I admit that this rule isn't applicable since a long time ago! Many students return back way more damaged books than this one ... and I always forgive them, it is most always by accident ...

Professor Haîyang replied in a firm tone:

- The rules are written to be followed, Miss Guendolyn!

Miss Guendolyn's cheeks turned all red:

- Certainly, yes ... but the drawings in this book can be erased ... they are only on the empty sides ... and it's only 2 pag...

Professor Haîyang interrupted the Library assistant politely:

- I am sorry Miss Guendolyn ... but the rules are for everyone, without any exceptions!

Dalya defended herself:

- It was only an accident Professor Haîyang!! My little sisters dra...

Professor Haîyang decided in a determined tone:

- You are both in detention ... for 4 months!

At this instant, Dalya and Amira exchanged a confused look. The decision of Professor Haîyang was absurd. Unable to contain her anger, Amira exclaimed in a shocked tone:

- What have I done? ... I didn't even speak!

Friday, September 09th, 1892.

After their Latin course, Dalya and Amira headed toward the school kitchen. And this time, Dalya was worried:

- I wonder what task the Cook Chef will impose on us again ...

Amira thought aloud:

- I admit that of the two of us, you have suffered the worst detention tasks! ... Storing the Pantry on a slippery floor ... it was insane!

Dalya sighed:

- And yet ... as soon as I managed to have a balance on my legs, the Cook Chef imposed on me a bucket of water to hold on top of my head!

Holding her laugh with difficulty, Amira replied:

- It was difficult to explain to the grand Mansion employees why you were all wet, every two days.
- They already think I'm strange ... a more or less incident will not change their opinion of me!

Approaching the kitchen, Amira tried to encourage her friend:

- Courage courage!

Opening the kitchen door, Dalya and Amira noticed that the activity in the school kitchen was well advanced. All the employees were busy cutting, roasting and cooking food.

Dalya and Amira stepped into the kitchen, among the counters and kitchen aides. Arriving at her usual place, Amira found a large basket of peas. She held an amused laugh:

- Well ... I think the Cook Chef wants to train me to peel all the vegetables!!

Needing no orders to work, Amira sat in her usual chair; she put on her gloves and she began removing peas. Amira was delighted:

- It's easier than tomatoes!!

Dalya sat on a chair near her friend, waiting for her new task. And since a while now, Dalya's mind was occupied by a strange thought:

- Don't you think that the behavior of Professor Haîyang is weird? Especially toward both of us? ... It looks like as if she tries to inflict detentions on us for a nothing!! ... You didn't even speak, and you ended up with a 4 month detention!! And this, at the first day back to school!!

Amira poured peas in a container, and the residue in another one:

- I admit it's a little weird coming from Professor Haîyang ... it surprised me that she inflicts these detentions on us... but some teachers are naturally wicked and they enjoy torturing their students ... and the best examples are the History and Geography teachers ...

Dalya thought for a second:

- No ... I don't think so, no ... Professor Haîyang isn't like them ... she doesn't seem to be mean and wicked ...
- She is not wicked; she just imposed on us almost 11 months of detention!

At this remark, Dalya and Amira laughed at their misfortune. When the silhouette of the Cook Chef approached them, Amira whispered to Dalya, with a discreet nod:

- Good luck!

When the Cook Chef finished giving his instructions to an assistant, he came near Dalya. With all her heart, Dalya prayed for a task easier than storing the Pantry on the slippery floor and with a bucket of water on her head. The Cook Chef pointed out a corner to Dalya, next to her friend Amira. A strange object was set up there, and a little stool placed in front of it.

- The kitchen of the Royal Georgetown College prepares its own butter flavored with herbs ... we pour the cream into two jars, firmly closed ... and we shake both jars for a few hours, by the time the little butter grains come off the liquid ... then we filter the liquid, by using a clean and thin cloth ... we rinse off the butter with cold water ... and we add salt and herbs to the butter ...

Dalya still didn't understand her new detention task. The Cook Chef asked her to sit on the little stool. Dalya complied immediately.

- Your task is to shake the two jars ... at the same time, in opposite direction. Explained the Cook Chef.

The movement was very simple, pull and stretch both arms to shake the cream. That's all. Dalya was delighted that her new job was less complicated than the previous ones. Before leaving, the Cook Chef ordered her one last time:

- Shake without a stop ... your hand move must be strong ... always in opposite direction!
- Yes, Chef! Dalya answered, while hurrying up.

When the Cook Chef went back to his kitchen aides, Dalya continued to do her job. Amira approached her basket of peas and her chair near her friend:

172

- It appears to be easier than the previous detention!! You were worried for nothing, earlier!

Pulling and stretching both arms, forward and backward. A simple movement. Dalya replied to her friend in a happy tone:

- It's much easier, I admit!

Amira chuckled:

- One more week in the Pantry, and your back wouldn't have endured one more fall!
- My butt too!

The two girls giggled, as they completed their detention. One was peeling peas. And the other one was pulling and stretching both her arms to shake the butter.

Chapter 36

A Chargé de Mission

Saturday, September 10th, 1892. At the French neighbor's house, les Poirier.

When Dalya walked into the office of the young Richard Poirier, it was unoccupied. She took a few steps inside, and she put down the silver tray, not on the desk table this time, but on a small table near a chair, and she turned around to leave the office. Except that one thing caught her attention. On the desk table of Richard Poirier, multiple folders and papers were spread. Dalya approached and she read:

At the Republican convention in Minneapolis, in Minnesota, President Benjamin Harrison came first, in the first round without real opposition...

Dalya had read some articles in the newspapers about the presidential elections of this year. When a voice interrupted her thoughts.

- Good morning.

Dalya turned around to find herself in front of Richard Poirier, he was smiling at her. He held in his hands, several books he had brought from the Library downstairs.

- I brought your tea.
- And a cake with it? Richard asked with amusement, while putting down the books on his desk.
- Certainly. Dalya smiled.

When he sat on the chair in front of his desk, Dalya hesitated a few moments before asking:

- You ... are you working on the new presidential elections, which will take place this year?

Although surprised by Dalya's curiosity on this subject, Richard answered:

- Yes, I am writing a report on the unfolding of this election ... this is a very important event ... both Houses of Representatives need a full report ... Mademoiselle is interested in politics?
- I read the newspapers almost every day ... I like to be updated of what is happening around.

Richard asked in an amused tone:

- And in your opinion, Mademoiselle ... who do you think will be our next president?

Having followed this affair since many weeks, Dalya replied without hesitation:

- The Democrats selected former President Cleveland as a candidate in this election ... and it will be a nice victory and good revenge of the 1888 election. The issue of customs duties had played in favor for the Republicans before, but the various changes made under Harrison's administration made the imported merchandises so expensive, that many voters cited in newspapers, wanted a revaluation of those customs duties ... so then I support Mr. Grover Cleveland as future president!

Richard Poirier observed Dalya for some long seconds, in a fascinated stare. He really misjudged this little girl. Richard straightened up on his chair; he took a book and looked for a specific page:

- Anyway, I can confirm that this election is a real headache! ... Reviews and statistics are opposing ... it doesn't make my job easy! ... The tea and the cake arrived at the right moment!

Dalya walked closer to the desk table:

- Your job is to write reports for the Government?

Richard hesitated a few seconds before looking at Dalya and answering her:

- In a way ... yes ...
- So then, you are a State Secretary? Dalya asked.

The young man was proud, knowing that Dalya was interested in his work. Richard let out an amused laugh, while pulling a paper from a folder:

- I have underestimated your political knowledge, Mademoiselle. I am precisely a Chargé de Mission, for the Government.

Dalya remembered having heard Mrs. Glorina talk about the young Richard Poirier's job. He worked very hard, often until late at night, and relentlessly.

Not wishing to disturb him more in his work, Dalya turned around and she was about to leave the office, when Richard's question stopped her:

- How is your back to school going on?

Dalya was somehow surprised by Richard's question. She didn't expect the young man to be interested in her studies. Dalya answered, after a few seconds of hesitation:

- Very well, thank you ... each new school year, my tutor, Professor Canfield adds me more courses than the previous semester. This time, I have the civilizations class ... and at the first look on it, it doesn't seem to be an easy course.

Richard relaxed on his chair. And without taking his eyes away from the paper he was holding in his hand, Richard answered Dalya:

- The civilizations course requires learning by heart the history of several eras. After a while, you will notice that it is one long history that repeats itself. I was aware that Mr. Iskander Balthazar was a big admirer and curious about civilizations ... in the Library of the grand Mansion, there surely must be several books about it ...

The young man looked up toward Dalya, and he smiled:

- And I have no doubt that you will succeed this class, better than anyone!

Was it because of the intense stare of Richard Poirier, or his intimidating smile or his unexpected encouragements ... anyway, at this instant, Dalya felt her cheeks become all red. She thanked him with a shy smile. Then she left the office, under the amused and pleased stares of Richard Poirier.

Chapter 37

Chess Pawns: the Tower and the Bishop

Wednesday, September 21st, 1892. In the Law firm.

September announced the new colors of autumn. The weather was getting colder and rainy. The sky was of a gray mood. The trees were preparing to undress off their foliage.

Late this afternoon, the Lawyer Mr. Ernest Laszlo asked his assistant and right hand lawyer Sloan Wilfrid for an update session on the files and the work at the Law Firm. And as Mr. Ernest Laszlo enjoyed it, a Chess game was going on.

This time, Sloan Wilfrid was determined to win, using the Chess pawns of the Tower and the Bishop. He had practiced and learned by heart almost all the strategies of these two important Chess pieces during the long hours of the free summer months. The Tower pawn was very effective, and the Bishop piece was very fast.

While proudly moving the Tower two squares away, Sloan Wilfrid asked his employer, sitting in front of him:

- I have revised the case we have on Friday afternoon ... do you wish that I reinforce the defense, Monsieur Ernest?

Without even a second to think, Mr. Ernest Laszlo moved a pawn to the left:

- No, it will not be necessary. The judge has already been informed of the matter.

Sloan Wilfrid decided to use the Bishop pawn. He moved it 3 boxes to the right. Mr. Ernest asked:

- Have you finished collecting the papers for the Pennsylvania file?
- Almost, Monsieur. I will have to travel for a day to this city, to get the ownership land certificate from the city administration. It is the only paper that is missing to complete the file.

Mr. Ernest Laszlo moved a pawn:

- Good ... good ... make sure that the land certificate spells correctly the name and the property number ... I don't want a writing error delaying us in this file.
- Understood, Monsieur Ernest ... be reassured!

Sloan Wilfrid felt lucky on that day. The Tower and Bishop pawns were very effective. He had already won almost all the soldiers pawns of his opponent. There were only a few tours left of the strategy, to win this Chess game ... finally!

Except that before Sloan Wilfrid could move his Bishop pawn, to swallow the Knight pawn of his employer, the secretary of Mr. Ernest Laszlo entered the office.

- Sorry to disturb you, Monsieur Ernest ... I received urgent messages to transmit to you.
- From who?

The secretary came close to the Lawyer, and she handed him two small notes:

- A message from Mr. Marius and another one from Mr. Quentin ... the messenger is waiting outside to confirm an answer.

Mr. Ernest Laszlo took the 2 little papers, and he carefully read them silently. Sloan Wilfrid stretched his neck vainly; he was unable to read the content of the message.

At this moment, curiosity startled in Wilfrid's mind. He managed himself all the court files of the Law Firm, and Mr. Ernest Laszlo consulted him in all matters, as private as they can be. So then, what could this urgent affair be between Mr. Marius, Mr. Quentin and Mr. Ernest Laszlo? Why was Sloan Wilfrid sidelined for the first time? And above all, what secret was Mr. Ernest Laszlo hiding? What was happening?

When Mr. Ernest Laszlo finished reading the two notes, a strange thing happened ... Mr. Ernest Laszlo let out a joyful and diabolical laugh. A laugh that was rarely heard. A laugh that didn't predict anything good. And at that instant, Wilfrid's doubts were confirmed ... Ernest Laszlo was up to something. But what was it? Why? And against whom? Sloan Wilfrid needed to find out, and quickly!

Mr. Ernest Laszlo wrote a reply, and he handed it to the secretary:

- Give this to the messenger. An immediate return to Mr. Marius and Mr. Quentin!
- Right away, Monsieur.

When the secretary closed the office door, the Chess game continued. Although in a very different atmosphere than what it was before. Sloan Wilfrid was disturbed. Curiosity itched seriously Wilfrid's brain, because of the joyful smile and strange attitude of Mr. Ernest Laszlo. Sloan Wilfrid pulled himself together, and he announced while moving his pawn:

- The Tower ... 3 squares forward.

You would not be surprised to know that this Chess game ended very quickly ... only 1 minute after Wilfrid's move. After swallowing the best assets of Sloan Wilfrid, the Tower and the Bishop, the Lawyer Ernest Laszlo shot the king of Wilfrid, affirming cheerfully:

- Checkmate!

Sloan Wilfrid lay back on his chair, shocked and disappointed. 3 summer months to review and learn by heart the best Chess strategies. 3 training months to win this Chess game, just once. Except that the Tower and the Bishop of Sloan Wilfrid didn't survive long against the cleverness of Mr. Ernest Laszlo.

Chapter 38

The Safoubri

Friday, September 30th, 1892.

At the end of her classes, Dalya returned straightaway to the grand Mansion. It was the arrival day of her mother's family; her grandmother, her uncle, her Aunt and her little family.

Dalya put down her bag in the living room of the grand Mansion, and without changing her school uniform; she went straight to the annex house. As far as her memories could bring her, Dalya remembered only vaguely her mother's family. And as strange as it may be, a feeling of anxiety invaded Dalya, whenever she thought of her mother's family. Why this feeling of anxiety? Dalya didn't know. Yet, she was not reassured about that visit...

Holding back her anxiety and trying to smile, Dalya walked up the stairs of the annex house.

As soon as Dalya appeared in the living room, all the conversation stopped, and all eyes looked at Dalya. Instantly, Dalya's mother stood up quickly, and she introduced her daughter:

- And here is my jewel! My dearest daughter ... Dalya!

Dalya was not surprised by her mother's kindness. In public, Mrs. Augustine always behaved as an exemplary mother, loving and caring. In private, it was an entire different attitude...

Dalya's twin sisters were sitting on little cushions, next to the fireplace, and they were eating their cakes, with an unusual and weird calm. The little twins observed the new visitors with a mute gaze, not daring to come close to them. Dalya's father was comfortably relaxed in a chair near his little twins. And when he noticed Dalya, he announced in a proud voice:

- My dearest daughter ... who will make me a rich man!! I shall soon have this fortune!!

Smiling nervously, Dalya stepped forward to greet her grandmother. Her name was Mrs. Medusa Safoubri. She was an old woman, a small size, very fat, with orange curly hair, and a very tanned skin. The grandmother had small crow black eyes, reflecting a severe and diabolic look. Dalya remembered having seen that look before ... it was the same diabolic eyes of her own mother, Mrs. Augustine!

Another detail caught Dalya's attention. She noticed that her grandmother's clothes were very dirty. The old woman was wearing a long dress tainted and dirty, a crochet shawl undone and with holes, big black shoes covered with dust, and a veil on her head which seemed never to have been washed before.

And when she came close to her grandmother, Dalya felt a strange smell emanating from the old woman; a stinky stench. Dalya had to hold her breath. Immediately, thousand questions invaded Dalya's mind:

- I always heard my grandmother was rich ... why does she wears dirty clothes then? ... And why is her smell unbearable? ... It seems like she never had a bath in her life ... she's rich, isn't she? ... This is strange ... but Lalla Fatim Fadl, the flower vendor at the market, she is a very poor woman, yet Lalla Fatim Fadl always dressed in very clean clothes and she always smelled very good! ... I now understand why the little twins Ari and Adi are sitting far away ...

With a diabolic and severe look, the grandmother observed Dalya from head to toe. Dalya smiled nervously:

- Welcome to Georgetown, grandmother ...

The old woman didn't say a word, but she continued to examine Dalya with an evil and arrogant look. And because of the old woman's stinky smell, Dalya had to move away from her, to breathe some fresh air.

Dalya turned toward a man sitting near the grandmother. And at first sight, Dalya guessed that it was her only maternal uncle.

Dalya's uncle appeared somehow weird. He significantly resembled the grandmother, small size, very fat, and small crow black eyes. The uncle was also wearing very dirty and tainted clothes, just like his own mother, although he had a less stinky smell than his mother. However, Dalya noticed that her uncle was ... abnormal. He displayed an idiot smile, his nose was flowing, and he dried his nose with his fingers.

Dalya was never disgusted and repulsed before, except this time. She avoided shaking her uncle's hand. Dalya greeted her uncle with a little smile:

- Welcome, Uncle Duroc Safoubri ...

And his name was weird too. Dalya thought for a moment:

- Duroc Safoubri ... Duroc ... isn't it the name of a pig's breed at the farm of Mr. Aymeric?

Duroc let out a stupid and silly laugh. And Dalya thought silently:

- He is the favorite son of my grandmother ... Mother always said that her brother was a mature and smart man ... he doesn't even look like a man, and clearly far away from being mature and smart! ... What makes him my grandmother's favorite?... It's true that he weirdly looks like the pigs in Monsieur Aymeric's farm!!

Dalya turned toward her only maternal Aunt, Claudine Safoubri. A young woman, long and very thin, ashy blond hair, a thin mouth, and a big hooked nose. Claudine Safoubri looked exactly like her sister Augustine. She was wearing a flowered dress, clean clothes unlike the grandmother and her brother. She seemed normal ... for now, thought Dalya.

When she came close to her Aunt, Dalya greeted her politely:

- I am pleased to see you au...

Claudine jumped happily and she interrupted Dalya:

- Me too, my son will go to a private school, like you!! ... Me too, my son will wear a school uniform, like you!! ... Me too, my son will have many classes, like you!!

Dalya didn't understand why all the sentences of her Aunt Claudine, included the words: "me too" and "like you". Dalya hesitated to find an answer:

- Yes ... I ... it would be nice ... yes ...

Aunt Claudine turned toward her sister Augustine, and she continued in a piercing voice:

- Me too, I have a gifted and intelligent son, just like your daughter!! ... Me too, my son will succeed, just like your daughter!! ... Me too, I also have a jewel ... my dear son Hugo!!

In all her life, Dalya had never heard the words "me too" and "like you", so abundantly, and in one conversation. Claudine didn't even breathe between her sentences:

- Me too, I live in a big house, like you ... me too, I also have a big garden, like you ... me too, my husband is a worker and a gifted man, like yours ... me too, my son is calm, like yours ... Me too ... like you ... Me too ... like you ... Me too ... like you ...

At a moment, Dalya felt dizzy while following her Aunt Claudine words. While observing her Aunt, Dalya realized something weird. She thought:

- *With each sentence, she say, "like you" ... it seems that Aunt Claudine compares herself to my mother ... me too my house, me too my husband, me too my son ... I never thought I will meet anyone as jealous as Aunt Claudine ... it looks like Aunt Claudine tries to have all the things that her sister Augustine has ... she doesn't even breathe between her comparison sentences... it looks like she will choke from jealousy ... it's incredible to be jealous this much! ... And I thought for a moment, that my Aunt seemed normal?!*

Dalya pulled herself together. She turned toward her Aunt's husband, while the young woman continued to speak:

- Me too, I have a pink dress like you ... Me too, I cut my hair like you ... Me too ... like you ... Me too ... like you ... Me too ... like you ...

Her Aunt's husband, Mr. Henrik was a man in his mid-thirties, normal size, brown hair and a simple look. Dalya had heard that her Aunt's husband, Mr. Henrik was a Hotel Butler. And it showed in his suit and bow tie, neat and clean. Mr. Henrik drank his tea, with a poised attitude, smiling occasionally to his wife's words. And as much as Claudine was a chatty woman, Henrik was a quiet man ... way too quiet ... a disturbing calm, and not reassuring at all, thought Dalya.

Dalya's cousin was sitting next to his father. Hugo was an 8 years old boy, a pale skin, brown eyes, a shy and quiet look, with a nice clean outfit, and a small cap on his head. Dalya came close to him, and she greeted him while shaking his hand:

- Good morning! I'm glad to meet you, Cousin Hugo! I hope you will have a nice time, here at Georgetown City ...

The little cousin smiled shyly. He remained silent and almost invisible.

After a few minutes, listening to the conversations between her parents and the new visitors, Dalya left the annex house, on the pretext of having homework.

In the way back to the grand Mansion, Dalya's mind was filled with thoughts. Her mother's family inspired neither trust nor assurance. But appearances can be deceptive, and Dalya hoped her worry was wrong.

1 week later. Saturday, October 08th, 1892.

Dalya visited the French neighbors, Les Poirier. It was always a pleasure for Dalya to help Mrs. Glorina prepare her dishes. At the end of this afternoon, Mrs. Glorina gave Dalya a large basket filled with a chocolate cake:

- I'm sure your adorable little sisters will love this cake!

Dalya couldn't hold an amused laugh:

- Adorable ... I don't know about that. But they will devour this chocolate cake, for sure!

After greeting Mrs. Glorina, Dalya left toward the grand Mansion. Arriving at the annex house, Dalya found her little twin sisters and her little cousin, sitting around the dining table in the kitchen. It was time for snack, and Aunt Claudine served the children warm milk with cinnamon, and buttered bread with jam. Dalya greeted everyone, and she asked:

- My parents are not here?

The Aunt Claudine poured milk in glasses, and she replied:

- They went to downtown city ... with your grandmother and your uncle ... to settle some papers ... I stayed to take care of the children ...

When Dalya placed the basket on the kitchen table, she announced:

- I came at the right time, apparently! ... I brought you cakes that I and Mrs. Glorina prepared this afternoon.

As soon as Dalya unwrapped the cake, the little twins had their eyes wide open:

- Oh!! ... Good cake!! ... We want cake!!

Dalya laughed:

- Yes, I was expecting this request! ... Do you want some too, cousin Hugo? A slice?

The little cousin Hugo replied with a shy smile. Aunt Claudine jumped and she exclaimed cheerfully:

- It looks like a delicious cake!! ...

Dalya explained to her, while serving her little sisters and her cousin:

- Yes ... the neighbor, Mrs. Glorina explained all the ingredients and the method for preparing it. It sounds difficult, but in fact it's simple when using the bain-marie method to melt th...

The Aunt Claudine interrupted her:

- Me too, I know how to prepare this cake! ... Me too, I use the bain-marie to melt the chocolate! ... Me too, I know how to make many chocolate cakes! ... Me too ... Me too ... Me too ...

While serving a slice of cake on her cousin's plate, Dalya went silent and she listened to her Aunt Claudine speaking without a pause or a breath of air between her sentences.

The little twins devoured their cakes with marveled eyes, and the little cousin seemed to like the cake, too. Dalya sat next to her little sisters, she served herself warm milk, and she observed for some long seconds her Aunt Claudine speaking:

- Me too, my cakes are very delicious! ... Me too, I have a large cake serving plate, decorated just like this one ... Me too, I have big wood spoons, just like those! ... Me too ... Me too ... Me too ...

Dalya had never heard anyone speak without interruption, that much. And above all, never Dalya had known someone so jealous and envious. While her Aunt spoke, Dalya thought in a silent voice:

- *But why is Aunt Claudine so jealous? ... yet she has a family and a much better life than my own parents ... her husband is yet a Hotel Butler, unlike my father who is only a vegetable seller and a restaurant courier ... the little cousin Hugo appears to be much quieter and nicer than my sisters twins who invent fooleries every hour ... but then, what is Aunt Claudine so jealous about?*

An outsider voice interrupted Dalya in her thoughts and Aunt Claudine in her repetitive comparison:

- It looks like a delicious cake!!

Aunt Claudine's husband, Mr. Henrik appeared in the kitchen of the annex house. He immediately sat down on a chair near his son:

- I finished a deal in downtown city, much earlier than I thought.
- Would you like some cake? And something to drink? Dalya asked him
- Such a cake cannot be refused! Mr. Henrik exclaimed

When Dalya was cutting a slice of cake for her Aunt's husband, the man asked her:

- You are living in an immense Mansion ... don't you get lost, there?

Aunt Claudine served milk to her husband:

- I would certainly get lost in that Mansion!!

Dalya smiled:

- Actually, I spend my days in only some rooms of the grand Mansion; the Library, the living room, the dining room and my bedroom ... I don't visit the other rooms ... I come in often tired of my classes in school ...

Before Mr. Henrik could say a word, his wife Claudine jumped:

- Me too, my son will study in a big school, like you! ... Me too, my son will grow up to live in a huge house, like you! ... Me too ... Me too ... Me too ...

It was an attitude that Dalya thought to be abnormal. Aunt Claudine was not only jealous of her sister Augustine, but also of Dalya Bouvard. And this attitude of comparison and jealousy, it annoyed Dalya and made her feel uncomfortable.

While tasting the cake, Mr. Henrik asked Dalya, ignoring his wife's words:

- It seems to me that there are many employees in the grand Mansion, isn't it?

Dalya was glad the conversation changed away from the comparisons of her Aunt Claudine, she replied:

- Yes, they were the employees of Late Mr. Governor ... and they are still working at the grand Mansion, until the appointment of the Heir.

Aunt Claudine jumped out of her chair:

- Me too, I am Heiress like you! ... Me too, I will receive an inheritance from a relative of my husband, and a big fortune, like you! ... Me too ... Me too ... Me too ...

Mr. Henrik continued to ask Dalya:

- And do all the employees live in the grand Mansion?

Dalya explained:

- Yes, the employees' rooms are at the ground floor ... and they get together for meals in the big kitchen ... there is a large dining table in the kitchen ...

Mr. Henrik relaxed in his chair:

- I guess the grand Mansion employees are very well paid, aren't they? So as to take care and watch over an immense place?

Dalya smiled nervously:

- I never dared to ask this question ... but I think so, yes ... the grand Mansion is immense to take care of.

Mr. Henrik was curious:

- How much is their salary?
- I don't have the faintest idea. Dalya replied uncomfortably.
- And ... how many years they have been working in the grand Mansion?

Confusion settled in Dalya's mind at that moment; her Aunt Claudine's husband asked very specific and weird questions, he was curious about the lives' details of the employees at the grand Mansion. Details that Dalya has never dared to ask, let alone think of. She tried to answer politely anyway:

- The employees have been working since a long time at the grand Mansion ... since the time when Late Mr. Governor lived there with his wife, Mrs. Irea Senderlson ...

Mr. Henrik's curiosity was increasingly abnormal:

- If the employees have long worked in such a prestigious place ... and with their excellent salary ... the employees of the grand Mansion, must have some quite personal fortunes, isn't it right?

Without any answer to this question, Dalya could only display an uncomfortable smile. Mr. Henrik wasn't embarrassed to ask her more questions:

- Who gives them their salaries, at the end of every month?

Dalya hesitated for a few seconds:

- Mr. Bûchebois is the responsible of the grand Mansion and its management ... I guess he is the one who handles the employees' salaries ... I think ...

Mr. Henrik ate his cake, while asking:

- And ... do the employees receive bonuses? ... At the end of year or for holidays?

Dalya had not a clue about it. And for once, she was relieved that her Aunt Claudine interrupted the weird curiosity of her husband, exclaiming joyfully:

- Your mother told me you bought an entire wardrobe of Mrs. Lancel store ... Me too, I know very well the fashion couture of Mrs. Lancel! ... Me too, I am going to get myself an entire wardrobe from this shop! ... Me too, I will have large closets to store my entire wardrobe! ... Me too, I will have a house, just like this one ... Me too, I will have an heritage like you ... Me too ... Me too ... Me too ...

Chapter 39

Advice from Lyor

Thursday, October 13th, 1892. At the Law Firm.

The end of the afternoon was quieter than the morning. All the employees were sitting in their offices, head focused in their files. Lyor Laszlo was only a few pages to finish his due report. He went to prepare his 6th cup of coffee. Except that before arriving at the counter, in a corridor, Lyor met Mr. Frank Hatton, the manager of the newspaper The Washington Post Company, supported by the Holding BalthEnterprise.

Lyor appreciated very much Mr. Frank Hatton; he knew him since long ago, and he read this newspaper every morning, without skipping a day. Mr. Frank Hatton was well known for his integrity and professionalism in the press milieu. Lyor hurried to greet him:

- Good evening, Mr. Hatton!!

He was an old man, a small chubby size, but a light march, with a large mustache, impeccably arranged hair, and a beautiful elegant black suit that reinforced his grand allure. The man turned around:

- Lyor Laszlo, it is a pleasure to meet you, young man!
- Me too as well, Mr. Hatton!! ... And I congratulate you for the scoop of the Wallgate case!

Mr. Hatton held an amused laugh:

- We worked on it secretly for months. It was difficult to keep the secret. But we managed to uncover the entire affair.

Lyor admired Mr. Hatton:

- The Country needs a media as upright and serious as your newspaper, Mr. Hatton! It is important to keep people informed and alert on what is going on. Your newspaper is a reference. I cannot start my day without reading your newspaper, Monsieur!

Mr. Hatton smiled at him:

- I am delighted to have a loyal reader such as you.

Lyor was curious of Mr. Hatton's visit to the Law Firm:

- What can I do for you, Mr. Hatton?

Instantly, Mr. Hatton's face changed, his smile became nervous:

- I came ... to meet your father, Mr. Ernest Laszlo ...

- He is at his office for a meeting ... it should end in 30 minutes ... but if you are in a hurry, I can help you with anything, Mr. Hatton ...

After a few seconds of hesitation and nervousness, Mr. Hatton decided to talk to Lyor:

- Well ... as you know ... since the start of the newspaper, many years now, I have refused the paper to be sponsored by advertising ... so that the paper preserves its integrity and does not yield to the blackmailed opinions of the advertising investors.
- Yes, I'm well aware of that, Mr. Hatton.

The old man continued to explain to Lyor:

- And that is the reason why the Late Mr. Governor Iskander Balthazar had decided to take on all the expenses of the newspaper ... without ever making an opinion on the articles or the voice of the newspaper ... he was a man who had the same vision as me; bring close the real and true information, to the readers!

Lyor still couldn't understand the reason for Mr. Frank Hatton's visit to the Law Firm. But he was soon about to find out.

- It happens that ... the new decision maker ... Mr. Ernest Laszlo wishes to sponsor the newspaper through advertising ... he spoke to me about it, several weeks ago, and I have made my wish clear, I don't want to be under pressure and the influence of advertising investors ... I would like to keep doing my job, freely and without influence!

Mr. Hatton appeared in a serious and somber air:

- I guess Mr. Ernest Laszlo didn't like my objection to his idea ... so then, he decided to delay the salaries of the newspaper's employees ... it's been 4 months now, since my employees have not been paid.

Lyor finally understood:

- And you came to the office today, to convince my father to pay the salaries of the newspaper's employees!
- Exactly! Mr. Hatton sighed.

The abuses of Ernest Laszlo were not a new thing for his son Lyor. Having lived and worked with his father for years, Lyor was aware of the pressures that his father would make, to reach all his goals. Mental and financial pressures.

Lyor affirmed to the man, with a decided tone:

- I will speak to him about it, Mr. Hatton! ... The salaries' delay must be caught up, and the newspaper must keep its integrity!

Mr. Frank Hatton was known to be a proud and incorruptible man. But to save the salaries of his employees, Mr. Hatton forced himself to come to the Lawyer's office, trying to find a compromise.

And at this moment, Mr. Frank Hatton seemed somehow relieved by Lyor's answer. He smiled at him:

- I leave the future of the newspaper in your hands, young Lyor Laszlo.
- And you will not be disappointed, Mr. Hatton!

Several minutes later.

Lyor Laszlo had practiced several times his argument in his private office. To convince his father to pay the salaries of the newspaper employees and not to pressure Mr. Hatton to accept sponsors ... it didn't seem to be an easy task.

After several minutes of thinking and careful choice of words, Lyor breathed a long shot, and he left his office. Thinking he would be in his bureau, Lyor met his father in the corridor, while he was ordering one of the employees:

- Correct this paragraph ... and the last sentence of the pleading is to be rewritten ... insert the suspect's name in the places I mentioned ... I want this report corrected, on my desk, in 1 hour.
- Yes, Monsieur.

Mr. Ernest Laszlo turned around to take his coat and hat from his secretary's hands, and he headed toward the exit of the Law Firm. The situation of the newspaper was urgent, so then Lyor decided to reach his father at the end of the corridor:

- If you have 5 minutes, Monsieur, I would like to inform you of the situa...
- I have 2 minutes. What is it about?

While Mr. Ernest Laszlo was wearing on his coat, Lyor gathered his strength and courage:

- About Mr. Frank Hatton's newspaper ... The Washington Post Company ... it's a well popular newspaper ... its articles are accurate and impartial ... I've heard that the newspaper is very appreciated by the public, because of its neutrality ... I think if the advertisers sponsor it, the newspaper will not survive ... its popularity will certainly decrease...

Noticing that his father issued no comment, Lyor continued to defend his idea:

- And ... on the accounting's report, I had noticed that salaries were delayed for the 4th month ... I wanted to suggest to you, to pay 2 months, next week, in order to gain more employee's productivity ... Monsieur Franck Hatton will certainly appreciate this gesture toward his employees ... he is a man with great analytical intelligence, he will be to you an excellent counselor ...

At this moment, Mr. Ernest Laszlo stopped walking in the corridor and he turned toward his son Lyor:

- So then ... if I correctly understand ... you advise me not to force the newspaper to accept the sponsorship of advertisers, and to pay the delayed salaries of its employees?

Lyor affirmed with a sure tone:

- Yes, Monsieur. I think it would be beneficial for the newspaper, but also for the image of the Law fir...
- And in what position do you advise me?

The employees of the Law Firm went silent instantly, feeling the anger coming out of their employer. Lyor Laszlo was confused by his father's comment:

- I am sorry, Monsieur ... I don't understand your questi...

The Lawyer smiled:

- Because you think my decisions should be corrected ... why don't you go and sit in my office's chair and manage yourself this Law Firm business and BalthEnterprise?
- It was not my intention to correct you, Monsi...

In an instant, and in front of all the employees of the Law Firm, Mr. Ernest Laszlo exploded with rage at his son Lyor:

- YOU FORGET THAT YOU ARE AN INSIGNIFICANT EMPLOYEE IN THIS OFFICE LYOR! ... YOU ARE NOT WORTH MORE THAN THESE EMPLOYEES! ... YOU HAVE NO EXPERIENCE, NO EXPERTISE, NO ABILITY, AND CERTAINLY NO VISION OF THE MANAGEMENT! ... SO THEN SPARE ME YOUR IDIOT ADVICES AND JUST DO THE PAPERWORK JOB ASSIGNED TO YOU!!

Immediately, Mr. Ernest Laszlo wore his hat in a quiet move, and he left the office, displaying a proud smile and pleased to have humiliated Lyor. A heavy silence filled the place. All the employees watched discreetly Lyor Laszlo, who had remained standing, frozen and struck by his father words. The employees didn't attend the first or the last Lyor's public humiliation by his father. They got used to it.

Chapter 40

A conversation

Friday, October 14th, 1892. At the grand Mansion.

Late in afternoon, while Dalya was about to walk up the hall stairs, to join her bedroom, some unusual whispering caught her attention. She thought she heard the voice of her Aunt's husband, Mr. Henrik:

- Don't worry, everything will go as planned ...

Dalya continued up the stairs, thinking that her brain is imagining things and voices. At the 5th step of the hall stairs, the voice of Mr. Henrik was confirmed:

- I promise you ... trust me, and you will not be disappointed ...

This time, Dalya froze on the hall stairs, not daring to go a step further. Her brain was intact though, it was indeed the voice of Mr. Henrik. Dalya was curious on why her Aunt's husband was in the grand Mansion, and especially who he was speaking to.

Dalya turned around and she came down the stairs in discrete steps, to seek the source of the conversation. The voice of Mr. Henrik guided Dalya.

- I know you are worried ... and I understand you, perfectly well ... but I reassure you ...

Dalya discovered the shadow of two silhouettes in a corner, down the hall stairs. The Library was the nearest room to these two silhouettes, Dalya slipped to hide inside the Library, while keeping the door slightly open, to hear what was going on. By looking discreetly, Dalya could clearly see the silhouette of her Aunt's husband, Mr. Henrik. Brown hair, and a beige suit.

Except that the second silhouette was hidden by Mr. Henrik's body, and despite Dalya tried to stretch her neck and her eyes, she didn't manage to find out who Mr. Henrik was speaking to. When all of a sudden, the second voice said:

- You don't know what her reaction will be ... she will be very upset to hear this news!

A shiver ran over Dalya, from head to toe. Dalya recognized the 2nd voice ... it was ... Océanie Shell, the help cook of the Grand Mansion!!

Thousand questions invaded Dalya's brain, in a second. Why was Océanie discussing with Mr. Henrik? What were they talking about? Did they know each other before? Why were they hiding to have this conversation?

Dalya had to expel and repress these questions, in order to focus and hear what Mr. Henrik and Océanie were saying. It seems that Mr. Henrik tried to reassure Océanie:

- My decision is already made ... I've thought about it long and hard, believe me!

The voice of Océanie was nervous:

- And what if she refuses? ... And what if she holds you? ... And what if she makes a scandal? ... And what if she forces you t..

Mr. Henrik interrupted her with a little discreet laugh:

- And what if I don't want to stay with her?

Océanie fell silent for a long second. Dalya still couldn't understand the topic of their conversation. But who were they talking about? Who is she? Dalya stick her ear on the door to better understand.

- Océanie ... for the 100th time, trust me ... I will not disappoint you, my darling!

This word may have calmed Océanie, but it resonated in Dalya's brain, like a knock on her head. Did Dalya heard right? Mr. Henrik called Océanie ... his darling? Dalya was struck by lightning and shocked. Dalya looked through the door's opening, to observe the 2 silhouettes. Mr. Henrik put his hands on Océanie's shoulders and he said with a whispered kind voice:

- Life with my wife became unbearable since many years now. And I admit that since I have met you here in the grand Mansion, I am eager to leave my wife. I think only about one thing ... to be with you, my darling.

Dalya turned around and she put her hand over her mouth to prevent any surprise sound coming out of her. Mr. Henrik will leave his wife Claudine to be with Océanie!! ... Of all the possibilities, Dalya had never thought to hear such a conversation. Dalya quickly pulled herself together and she looked through the door opening. Océanie smiled and she seemed overjoyed.

- So then, you will ask for divorce? Océanie asked.
- Yes! Mr. Henrik stated with a sure tone.
- And your child?
- I will visit my son Hugo, whenever I can. But he will remain with his mother. And I will send him his pension every end of the month.

At that moment, Dalya's head was dizzy; one because of the conversation she had just heard, and two because of all the questions that appeared in her mind.

Océanie remained silent, thinking for a moment, and then she asked:

- And after that?

Mr. Henrik came close to Océanie and he lifted her chin, so she can look at him in the eyes.

- First, I must settle my situation in this city ... I cannot live in the grand Mansion ... and I cannot live in the annex house with the Bouvard family ... do you understand, my darling?

191

... that's why I asked you for this service ... I don't want to create more worries for anyone ... I want to resolve my divorce as quietly and quickly as possible ... and to settle in this city with you, I need you to do me this little favor ...

Right away, Océanie took out of her apron's pocket, a rectangular package. Dalya clearly noticed the package, but she didn't know what it contained. Océanie handed the package to Mr. Henrik. He took it happily, and he spoke to Océanie with a cheerful tone:

- And after I settle my situation in this city ... we'll get married, my darling. And I promise to make you the happiest woman in the world!

By hearing these words, Dalya could clearly see Océanie blushing, her eyes shining with joy and she was so happy. Mr. Henrik asked her:

- And now, do you trust me, my darling?
- Yes!

When Mr. Henrik and Océanie left their hiding place, each taking an opposite path, Dalya turned around and she looked for the nearest chair in the Library. Her legs didn't hold her anymore. Her brain was dizzy. Her hands trembled. And her heart almost stopped. The conversation that she had just heard between Océanie and her Aunt's husband left her all confused and trembling. Dalya thought aloud:

- But ... he is already married ... he seemed thoughtful and caring toward my Aunt ... but then Océanie ... He will divorce for ... but ... the package that Océanie gave him ...what favor will Océanie do to him? ... he will divorce my Aunt ... he called Océanie his darling ... several times, I didn't misheard it ... he cheats on my Aunt ... with Océanie ...but it's ...

After several minutes, Dalya decided to go up to her bedroom. No other subject filled her mind, except that conversation. The snow Panther waiting for Dalya in the corridor near her bedroom, she straightened up when she noticed the little girl. Inside the bedroom, Séraphine followed Dalya in slow steps. Without daring to make any sound, the snow Panther perfectly felt Dalya's worry. Séraphine didn't take her eyes off the little girl.

- What should I do? ... Warn my Aunt? ... She will not believe me ... tell my mother? ... She doesn't even speak to me ... what should I do? ... Talk to Cristelle? ... No, it's a bad idea, Cristelle already hate Océanie because of me ... so what to do? ... I cannot say anything to my father, he hates my Aunt ... what should I do? ... I shouldn't have heard this conversation ... but what do I do now? ... Should I intervene or not? ...It's not my business ... but ... he is my Aunt's husband ... and she is Océanie ... what should I do?

Dalya was worried and troubled by this conversation. And the night promised to be very long for Dalya Bouvard. She turned around hundreds of times in her bed, she couldn't sleep. Questions revolved like a whirlwind in Dalya's mind. After a long moment of thinking, Dalya finally decided to do nothing and wait. Just wait, to see more clearly through it.

Chapter 41

A missed meeting

Saturday, October 15th, 1892.

At 4:52 PM. The weather announced a probable rain, more cold wind breezes were blowing and the sky was blackened. The streets of Georgetown City were full of passersby. Richard Poirier walked down the steps of the Interior Ministry with hurried steps. It was not the probable rain that made him running. Richard checked his watch, and he was in a hurry for a very different reason. When a voice called him:

- It is true that you are invisible most of the time! One meets you only rarely!

The young Richard Poirier turned around to be in front of the Prime Minister's office employee. The Secretary General was followed by two bodyguards. He caught up with Richard at the stairs, and he continued:

- You did a great job in your report of the presidential elections ... the Prime Minister was very impressed by your analysis!
- Thank you, Mr. Secretary. Richard replied, bowing his head in a respectful move.

The man put a hand on Richard's shoulder, and he continued:

- Your report helped us to resolve the situation before it escalates. We avoided a diplomatic crisis.
- That is my duty, Mr. Secretary.

The Secretary General went down the huge stairs of the Ministry, followed by his two men, and still addressing Richard Poirier:

- I heard that the Security Minister instructed you about the new immigrants' case ... the new Law project.
- That's correct, Monsieur. I'm trying to collect all the information needed to my report.
- It is a crucially important matter, Richard. It will reflect not only the image of the Government, but of the entire Country.
- I understand, Mr. Secretary. I will give my notes on the subject in the upcoming days. With the best possible recommendations.
- Well, excellent ... keep up the great work!
- Certainly, Monsieur.

Before the Secretary General went inside a black car parked right in front of the stairs, he turned to Richard Poirier:

- Join me for dinner, Richard.

The young man hesitated a few seconds to rephrase his answer:

- Thank you, Mr. Secretary. I am sorry not to be able to accept your invitation today ... I have an important appointment.

The Secretary General insisted, while handing his files to his assistant:

- Are you sure, Richard? ... The roast turkey of my Cook Chef is a pure delight!
- I am sorry to miss it, Mr. Secretary.

Before the man went to his car, he greeted Richard:

- Another time, then. Please express my greetings to Mrs. Marianne Poirier, your mother.
- I certainly will, Mr. Secretary.

Richard had to do only a few more steps to the left to find his car and his driver. As soon as he sat inside the car, Richard checked his watch. It was 4:58 PM. He ordered the driver:

- Home ... and quickly, please.

A hurried allure, an impatience to reach home, the driver ordered to speed up ... what could be this so important meeting that Richard Poirier didn't want to miss, to even refuse a dinner with a high profile person?

As soon as he arrived at the Poirier family house, Richard came out of the car. When he entered the living room, Richard was curious not to feel the usual delicious smell. He put down his files and his coat, before greeting his mother. Mrs. Marianne Poirier was sitting by the fireplace in the big living room. She was reading a book, while drinking a hot tea.

- Good evening Mother. Your day went all well, I hope?

Mrs. Marianne Poirier answered her son with a caring smile.

- Have you received any visits today?

Mrs. Marianne shook her head in a negative answer, before she continued reading her book. While his mother was busy, Richard was too curious and impatient to wait. He walked toward the kitchen.

- Good evening Mrs. Glorina.

The woman was preparing soup for tonight. She looked up and smiled:

- Good evening Mr. Richard. Glad to see you back home, so soon. Dinner will be ready in almost an hour. Should I serve you with Mrs. Marianne?

Richard examined the entire kitchen with a single glance. You would have thought that he was looking for something. A few long seconds later, Richard was forced to answer:

- Yes ... I ... I will have dinner with mother, tonight ... thank you.

Mrs. Glorina stirred the soup that was cooking, saying:

- As you wish, Monsieur. Mrs. Marianne will certainly appreciate tonight's soup. Nothing warms better than a good hot soup with mushrooms, cream and fine herbs.

Before closing the kitchen door, Richard paused, and he asked Mrs. Glorina, with a much natural voice as possible:

- Mademoiselle Dalya Bouvard ... isn't coming today?

While peeling carefully the mushrooms, Mrs. Glorina naturally replied:

- No Monsieur. I met her yesterday on the way back home. She informed me that she had a catch-up course at her school.

At that precise instant, when Mrs. Glorina looked at Richard, the woman was surprised and astonished by the disappointed reaction of Richard Poirier. And without realizing it himself, Richard murmured in a little disappointed voice:

- That's too bad.

Mrs. Glorina observed him with a curious look. It was an unusual attitude coming from the young man. Richard Poirier pulled himself together at once, and he hurried to answer in a natural tone:

- I ... I will be in my office. When dinner is ready, please let me know.
- Understood, Monsieur.

When Richard closed the kitchen door, Mrs. Glorina thought aloud:

- It's ... strange ... very strange.

One Saturday later. Saturday, October 22nd, 1892.

A 5:20 PM. Dalya ran to the French neighbors' house, Les Poirier. She was holding a big basket full of pears. When she was greeted at the kitchen door by Mrs. Glorina, Dalya was still breathless from her race:

- I ... I'm sorry for... being … late ... Mrs. Glorina.
- No worries, Mademoiselle!! Mrs. Glorina reassured her.

Dalya placed her basket full of pears on the kitchen table.

- I brought you fruits from the garden of the grand Mansion ... Mr. Gardener picked them up for me.

While examining a fruit, Mrs. Glorina exclaimed:

- I've never seen pears as big and beautiful as these!
- Mr. Gardener is good at gardening and also at growing fruits and vegetables.

Mrs. Glorina was fascinated by the fruit. Dalya sat down a few moments to catch her breath, while Mrs. Glorina washed 3 pears.

- How is Madame doing today?
- Better, Mademoiselle. Mrs. Glorina replied, before continuing with an innocent laugh:
- Mrs. Marianne was curious to know what cake we will bake today. She insisted on sitting in the living room, so she can be close to come and help us in the icing of the cake. Honestly, I am delighted that Mrs. Marianne assists us here in the kitchen. It's so good for her to get out of her bedroom and get busy at something other than her illness!
- Yes, it's true Mrs. Glorina. I will move a lounge chair to the kitchen. She will be more comfortable in it.

Mrs. Glorina dried up the fruits. Dalya wore her white apron, and she asked hesitantly:

- Is ... is Monsieur Richard at home, today?

Mrs. Glorina answered, while placing a few containers of different shapes on the table:

- No ... he warned me that he had an important meeting today. He may be late this evening.

When placing a flour container on the kitchen table, Mrs. Glorina noticed that Dalya's smile faded away, in a second. Spontaneously, Dalya murmured in a disappointed voice:

- That's too bad.

At that precise moment, Mrs. Glorina froze in her place, standing in front of the kitchen table, holding the butter in one hand and the milk in another hand. The woman was surprised and confused by what she watched and heard. Mrs. Glorina thought aloud, with a confused laugh:

- That's quite funny ... you've both had the same reaction, you've both said the same words!

Dalya didn't understand what Mrs. Glorina meant. However, Mrs. Glorina giggled while putting the ingredients on the kitchen table:

- I may be wrong ... but I feel that something else besides the cakes, is cooking in this house...

And Mrs. Glorina was well right. Something was growing in the French family house, Les Poirier. Something was growing between a 14 years old girl and a young gifted man...

Chapter 42

Confusion

Sunday, October 23rd, 1892.

The weather was milder at the end of October month. The blue sky was adorned with several white and gray clouds; the wind blew a soft but strong air. It was a beautiful calm day.

Dalya had finished her school homework quicker than expected. She decided to join her little twin sisters and her cousin, at the annex house. From afar, Dalya could see her little sisters wearing matching uniforms as usual; pink coats and white caps. The little twins and the cousin were playing ball in the garden of the annex house. As soon as they noticed their older sister, the little twins ran to greet her with screams and jumps in the air:

- Dindin!! Dindin!! Dindin!!
- Always in a good shape, little twins! Dalya laughed, while kneeling down to hug them.
- Yes!! You play with us? Please!! Please!! Please!!

Dalya greeted her little cousin:

- Good morning Hugo.

Her cousin replied to her with a joyful smile. At that moment, a small item caught Dalya's attention. Her little cousin was wearing around his neck a soft cotton scarf, in blue and bronze color lines, and at each end of the scarf was sewn a flying eagle. This scarf seemed familiar to her, Dalya remembered to have received the same scarf as a birthday present from the Dean of the Merchants, Mr. Kenan Einsenberg. Dalya smiled, noticing that her little cousin Hugo had the same scarf as she had. It was a funny coincidence!

The little boy informed Dalya:

- We were playing ball ... my parents went Downtown with your father ... and your mother is in the kitchen inside ...
- A perfect day to play, then! Dalya exclaimed before continuing:
- It seems there is a good wind today ... would you like to make kites and fly them up?

Immediately, the little twins jumped yelling:

- Yes!! Kite!! Kite!! Kite!!
- That sounds like a good idea. The cousin said.
- Perfect! I will get the equipment and I'll be right back. Dalya affirmed.

After a few minutes, Dalya returned back from the grand Mansion loaded with papers, sticks of wood that she took from the fireplace wood stock, pens and ribbons, succors and glue ... Dalya sat down in the garden of the Annex house. The little twins and the cousin joigned her.

Dalya gave each one of them a big blank paper to draw on it, while she got busy to create a wood stick cross to hang the kite paper on. The little twins worked on it seriously. They drew hearts, roses and stars. The cousin also seemed to enjoy this activity. Dalya asked him:

- Did you visit downtown?

While drawing several types of cars on his big paper, the cousin replied:

- No, not yet.

Dalya fixed the first kite, and she exclaimed:

- Well ... we have to show you around our city. You'll love it. There are huge gardens, several strange and immense buildings. And you will surely enjoy observing the different cars passing in the street!
- Yes, it's true that you have so many cars in this city! Answered the cousin.
- You like cars, don't you? Dalya asked, while smiling at the paper her cousin drew.
- Yes, cars are super great! Exclaimed the little cousin.

Dalya prepared the second kite's sticks:

- We can go on a tour of the city next weekend. The little twins love downtown ... especially because I buy them candies. There are benches where to sit on, at the Toscana restaurant street. We can sit there and watch the cars, if you want?

The little cousin smiled and was enthusiastic about this idea:

- Really?! That would be great, yes!! And I'll bring my sketchbook too!!
- The cars go fast; can you draw them so quickly? Dalya asked all curious and amused.
- Yes!! I observe them for an instant, and afterward I quickly draw what I remember!!
- Well, in that case, you will be served the next weekend!! Don't forget your sketchbook!!

The little twins had almost finished coloring their papers. Dalya finished fixing the third kite, and she asked her twin sisters:

- Have you finished filling your papers, so I can glue them to the cross that I made?
- Yes!! Finished!! Finished!!

When Dalya was about to stick her little sisters paper into the wood cross, the little cousin who was still drawing his cars, said in a natural voice:

- Mom and Dad went downtown to pay for our new home ... in the new town where we will move out ... a city called Florida.

At that moment, it was as if Dalya was struck by a lightning. She stopped in her move, thinking that her ears misheard something. And to be sure of it, Dalya asked again her little cousin:

- They went ... your parents ... they went to pay for a new home in Florida? ... You are moving to Florida?
- Yes ... I heard my parents speaking, this morning. They will pay today, for our new home in Florida. Dad found a great job in this city! ... And your father took my parents to meet a Monsieur ... someone called Sprint.

Dalya knew very well Mr. Sprint. He was a real estate agent, specialized in sales and purchases of the houses.

- Dad said it was a beautiful big house ... and I will have a large room, just for myself ... Dad's work is close to a beach ... he said that we will often go swimming in the beach, and eating ice cream! Exclaimed the little cousin, all joyful.

Dalya tried to smile at her little cousin Hugo. She fixed the 2nd Kite of her little twin sisters, her mind occupied by a weird thought.

When Dalya heard the conversation between her Aunt's husband Mr. Henrik and the Mansion's employee Océanie, Dalya understood that Mr. Henrik would leave his wife Claudine and he will settle with Océanie, here in Georgetown city. And now, Dalya heard a different story from her little cousin; Mr. Henrik went to pay for a home in Florida, he found a job in that city, and he planned to settle there with his wife and son.

What is going on? ... what is happening? ... Which scenario to believe about Mr. Henrik?

And besides that, the thought that tormented Dalya the most was; when Mr. Henrik complained of the high cost of homes, and not having enough money to pay for one. Only few days ago, Dalya clearly heard Mr. Henrik speaking with her father, that he couldn't buy a house.

And today, Mr. Henrik was paying for an entire house in Florida! ... It was a large sum of money ... But, where did he get all this money from? ... How and when?

Chapter 43

5:00 PM

Saturday, October 29th, 1892. At the French neighbors' house, Les Poirier.

Richard Poirier had a file of more than 300 papers to read. He wrote his notes on the blank edges of the pages. The file including his notes, had to be given to the Ministry of Interior department, first hour Monday morning. It promised to be a busy working weekend. This report was urgent and important.

Richard was at page 47. He was trying to focus on his reading, since several minutes now, but his eyes kept looking at the small clock placed on his desk. It seemed that Richard Poirier was impatiently waiting for the clock needles to reach 5:00 PM. Richard had no appointments at this time. And yet ... he looked forward to 5:00 PM impatiently.

Richard has become used to a scene for several months now; he was looking forward to getting to 5:00 PM ... because he would feel the smell of a prepared cake, coming out of the kitchen. Because after few minutes later, his office door should open. Because a strange little silhouette all covered with flour, jam, butter and eggs, should come into his office. Because Richard was curious to taste her cakes, although they were always imperfect; too sweet, too cooked, too soft, too hard. Because Richard had missed 2 Saturdays without meeting this strange little silhouette. Because despite Richard would have, at each meeting, a tight throat and a clumsy attitude ... he was anxious that his clock strikes 5:00 PM.

A few seconds after 5:00 PM, a delicious smell invaded the office and the brain of Richard Poirier. It was impossible for him now to focus on a single word in the file. He read the same sentence several times, without understanding the meaning.

When the door opened, Richard Poirier straightened up on his chair. And like the previous times, she entered the office, displaying a nervous shy smile:

- Good evening!

It has been 2 Saturdays now, that Richard hadn't met her in his house. The words flowed from Richard Poirier, and he wasn't able to control them:

- Good evening, Mademoiselle Dalya ... it has been a long time.

At this comment, Dalya blushed. She didn't know that Richard Poirier has realized her absence. She let out a nervous giggle:

- Yes it's been a long time ...

Richard continued reading, displaying a serious calm air.

- *What was I reading again?* He thought.

Although he lost the thread of his reading, several minutes before, Richard pretended to read his file. Meanwhile, Dalya walked not toward the office desk in front of Richard, but toward a small table near a big chair, and she put down a silver tray. Dalya announced to him with amusement:

- To avoid any incident ... it is better to keep the teapot away from your office desk!

Richard smiled politely; he tried to answer in a natural voice and hide his tense throat:

- Thank you, Mademoiselle.

Dalya poured the contents of the teapot in a porcelain cup, while explaining:

- Mrs. Glorina prepared for you a delicious hot chocolate; with 2 coffee spoons ... she thought that it will help you better work, tonight.

Richard took a quick glance at the porcelain plate:

- And today's cake?

Dalya felt her cheeks blushing, she was glad that Richard was interested in what she cooked.

- It's a charlotte biscuit cake with pears ... Mrs. Glorina taught me to straighten up the biscuits today.

Without taking his eyes off the file, Richard said:

- I guess it must be a delicious cake ...

Dalya sighed:

- Delicious ... and incredibly difficult to make!

Richard smiled. Was he smiling because of Dalya's comment, or was he smiling because he was delighted to see her again after 2 missed Saturdays, or was he smiling because he read the same sentence for the 10th time, without understanding its meaning? Richard Poirier himself didn't know the answer to this question.

When he looked up at Dalya, he noticed that the girl's attention was toward something specific. Dalya inclined her head to read a book title that Richard had in the small Library of his office.

- The big jump ... of Mr. Steve Havel!! Have you read this book? Dalya asked curiously.

Richard, still sitting in front of his desk, holding firmly his file, he replied in a natural tone:

- Yes, several times. I frequently reread it to refresh my brain. And you? Do you know about this book?

- It is my favorite!! Dalya exclaimed happily. I found it in the Library of the grand Mansion, one evening ... the author is very funny, sincere and clear. His book is inspiring and very ... very ...
- Very practical. Richard finished her sentence.
- Yes!! Exactly!! Dalya jumped.
- He has written several other books, did you know that? Richard informed.
- Really? Are you sure? I found only one book at the grand Mansion ...

Richard pointed at a lower shelf on the right:

- In that corner ... there must be 3 other books by the same author ...

Dalya bent down and she searched among the books. And she was surprised to find other works of her favorite author. Richard put down his file and said:

- Since you enjoy this author's work, you can have his books. I offer them to you.

When she turned around toward Richard, Dalya was speechless:

- You are ... serious? ... You offer me these 3 books? ... To me?
- You seem to enjoy reading. And I've already read these books...they will be helpful to you.

Dalya took the 3 books in her hands, as if they were the most precious gift that one could offer her.

- Thank you!! Thank you so much!! He's my favorite author!! Thank you so much!!
- With great pleasure, Mademoiselle.

When Dalya left his office, Richard Poirier observed the door for several minutes, being lost in his thoughts.

Did Richard read these books before? No. Did Richard knew about the author? No. Did Richard knew he had these books in his Library? He realized they were, only just seconds ago. Does Richard read books in his free time? ...No. One, he doesn't have any free time, and two, his only reading is related to his work at the Government. And yet, Richard was delighted to have made Dalya happy, by offering her these books.

Given the long night of work waiting for him, Richard continued his reading. After several minutes of focus, Richard Poirier realized he had to restart the report ... from the beginning! He had never lost track of his reading that much, before. Richard Poirier lay back on his chair and sighed:

- What is wrong with me?

Chapter 44

On the roof of the grand Mansion

Wednesday, November 02nd, 1892.

Back from school, Dalya enjoyed the calm on the road of Dumbarton Oaks Park. The path was dotted with spacious gardens and peaceful trees, a fresh smell of earth and grass, was coming out from the ground. The gray sky predicted assured soon rain.

When she reached the big entrance of the grand Mansion, Dalya noticed the snow Panther.

- Good evening Séraphine. Dalya greeted her, as usual.

Except that for once, Séraphine ignored Dalya's presence. Approaching the snow Panther, Dalya noticed that Séraphine had her eyes focused and upraised toward the sky. The snow Panther let out a long worried meow, without taking her eyes away from up.

When Dalya followed Séraphine's look, she noticed the kite of one of her little twin sisters, stuck at the grand Mansion' roof.

- The kite surely escaped from my little sisters' hands ... we are lucky that the wind have stopped it on the roof of the grand Mansion.

The weather soon became gray; a few drops of rain were already falling from the cloudy sky. Dalya decided to get changed in her bedroom, she wore her big coat, and she walked up the many stairs toward the Grand Mansion's roof.

- I better pick this kite before it is all wet of rain!

After a few minutes, Dalya finally opened the door of the roof. She walked to where the kite was hooked. When suddenly, Dalya noticed a familiar silhouette on the roof, near the kite. Dalya barely recognized her. While coming close in slow and hesitant steps, Dalya discovered a young woman, with chestnut hair, wearing a long white thin robe.

- Océanie? ... You too have seen my little sisters' kite? ... Well, we had the same thought, you and me. I came up to take it before the rain w…

Dalya stopped. When Océanie turned around toward her, Dalya immediately felt that something was wrong. Océanie had a very pale face, her eyes were red, tears flowed down her cheeks, a white pale mouth. Océanie was shivering with cold; her robe was so thin that Dalya could clearly see goosebumps on Océanie's skin.

A 2nd meow came out of Séraphine, who stayed down at the grand Mansion's garden. And at that moment, Dalya realized that the snow Panther was not watching the kite stuck on the roof, the creature was watching Océanie who was there too.

In a worried voice, Dalya asked:

- Océanie ... what's going on? ... What are you doing here on the roof of the grand Mansion?

Amid the silent sobs, Océanie whispered in a trembling voice:

- He ... he took everything ... he ... he took everything ...

When Dalya made a step closer toward Océanie, the young woman stepped back, crying and shaking. Dalya warned the young woman:

- Océanie ... you are too close to the roof edge ... be careful please ...

Except that Océanie was well aware of being close to the roof edge. In a second, a wave of fear invaded Dalya. She didn't understand what put Océanie in this state, but Dalya could clearly perceive Océanie's intentions. Dalya tried to stay calm and immobile:

- Océanie ... it's cold, and you are wearing thin clothes ... come with me inside ... the Cook Chef will prepare for us a good hot chocolate cup ... and Igor will light up the firepla...
- He took everything ... he took everything ... he took everything. Océanie repeated in a lost voice.

Dalya stressed out, because she was trapped in a dangerous situation. She couldn't leave Océanie and go ask for help from the employees. Dalya tried to stay still, while Océanie cried and repeated:

- He took everything ... he ... he took everything ...

At this moment, as if the sky felt Dalya's anxiety, a loud 3rd meow was heard from down the grand Mansion's garden. Dalya inclined her head down. And as soon as the snow Panther and Dalya exchanged a look, Séraphine ran straightaway inside the grand Mansion.

Dalya hoped with all her heart that the snow Panther have understood her urgent need. And in order to gain more time, Dalya tried to calm the sobs of the young woman:

- You should cover yourself, Océanie ... you might get sick ... it's very cold.

Dalya took off her coat, and she reached out to Océanie. But the young woman took several steps back, and she screamed:

- Don't come close!! ... Don't come close!! ... Don't come close!!

Dalya's heart almost stopped. Océanie was dangerously close to the roof edge. Dalya froze in her place. She put her coat down, and she tried to reassure her:

- Understood ... alright ... alright … I will not come near you anymore ...

A few whispers were heard down the grand Mansion. Dalya looked over the roof, and she noticed the snow Panther pulling Cristelle by her apron to the garden outside the grand Mansion. Cristelle followed the Panther with upset steps:

- Séraphine!! But where are you leading me? ... It's going to rain soon and you want to play outside? ... This is ridiculous ...why are you pulling me by the apron? ... What do you want now? ... Come on my beautiful, let's go insi... Oh my Goodness, what are you two doing on the roof of the grand Mansion? ... Come down immediately!! Mademoiselle Dalya!! Océanie!!

A second voice added to that of Cristelle. The head of the grand Mansion asked all curious:

- Cristelle ... why are you yelling? ... what is happeni...

Mr. Bûchebois froze, raising his eyes upward:

- What are they doing on the roof, both of them?

The voice of the Cook added:

- Cosa sta succedendo? *(What is going on?)*

Igor was also heard:

- It must be really important for Séraphine to force us outside in this weather. It will rain soo...

All the employees of the grand Mansion froze, their eyes fixed upward. They didn't understand Dalya and Océanie's presence, on the roof of the grand Mansion, in such weather. They were all worried about this unusual scene. And despite that the employees were far down the grand Mansion, Dalya was reassured that Séraphine understood her urgent need and searched for help.

A few drops of rain touched Dalya's face.

- Océanie ... it will rain soon ... let's go inside, please ...

Océanie was still shaking and tears still covered her cheeks:

- I ... I lost everything ... he ... he took everything from me ...

Dalya had no other idea, than distract and try to keep Océanie away from the roof edge:

- What did you lose? ... Who took everything from you? ... Who is he?

Océanie didn't seem to realize what she was saying. She was crying aloud:

- I gave him everything ... everything I had ... He took everything ...

The rain was pouring down, right now. In seconds, Dalya felt her clothes all wet. Cristelle screamed:

- Mademoiselle!! Océanie!! You'll catch a cold!! Come inside!!

At this instant, Dalya noticed the silhouette of the Gardener behind the door of the roof. He pushed the door with a silent move, and he came forward in slow and silent steps toward Océanie, who had her back turned on him. The Gardener signaled at Dalya not to reveal his presence to Océanie. Dalya knew what she had to do; gain more time for the Gardener!

- Océanie ... there is a solution to every problem ... I can help you ... tell me what is going on ... what put you in this state?

The young woman was exhausted, her tears tangled with the rain drops, which fully wet her:

- I gave him everything ... I was wrong ... he took everything ... I have nothing left now ... nothing left ...
- Who is he? Dalya asked.

The Gardener stepped forward without a sound. Océanie continued to tremble and cry:

- He took everything ... I am a poor idiot ... I don't deserve to be loved ...

Although she didn't exactly understand the matter, Dalya replied as best as she could:

- You deserve to be loved, Océanie! And you will be loved! ... you are not an idiot ... don't say that … please calm down now, and come with me insi...

Océanie interrupted her while crying:

- No one will ever love me ... no one will ever love me ... I'm an idiot ... I'm an idiot …

In a second, Océanie moved back 2 steps toward the edge of the roof. Her bare feet were now on the thin edge of the roof. Still down at the grand Mansion's garden, the employees screamed in one voice:

- NO OCÉANIE!! DON'T DO THAT!!
- OCÉANIE!! PULL YOURSELF TOGETHER, PLEASE!!
- NO NO OCÉANIE!! STEP BACK!!
- BE CAREFUL OCÉANIE!!

At this instant, the Gardener behind Océanie froze up, not daring to move. Fear invaded Dalya, and she yelled with a trembling voice:

- Océanie!! ... I don't know what exactly is happening. Maybe you may have made a mistake ... I beg you, Océanie, do not correct it by making another mistake!!

Océanie looked at Dalya and smiled at her sadly:

- You are nice to me ... even though I was hurtful and mean to you ... why so?

Dalya's answer didn't need a second:

- Mistakes don't make you a bad person ... you're a human being, Océanie, you have the right to make mistakes.

The Gardener approached 3 mores steps closer. Dalya continued to distract Océanie:

- And I confirm to you that you are not a bad person, Océanie ... the person who made you in this state, is the wrong person!!

Océanie let out a sad and painful laugh:

- He really took everything ... I gave him everything ... but really everything ... I'm an idiot ... a poor idiot ... I don't deserve to be loved ...
- You did nothing wrong, Océanie!! ...You're not an idiot, believe me ... it may be just a mista...

But before Dalya could complete her sentence, the events happened in a split of a second. Océanie walked back a step toward the void, and instantly her body disappeared from the roof of the grand Mansion. Screams were heard below. Séraphine let out a loud roar. Dalya's heart stopped beating, her legs didn't hold her anymore, and Dalya fall down on the roof ground.

After several long and difficult seconds of a heavy silence, Dalya's brain recovered. She noticed that the Gardener was strangely lying down on the roof ground, and he was holding something over the roof edge of the grand Mansion ... Océanie!!

The Gardener was holding Océanie's arm, the young woman was hanging in the air, unconscious. The Gardener immediately screamed:

- BUCHEBOIS!! THE HAY!!

The employees of the grand Mansion lost no time to gather themselves up. They instantly understood the Gardener's order. The head of the Mansion Mr. Bûchebois, the Cook and Igor ran to the adjacent garage. Cristelle ordered the snow Panther:

- Séraphine!! Follow me!!

The maid and the snow Panther ran inside the grand Mansion. Dalya stood up quickly and approached the Gardener. Océanie fainted and her body was becoming heavier. The rain made the roof ground slippery. As soon as the Gardener felt his own body sliding down toward the roof edge, he yelled:

- DALYA!! MY FEET!! THE ROPE!!

Dalya didn't need to be ordered twice; she had to stop the Gardener from sliding above the roof. Dalya grabbed the end of a rope; she wrapped the Gardener's 2 feet with the rope, and then she ran to attach the other half of the rope around a fireplace pole.

Dalya returned back near the Gardener, who was still holding Océanie's arm. But the rain was sliding his hands. The Gardener grabbed Océanie's arm with such a strong move, to the point of cutting blood out of it, fearing to let her go out from his hands. The Gardener screamed:

- BUCHEBOIS!!!

The head of the Mansion Mr. Bûchebois appeared, followed by the Cook and Igor. The 3 men were holding several large hay bags, which they put just below where Océanie was suspended. Cristelle and the Panther also appeared, from inside the grand Mansion. The maid and the Panther were loaded, arms hands and teeth, with cushions and pillows that they threw on the hay.

- BUCHEBOIS!!! HURRY!!! Screamed the Gardener.
- HANG IN THERE, WEIL!! The head of the employees yelled, before running to the garage for a second time, followed by the Cook and Igor.
- WE ARE ALMOST THERE!! Cristelle screamed while entering the living room, followed by the Panther.

Dalya bent down to reach Océanie. But being away, Dalya couldn't help the Gardener hold up Océanie. The Gardener felt Océanie's arm sliding out of his fingers. And soon, because of the rain, he held her only by the handshake. The Gardener screamed:

- BUCHEBOIS!! I WILL LET GO!!
- WE ARE COMING!! WE ARE COMING!!
- HOLD ON!!
- ONE SECOND!!

The 3 employees left the garage, loaded with large hay bags that they threw at the exact location. The snow Panther outran Cristelle, and she threw the pillows clung to her jaw. Cristelle nearly fell while running; she threw the rest of the cushions on top of the hay bags. The head of the grand Mansion Mr. Bûchebois screamed:

- WE ARE READY!! LET HER GO!!

The Gardener didn't need to be repeated a 2nd time. And anyway, the rain left him no other choice, Océanie's hand slipped from his fingers in a second. Océanie landed safely on the hay bags and the gathered cushions and willows. Immediately, the employees of the grand Mansion surrounded her. Dalya ran to remove the rope around the fireplace pole. The Gardener sat down to catch his breath. When Dalya returned to him, the Gardener untied the rope at his feet, and he said in a serious grave tone:

- It was just right ... one more second and we would have lost her!
- Yes ... it was just right. Dalya repeated breathlessly.

The Gardener and Dalya returned inside the grand Mansion, and they joined the other employees gathered at the door of Océanie's room. As soon as she noticed them, Cristelle gave big towels to Dalya and the Gardener. Everyone was wet with rain from head to toe.

Dalya stood still on the door of Océanie's room. They have lay down Océanie on her bed; she looked pale, blue lips, sleepy and quiet. Cristelle replaced Océanie's soaked robe with another dry one, and she covered her in a warm blanket. Then, Cristelle announced in a serious and worried voice:

- Mr. Bûchebois ... she has fever, her body is burning, and her lungs emit a sound with every breath ...

One look was enough between the head of the Mansion and the Gardener, for the Gardener to say in a decided tone:

- I will change my clothes and I will bring the doctor ... right away!

When the Gardener disappeared down the corridor, the head of the Mansion Mr. Bûchebois ordered Igor:

- Lighten up all the chimneys in the employees' rooms ... and the fireplace in Mademoiselle Dalya's bedroom. We are all soaked in rain; we need to prevent anyone from getting sick.
- Understood, Monsieur! All the bedrooms!

The Cook and the head of the Mansion exchanged an accomplice look. And without the need for words to understand each other, the Cook announced:

- A hot soup with chicken and vegetables ... with pepper and a pinch of red pepper, to warm up everyone!! ... I will start right away!!

The head of the Mansion came close to Dalya and he asked her in a calm but worried tone:

- What happened, Mademoiselle? Why were you with Océanie on the roof?
- I came up to the grand Mansion's roof, to take back my little sisters' kite ... the kite was stuck there ... that's where I found Océanie ... she was shaking and crying, she spoke incomprehensible sentences ... it's only after a while, that I realized that Océanie wanted to ... she wanted to ...
- Jump off the roof. The head of the Mansion finished Dalya's sentence.
- Yes, Monsieur. And luckily, Séraphine realized that I needed help.
- This Panther is an angel from heaven!! Cristelle stated adding another towel on Dalya's shoulders. Cristelle continued:
- We were having tea in the kitchen; Séraphine came in and she pulled me outside!!

The head of the grand Mansion hesitated a few seconds, before daring to ask:

- Mademoiselle ... do you know why Océanie was in such a state? What could have led her to end her life?

At this precise moment, Dalya gathered all her strength and she answered with a natural tone:

- No, Monsieur. I don't know what could have led Océanie to such a state.

The head of the grand Mansion observed Dalya for a long second. Mr. Bûchebois was sure and convinced that Dalya knew more than what she was saying. Except that Dalya didn't want to reveal Océanie's secret, and she preferred to stay silent, at least that night.

The head of the grand Mansion insisted no more. There was already enough to be busy with, that night. Mr. Bûchebois turned toward the maid:

- Cristelle ... lead Mademoiselle to her bedroom, so she can change her clothes and rest. I will stay with Océanie until your return.
- Yes, Monsieur. Cristelle answered.

Mr. Bûchebois spoke to Dalya with a formal tone:

- Dinner will be served in your bedroom, Mademoiselle. If you need anything, let us know.
- Thank you, Mr. Bûchebois.

But before Dalya could walk away, the head of the Mansion said in a caring voice:

- And Mademoiselle ... because of your presence, at the right time and at the right place, a life was saved today. Thank you for your help.

Dalya smiled to him shyly, before following Cristelle.

When she arrived in her bedroom, Dalya realized how much she was all wet. She took off all her clothes that Cristelle removed, and she put on her pajamas. Shivering with cold, Dalya decided to put on socks and wear a night bonnet. Igor had already lit up the fireplace of her bedroom. Dalya sat on a large chair by the fireplace, to warm up. Before Cristelle left the bedroom, she whispered in a trembling voice:

- You ... you saved a life, Mademoiselle!!
- I've only distracted and delayed her. Fortunately, Mr. Gardener climbed back on the roof, on time.

Cristelle sighed:

- It's a terrible incident, Mademoiselle. Never such a thing happened at the grand Mansion. I was so scared for you too, as well. By the grace of Heaven, everyone is safe ... by the grace of Heaven!!

When the bedroom door closed, Dalya relaxed on the big chair, and she observed the fire in the chimney. Hundreds of questions invaded Dalya's brain:

- *To end her life, Océanie must have had a serious problem ... she repeated on the roof some strange words ... he took everything ... he ... so it's all because of a man ... a man took something from Océanie, and she was so troubled that she wanted to end her life ... but who is this man?... and what did he take from her?*

After several minutes of thinking, a shadow of an idea was forming in Dalya's mind. And she was interrupted by Cristelle's arrival with a dinner tray, which she placed in front of her.

- Here you go, Mademoiselle ... a big bowl of soup ... hot and spicy! ... I know you don't like hot spices, but Mr. Bûchebois insisted that everyone have some of it tonight! ... He doesn't want to have another sick person, in the grand Mansion!!
- Thank you, Cristelle. Don't worry, I will finish the soup.

Some minutes later, when Dalya finished her dinner, she heard a strange voice outside the grand Mansion. Dalya jumped and rushed to the window. The Gardener opened the car door to a gentleman, who entered inside of it, and then the Gardener sat in the front, and they left the grand Mansion.

- He certainly must be the doctor who came to examine Océanie!

Dalya wore her robe, and she ran toward Océanie's room. At the door of the employee's room, Dalya noticed Cristelle sitting on the edge of the bed where Océanie was still lying asleep; a towel was placed on her forehead. The Cook, the head of the employees, and Igor, they were all surrounding Océanie's bed. They all had somber and worried faces.

It was Igor the first who broke the heavy silence:

- What happened to her?! ... a few days ago, she was laughing and normal ... what happened?!

The Cook replied:

- No one knows what forced her to end her life.

Igor insisted:

- But yet she lives with us! ... We could have seen this coming! ... if she had a problem or a worry, we would have known about it!

Cristelle observed Océanie for a moment:

- It's weird ... Océanie has always been very talkative, she tells everything that happens ... it's weird that for once, no one knows what happened to her ...

The head of the grand Mansion thought aloud:

- The doctor confirmed that she have an severe bronchitis ... and in addition to the physical illness, Océanie will struggle to heal her mind ... wanting to end her life, means that something went wrong in her mental ... holding on to life will not be so simple ... the doctor warned me that she might enter into a long depression ... there is no medication for this disease ... it will all rely on her will to survive!

After a few minutes of a heavy silence, the Cook affirmed in a determined voice:

- If she enters into depression ... then we must be prepared! ... And we will help her get out of it! ... I will change the menu for the next days... several hot soups, more vegetables with hot spices, ginger teas ...

Cristelle wet the towel and dried it, before putting it back on Océanie's forehead:

- We will watch over her, Mr. Bûchebois. I will make sure that she takes her baths and her meals.

Igor announced:

- I will keep all the fireplaces lit, in every room, Mr. Bûchebois. Especially this week.

Dalya stepped near Océanie's bed, and she affirmed with a sure voice:

- Océanie survived her roof fall ... she will also survive the severe bronchitis and depression ... It may take her some time, but she will survive!

All eyes turned toward Océanie Shell. The Challenges ahead of the young girl were huge and painful. However, all the employees of the grand Mansion, including Dalya Bouvard ... they were all willing to help Océanie, the best they could.

And as much as the employees were decided to take care of Océanie, during her recovery time, the little Dalya Bouvard was determined to help too ... in her own way.

When she went to her bedroom, Dalya had only one idea in her mind; The Excelbox. As strange as that box was, the Excelbox was always gifted to help in the most difficult times.

In the bedroom, on the office desk, a gray metal box was recharging on the night's light. The Excelbox released off a powerful and serene strength that no one could explain or understand. Dalya approached it; she wrote on a little paper:

What is the 3ʳᵈ clue?

When she introduced the paper into the rectangular opening of the box, Dalya closed her eyes and she prayed with all her heart:

- I need something to help Océanie ... please ... please ...

The Excelbox took the paper, and heard the little girl's prayers. After a blinding light emanating from within the Excelbox, the opening let out an answer:

How long before a heart will heal?

5, 14

Standing still, reading the clue several times, some words held Dalya's attention:

- A heart will heal ... a heart will heal ... a heart will heal!

All of a sudden, Dalya jumped; she knew exactly what to do:

- I know how to help Océanie!

Chapter 45

Depression

Wednesday, November 09th, 1892. In the evening, at the grand Mansion.

Cristelle put the dinner tray on the bedside table near Océanie, who was lying down on her bed. Since the incident at the Grand Mansion's roof, Océanie remained silent and motionless entire days and nights, lying down on her bed.

Since several days now, Océanie's eyes were opened, but her gaze and her mind were lost and far away. She had lost interest in everything; meals, work, discussion, and even in life. Océanie appeared to be a body drained of all emotion. Her moves were heavy, and the words seemed so difficult for her to pronounce. Océanie drowned in a sea of sorrow, and coming back to the surface seemed almost impossible for her. Depression is a much cruel and difficult disease than you might think...

Cristelle came near her and she put her fingers on Océanie's forehead:

- Your fever is well down ... and you sweat a lot less.

Paralyzed, Océanie stared at the fire in the chimney, with a lost gaze. And despite the sad unchanged state of Océanie, Cristelle rejoiced:

- Your bronchitis is gone!! ... At this rate, by following the doctor's treatment, you will be in a good shape in a few more days!!

All the employees of the grand Mansion were worried about Océanie's health. And everyone did their best to help her heal. The head of the grand Mansion took on all Océanie's tasks, the Cook prepared the meals especially for her, Igor made sure that Océanie's chimney never lack of wood logs, Cristelle helped her to eat and take baths, the Gardener took care to bring her flowers bouquet from the garden every day. Even Dalya visited Océanie's room every day, to check on her and help in whatever she could.

- There is a good soup of broccoli and cream, tonight!! Exclaimed Cristelle.

Océanie remained mute and immobile. Cristelle then sat down near her on the bed, and she helped her eat her dinner.

- Did you read the books I brought you earlier? Cristelle asked her, while making her eat a spoonful of soup.

With a lost spirit, Océanie didn't hear Cristelle's words. Yet, Cristelle continued:

- It's Mademoiselle herself who chose these books from the grand Mansion's Library ... she told me they were very funny stories ... and I even remember seeing Mademoiselle laughing aloud once, reading one of these books ...

Océanie ate her soup, without speaking a word. It's been many days now that Cristelle was trying to take out Océanie from her absent and lost state, but without any success. Cristelle wouldn't give up yet.

- After your dinner, I will help you take a hot bath! The Cook prepared for you a chamomile tea; to be taken after the bath ... and I will add some wood logs in the fireplace ... a good night sleep will do you so much good, that's for sure!

The silence remained Océanie's answer. Cristelle forced her to finish her soup bowl, before removing the dinner tray.

After taking her cloth off and placing her on the tub, Cristelle soaped and washed Océanie, from head to toe. Only Cristelle's words filled the silence of the room:

- Did you know that I too have used this soap!! ... This is the best product on the market, right now!! ... it has lemon ... it smells very good ...

Several minutes later, after the bath, Cristelle helped Océanie get dressed in her pajamas. Cristelle covered her in a large soft cotton robe, and she made Océanie sit to dry her light brown hair. And while Océanie slowly drank her soothing tea, Cristelle asked her:

- You should change your hairstyle ... what do you think about it? ... I know a very talented hairdresser ... she is the personal hairdresser of the Attorney General's wife ... I can ask her to come here to the grand Mansion, and make you a nice haircut ... would you like that?

Although Cristelle tried all of her best to take out Océanie from her immobile and silent condition, but no discussion and no subject could help. After Cristelle finished drying Océanie's hair, and the young girl drank her entire cup of tea, Cristelle then lead Océanie toward her bed, and she put the covers on her:

- After this dinner and this hot bath, you will have a good night sleep ...

Before turning off the lamp light and closing the door of the bedroom, Cristelle observed the thin emotionless silhouette of Océanie, for a long second, and she sighed sadly:

- Océanie ... Océanie ... what happened to you?

Chapter 46

Océanie's remedy

Friday, November 11th, 1892. In the house of the French neighbors, Les Poirier.

Friday, November 11th, 1892. In the house of the French neighbors, Les Poirier.

The afternoon's cake was particularly difficult to achieve; a white chocolate soufflé. Despite the complexity of the cake, Dalya was happy to attend and observe Mrs. Glorina preparing it. After Mrs. Glorina put the mold in the oven for baking, Dalya exclaimed:

- It will be a delicious cake.
- Certainly Mademoiselle! Mrs. Glorina smiled before continuing:
- The baking should last 20 minutes. I will go out to wash and hang these kitchen towels, before the chocolate sticks on them!!
- I will watch over the cake, Mrs. Glorina. Dalya proposed.
- Thank you, Mademoiselle!! ... at 20 minutes, use two small towels to take it out of the oven ... and be careful, it may be hot!!

When Mrs. Glorina walked out of the kitchen, Dalya washed some cooking utensils, and she cleaned the kitchen table. Then, she sat down in front of the oven, waiting for the cake's baking.

After a few minutes, Dalya decided to visit Mrs. Marianne Poirier who was in the living room, just near the kitchen. The great woman was sitting in an armchair in front of the lit fireplace, wearing a velvet robe and a light blanket on her legs; she was reading a book attentively. Mrs. Marianne Poirier was not alone in the living room; Richard Poirier was sitting behind an office desk, busy writing reports, in front of a stack of files on the table.

Once Dalya appeared in the living room, Mrs. Marianne Poirier greeted her with a smile. Dalya announced in a proud voice:

- The cake will be ready in a few minutes.

Mrs. Marianne Poirier smiled. Richard threw a discreet look at Dalya, before continuing to work.

Except that instead of returning back to the kitchen to watch over the cake, Dalya remained standing, she hesitated a few seconds before coming close to Mrs. Marianne Poirier. Then, Dalya whispered few words in the great woman's ear. Richard tried very hard to focus on his report in front of him, but he failed. He was curious about the strange whispers between the little girl and his mother.

A few seconds and a few whispers later, Mrs. Marianne closed her book, and she slowly stood up from her chair. Mrs. Marianne walked toward the Library of the living room, and she stopped in front of it, while searching by look for specific books. When the great woman pointed to a higher shelf, Dalya understood what to do. The little girl climbed on a small scale and she reached the top shelf. Dalya asked Mrs. Marianne which exact book she wanted:

- This one?

After several directions of Mrs. Marianne, Dalya came down the small scale, holding 3 books. Mrs. Marianne returned to sit back on her chair by the fireplace, followed by Dalya. The great woman opened one of the books right to a specific page, and she handed it to Dalya. After reading the presented page, Dalya was confused and surprised:

- Red meat ... dates ... beets ... I don't understand how they can be useful.

Mrs. Marianne took a 2nd book, she flipped the pages and she pointed to a paragraph to read. After a few seconds, Dalya murmured:

- Because they are rich in Iron ... and Iron is an essential food for helping th...

When suddenly, Dalya understood what Mrs. Marianne was explaining to her. She jumped all happy to have found a solution to a problem:

- Red meat!! Dates!! Beets!!

Mrs. Marianne smiled, happy to have answered the question of the little girl. Dalya turned around and she shyly asked Richard for a paper and a pencil to note. When he handed them to her, Richard still didn't understand what was happening between Dalya and his mother. But he followed the scene with all his attention.

Dalya immediately began to copy informations from the books. And from time to time, Mrs. Marianne would point her finger on what Dalya should write. After several minutes and notes, Dalya exclaimed all happy about her discovery:

- These are really valuable tips!! ... They will certainly help her so much!! ... Thank you Madame ... thank you very much Madame!!

At this instant, Dalya firmly hugged Mrs. Marianne Poirier in her arms, in a spontaneous way. And it was an unusual thing for the great woman ... it has been long ago since Mrs. Marianne had receive a firm hug. And a few steps away, sitting on his desk, having lost his focus on his work several minutes ago, Richard Poirier smiled discreetly.

When suddenly, a strange smell invaded the living room of the Poirier house. Richard thought aloud:

- It seems that ... it seems that something is burning ...

In a sudden leap, Dalya jumped and screamed:

- THE SOUFFLÉ!!! NO NO NO!!! THE SOUFFLÉ!!! NO NO NO!!!

Dalya ran toward the kitchen to rescue the cake that was over 30 minutes in the oven. Madame Marianne Poirier giggled, while continuing her readings. Richard continued his work and he sighed with an amused air:

- It seems that we will have our tea without a cake, today!

Later, in the kitchen of the Grand Mansion.

- How is she doing? Asked the head of the grand Mansion as soon as Cristelle entered the kitchen.
- Océanie is not better than yesterday! Cristelle sighed.
- The doctor warned us that her illness won't be easy to heal. Replied the Cook in a sad voice.
- She remains motionless and silent ... it's been many days. Igor wondered in a worried tone.
- Physical health seems much easy to heal than mental health. The Gardener affirmed in a serious tone.
- But then, besides medicines prescribed by the doctor, what can we do more? Cristelle asked.

The employees of the grand Mansion did all their best to help Océanie recover from her fall. But despite all the care and support provided, Océanie's state worsened more each day. After a heavy silence, the head of the grand Mansion ordered:

- Igor ... I want you to lit the fireplace in the living room, tomorrow morning ... maybe Océanie would sit in the living room, instead of spending her entire days locked in her bedroom ...
- Certainly, Monsieur! Igor replied with an enthusiastic tone.
- That's an excellent idea!! Exclaimed the Cook.
- I will serve her breakfast in the living room, then! Cristelle decided.
- I can move the big sofa and the covers to the living room as well. Answered the Gardener.

A little voice interrupted the employees' conversation in the kitchen.

- Good evening!

The employees greeted back Dalya, who was standing at the kitchen door. The head of the grand Mansion Mr. Bûchebois asked her:

- Would you like to be served dinner in your bedroom, Mademoiselle?
- Yes, Monsieur. Thank you.

The head of the grand Mansion didn't get used yet to the manners and courtesies of the little girl. He bowed his head answering in a formal voice:

- Understood, Mademoiselle!

While Mr. Bûchebois prepared Dalya's dinner tray, the Cook was in charge of serving the soup in a bowl, Igor was preparing the dinner table for the employees, and the Gardener was cutting slices of bread, Dalya remained standing near the kitchen's door. Cristelle realized that the little girl was hesitant to say something, she asked her with an encouraging tone:

- Would you like something else, Mademoiselle?

At this instant, Dalya approached Cristelle, and she handed her a small paper:

- The French neighbor, Mrs. Marianne Poirier ... she was a nurse before ... I asked her what we could do to help Océanie in her illness ... and she pointed out some books, from where I took these notes ...

Immediately, the Cook, the head of the employees, the Gardener and Igor, they all left their work and came near Cristelle, so as to read the paper handed to her by Dalya:

List of food to help the body, heart and immune system, to overcome a difficult period of convalescence:

- *Breakfast: scrambled eggs with olive oil, cumin and salt, whole wheat bread, coffee with cinnamon.*
- *Between meals: Dates stuffed with walnuts*
- *Lunch or dinner: Red meat, Tihal, spinach, vegetables baked in oven, rice and pasta*
- *3 glasses of juice a day: beets, oranges, and carrots*
- *Evening herbal tea: a few slices of ginger, honey, lemon zest, black pepper seeds.*
- *Gabrielle Noir perfume*
- *Mixture of Sellou with honey*

Cristelle was the first to act:

- Red meat?!

Dalya explained with a sure tone:

- Yes! Madame told me that red meat contains Iron ... which helps the proper functioning of the body ... the Iron helps carry oxygen throughout the body; it eliminates fatigue and gives more physical and mental energy!!

The head of the grand Mansion asked curiously:

218

- Perfume? ... Why? … How can that help Océanie?

Dalya smiled:

- I was surprised too when Madame recommended me perfume in this list ... she showed me a book; the Aromachology ... it is the science of aromas and odors psychology, it was written that the fragrant molecules have a real influence on our mental ... there are scents that make you Zen, stimulating citrus smells, sweet fragrances to make you feel reassured, and other smell to calm anxiety and anger ... Madame advised me the name of this fragrance ... Gabrielle Noir ...

The five employees were speechless in front of the little girl's explanations. And immediately, the head of the grand Mansion addressed Cristelle:

- Any idea where to find this perfume?

Cristelle replied very sure:

- In one Place! At Mr. Arthur Boy Capel shop!

The head of the grand Mansion displayed a surprised smile; he never thought that a simple product could have such beneficial effects. Continuing to read the list, Igor thought aloud:

- Tihal? What is that? I never heard such a name!

The Cook explained:

- Tihal ... that's stuffed veal spleen, with herbs and hot spices ...

Igor said in an amused tone:

- This looks very delicious!!

Staring at the paper, the Cook affirmed:

- I can cook all these food ... eggs, bread, vegetables, juices, pasta ... it's easy to do!
- Igor …Tomorrow, you will have some shopping to do! Said Mr. Bûchebois.
- Understood, Monsieur! Tomorrow morning, I will go! Said Igor.

The Gardener pointed an ingredient on the list:

- And for ginger … tomorrow afternoon, I will ask a friend of mine, to give me some roots.

Cristelle asked:

- Mixture Sellou with honey … What does that mean?

Dalya said:

- Madame explained to me that it was an ancient recipe of grounded seeds mixed with honey ... a doctor of Arab origin offered it to his patients, to speed up their healing. Except that Madame doesn't know the ingredients of this mixture.

The Cook rubbed his forehead for a moment:

- I don't remember having heard of this mixture before ... Sellou ... not in the grocery stores nor in the Saturday market ... not even in th...

Instantly, Dalya jumped and she interrupted him:

- The Saturday market!! Lalla Fatim Fadl at the market!! ... She often prepares remedies, and she is of Arab origin ... She must surely know the recipe for this mixture! ... I will ask her tomorrow!

This list of foods to buy and special recipes to prepare, gave a shot of motivation and hope to the employees of the grand Mansion. They divided the list of things to buy and prepare. As of now, everyone knew how to better help Océanie to recover and heal.

The next day. Saturday, November 12th, 1892.

Dalya woke up early, she wore her weekend clothes, she took her breakfast quickly, and then she left the grand Mansion. When she passed the front door, two tiny silhouettes ran to her:

- Dindin!! Dindin!! Dindin!!

Dalya's twin sisters clung to her legs. Dalya replied:

- Good morning Ari!! Good morning Adi!!

Starring at their big sister, the twins begged her:

- Spend day with you Dindin? Please!! Please!!

Dalya tried the best she could to detach her sisters off her legs:

- I'm busy today!! ... I have an important task to do in the market!! ... I will bring you candy ... go play ball with our little cousin Hugo ... I will see you later ...
- No no!! Cousin went with his parents ... to shopping ... cousin is busy!!
- Please Dindin!! Please!! ... Spend day with you Dindin!! ... Please!!!

The little twins were real glues. And at two, they were unbeatable. Dalya sighed annoyed. A second of thinking after, Dalya knelt in front of her little twin sisters and she spoke to them in a serious voice:

- I'll take you with me, on one condition! ... You need to be calm and do no fooleries... nice obedient girls today!! ... Statues today! ... Is that clear?
- Yes!! Clear!! Screamed the little twins with a serious air.

When Dalya continued her way out of the grand Mansion, Adi whispered to Ari:

- What is statue?

Ari replied in a sure voice:

- It is a fruit!

And despite that the little twins were unaware of what being a statue meant, they were happy to visit the Saturday market. The two little twins followed their older sister Dalya. And the day promised to be long and busy...

The road of Dumbarton Oaks Park was splendid on that Saturday morning. Despite some cold breezes, the sky was a beautiful blue, without a cloud, and the sun shone with all its might.

Several minutes of walk later, when they arrived at the market in front of the Toscana restaurant, Dalya led her little twin sisters, straight to the kiosk filled with flowers. It was the most beautiful kiosk of the Saturday market. All kinds of beautiful flowers in fresh colors and sweet scents.

- Good morning Lalla Fatim Fadl!!

Lalla Fatim Fadl was a grand old woman, with beautiful facial features, despite her advanced age. She wore a long pale pink dress, a large gray apron, and a small green scarf holding back her long white gray hair. The grand woman was arranging a large bouquet of twenty tulips in a water-filled container.

- Moonlight!! Welcome!! Welcome!! Exclaimed Lalla Fatim Fadl, as soon as she noticed Dalya.

The little twins approached the grand woman, and they hugged her in their arms. From Lalla Fatim Fadl emerged a floral and a sweet odor. And the little twins confirmed it, exclaiming:

- Oh!! ... Lalla Fatim smells very good ... smells very very good!!

At this instant, Dalya remembered her maternal grandmother. Mrs. Medusa Safoubri looked very different from Lalla Fatim Fadl. The two old women were the same age. Yet, the poor flower seller was cleaner and she smelled much nicer than the rich grandmother. Since the visit of the Safoubri family, the little twins didn't get a centimeter close to their maternal grandmother; her clothes were always dirty, and her smell was terrible. Dalya couldn't understand why and how her grandmother was in such a state.

Lalla Fatim Fadl kissed the little twins with love and tenderness, and she laughed:

- And you're the prettiest, my treasures!! ... How about I make you flower crowns? ... Would you like that?

The twins jumped joyfully:

- Flower crown!! Yes Yes Yes!! Flower crown!!

- Very well then! Lalla Fatim Fadl laughed.

Dalya sat on an empty box near the grand woman. Lalla Fatim took a few long-stemmed flowers and she began to make the crowns. The twins walked away a few steps toward the fruit vendor. Dalya kept an eye on her little sisters, and she seized the opportunity to start a subject with the grand woman.

- Lalla Fatim ... I have seen you once, preparing a mixture to clear the Dean of Merchants throat.

While delicately tying the stems, the grand woman replied:

- Yes, Mr. Einsenberg still needs it sometimes ... it's very beneficial for the throat ...
- Do you know other remedies too?

By hanging a few flowers on a crown, the grand woman smiled:

- Some, yes ...

Dalya noticed the fruit vendor offering pears to her little sisters. The twins ate them at once, while giggling. Dalya continued:

- And where do you know these remedies from?

Lalla Fatim smiled proudly:

- In the Country where I come from, people often use the benefits of nature to heal and cure their illnesses ...

Dalya asked:

- Lalla Fatim ... do you know anything about the Sellou mixture?

At that instant, the grand woman stopped and she turned back to the little girl:

- Absolutely, yes ... it is one of the most effective remedies for the ills of the body and the mind ...

The twins moved to the vegetable seller's kiosk, who greeted them with a smile. Dalya continued her conversation with the grand woman:

- There is an employee at the grand Mansion, where I live now ... the doctor said she suffers from depression ... and a neighbor who was a nurse before, she told me about this mixture... but I don't know the ingredients ...

Lalla Fatim let out a happy little laugh:

- Well then, you asked the right person, Moonlight!! ... I will tell you all the ingredients and the preparation method of this mixture!!

- Thank you very much, Lalla Fatim ... It's very nice of you!! This remedy will help so much the employee of the grand Mansion!!

The grand woman had completed a crown, and she began to make a second one:

- There are several ingredients and a long preparation ... so listen to me carefully ...

Instantly, Dalya took out from her pocket a pencil and a notebook:

- Yes, Lalla Fatim ... I will write everything!

While Dalya was about to write the grand woman's explanations, the little twins were standing in front of the kiosk of the milk and cheese merchant. The seller served some clients, while telling jokes to the little twins.

Lalla Fatim Fadl began:

- First, the ingredients ... almonds, sesame seeds, backed flour, anise, cinnamon, Arabic gum, melted butter, pollen grains ... you can even add dried fruits ... all these ingredients should be grilled over low fire and grounded into a powder ... and in the end, you double the amount of honey to the mixture ... let's say 2 tablespoons of Sellou with 4 tablespoons of honey ...

Dalya asked while writing:

- How often a day should we take this mixture of Sellou?
- As many times as needed ... I recommend a small bowl, 2 times a day ... with a glass of fresh milk or yogurt!

Several minutes later, Dalya filled her paper. Fatim Lalla told her one last recommendation:

- The most important thing is that the oven fire should be low heat ... otherwise the ingredients will burn and will no longer have a taste or usefulness! ...
- Understood Lalla! Low heat! Dalya affirmed by highlighting this sentence on her paper.

The grand woman had finished the two crowns, and as soon as she called them, the little twins approached the kiosk of Lalla Fatim Fadl. But before the grand woman could offer them the flower crowns, Dalya exclaimed in a surprised tone:

- But ... what ... what did you do?

The little twins had their mouth full, munching fresh strawberries. And they both had well-filled and enlarged bellies. Ari and Adi answered in a satisfied and full tone:

- We ate!
- Great food!

Dalya still couldn't understand what her little sisters had done:

- And what are you holding, both of you?!

The twins had their hands packed of large bags filled with fruits, vegetables, cheeses, herbs, spices, bread and milk. Their mouth still full, Ari and Adi explained to their older sister, cheerfully and proudly:

- Fruits for cake ...
- Vegetables for soup ...
- Ceese ... delicious Ceese ...
- And bread!! ... Hot bread!!

Dalya stood up:

- But ... How did you get all these things? ... With what money?

Mouths full of bread parts shared between them, the little twins replied in a natural tone:

- Gifts!

Because you see, when Dalya was busy writing the mixture's recipe ... the little twins visited almost all the kiosks of the Saturday market. And all the merchants loved the little twins so much; they offered their merchandise to them, to eat or to takeaway.

Dalya screamed all furious:

- I LET YOU ALL ALONE ONE MINUTE AND YOU RAID THE ENTIRE MARKET?!!

The twins didn't understand their older sister's anger. Ari and Adi observed Dalya for a moment, then they asked her, while handing her a fruit:

- You want strawberry?

Lalla Fatim Fadl struggled to hold her laugh. She placed the flower crowns on the heads of the little twins:

- They are such cuties these little ones ... nobody can refuse them anything!

Receiving 2 pears was one thing, but to receive bags all filled with goods for free ... it was quite another thing! Dalya had so much trouble holding her anger:

- Ari!! Adi!! ... You must return all these products to the merchants!! You cannot go around the kiosks and take things for free!!

The little twin defended themselves passionately, between two bites of cheese:

- But we did nothing!! Mr. Choux gave us strawberries!!
- Yes!! And Mr. Aymeric gave Ceese!!
- And he gave milk too!!

Dalya got angry:

- I don't care and I don't want to know!! Return these bags immediately to the merchants!! I asked you to be statues today!! But what was I thinking, to bring you here today?!

At this precise moment, Adi turned toward Ari, and she whispered in a serious tone:

- Where is fruit statue?

Ari finished her mouthful of cheese, and she replied:

- Fruit statue ... no it is not the season of fruit statue, now ... next month ... next month...

Chapter 47

Dalya and Océanie

Friday, November 18th, 1892. In the grand Mansion.

The sky was dark. The clouds covered the entire atmosphere. The wind and rain were falling in each ones turn, on Georgetown city. It was a cold day.

The employees of the grand Mansion were each busy in their work. The Cook was finalizing his meals by adding the last ingredients, the Gardener was busy closing the windows' shutters to avoid the wind knocking, Igor was loading wood logs in different fireplaces, and the head of the grand Mansion was preparing the dinner's trays and the employees' table.

Cristelle undertook to help Océanie eat her dinner. When she took the prepared dinner tray, Cristelle displayed a joyful smile and she entered Océanie's bedroom:

- Here I am again, dear!! ... Tonight, there is a delicious gratin of vegetables and béchamel sauce, with fine herbs ... Igor may devour the entire gratin plate, so I served you first!

And as usual, since many days now, Océanie was lying down on her bed, watching the fire, her gaze and her mind lost. Cristelle placed the tray in front of Océanie, and she didn't lose her enthusiasm:

- And the Cook prepared for you a chicken fillet, very soft and delicious! ... Marinated in a sauce which I wasn't able to remember the name ... The Cook is quite funny, I can barely understand what he says! ... But how could you manage to help him in the kitchen?

Océanie remained motionless and silent, despite the efforts of Cristelle to make her speak and react. Suddenly, Cristelle realized that something was missing from the dinner tray:

- The bread!! ... Bread is missing!! ... Essential food for survival!! ... Wait for me a minute, I will warm it for you!

When Cristelle left Océanie's bedroom, she met Dalya in the corridor:

- Mademoiselle!! I was just about to bring you your dinner tray, in few minutes.

Dalya smiled:

- Thank you, Cristelle. The head of the employees, Mr. Bûchebois brought me my tray in the dining room. Bread was missing; I came looking for some of it.

Cristelle exclaimed:

- How dizzy am I!! ... I also forgot the bread in Océanie's tray. I will warm bread for you in a minute, Mademoiselle!!

Dalya asked:

- How is she doing?

The face and the voice of Cristelle darkened:

- There is no change, unfortunately. I try to get her out of her state, but it's like talking to a marble statue. It's been several weeks now, that she is quiet and motionless. If I could just know what is happening inside her head ...

Dalya displayed an encouraging smile:

- She will recover, Cristelle ... she just needs a little more time.
- May Heaven hear you, Mademoiselle!! May Heaven hear you!!

Before Cristelle disappears into the kitchen, Dalya said:

- I will visit Océanie for a minute ...
- ... While I warm some bread for both of you! Excellent idea, Mademoiselle!!

When she entered the employee's bedroom with a shy step, Dalya approached Océanie and she smiled at her:

- Good evening Océanie ...

The young girl didn't emit any sound or move. She stared at the fireplace, with a blank stare. Dalya asked:

- Are you cold? ... Do you want me to add wood logs in the fireplace?

Dalya realized that she was talking to a motionless statue. Yet, she was not discouraged:

- Your face looks good ... your cheeks are significantly pinker than before ... The good recipe of Lalla Fatim Fadl and the meals of the Cook, have done you real good! ... Tonight's gratin is delicious ... the Cook added plenty of cheese in it! ... I guess you too, like to have plenty of cheese in your meals, don't you?

Océanie seemed to be in another world, she didn't even realize the presence of Dalya in her bedroom. The mind of Océanie was occupied by dark ideas. Despair and sadness prevented Océanie from paying attention to what was happening around her.

For weeks now, the employees of the grand Mansion tried all their best to help Océanie to recover. Without being able to succeed, no one could understand what could have caused her condition. They were all unaware of what had happened ... all, except Dalya Bouvard.

Since the incident on the roof of the grand Mansion, Dalya connected some events with each other. And as incredibly smart as she was, Dalya guessed the cause of Océanie's state. Since many weeks now, Dalya didn't dare to speak of it nor to the employees, nor even to Océanie. Until tonight...

In a moment, Dalya gathered her courage, and she spoke to Océanie in a convinced voice:

- He doesn't deserve you. You are way too good for him.

For the first time since so long, Océanie took off her gaze focused toward the fireplace, and she observed the little Dalya Bouvard.

And for the first time since so long, Océanie Shell smiled. A little smile. A little light appeared after the long dark weeks. Dalya didn't say a single more word. It was useless. Because Dalya Bouvard and Océanie Shell understood each other, straight away.

At the end of that day, the clouds in the sky seemed so many and impenetrable ... except that a brave little ray of sunshine made its way through the chaos. There is one thing you must always be sure of ... dear reader ... when we hit rock bottom, we don't have any other choice but to go back up to the surface!

Chapter 48

A return to the market

Saturday, November 19th, 1892.

On that day, the weather was cheerful; a sunny beautiful blue sky and a cool breeze that touched your skin occasionally.

Dalya woke up very early this morning. She wore her overalls, her white shirt, her cap and her boy's shoes. And after quickly eating her breakfast in the dining room, she took her bag and left the grand Mansion, heading toward downtown.

Several minutes of walk later, Dalya arrived at a place that was familiar to her; the market in front of the Toscana restaurant. The activity was already noisy; kiosks were installed since a while now, the merchandises were well-ordered on the counters, and the vendors were busy serving customers.

Walking between kiosks, Dalya greeted several merchants and sellers. Dalya liked this place since the time she worked here with her father. When a familiar voice from behind retained Dalya; it was her classmate Amira Mounier. And for once, Amira had abandoned her little pink dresses and elegant hats. Amira was wearing black pants, a turtleneck sweater, and boots. Amira had arranged her long braids into a bun, and she wore a big hat that seemed to belong to her father. She walked toward Dalya with an enthusiastic step:

- Good morning!! I've just arrived here a few seconds ago, too!!
- Good morning Amira. Dalya smiled back at her.

Dalya asked her friend Amira the same question for the 15th time:

- Are you sure you want do this with me? ... we will work most of the day ... and I'm used to work in the market ... you're sure you want to spend your Saturday with me, here?

Amira jumped:

- Of course, yes!! And I insist!! ... I have never worked before ... my father was so proud of me when I told him that I will work at the Saturday market ... he even made us sandwiches for lunch, for you and me ... it will be a great working day!! ... I will be very useful to you, believe me!!

Dalya laughed:

- Well ... alright then ... as you wish.

Followed by Amira, Dalya walked toward the kiosk of Mr. Choux. He was a nice man, liked and respected by everyone. His kiosk was well filled with vegetables of all kinds and shapes. When he noticed Dalya, Mr. Choux greeted her cheerfully:

- Good morning young demoiselle!!
- Good morning Mr. Choux. Dalya smiled at him. Here is my friend Amira, she will help me in our work today.
- Good morning to you too, young girl!!
- Thank you for accepting my offer, Mr. Choux. Said Dalya.
- With great pleasure, young demoiselle!! Mr. Choux affirmed with a caring voice, before continuing:
- I have prepared for you a work table, and two chairs ... the water-filled buckets are in the back ...

Dalya and Amira settled behind the table adjacent to the kiosk of Mr. Choux. Dalya took out of her bag a large plastic tablecloth, and two knives that she borrowed from Cristelle in the grand Mansion. And Amira took out of her bag two white aprons, two pairs of large gloves, and a large roll of small plastic bags, she brought from her home.

When the little girls wore their aprons and gloves, they settled the tablecloth on the table. Immediately, Mr. Choux placed before them a large basket of several different vegetables:

- And here you are demoiselles ... your first basket!
- Thank you, Monsieur. Replied the little girls simultaneously.

Dalya turned toward Amira:

- So, you will peel the vegetables, I will cut them into small pieces ...

Amira finished the sentence:

- ... And we will put everything in a small bag!

Dalya smiled:

- It's the only idea I had to earn more money and faster ... I hope it works!
- Of course it will work!! You'll see!! Amira reassured her in a determined tone, adding:
- With the 11 months' detention we had at school, I can guarantee you I'm the best vegetable peeler of the entire city!!

Dalya Bouvard and Amira Mounier began their work day, with a joyful determined laugh. One had to peel vegetables, and the other one would cut them into small dices.

After several minutes of work, Dalya and Amira had peeled, diced and filled 3 small bags of mixed vegetables. Mr. Choux, at the kiosk near them, was busy serving a customer. When Dalya noticed that the client, waiting for her order, was observing the small bags of diced vegetables, with a curious and confused look. Dalya explained to her:

- This is an ahead prepared soup.

The client approached the table of the little girls, and she asked curiously:

- An ahead prepared soup? ... How is that?

Dalya continued:

- The vegetables are peeled and cut in dices ... customers will only boil the vegetables in hot water, add spices ... and their soup is ready!

Immediately, the client turned around and she yelled:

- Margaret!! Come over here for a second!!

A 2nd woman approached. Her friend asked her:

- Margaret ... don't you have unexpected guests for tonight's dinner?
- And I stressing enough about it! I have so much work to prepare for this dinner! I don't even know where to start!!
- Look at these ... an ahead prepared soup ... the little girls peel and cut the vegetables for you ... you only have to add spices, boil it in hot water and serve your soup ... it will leave you time to prepare something else.

The 2nd woman took a small diced vegetables bag in her hands, observing it as if it was the most ingenious solution to her unexpected dinner problem. She asked Dalya:

- How much for this bag?
- 7 cents.

Immediately, the 2nd woman replied:

- I'll take 5 bags then!

The first client laughed:

- But I also want some!! You leave no bags for me!!

The 2nd woman exclaimed, all delighted to have one less chore to do for tonight:

- Christine ... my dinner is more urgent than yours!

Dalya announced to the first client:

- If you have other shopping to do in the market ... came back to our kiosk in 10 minutes and we will have prepared you more bags ... how many do you want?
- 3, please. And if possible without onions? My little boy doesn't like them.
- Understood!! 3 bags, no onions!!
- I will get some mint and come back ...
- Perfect. In 10 minutes, your bags will be ready!

When both clients paid Dalya and continued their shopping at the market, Amira hurried to peel more vegetables, thinking aloud:

- 8 bags of vegetables ... 7 cents ... it's 56 cents ... 50% to the vegetable vendor, Mr. Choux ... that's ... that's ...

Amira froze in her move a few seconds, before turning back to Dalya, eyes wide open with surprise:

- That's 28 cents in 1 minute!! ... It's awesome!!

Dalya cut the potatoes faster, and she laughed:

- The day promises to go on very well!!

Dalya and Amira didn't need to explain to passersby the idea of their ahead prepared soup bags. Their first two customers took care of that, joyfully and gladly. Conversations in the market were quickly infiltrated with the idea of ahead prepared soup bags. And orders were soon to increase...

In the street in front of the market. At the Toscana restaurant.

A car stopped at the Toscana restaurant. Sloan Wilfrid came down first, and he hurried inside the restaurant. Lyor Laszlo followed him with a slower pace. Wilfrid took off his coat and hat, and he handed them to the valet, then he walked to his usual lunch table. When Lyor sat near him, Sloan Wilfrid exclaimed while taking the menu from the server's hands:

- I am so hungry!! ... I thought the court hearing would last forever!!

Lyor took the menu card, and he said with a tired tone:

- Yes ... the judge took all his time to decide ... yet the case was very clear and obvious.
- It was not about the case, Lyor. The judge wanted to show his skills in front of our client ... there were rumors circulating in recent months, about the proximity between the judge and our client's nephew ...
- So then ... he kept us 5 hours for an audience, just to prove that he was competent and impartial? Lyor wondered, with a little laughter.
- Yes!! Wilfrid sighed. I've almost fainted at the Court exit, my stomach couldn't hold any longer.

Asking for the headwaiter, Wilfrid said his lunch order:

- I would like ... a broccoli soup with cheese ... a potato puree dish and vegetables sauté ... and stuffed chicken, with white sauce ... 2 mushrooms quiches ... a lasagna with eggplant ... and for dessert, I will order later. But please bring me as soon as possible the broccoli soup, with slices of buttered bread. Please.
- Immediately, Monsieur.

Lyor also made his lunch order, with much less dishes than Sloan Wilfrid. A few minutes later, when they were served soup, Sloan Wilfrid hurried to taste it. At the first spoonful, he uttered a long sound of delight. Lyor laughed:

- Did you recover your full strength?

Sloan Wilfrid replied with an amused smile, and he continued to eat his soup, with slices of buttered bread. In less than 5 minutes, Sloan Wilfrid had finished his soup bowl, even before Lyor completed half of his. Sloan Wilfrid relaxed on his chair and he sighed cheerfully:

- I can finally feel my heart beating again ... 5 hours of aud...

Sloan Wilfrid paused for an instant; his eyes froze in front of the restaurant's large windows. After a few seconds, Wilfrid shook his head, and then he continued:

- 5 hours of audience almost ki...

For the 2nd time, Sloan Wilfrid stopped still in front of the window. Lyor wasn't listening to him, being busy eating his soup and reading a newspaper. Wilfrid shook his head in disbelief, a second time, and he finished his sentence:

- 5 hours of audience almost killed me ... I no longer felt my le...

This 3rd time, Lyor Laszlo realized that something was wrong. He turned toward Sloan Wilfrid:

- What is going on?

The young Lawyer, Sloan Wilfrid straightened up on his chair, he looked shocked, and his eyes were focused through the windows of the Toscana restaurant. Lyor repeated his question:

- Wilfrid ... everything is alright?

Sloan Wilfrid thought aloud:

- But ... it is not possible ... is it really her? ... Is it really what I see?

At this instant, Wilfrid doubted his eyes, and with a quick move, he stood up. Lyor asked him all curious:

- Where are you going? ... What is going on?

Wilfrid replied with an amused laugh:

- I have to check something ... either I have seen the insane ... or I have to recheck my brain!

At the end of his words, Sloan Wilfrid walked toward the exit of the Toscana restaurant. For Sloan Wilfrid to interrupt his lunch, despite his hunger, it must have been something really important. Lyor was curious, he put down his newspaper and he followed him outside the Toscana restaurant.

Dalya closed the bags of vegetables cut into cubes. And it was well-confirmed; Amira was indeed the fastest vegetable peeler of the entire city. She was proud to help her friend Dalya, and happy to work for the first time in her life. When Dalya gave 3 bags to a client, she put the money in the pocket of her apron, thinking aloud:

- At this speed ... we'll have at least half the amount of money needed ... in no time!!

Amira finished peeling the potatoes, she lifted up her hands in a victory form, while exclaiming cheerfully:

- We will succeed!!

Dalya and Amira laughed for a moment, when a calm and familiar voice interrupted them:

- Good morning, Mesdemoiselles.

Immediately, the two girls went mute, their laugh disappeared and they were paralyzed in their chairs. Neither Dalya nor Amira didn't dare to say a word or make a move. Sloan Wilfrid stepped close to their work table, and he explained his presence in a calm voice:

- I was at the Toscana restaurant, right in front ... for lunch. And I noticed you through the windo...

But before Sloan Wilfrid could complete his sentence, Lyor had arrived within seconds, wondering at the presence of Dalya Bouvard in the middle of the market, wearing an apron and gloves. Lyor was surprised:

- But ... what are you doing here?

Dalya answered Lyor, without hesitation:

- I am taking a bath.

Given the confused look of Lyor Laszlo by this reply, Dalya continued:

- I am working, abruti!

Lyor didn't know if he was exploding because Dalya called him abruti, or because she was working at the market. Anyway, Lyor yelled:

- How is ... you ... But what's this ... what is wrong with you?! Are you insane?! You're an Heiress!! You cannot work here!!

Dalya defended herself with absolute confidence:

- And so what? Since when work is a shame? I remind you that I'm not an Heiress yet!

Lyor exploded with anger:

- Do we always have to find you in the most insane places and situations?

234

Amira whispered to Dalya in a worried tone:

- Your legal guardian, will he bother us for long? ... Because we are already 3 bags late ... the clients will soon come pick them up.

Dalya raised her knife and she pointed it at Lyor, in a threatening tone:

- Disappear of my sight, Lyor!! I'm busy today!! I have no time for you!!

Sloan Wilfrid didn't hold his amused laugh. But Lyor was forced to hold his anger; he turned around and he left toward the Toscana restaurant, while muttering angry words on his way:

- Crazy!! Insane!! Sick!! Working in the market!! An Heiress!!

After Lyor left, Sloan Wilfrid recovered from his laugh, and he observed Dalya who was filling a bag of diced vegetables. Dalya hurried to explain to him:

- These are bags of ahead prepared soup. We peel the vegetables and cut them into small cubes ... customers will boil these vegetables, and just add spices ...
- And their soup is ready in minutes and effortlessly! Amira exclaimed in a proud tone.

Sloan Wilfrid crossed his arms and he thought aloud, while observing the bags filled with diced vegetables:

- It is ... I admit that it is a very smart idea ... Mesdemoiselles!

Dalya and Amira exchanged an accomplice and a proud look. Sloan Wilfrid understood the work that Dalya was doing in the market. However, he was also curious about her reasons. Sloan Wilfrid spoke to Dalya in a thoughtful and serious voice:

- Mademoiselle ... May I know why are you here in the market? ... Why are you working today?

Dalya looked at the young Lawyer, unable to find the exact words to answer him. The last person she thought she would meet in the market was Mr. Wilfrid.

Having known Dalya Bouvard for the 3rd year now, Sloan Wilfrid recognized the hesitancy and anxiety of the little girl, to answer his question. And Sloan Wilfrid thought that something must have forced Dalya to work in the market. He approached and he whispered to Dalya with a serious voice:

- Mademoiselle ... how much money do you need?

Dalya became silent; she didn't dare to pronounce the amount of money she needed. And since she was little, Dalya Bouvard was always embarrassed to ask for money, from anyone. However this time, Dalya really needed this money, and urgently. After several seconds of silence, Dalya finally found the best answer to give to the Lawyer:

- I need ... I need you to buy me some vegetable bags, Monsieur Wilfrid.

Of all the answers that Sloan Wilfrid hoped to hear, this answer hit him like lightning. Dalya Bouvard never stopped to surprise and amaze him, since their first meeting. For a few seconds, Wilfrid observed the little girl, with a fascinated stare. He smiled tenderly at her:

- Understood, Mademoiselle. I will buy you 7 bags of diced vegetables.

Dalya smiled back at him:

- Thank you, Monsieur. When you finish your lunch at the Toscana restaurant, your bags of vegetables will be ready for you.

Wilfrid bowed his head in greeting her. And while returning to his lunch, Wilfrid heard the voice of Dalya and Amira, active and hardworking:

- Here are the potatoes!
- The carrots are peeled ... they're yours!
- Alright, the second bag of the client is filled ... I need zucchini Mr. Choux!
- Bring me the peppers too ... I need some!
- Here are your zucchini demoiselles!
- Thank you, Mr. Choux … carrots cut ... we still have to fill 11 bags!

When Sloan Wilfrid returned back inside the Toscana restaurant, he observed the little girls working in the street in front of him, while he slowly moved the spoon in his potato puree plate. After a long silence, Wilfrid thought aloud:

- One must admit that ... this little girl never stops to impress ...

Lyor sighed in an exasperated tone, while torturing his meat steak:

- Really?! ... That little girl impresses you?! … yet she shook upside down my life and my career !

Sloan Wilfrid stared at the activity of the vegetable kiosk in front of the restaurant. After a moment, Wilfrid whispered in a convinced voice, and a determined smile:

- Oh ... and she will shake many more things, Lyor ... she will shake many more things!

Lyor continued reading the newspaper, while finishing his lunch. While Sloan Wilfrid had an idea in his mind; he called the headwaiter with a sign:

- I need a service, from the Toscana restaurant ...
- Of course, Monsieur. What can we do for you?

By the end of the working day, Dalya and Amira helped Mr. Choux to close his kiosk and gather his wagon, and they left the Saturday market, back toward their homes.

- So ... have we made enough money today? asked Amira.

Dalya showed her friend the purse full of money:

- Not only cents but dollars too!! Dalya answered with a proud tone.

Amira jumped on the sidewalk:

- And this is only our first day! It's awesome!! We will succeed Dalya!! Without a doubt!!
- Thank you for helping me today, Amira.
- It was my pleasure to work with you at the market!! My father will be so proud when I tell him what happened ... clients ... the money we collected ... the funny incident at the fish kiosk ...
- It was the best scene of the day!! Dalya laughed. Did you see the sardines jumping in the air?
- Of course! Amira laughed. The shrimp also flew!! Flying fish!!

The road back home was filled with laughs and pride. Dalya and Amira were happy with the money they had collected, and the success of the idea of the ahead prepared soup.

Later that day. In the kitchen of the Grand Mansion.

The kitchen of the grand Mansion was very quiet in this late afternoon. The Cook was stirring the soup in a large pot, Cristelle was setting up the dinner table for the employees, and the head of the grand Mansion was preparing the tray for Mademoiselle Dalya and Océanie.

When the kitchen door opened like a thunder:

- You'll never guess who I met in the market, in front of the Toscana restaurant!

Igor seemed happy to bring news for once. The Cook replied, while continuing to stir the soup:

- A Governor?

Igor put his shopping bags and baskets:

- Even better!

The head of the Mansion readjusted the plates in both trays:

- A Congressman?

Igor couldn't contain his laugh:

- Even better!

Cristelle sighed in a bored voice, placing cutlery on the table:

- The president of the United States?

This time, Igor could hardly retain his agitation, he screamed:

- Dalya Bouvard!

Instantly, all the employees froze in their moves. The Cook was the first to recover:

- What was she doing in the market?

Igor sat near the kitchen table, and he proudly described his discovery:

- I was shopping at the market, as requested ... when suddenly, I turn around, I find her sitting behind a table covered with a large tablecloth, near the vegetable kiosk ... she was wearing an apron and holding a knife in her hand ... she was working at the market today!

Cristelle bit her lips, at that instant. Dalya had actually asked her for a large tablecloth and two kitchen knives. Except that Cristelle was unaware that Dalya would use them ... to work in the market!

The head of the grand Mansion and the Cook exchanged a confused and puzzled look.

- Are you sure it was her ... Mademoiselle Dalya Bouvard?
- As sure as the sky is blue! Igor replied with a sure tone, before continuing:
- And she was not alone, by the way! there was her friend ... the girl with long braids ...
- Amira Mounier? Her classmate? Asked the head of the Mansion.
- Yes, that girl was also present with her!! They both worked at the market!!

The Cook thought aloud:

- But ... working il mercato? ... Why? Perché?

Igor relaxed in his chair, and he answered in an amused voice:

- I don't know ... that girl is very strange ... I think she doesn't have the same brain as we do!

Cristelle asked with a hesitant voice:

- And ... what ... what was she working on, in the market?
- It took me some time to understand their work ... Dalya and Amira were peeling vegetables, cutting them into small dices, and filling up little plastic bags of diced vegetables ... they sold these small bags as an ahead prepared soup ... clients would only add spices, boil the diced vegetables in hot water ... and finally, serve the soup!

Cristelle's legs couldn't hold her anymore. She sat on the nearest chair. Her face turned pale and she lost her words. The head of the grand Mansion was surprised by what he was hearing:

- An Heiress selling ahead prepared soup ... in the market!

The Cook had wide open eyes with surprise:

- I admit ... it's quite a smart idea ... buy a bag of vegetables peeled and cut in advance ... it's a time saver to prepare something els...
- Ferrero!! Exclaimed the head of the grand Mansion. You forget that she is an Heiress!

Immediately, the Cook pulled himself together:

- Dio Dio!! Yes!! An Heiress who works at the market!! ... Stolto!! Pazzo!! This is insane!!

The head of the grand Mansion asked in a worried voice:

- Cristelle ... were you aware of her work? ... Did she spoke to you about it?

The words were hard to come out of Cristelle's mouth, she jumped:

- No ... no, Monsieur ... I knew nothing about her work! ... I have just discovered it, right at this instant, as all of you!

The Cook turned toward Cristelle:

- Do you know why she worked at the market, today?

But before Cristelle could answer no, a little silhouette appeared at the kitchen door. Since the head of the grand Mansion prevented her from being in the kitchen, Dalya never dared to enter inside. Therefore, at the door step, Dalya Bouvard displayed a proud and innocent smile:

- Good evening!

The employees of the grand Mansion became silent, instantly. With all the confused and worried looks that turned toward her, Dalya felt tension in the air. Yet, Dalya said in a spontaneous voice:

- I just wanted to inform you that I came back. I will be in my bedroom.

None of the employees spoke or moved. Only the head of the grand Mansion replied in a formal tone:

- Understood, Mademoiselle. We will serve you dinner in your bedroom, if you wish.
- Thank you, Mr. Bûchebois.

When Dalya walked away, a heavy silence filled the kitchen for many minutes. Igor broke the silence with an amused laugh:

- This is unheard of!! An Heiress working at the market!! The Late Governor's Heiress working at the market!!
- That's strange ... unusual. Mr. Bûchebois thought aloud.
- Yes! strano ... very strange. The Cook replied in a serious voice.

Only Cristelle remained silent, between the astonishment of Mr. Bûchebois and the Cook, and between Igor's laugh.

Chapter 49

Thanksgiving

Thanksgiving holiday. Thursday, November 24th, 1892.

The air was fresh; a beautiful shining sun reigned over a blue sky. The birds were singing in a good mood, for their last Autumn outing. The Gardener had spent several days earlier to clean the garden of the grand Mansion, from fallen leaves. The landscape was about to change its dress and welcome winter.

It was a great day of celebration. After breakfast, Dalya went up to her bedroom and she wore a pretty cream dress that the stylist Mrs. Lancel insisted on including in Dalya's wardrobe. As well as small beige shoes and a gray cardigan with gold buttons. Dalya gathered her hair up in a bun.

Going down the hall stairs of the grand Mansion, Dalya was called by a cheerful and familiar voice:

- How beautiful you are in this dress Mademoiselle!!

Cristelle was coming out of the living room. Dalya greeted her, while blushing slightly:

- Thank you, Cristelle. I thought it would be a good occasion to wear a dress.
- And you did very well Mademoiselle!! I must admit that Mrs. Lancel has an excellent taste!!

Approaching the little girl, Cristelle adjusted Dalya's dress knot:

- I am glad that you will spend Thanksgiving lunch with your family, at the annex house.
- Me too!

Since she lived in the grand Mansion, Dalya felt being far from her family, although the annex house was just close. The only contact Dalya had with her family was her little twin sisters, who visited her often. Her father spoke no word to her, only giving her cold stares. And her mother was avoiding her like the plague. Dalya hoped that on this holiday, her parents would be more warm and welcoming.

Midday. The Thanksgiving lunch. In the annex house.

When Dalya crossed the garden of the annex house, two small silhouettes welcomed her with screams and jumps. Ari and Adi were both dressed in light green dresses, pink butterfly hairbands holding their light brown hair, and shiny beige shoes.

- Dindin!! Dindin!! Dindin!!

- Good morning Adi ... Good morning Ari!!

When she knelt to kiss her little sisters, Dalya greeted her little cousin who joined them in the garden:

- Good morning cousin Hugo!

The little boy answered with a happy smile. He was wearing an elegant blue suit, and a cap on his head. Around his neck, the cousin Hugo wore a scarf in blue bronze colors, with drawings of flying eagles stitched on the edges.

- I'm glad you are spending the Thanksgiving holiday with us this year!! I'm sure you will like it!!

The little twins were eager to tell their older sister about the feast preparations:

- Dindin!! There is big turkey ... very big!! With stuffing inside!!
- And potatoes ... and small cabbage ... and carrots ... and zucchini ... and pumpkins ...
- There is bread Corn ... and tart with pecan caramel ... very very good!!
- Other dessert ... chocolate cream!! Sweet and good!!
- And also red sauce!!

Dalya laughed:

- The red sauce is the cramberries ... it is clear that you are already hungry, little twins!!

The cousin Hugo laughed too:

- Mrs. Augustine banned them from entering the kitchen ... Ari and Adi wanted to taste everything ... that's why we are playing outside in the garden.

Dalya knelt down:

- Ari ... Adi ... you will continue to play in the garden ... and I will help our mother for the lunch feast ... it should be soon ... and if you don't do anything silly, I will serve you first, and I will double your desserts' portion!

The little twins had eyes wide open and joyful smiles:

- We have lots of desserts?
- We served first? Soon?

Ari and Adi continued playing with their little cousin, while Dalya entered the annex house. She went immediately to the kitchen, sure to find in her mother.

- Good morning mother!! ... Happy Thanksgiving!!

Mrs. Augustine didn't reply to her daughter's greeting. And Dalya was used to it, since always. Mrs. Augustine wore a mustard-colored dress and a white apron. She had just taken out the Corn bread from the oven, a few seconds ago, and she was cutting it into cubes. The kitchen was a mess. Immediately, Dalya began to wash dishes and set the lunch table, while her mother was busy finalizing the meals.

Several minutes later, when Dalya finished arranging all cutlery and plates on the lunch table, Mrs. Augustine was almost done too. Dalya asked her mother:

- Would you like me to fill the chocolate cream in the verrines?

Without even looking at her daughter, Mrs. Augustine answered with a stressed voice:

- And put whipped cream on top, with a cherry ... make sure 2 verrines per person ...

Dalya was delighted to help her mother for the feast lunch, while her father was giving a guided tour around Dumbarton Oaks Park to the guests. Dalya was aware that the visit of the Safoubri family, caused her mother big stress. Mrs. Augustine wanted everything to be perfect for her family, and she had never appeared so tense and anxious.

After having filled all the verrines and put the cherries on top, Dalya placed the vegetables dishes and sauces on the table. Mrs. Augustine put the big turkey in the middle of the table. When a silhouette entered the kitchen and said in an angry mean voice:

- That's a way too big turkey! Why didn't you cook a smaller one?!

Generally, people make a clothing effort to celebrate a holiday. The grandmother Safoubri was an exception. The old woman was wearing a long black dress tainted with dust, a holed shawl that seems never to have been washed before, her curly orange hair overflowed in all directions. Dalya still couldn't understand why her rich and wealthy grandmother dressed in very dirty clothes, with holes. But what concerned Dalya the most was the terrible odor that emanated from her grandmother. Dalya thought:

- *She can take a bath every day ... she can put on perfume or essential oils ... why does this terrible smell sticks to her skin? ... Is she even aware of her smell? ... Or no one has dared to talk to her?... she is rich, yet stingy ... how come she is so rich and doesn't buy new proper clothes?*

The grandmother stepped into the kitchen, and she settled in a chair at the lunch table, addressing her own daughter with an arrogant tone:

- Augustine ... why didn't you cook a smaller turkey?! ... It's a waste of food ... Don't you ever think properly?

Mrs. Augustine became pale and she lost her words. Dalya stood still in her place. Knowing very well the hard difficult nature of Augustine Bouvard, Dalya would have never believed to see someone criticize her mother. Except on that day...

By placing the corn bread plate on the lunch table, Dalya observed from afar her maternal grandmother, who continued to speak in a spontaneous harsh and cruel tone:

- It is useless to have cooked so many desserts! ... But when will you ever learn to prepare a feast menu Augustine?!

A strange thought came to Dalya's mind, at that precise moment. Dalya heard this sentence before ... "when will you ever learn"...

When the rest of the guests entered the kitchen, Dalya pulled herself together.

- Oh!! Me too, I cook the same meals at Thanksgiving!! ... Me too, I have the same decorated plates with the same patterns!! ... Me too, I have a dress of the same color!! ... Me too, I have the same glasses like those!! ... Me too ... Me too ... Me too...

Aunt Claudine didn't stop her comparisons on every detail of the Bouvard family life. She sat on a chair at the table, and her husband joined her. Mr. Henrik seemed in good spirits, he displayed a strange smile, proud and arrogant.

Dalya's father invited his brother-in-Law to sit on a chair, but the unusually kind voice of the grandmother interrupted him:

- Come my adored son ... come and sit near your mommy ... I hope this lunch pleases my adored son ... you deserve the best feast lunch ...

Duroc Safoubri preferred to sit near his mother. And by the way, he followed his mother like a shadow. Since their arrival in the annex house, Dalya noticed that the grandmother had her eyes only for her son, even ignoring the presence of her other daughters Claudine and Augustine. She spoke in a kind voice toward her son Duroc, but she addressed her two daughters with harsh looks and criticism.

The little twin came to the kitchen too. Dalya helped her sisters to sit at the end of the long table, next to their little cousin Hugo.

- We are happy to welcome you on this festive day!! It is a great pleasure that you joined us!!

Antman Bouvard smiled happily, while cutting the big stuffed turkey. All the guests served themselves to the dishes around the table. Dalya made sure to fill the plates of her sisters and her little cousin.

- The turkey is too dry ... you should have marinated it with a sauce the night before ... why haven't you thought about it?

The grandmother observed her daughter Augustine with a severe and insistent gaze, waiting for an answer to her question. Mrs. Augustine became pale and she whispered in a confused tone:

- I ... I did ... maybe not enough ... sauce ...

Dalya's father moved forward a bowl toward the grandmother, releasing a nervous laugh:

-   With the cramberries sauce, the turkey meat is delicious!! You should try it!!

Except that the grandmother stared at her daughter Augustine in a cold look:

-   You forgot again to marinate the turkey!! ... But why did you forget?

Dalya choked on a bite of Corn bread, she didn't believe her ears. Dalya had previously heard that same illogical question ... "Why did you forget?"

The grandmother poured a spoonful of sauce on her slice of turkey, thinking aloud:

-   You have never succeeded at cooking a simple holiday dish, Augustine ... since always, you are an incapable, Augustine ... an incapable ... I don't even know how you feed your family ... an incapable ...

Dalya took a long sip of water to lower the bite of turkey stuck in her throat. The word "incapable" that her grandmother said, Dalya had also heard it many times before ... and it was a weird thing.

The grandmother pampered her son like a spoiled baby. Duroc Safoubri ate with his two hands, his mouth full, his cheeks puffed, his shirt was full of sauce and stains. And despite his mature man size, Duroc looked like an idiot. The grandmother ordered her daughter in a cold tone:

-   Augustine!! What are you waiting for to fill your brother's plate? ... Do I always have to tell you what to do? ... Can't you ever think of yourself?

Mrs. Augustine tried to smile, and fill the plate of her brother Duroc, without daring to say a word. The violent nature of Augustine Bouvard was repressed by the harshness of her own mother, Mrs. Medusa Safoubri.

The meal continued yet in a calm air. Mr. Henrik and Dalya's father were talking about the new house that Mr. Henrik bought in Florida.

-   What is your idea about the roof of the house? Mr. Henrik asked Antman.
-   In Florida, there is never any snow, but I heard there was a lot of rain ... the ideal would be that you put a layer of black tar paint on the roof ... it will save you from having rain leaks!
-   Great idea, you're right, Antman. And ... do I need to varnish the windows too?
-   Certainly!! But you will not need a black paint, use only white glue ... it will work well and will cost you almost nothing ... tomorrow we will go to downtown, to show you which products to use.
-   Yes, that would be perfect! Thank you, Antman. I hope I can renovate my new home in less than 2 weeks ... I am starting my job right after.
-   Don't worry Henrik. This annex house was inhabitable, and I was able to renovate it myself in one week. Your new home will be ready in no time!

Several days before, nearly all Dalya's doubtful questions were answered about this new home in Florida.

The little twins and the cousin Hugo ate with big appetite, without worrying about the conversations around the table. Ari and Adi had almost finished their meat, they asked for more. By serving them vegetables and Corn bread, Dalya asked her little cousin:

- Do you want some more of the Cramberries sauce? Would you like me to serve you some turkey with stuffing?

Before the little cousin could answer, his mother, Aunt Claudine jumped joyfully:

- Me too, I cook the same delicious Cramberries sauce!! ... Me too, I prepare the same stuffed turkey!! ... Me too, everyone loves the Corn Bread that I bake!! ... Me too ... Me too ... Me too ...

Dalya and her little cousin exchanged an uneasy smile. Without waiting for the little boy's answer, Dalya amply filled his plate.

The Thanksgiving Lunch took place in a very weird atmosphere. Dalya ate her food silently, observing the different attitudes. The grandmother criticized everything her daughter did:

- Vegetables are too marinated in oil ... you shouldn't have cooked the zucchini with the carrots ... when will you ever learn, Augustine?! ... The Cramberries sauce is too bitter ... why didn't you think of preparing another sauce?!... what is that? Baked potato in the oven? Do you ever think before cooking, Augustine? ... The turkey stuffing is too salty ... you have always been an incapable and you will always be, Augustine ... This Corn Bread is too dry! ... What a meal! Such a shame! Incapable Augustine ... incapable!

Mrs. Augustine remained oddly silent, displaying a nervous and anxious smile during the entire lunch time. And for Dalya who was used to hearing her mother scream and explode without any restraint, Dalya was very surprised of Augustine's sudden calm.

And that was not all; the grandmother radically changed the tone of her voice in a second, when she spoke to her son Duroc:

- Eat my adored son ... take all the vegetables you want, they are good for your health ... how adorable my beloved son is! ... Would you like me to serve you more sauce? ... Finish your plate my angel ... there will be plenty of desserts just for you, my adored son ... eat some Corn bread; it's very good for you!! How cute my beloved son is ... a real angel!

Dalya leaned a little bit to observe her uncle Duroc, sitting at the other side of the table. Dalya couldn't understand the grandmother's worship for her son. His shirt was all dirty, his face all tainted, his hands were filthy, and he laughed loudly letting appear all the food in his mouth. Duroc Safoubri looked far away from a mature man and an angel.

The Safoubri were a very special family. By serving herself some vegetables, Dalya was almost dizzy trying to follow the words of her Aunt Claudine:

- Me too, I cook the vegetables in the oven just like that!! ... Me too, I marinate them with olive oil just like that!! ... Me too, I cut the vegetables into slices just like that!! ... Me too, I add herbs!! ... Me too ... Me too ... Me too ...

Dalya slowly ate her meal. She couldn't understand the excessive jealousy of her Aunt Claudine toward the Bouvard family. Dalya wondered if the Aunt Claudine was ever tired of her jealousy. In front of the relentless energy of the young woman, Dalya was convinced that there was no cure for Aunt Claudine's jealousy.

Sitting a few chairs away, Dalya's father and Mr. Henrik were busy discussing the renovation of the new home recently purchased in Florida. Dalya observed for a few minutes her Aunt's husband. From the outside, Mr. Henrik appeared to be an honest and a respectable man. But in the inside, he was a very different man. The poised and calm attitude of Mr. Henrik inspired no trust ... and that, Dalya guessed it at their first meeting.

Only the little twins and the little cousin enjoyed this festive meal. Ari and Adi loved turkey with stuffing and the Cramberries sauce. They laughed while exchanging their forks full of turkey bites. The little cousin smiled, watching the game of the little twins, while serving himself for the third time vegetables and corn bread.

Dalya ate in silence her Thanksgiving meal. And as unexpected as it was, this lunch revealed many things ...

At the end of lunch, Dalya's father invited everyone to have tea and dessert in the living room. And you may have thought that the attitudes would improve and lighten up after a delicious meal ... but no. The same behaviors were repeated.

- I hate pecans! ... You forgot as always ... you will never learn anything, Augustine?!... And what is this chocolate cream? ... A cherry on top, that's ridiculous! ... the whipped cream is too light ... the tea is too sweet ... incapable, Augustine ... good for nothing ... all these years, and you haven't learned anything good!

The grandmother shot her daughter Augustine with bloody critics, relentlessly and ruthlessly. Mrs. Augustine remained silent, displaying a nervous smile, while serving dessert and tea to the guests. And a second later, the grandmother radically changed her tone:

- How adorable my son is! ... Serve yourself more pecan pie ... you love pecans, my dear Duroc ... take as much chocolate verrines as you want ... my adored son ... would you like me to serve you some tea? ... How many sugar cubes do you want? ... my angel!

Dalya couldn't watch her uncle Duroc without feeling disgusted. His entire shirt was tainted by the lunch meal, and now adding desserts stains. His big belly was growing and overflowing off his pants. His face was smeared by the sauces, his hands were busy eating the nuts pie without a fork or a politeness. Dalya had never met someone who looked as disgusting as Duroc Safoubri, eating with savage manners.

- Me too, I bake the pecan pie!! ... Me too, I prepare it with caramel sauce just like that!! ... Me too, I have a pretty teapot and cups service just like those!! ... Me too, I put the chocolate mousse into verrines just like that!! ... Me too, I have lace napkins just like these!! ... Me too, I decorate the whipped cream with a cherry on top like that!! ... Me too ... Me too ... Me too ...

Dalya thought that since her arrival in Georgetown city, Aunt Claudine had certainly reached the one million "me too" expression. The jealousy and the comparison were the only words that Aunt Claudine pronounced. At a moment, Dalya even wondered if her family had something that Aunt Claudine didn't claim to already have...

After serving chocolate mousse to her younger sisters and her little cousin, Dalya sat near them to drink her hot tea. Meanwhile, her father explained to Mr. Henrik that he had to plant citronella around the house in Florida, because the mosquitoes were very present in that area. Mr. Henrik listened carefully to all Antman's advices, while asking more specific questions.

Several minutes later, the desserts plates and verrines were empty, and bellies were well filled. Everyone was talking and enjoying the calm of the afternoon.

Mrs. Augustine retired to the kitchen to arrange the rest of the meal. Aunt Claudine and the grandmother were discussing the decoration of the new house in Florida. And Dalya's father refilled Mr. Henrik's tea cup.

- Dindin!! Dindin!! Can we have lemon juice?
- Please ... belly hurts ... a lot ...

The little twins ate so much at lunch; their little bellies were clearly bloated over their dresses. Ari and Adi were lying on the divan, looking exhausted and sleepy. Dalya laughed at the state of her little sisters:

- I told you not to eat too much too fast ... the turkey wasn't going to escape!! ... When I was saying eat slowly, was anyone listening to me? ... No!!

The twin caressed their puffy bellies:

- Sorry Dindin!! Sorry!!
- lemon juice ... please ...
- Last time we eat a lot ...
- Turkey was very good ... very very good ...
- Belly hurts ...
- Lemon juice ... Lemon juice ... please ...

Dalya reassured her little sisters, while standing up:

- Alright ... alright ... I will bring you some lemon juice to help you digest.

Before entering the kitchen, Dalya heard the angry and whispered voice of her mother Augustine:

-   You ate almost all the pecan pies!! I didn't cook them only for you!! Aren't you ashamed?! You should have left a slice to the others!

Duroc Safoubri answered his sister Augustine, in an arrogant tone:

-   Why do you care? ... And even if I ate the entire pies all by myself, why do you bother?

Dalya didn't dare to enter the kitchen and interrupt the conversation; she hid in a corner under the stairs.

-   What do you want now? Augustine asked her brother impatiently.
-   More pies, you idiot! Duroc let out a silly mean laugh.

For Augustine Bouvard to be called an idiot, Dalya felt that her mother was about to explode with rage. Except that for the first time ever, Augustine retained her anger, and she displayed a forced smile to answer her brother:

-   I have no more pie! ... Go back and sit in the living room ... you ate enough for today!
-   Wrong!! Yelled Duroc. You hid a pie in the oven!! I saw you earlier!!

Dalya never thought her uncle was hungry as an ogre. Augustine breathed a long shot, and she spoke in a forced calm voice:

-   Duroc ... you alone ate the 3 pies that I have served in the living room ... it would be polite to leave one pie for the others ... it would be generous of you, don't you think?

At this moment, Dalya could clearly see the anger on her uncle Duroc's face. His cheeks became red and inflated. But before Duroc could say a word, the grandmother came in the kitchen.

-   What is happening here? Why is my beloved son delayed in the kitchen ... my adored son should rest in the living room after such a meal ... and you, Augustine, what are you doing here, leaving your guests alone in the living room?! ... you will never learn good manners! ... definitely it was a waste of time to have you as a daughter... a good for nothing!

Dalya froze in her hidden place, paralyzed by what she was hearing. Dalya never thought that her grandmother could treat her daughter Augustine in such a hard mean way. And also, Dalya never thought that her mother Augustine would accept being insulted and criticized by anyone.

Yet, Augustine Bouvard decided to explain to her mother, in a trembling voice:

-   I ... I was arranging the rest of the meal ... for tomorrow ... and Duroc wanted ... a ...

When suddenly, Duroc jumped and he complained with a fake voice:

-   She refused to give me a pie that she hid in the oven!! She said I was selfish!! She said that I shouldn't have eaten all the pies!! She said that I was a rude boy with no good manners!! She yelled at me!! She said that I ate too much, without caring about the others!!

Augustine tried to defend herself as best as she could:

- This is not what I said ... I only asked him to ke...

The grandmother observed Augustine with a diabolic look. And that look ... Dalya knew it very well, having received it from her own mother Augustine.

In a second, the grandmother came close to her daughter Augustine, and she pinched her cheek, with a move so strong, that Augustine was paralyzed trembling in her place. The grandmother whispered in a menacing voice:

- Listen carefully to me, you idiot ... you give my adored son everything he desires ... and if he wants to eat all the meal on the table, he has the right to ... because, you need to understand something important, Augustine ... you will never have the same value as my beloved son Duroc ... you are an idiot, Augustine ... you are a nobody, a vermin, an incapable, and an ignorant!!

Even from afar, Dalya could clearly see that her mother was suffering while the grandmother pinched her cheek even harder. And this pain, Dalya could remember it too, for having endured it many times before.

When the grandmother released her daughter's cheek in a violent move, Augustine nearly tripped and she fall on the ground. Her cheeks were red, and her eyes filled with tears. With a trembling move, Augustine stood up, she took out of the oven a pecan pie, and she gave it to her brother. Duroc displayed a triumphant diabolic grin. He took the cake with a brusque move:

- You heard well, you idiot ... you must give me all that I want!! ... And if my mommy says I can eat the entire meal, I have the right to!! ... you idiot!!

The grandmother observed her daughter Augustine with a disgusted diabolic look, before taking her adored son toward the living room:

- Come, my angel ... let's go back to the living room, so you can eat the pie as you like ... how handsome my beloved son is ... you deserve this pie ... come, my angel ...

Duroc and the grandmother disappeared into the living room. Remaining alone in the kitchen, Augustine dried her tears, and she continued to store the leftovers from the Thanksgiving lunch.

Standing still in her hidden place, Dalya had some hard time to believe the scene and the conversation that had just happened in front of her. Dalya was shocked.

After several seconds of hesitation, Dalya didn't dare to enter the kitchen and face her mother. She returned with discreet steps, to her place in the little living room. The grandmother proudly observed her beloved son who was eating the pecan pie ... with both hands!

Her little sisters were still lying down on the divan. Dalya pulled herself together and she told them in a normal voice as possible:

249

- I didn't find any lemon juice in the kitchen ... I will serve you some tea ... it contains chamomile and lemon slices ... it will help you to digest.

The end of Thanksgiving Day.

Going up the stairs of the grand Mansion's hall, Dalya had her mind busy. The Thanksgiving lunch of this year had unveiled many things and attitudes.

The fireplace in her bedroom was lit, warming the room with a soft air. Dalya was about to change her clothes when someone knocked on the door.

- Come in.

It was Cristelle, the maid of the grand Mansion. She displayed as usual, a joyful smile.

- Good evening, Mademoiselle. I wanted to know if you would like a cup of tea after your Thanksgiving meal?

Actually, Cristelle knew that Dalya was stressed out because of this Thanksgiving lunch. Her relationship with her parents has worsened since she was appointed Heiress. And Cristelle was well aware of that. Therefore, the maid patiently waited for Dalya's return back home, in order to be reassured that the meal went well.

Dalya replied in a small voice:

- It would be nice, thank you.
- Understood Mademoiselle, I will make you a nice hot tea. With such a big meal on this festive day, nothing is better than a good tea for a good night's sleep!

While Dalya was changing her clothes to put on her pajamas, Cristelle added a few pieces of wood logs in the fireplace. The maid observed Dalya from afar. The little girl had a lost and sad face. And as curious as she was, Cristelle decided to find out a little more:

- I hope lunch at the annex house went well. Here, we had a thin turkey. The Cook overcooked it. But the stuffing was delici...

After a while, Cristelle stopped talking. It was clear that Dalya didn't even listen to her, she was lost in her mind and strangely silent. It was a very unusual attitude coming from Dalya. Something went wrong during the holiday meal in the annex house, thought Cristelle. After Dalya sat on her bed, Cristelle approached her:

- Is everything alright, Mademoiselle?

After a long second, Dalya answered with a convinced voice:

- Cristelle ... I think I understand why my mother always treated me so cruelly.

Of all the eventualities that Cristelle thought about, this answer was far from what she expected. Cristelle sat on the side of the bed and she asked:

- How do you know that, Mademoiselle?

Dalya explained what she discovered that day:

- Earlier on, I watched how my grandmother treated my mother. She screamed at her, she criticized everything that she cooked, she humiliated and demeaned her, she even pinched her cheek, because of a lie that my uncle said. Cristelle ... the way my grandmother treated my mother ... it was exactly the same way my mother treated me! ... The same words, the same pinching cheeks, the same tone of voice, the same meanness and injustice, the same diabolic look ...

Cristelle was surprised at what she was hearing; she lost her words, and her eyes looked shocked. Dalya continued:

- So ... I think that ... I think that my grandmother's education was the only way my mother knew how to raise me ... I understand why she was cruel to me.

Immediately, Cristelle jumped from the side of the bed:

- Oh but no, Mademoiselle! Your logic is very wrong! ... I allow myself to correct you on that! ... nothing should justify the meanness! ... nothing should justify violence! ... we shouldn't give excuses for cruelty!

Dalya thought for a moment, and then she asked:

- Even though my mother was, herself, raised in a cruel way? ... It's not her fault that she was tough and cruel with me ...

Cristelle explained in a sure tone:

- But Mademoiselle ... If your mother was cruelly raised by your grandmother, it gives her no right to abuse you in the same way! ... We all have our own brain, we must learn to differentiate the other peoples' mistakes and not repeat them!!

On this point, Dalya confessed that Cristelle was well right. If her mother suffered from the education of her grandmother, she shouldn't have inflicted on Dalya the same pain she herself suffered.

However, a final thought preoccupied Dalya's mind, and she asked Cristelle:

- But ... my mother cooked and cleaned the house for us ... so I shouldn't complain of her cruelty ... she did many things for me and my littl...

Cristelle dared to interrupt Dalya at once; she seemed determined to clear up the misconceptions of the little girl:

-   Certainly not, Mademoiselle! ... It's not because your mother fed you and washed your clothes, that she had the right to abuse you ... cruelty is nastiness, period. I am sorry to correct you, but nothing justifies or excuses the cruel attitude of your mother. And above all ... nothing should keep us silent about violence, no matter what the abuser do for us!

As sad as the truth may be, Dalya had to admit that Cristelle's answers were logical and right. Cruelty should never be justified or excused or protected!

Cristelle observed Dalya for a long second. And for the first time ever, the maid had pity on the little girl. Cristelle dared to say in a sad tone:

-   Mademoiselle ... I don't know how you survived the violence and abuse of your mother ... I can't imagine what she made you go through ... and I can't understand why your mother was so cruel and mean to such a lovely girl like you ... but, one thing I am sure about, you are so different from her ... and fortunately by the way!

Dalya smiled sadly, without finding any words to say. Cristelle dared to hug the little girl firmly, and she whispered to Dalya:

-   How strange it is, that sometimes beautiful roses can be born amidst the cruelest thorns.

Chapter 50

Ghosts

The day after Thanksgiving. Friday, November 25th, 1892. In the kitchen of the Grand Mansion. At the end of the afternoon.

The Cook was preparing tonight's dinner. Mr. Ferrero Lutché thought aloud:

- The soup is ready ... the slices of bread are cut ... the mixture of olive oil and herbs is ready ... I have only the plates and cutlery to arrange and ... Mademoiselle's tray to prepare ...

The Cook took out the plates to put them down on the large kitchen table, when suddenly; he remembered les Madeleines cakes in the oven:

- How dizzy am I! ... One more minute and Les Madeleines would have burned!

Dalya Bouvard enjoyed Madeleines cakes with tea in the late afternoon or with milk for breakfast. And the Cook always made sure to prepare a dozen a week, just for her. After removing Les Madeleines out of the oven, the Cook detached them from the mold; he placed them on a large plate, to cool down, before spreading the peach jam above.

The Cook finished arranging the dinner table for the employees, and Dalya dinner tray. Then, Mr. Ferrero decided to wash all the towels and cloths, outside the kitchen.

The end of the afternoon was very quiet and serene. The wind breezes were few. The gray clouds decorated the sky. The sun showed off softer and less intense colors.

Few minutes later, the Cook came back inside the kitchen, thinking aloud:

- The employees will be coming soon ... Mademoiselle Dalya must be hungry by this hour ... I'd better spread the mixture of oil and herbs on bread, and warm th...

When suddenly, the Cook stood paralyzed in front of the kitchen counter.

- But ... what ... where are ... but ... who took all the Madeleines?!!

With horror and astonishment, the Cook discovered that the big plate of Madeleines cakes, was completely empty!! All the Madeleines were gone!! No one has ever dared to steal anything from the kitchen, ever before. None of the employees, not even Igor who was often very hungry. And it was certainly not Dalya Bouvard; she always politely asked for a second serving, she would never have taken all the Madeleines.

The Cook remained shocked and frozen, in front of the empty plate:

- Who took all my Madeleines?! ... who?

A few minutes later. In the corridor of the upper floor of the Grand Mansion.

Every day at 7:00 PM sharp, the head of the grand Mansion took care of lighting all the candles of the grand Mansion. First, Mr. Bûchebois would lit the lamps of the lower floor which included the living room and the Library, and then the lamps of the upper floor which included the corridors and Mademoiselle's bedroom.

When Mr. Bûchebois made sure all the lamps were lit in Dalya's bedroom, he took one last glance at the room, before closing the door, and he continued to turn on the corridors' lights.

Suddenly, Mr. Bûchebois heard footsteps walking down the corridor. Turning right and left, Mr. Bûchebois couldn't see anyone. And that was weird. The footsteps sounded very clear. The head of the grand Mansion thought aloud:

- That must be my hunger imagining things ...

Seconds later, before closing the glass on a lit lamp, all of a sudden, the head of the grand Mansion jumped when he heard clear laughs and giggles. It seemed like little kids were laughing in the corridor. Except that ... one, there was nobody in the corridor, besides Mr. Bûchebois. And two, there were no children in the grand Mansion!

Mr. Bûchebois froze in his moves, and he turned all pale. Never in all his years of service in the grand Mansion, he never heard voices in an empty corridor.

Yet, Mr. Bûchebois pulled himself together, and he forced himself to light a 4th lamp in the corridor, thinking aloud with a trembling voice:

- It's just a trick of my mind ... it's just hunger imagining things ...

As soon as he finished his sentence, a clear sound of running steps and happy laughs, was heard in the corridor. Children voice was repeating aloud:

- Cakes!! ... Cakes!! ... Cakes!!

At this moment, the head of the grand Mansion fell to the ground, petrified and frozen. His legs held him no more, his throat tightened, his face turned pale, Mr. Bûchebois was trembling flesh and bones, looking right and left at the empty corridor:

- Who ... who ... who ... who is the ... the ... who is there?

Chapter 51

Chess Pawns: the Knight and the King

Monday, November 28th, 1892. At the Toscana restaurant.

After the end of a court hearing, Sloan Wilfrid and Lyor Laszlo went to the Toscana restaurant for lunch. Sitting in their usual table in front of the large windows of the restaurant, the two men waited for their meal. Lyor was correcting a few words in his notebook, while Wilfrid got busy reading a particular manual.

When they got served their salads, Lyor began to eat. Wilfrid was so absorbed in reading his manual; he seemed confused and serious. For the first time since ever, Sloan Wilfrid didn't care to eat. Curious and worried, Lyor asked him:

- What is going on?

Sloan Wilfrid put down his book in a frustrated move, and he sighed:

- Last night, I used the best Chess pawns ... the Knight and the King ... it's supposed to be the strongest pawns ... I applied the exact strategy in this book ... I was sure I would win against Mr. Ernest Laszlo ... and yet, I lost in less than 15 minutes!

Holding with difficulty an amused laugh, Lyor continued eating his salad:

- He is unbeatable Wilfrid! ... I told you that many times ... you tire yourself playing against an expert ... He is seriously unbeatable!

It is true that Lyor Laszlo had repeatedly warned Sloan Wilfrid, about his father's perfect mastery of the Chess game. With or without the best strategy manual, Ernest Laszlo was unbeatable at the Chess game.

Sloan Wilfrid lay back on his chair, and he started eating his salad. Except that after a few minutes of silence, Wilfrid put down his fork; he took on his manual, and he exclaimed with a decided tone:

- Nobody is unbeatable, Lyor! ... Nobody!

Chapter 52

Lyor's decision

Tuesday, November 29th, 1892. In the Law Firm.

It was a gray day. The sky was invaded by black and filled clouds. The wind was blowing hard, shaking the branches and leaves. A storm announced its coming very soon.

The activity in the Law Firm was noisy. All the employees were busy in their work. All the desks were packed with files, folders and papers.

Sloan Wilfrid has asked Dalya to visit him in the office after the Thanksgiving holiday. Aware of the difficult relationship between Dalya and her parents, Sloan Wilfrid wanted to be informed and reassured of Dalya's wellbeing. Since the first time he had met her, Wilfrid was watching over her, just like he had promised.

When Sloan Wilfrid headed toward the counter to serve himself some coffee, an unusual presence in the Law Firm, caught his attention. Mr. Eliott was leaving the lawyer Mr. Ernest Laszlo's office. Mr. Eliott and Mr. Ernest greeted each other, and they exchanged an accomplice smile.

And it wasn't certainly just a courtesy visit. For Mr. Eliott to come in the Law Firm, it had to be an important and urgent matter, Sloan Wilfrid thought. There have been some strange visits at the office, since several months now. Wilfrid tried by every way to learn more about these strange visits, but he didn't succeed. While observing Mr. Eliott leaving the office, Wilfrid thought:

- *There is something going on ... it doesn't feel good ...*

When suddenly, a little voice interrupted Sloan Wilfrid from his thoughts. Dalya Bouvard greeted him with her usual smile:

- Good morning Mademoiselle Dalya! It's always a pleasure to see you!
- Good morning Mr. Wilfrid. I hope I am not disturbing you.
- On the contrary! I expected your visit. How was your Thanksgiving lunch, at the annex home?

Dalya answered as naturally as possible:

- Very well Monsieur ... very well ...

Mr. Wilfrid smiled, because he was sure that Dalya was hiding the truth. He insisted to know:

- I hope that there were no incidents ... no mean attitude that has upset you, Mademoiselle?

Dalya tried to reassure Mr. Wilfrid with an honest smile:

- No, Monsieur ... there was no incident.

And this time, Dalya didn't lie. There were no incidents ... toward her! But what her mother had endured from her own family during this holiday meal, Dalya was still struggling to believe it. And yet, Dalya decided to keep it a secret and not to speak of it to Mr. Wilfrid. The Lawyer was hard to convince:

- I guess your parents understood the lesson ... once and for all?
- Yes, Monsieur. My father was busy discussing the renovation work with my Aunt's husband ... and my mother was ... she was busy serving the Thanksgiving meal!

A reassured smile displayed on Wilfrid's face; his threats were understood by the Bouvard parents, and he was pleased that Dalya was safe and sound.

- And what about your parents' guests? ... Your mother's family... Did they behave civilly?

Although Dalya was surprised by this question, she tried to answer naturally:

- Yes, Monsieur ... my mother's family ... my grandmother is ... nice ... and my maternal uncle is ... is ... nice ... my Aunt is ... also nice ... my Aunt's husband is ... very nice ...

While leaning on a corridor wall, Sloan Wilfrid retained with difficulty his amused laugh. It was clear that Dalya was a bad liar. The only qualifier she found to describe her mother's family, was nice. Four nice people in the same sentence, it was funny and weird. Yet, Dalya continued:

- My little cousin Hugo is quiet and polite. My little sisters are happy to have a good company to play with.

Wilfrid smiled:

- I'm delighted for your little sist....

Suddenly, an angry footsteps sound interrupted the conversation of Sloan Wilfrid and Dalya in the corridor of the Law Firm.

The young Lyor Laszlo was working quietly in his private office. He had just finished his argument for a case, and he was checking his work one last time.

When all of a sudden, the door of Lyor's office opened like a thunder. Mr. Ernest Laszlo asked in an accusing tone:

- Have you talked to the Manager of the Perlman Company?

Lyor stood up immediately:

- I met Mr. John Perlman before yesterday, at the Toscana resta...

Mr. Ernest Laszlo was impatient:

- Did you speak to him? Yes or no?
- Yes, we had a brief conversation before lunc...

The young Lyor didn't understand why his father was upset at a simple conversation. Mr. Perlman was a Manager of a Company belonging to BalthEnterprise. And at the Toscana restaurant, Lyor and Mr. Perlman met unexpectedly, and they had a brief but pleasant conversation. Mr. Ernest Laszlo exclaimed with an upset tone:

- And how dare you speak to a Manager?

The question seemed somewhat weird to Lyor:

- I've known Mr. Perlman since long time ago ... his son studied with me at the Colle...

Mr. Ernest interrupted him with a cold voice:

- I don't care if you have studied with his mother!! ... Did you advise him an internal recruitment for the new post of technical chief?

Sloan Wilfrid who was still standing in the corridor with Dalya, he had heard the conversation between the father and his son. Dalya didn't dare to move, but Wilfrid came close to Lyor's office and he tried to calm the situation:

- It was a brief conversation of 2 minutes only, Mr. Ern...

Except that Lyor decided to defend himself with a convinced strong tone:

- Yes, I did advise him an internal recruitment for the post of technical chief. An employee already knows the workflow and the workers' management, better and faster than an external person ... it will save Mr. Perlman so much time to form an externa...

Wilfrid tried to place a word, but he failed in front of Mr. Ernest Laszlo who exploded in anger:

- I HAVE HAD ENOUGH REPEATING IT TO YOU! ... YOU ARE AN INCAPABLE AND YOU KNOW NOTHING ABOUT MANAGEMENT! ... STICK THAT WELL IN YOUR HEAD, LYOR! ... YOU ARE NOT MANAGING BALTHENTERPRISE! ... AND YOU NEVER WILL! ... I'M THE ONLY DECISION MAKER! ... I AM THE ONLY AND THE LEGITIMATE RESPONSIBLE OF BALTHENTERPRISE! HOW MANY TIMES DO I HAVE TO REPEAT IT TO YOU!

After Mr. Ernest Laszlo left the office and slammed the door with a brusque move, Lyor Laszlo sat back on his chair with a crushed air.

Apart the anger scene of Mr. Ernest Laszlo, there was something very strange in the words of the Lawyer. Everyone, including you, dear reader ... you have very well read the Will of the

Late Mr. Governor ... Iskander Balthazar had appointed a sole and legitimate responsible of BalthEnterprise. Isn't it right?

Lyor had never been so angry in his life, up to this day. Yet, when Sloan Wilfrid opened the door of Lyor's office, he found the young apprentice calmly sitting in front of his desk, still in shock of his father's words. Sloan Wilfrid tried to play down the situation:

- It's a simple misunderstanding Lyor ... nothing is your fault ... I remember that it was Mr. Perlman who asked your opinion on the subject ... don't take at heart everything Monsieur Ernest say ... don't be ups...

Except that at this precise moment, Sloan Wilfrid stopped talking, he noticed that the young Lyor was staring at a silhouette standing by the office door. Dalya Bouvard.

Strangely calm, Lyor observed Dalya for many long tense seconds, with a furious stare. Dalya didn't dare to move or ask why was Lyor looking at her that way. When Lyor finally spoke, with a calm cold voice:

- She is the source of all my problems.

Instantly, Lyor took a paper and he started writing. Dalya was confused by Lyor's accusation, she instantly replied:

- But I didn't say anything ... I didn't do anything ... I haven't said a word!

Sloan Wilfrid understood Lyor's accusation. He walked close to Lyor's desk, and he explained to him in a calm and serious voice:

- She's not responsible for what is happening, Lyor. She didn't choose to be in this Will.

Lyor ignored his mentor, and he kept on writing. Given Lyor's silence, Wilfrid continued:

- I understand perfectly well your anger and your unease. But if you can be a little more patient, there are only a few more Challenges left. And she seems smart enough to succ...

Suddenly, Lyor stood up; he handed Wilfrid a paper, and he announced with a happy voice:

- Today and now … I am solving my problem, once and for all!

Worried about the strange attitude of his apprentice, Wilfrid read the content of the paper that Lyor handed him:

Hereby, I undersigned, Lyor Laszlo, officially and unquestionably withdraw from the responsibility of the "Will" of the Late Mr. Governor Iskander Balthazar. I give all the management rights to my father, Mr. Ernest Laszlo.

Wilfrid was struck by what he read:

- But ... Lyor ... you can't do this ... it's not legal ... you know the Law ... you have no choice but to remain her legal guardian ...

Lyor Laszlo let out a happy laugh:

- Wrong! It's perfectly legal! Last week casa, the Lawyer has asked to be excused from this function!
- Yes, but the Lawyer had a chronic illness that prevented him from continuing to represent his nephew! Replied Wilfrid.
- At this rate, this girl will drive me to a heart attack!! Lyor answered in an angry tone.

Dalya's heart tightened but what was happening in front of her; Lyor Laszlo will withdraw from the Will, and he will not be her legal guardian anymore. It is true that Lyor's character was difficult and hard, but it was a much more moderate character than that of his father. The idea that Mr. Ernest Laszlo would be her legal guardian frightened Dalya. She came close to Wilfrid, and trembled:

- But ... he cannot do this ... his name was in the Will ... I didn't say a word today ... I didn't do anything today ...

Wilfrid turned around and he gave an encouraging smile to Dalya. He understood Dalya's fear. What Lyor was about to do, would make the situation even more complicated for Dalya. Sloan Wilfrid took a long breath, and he addressed Lyor with a calm tone:

- Listen to me, Lyor ... we have to respect the last wishes of Gov...
- You ask me to respect his wishes at the expense of my career? Of my life? ... Wilfrid, I remind you that since the beginning of this matter, I have lost the bit of esteem from my father! He doesn't give me anymore files to manage!
- And I understand that perfectly well, Lyor. But believe me; retreating from the Will, it will only make things even worse!
- On the contrary, if I retreat from the Will, I won't be in a constant confrontation with my father, every single day because of BalthEnterprise!! And he can manage it as he pleases, without forcing me to sign sales contracts of factories!!

For the first time since long, Sloan Wilfrid was worried. All his words failed to convince the young Lyor Laszlo to reverse his decision. Yet, Wilfrid tried every possible argument:

- Lyor ... I am asking you, not as a tutor ... but as a friend ... don't do this ... you don't know the consequences of your decision ...
- I have no choice, Wilfrid. My career will be ruined!
- Can you at least wait until next week? ... We will think about it, in a more relaxed and calmer way? ... Please ...
- My decision is made Wilfrid! Lyor announced in a strong convinced tone.

At that moment, the young Lyor opened the door of his office and he asked the courier:

- Jack ... I need you for a second!

Under the worried and anxious looks of Dalya and Wilfrid, a young man came into Lyor's office. And he ordered him:

- This letter is to be legalized and sent to Court today! ... Don't come back to the office without having done it!
- Understood, Mr. Lyor! Right away!

Several hours later. In the grand Mansion.

As expected, a rain storm struck Georgetown city that night. The sound of dripping water, soaking the city in a quiet dark. The winter cold was becoming more and more present. Some thunder broke out occasionally, to remind you of the heavenly force.

In a bedroom of the grand Mansion, the fireplace was lit and well charged. Dalya Bouvard sat on the edge of a large window, admiring the view of the rain, listening to the lively fire in the fireplace. The snow Panther lying down in front of the fireplace, was watching Dalya with a worried look. Séraphine felt the anxiety of the little girl. Dalya had a thousand questions and worries in her brain:

- *I didn't say anything earlier, I didn't say a word ... it was not my fault that Mr. Ernest Laszlo reprimanded his son Lyor ... I didn't do anything ... but why Lyor decided to pour his anger on me? ... Why is he retreating from the Will? ...*

And a new subject preoccupied her mind:

- *And why does Mr. Ernest Laszlo treats his son so viciously? ... It's true that Lyor is often impatient and not so polite ... but he seems to be a great worker, and Mr. Wilfrid always tells me that Lyor is honest and smart ... so then, why does Mr. Ernest Laszlo humiliates and demeans his son Lyor at every possible opportunity? ... And what is the reason of the conflict between Lyor and his father? ... it must be serious and important for Lyor to decide to abandon his responsibility in the Will ...*

The night promised to be long, and Dalya's worries were growing:

- *If Lyor withdraws from the Will, everything will change ... I should answer directly to Mr. Ernest Laszlo ... I should submit to his orders ... I can hardly bear the temperament of Mr. Ernest Laszlo, his dark eyes, his humiliating remarks, his mean attitudes ... and to have him as legal guardian, it will be a real torture ...*

Sleep was slow to come. Dalya was worried and anxious; Lyor's decision would have a hard impact on her life. And although Mr. Wilfrid tried to reassure her that he would do his best to convince Lyor to reverse his decision, Dalya was afraid that it was impossible. Lyor seemed very angry and decided to abandon his role as her legal guardian!

Several minutes of silence later, Dalya felt a migraine. Because all these worries were too heavy for the brain of a little girl. And what the upcoming days announced ... was disturbing!

Dalya decided to return to her bed.

- *It is useless to worry now ... what is done is done ... Lyor has already decided ... and anyway, there is nothing I can do to fix things ... next week, Lyor will not be my legal guardian anymore, even before I answer the Third ques...*

When all of a sudden, Dalya stopped in front of her small desk. It is hard to believe how a small item could change the path of an entire life ... not only that of a little girl, but of so many other people. Although immobile and silent, the Excelbox radiated an unfailing wisdom and unnatural strength.

Under the light of the night, the box revealed its treasures and it was reloading. In a shiny metal, the Excelbox exuded an unbeatable force. On the edge, a small rectangular opening was always open and welcoming all doubts and questions. On the top side of the box, a transparent and light glass cage, in an oval form, stood up majestically. The cage being welded by four cylinders, in yellow gold forged in a shape of vine plant. The round clock inside the transparent cage indicated that night's date in its big needle:

$$November\ 29^{th},\ 1892$$

The small needle of the clock was fixed on a date that worried Dalya, increasingly:

$$December\ 12^{th},\ 1892$$

In all its splendor, the Excelbox was a fascinating and intimidating item. While observing the strange box, Dalya thought:

- *Could the Excelbox have a solution? A clue about what will happen in the upcoming days?*

Dalya approached the strange box, and she wrote with a trembling hand on a small paper:

$$What\ is\ the\ 4^{th}\ clue?$$

As soon as placed on the opening, the paper was swallowed inside. The Excelbox seemed eager to unveil her wisdom. A blinding light invaded the cage in an instant. And a small paper appeared on the opened edge of the box.

$$How\ long,\ the\ pressure,\ a\ heart\ will\ bear?$$

$$3,\ 5$$

At that moment, the snow Panther stood up and approached the little girl. Dalya sighed:

- How long a heart will bear the pressure? ... Sometimes less than we think ...

With a sad move, Dalya put down the paper on her desk, and she went back to sleep. Or at least hoping to sleep fast and calm the whirlwind of worry in her mind.

Except that this time, Dalya wasn't aware of a little important detail. The heart is an incredibly powerful organ. And as difficult as it is to believe, the pressure can sometimes be the best thing that could happen to us.

After providing the 4th clue, the Excelbox returned to its previous calm, reloading at the night's light. However, under its peaceful and silent air, the Excelbox predicted a tomorrow … much greater and larger than your own imagination ... dear reader.

Chapter 53

Disappeared

Thursday, December 01ˢᵗ, 1892. In the kitchen of the Royal Georgetown College.

Amira was peeling apples, sitting in her usual place of detention in the school kitchen. When suddenly, she jumped out of her chair:

- Maybe the Lawyer Ernest Laszlo will be so busy with the business of his Law Firm ... he will ask Monsieur Sloan Wilfrid to be your legal guardian!

Near her friend Amira, Dalya was sitting on a small stool:

- I don't know ... I hope so!! ... Anyway, Lyor was determined to let me down ... he wouldn't even listen to Mr. Wilfrid!! ... I didn't sleep at night ... Mr. Ernest Laszlo is 10 times worse than Lyor!

Amira took another apple to peel, and she exclaimed:

- Don't worry about Mr. Ernest! ... Trust Mr. Wilfrid, he has promised you to resolve the situation ... Everything will be fine ... Mr. Wilfrid had always protected and watched over you, and he will not stop now!

Dalya seemed worried by the turn of the events. But she was somewhat reassured by the words and encouragements of her friend Amira Mounier.

In the school kitchen, Dalya's task to complete her detention, was to shape the dough butter and take out of it the rest of the cream. The Cook Chef showed her the movement to do, and it was very simple; kicking strongly and straightaway toward the dough, so as to empty it of all the cream. And although her arms and hands ached at the beginning of this detention, Dalya didn't feel any more pain now.

At a moment, while peeling an apple, Amira began humming happily and discreetly:

- Our last week of detention ... our last week ... lalala ... lalala ... our last week of our detention ... lalala ... lalala ...

A smile escaped out of Dalya:

- I am happier than you are, Amira! ... I had painful detentions to do!

Amira thought aloud:

- Yes, I admit! ... Between cutting rice in two, arranging the Pantry on a slippery ground, counting the lentils ... you suffered the worst detentions ever!!

Dalya let out a discreet laugh:

- I would have loved to see Gael Benoble arranging the Pantry on the slippery floor, with a bucket of water on his head!

Without being able to retain her laugh, Amira replied:

- It would be so much fun to see! He wouldn't hold a second on his feet! ... And imagine if Lakita had to cut the rice in two?!

Dalya gave strong knocks to the dough butter, while laughing:

- She would surely have lost her power of observation and reporting back what she sees! ... It's a detention task that would have served to change her fault!

Amira and Dalya laughed a long moment. And luckily Dalya had some good company; she would not have managed to achieve the detentions alone. The moments of laughs and giggles with her Amira Mounier, made the detentions' hours went faster.

Later in the afternoon, in the Grand Mansion.

At 6:00 PM, after the end of her classes at school, Dalya returned to the grand Mansion. Tired from a long day of classes and detention, Dalya walked up to her bedroom to change her school uniform and take a nap before dinner.

When she arrived in her bedroom, Dalya put down her school bag on a chair in the living room. And before walking to the dressing room, suddenly, Dalya froze. She had noticed a strange thing. Dalya stepped back, and she walked toward the little living room. Usually placed there, a small item was no longer on her office desk...

At 8:00 PM. In the Grand Mansion.

Sloan Wilfrid entered the grand Mansion, with hurried steps. He had come as quickly as he could, after the Gardener of the grand Mansion, had left an urgent message for him, in the Law Firm.

When Wilfrid entered the living room of the grand Mansion, he noticed Dalya sitting on a chair surrounded by all the employees of the house. At first glance, Sloan Wilfrid noticed the worried and anxious state of Dalya, her face was pale and her hands trembled.

The Employees of the grand Mansion greeted Mr. Wilfrid, and they all had a troubled mine. Sloan Wilfrid realized that a serious concern was hanging over the grand Mansion, this evening. He approached Dalya and he gave her an encouraging smile:

- Good evening, Mademoiselle ... I came as soon as I got a message ... what's happening?

Dalya's entire body was shaking. And it looked like she needed a considerable effort to pronounce her words:

- It ... it disappeared ... Monsieur Wilfrid ... it disappeared ...

Wilfrid didn't exactly understand the information given by the little Dalya Bouvard, he insisted in a curious tone:

- What has disappeared?

Gathering her strength, Dalya whispered in a choked voice:

- The Excelbox disappeared!

The news was so shocking for Sloan Wilfrid, he could barely stand up. He sat on the nearest chair. Of all the possible problems, Sloan Wilfrid never thought he would face such a situation. A confused and shocked laugh escaped from him:

- The ... the Excelbox disappeared?!

Long seconds later, the lawyer pulled himself together with difficulty, and he asked Dalya in a serious tone:

- Did you carry it somewhere? Did you move it somewhere else other than in your bedroom? The grand Mansion's library? ... Did you forget it at school? Or maybe it's with your friend Amira?

Dalya became paler:

- No Monsieur ... since I've been living in the grand Mansion, I never moved the Excelbox from the office desk in my bedroom!

Sloan Wilfrid turned around to the employees. The head of the grand Mansion answered Wilfrid's question, even before the young Lawyer would say it. Mr. Bûchebois said with a serious voice:

- I vouch the honesty and integrity of all the employees working in the grand Mansion, Monsieur Wilfrid. Never any of us would be able to steal anything.

The lawyer replied with a polite smile:

- I have no doubt of that, Mr. Bûchebois. So is it possible that this box could have been stolen by an intruder?

The Gardener was the first to reply in a sure tone:

- I don't think so, Monsieur. The grand Mansion is well guarded, and nobody comes or goes out here, without anyone knowing it.

For a second, Sloan Wilfrid wondered aloud:

- It is possible that the thief got inside ... late at night ...

The head of the grand Mansion informed the young Lawyer:

- I make sure myself that all doors and windows are closed at night.

Sloan Wilfrid looked confused in his ideas:

- The Excelbox disappeared ... it has been stolen ... but how? ... and by whom?

Cook stated with a grave tone:

- Monsieur Wilfrid ... no item was ever stolen from the grand Mansion, since the time we were working here ... never such an incident has happened before!

Igor joined the discussion:

- And even assuming that the thief was able to enter the grand Mansion ... you all forget about Séraphine! ... The snow Panther prevents small snakes from entering the garden ... so a thief won't even make it ... nobody can escape from Séraphine!

The employees of the grand Mansion and the young Lawyer agreed with Igor. For a few seconds of thinking, Wilfrid thought aloud:

- So then ... this box might still be here, in the grand Mansion?

Cristelle replied in a trembling voice:

- It's just ... Monsieur, we looked everywhere in the grand Mansion ... we've searched all the rooms and the places ...

Instantly, Sloan Wilfrid stood up, and he ordered all the employees with a grave serious voice:

- Search again and again!! Day and night!! Every corner, every room, in the attic, at the bottom of the chimneys, in the garden ... this box has to be found!! Our future of all of us, depend on it!!

Chapter 54

One worry at a time

Friday, December 02nd, 1892. At the Royal Georgetown College.

This December morning was busy for all the students of the Royal Georgetown College. The exams of this semester were starting in all the classrooms, and in all levels. On the stairs and around the corridors, students had their noses glued to their books, trying to remember everything they could before the start of the exams.

A little silhouette stood outside the Mathematics classroom. Easily known with her long braids of light brown hair, Amira Mounier repeated in a low voice:

- A to the power 1 equals A ... A to the power 0 equals 1 ... 0 to the power N equals 0 ... 1 to the power 5 equals ... Good morning Dalya!! You are on time to review with me the Ma...

When Dalya Bouvard appeared in the school corridor, her friend Amira immediately asked her in a worried tone:

- You have dark circles and puffy red eyes ... what happened to you? Is everything alright?

Dalya had not slept a wink the entire previous night. She tried to answer in a natural voice:

- I ... I'm just a little tired.

This time, Dalya failed to perfectly lie. Instantly, Amira firmly took Dalya by the hand, and she led her toward the girls' bathroom. As soon as they were inside, Amira made sure that the bathrooms were empty, before turning toward her friend:

- Dalya ...you don't look just tired ... you're whacked!! ... You are pale, your eyes are red, and you seem not to have slept the entire n...
- The Excelbox disappeared.

These 3 words completely paralyzed Amira. She lost her voice, and recovered with difficulty:

- The strange box? ... The one that allows you to pass the Challenges ... disappeared where?

Dalya explained to her friend:

- It just disappeared ... the employees and I, we've searched for it all night ... that's why I didn't sleep at all ... I informed the Lawyer, Mr. Sloan Wilfrid ... he ordered us to continue the search for that box ... the grand Mansion has never been stolen before ... no one could have entered without passing through the snow Panther ...

When all of a sudden, Dalya choked, her throat tightened and she struggled to breathe:

- Without the Excelbox, I cannot pass the Third Challenge ... I looked everywhere ... I'm going back to my old life ... I'm going back to sleep on the kitchen floor ... my little sisters will return to our poor house with 2 rooms ... Ari and Adi ... I ... I ... I don't know where that box is ... I don... I ... I ... I ... don ... I ...don ...

Quickly, Amira led Dalya toward an opened window, and she ordered her:

- Breathe slowly, Dalya ... breathe ... slowly ... gently ... breathe ... close your eyes and breathe ... slowly ...

By following Amira's instructions, Dalya felt better after a few painful long seconds. Her breathing slowed, the fresh air appeased her panic attack, and she calmed down.

When Amira was reassured that Dalya's breathing was back to normal, she pulled out a strange little item from her bag and she gave it to Dalya with an encouraging smile:

- My best and only friend offered me this, one day ... and it helped me so much!

The item that Dalya held in her hand was familiar. Immediately, Dalya recognized it:

- This is the pressure ball of Mr. Iskander Balthazar ... I gave it you to de-stress and relieve pressure from your throat.

Amira smiled happily:

- And I still use it! ... Less to de-stress my throat, but mostly to de-stress from the exams!

A moment of complicity united the two students. Dalya squeezed the ball in her hand, and one had to admit that this hand movement made her feel good. Amira addressed her friend in a serious tone:

- Dalya ... we have a Mathematics exam, in half an hour. And like my father always tells me; let's handle one worry at a time. You have to pass this semester's exams, and you have to succeed! ... And after the exams, we will find a solution for the Excelbox problem!

Dalya felt supported and encouraged by her friend. Dalya squeezed the ball in her hand, and sighed:

- One worry at a time!

Amira answered with an enthusiastic and encouraging tone:

- Exactly! ... First, wash your face ... the cold water will wake you up.

And it was quite true. Dalya rinsed her face with cold icy water. Immediately, a freshness feeling invaded her and wiped the fatigue of the long sleepless night. Amira handed her a towel to dry her face, and she affirmed with a convinced voice:

- The employees of the grand Mansion and the Lawyer Monsieur Wilfrid, they will not let you down ... I am very sure of that! ... So let them search for that box, and focus on the exams! ... You have to succeed your semester!!

Leaving the girls' bathroom, Dalya was more motivated to pass the exams. Amira was an invaluable help to her friend. Walking toward the classroom, Amira pulled out a green apple from her bag, and she handed it to Dalya:

- Here, eat this apple ... you have one hour exam ahead of you ... 0 to the power 6 equals...?

Dalya said while chewing an apple bite:

- 0
- And 5 to the power 3 equals ...
- ... 125

The exams in the Royal Georgetown College were about to begin, in a few minutes. Dalya forced herself to focus on her answers. Because Amira Mounier's father was quite right ... Let's handle one worry at a time!

Chapter 55

A secret passage

Saturday, December 03rd, 1892. At night in the grand Mansion.

The day was very long for Dalya. One, because of her exams at school, and two because of the intense search for the Excelbox in the great Mansion. The exams were going on rather well, although Dalya had to focus all her strength on her exam papers. However, for the Excelbox...

- We will find it, Mademoiselle! ... we will find it! Cristelle repeated in a determined voice.

After Cristelle took the dinner tray and closed the bedroom door, Dalya put on her pajamas and she climbed on her bed. Her head was heavy and dizzy, her body was exhausted, and a good night sleep was required. So right away, Dalya turned off her bedside lamp.

Several minutes later, Dalya turned in her bed for the hundredth time. She hoped to have a good night sleep, but sleep was slow to come.

When suddenly, Dalya heard the creak of a wood door, and something moving in her bedroom.

- *It must be Séraphine who came inside, to lie down by the fireplace as usual.* Dalya thought.

Except that after a few seconds of silence, Dalya felt something coming up to her bed and approaching her. The snow Panther never came up to her bed before. It couldn't be Séraphine ... but so then, what was it?

Unexpectedly, the thing came close to her so fast, Dalya jumped rapidly and she fell out of her bed, on the floor. She quickly stood up and lit the bedside lamp with a trembling move. When a voice screamed all of a sudden:

- Coucou, Dindin!! Coucou, Dindin!!

Dalya's brain needed several long seconds to realize what was happening. Her little twin sisters were sitting on her bed, wearing their bright pink onesies and little shoes, their little hats didn't hold entirely their light brown curls. The little twins seemed happy to meet their older sister. They laughed simultaneously:

- Coucou, Dindin!! Coucou!! Dindin!!

Dalya sat back on her bed, and she asked in a confused voice:

- But ... what are you doing here? ... In the middle of the night? ... you should be in your bed, in the annex house! ... who brought you here to the grand Mansion? ... what are you doing here?

Ari and Adi exchanged an accomplice look, and they answered:

- We come to see you Dindin!!
- We bring this to you Dindin!!

It was only at that moment that Dalya realized her little twin sisters were holding in their hands a large plate covered with a white lace cloth. Dalya took the plate that her twin sisters handed her, and she found out a cake and a small fork. It was a strawberry charlotte cake with white cream and a cherry on top. The cake looked a little shaken, placed in reverse, and many crumbs on the side of the plate. However, Dalya took the fork, and taste it. And beside the mixed layout, the cake was very delicious.

- It's ... very very good! Dalya said between two bites.
- Yes!! Cake for you Dindin!! Cake for you Dindin!!

Dalya was touched by her sisters' kindness. The little twins jumped on the big bed, laughing happily:

- Cake for Dindin!! Cake for Dindin!!

At the 3rd bite, Dalya laughed too:

- This cake comes in a perfect timing. I needed it very much, especially after this long hard day ... between exams and my worries ... nothing is better than a delicious cake to cheer you up! ... Thank you Ari!! Thank you Adi!!

The twins stopped jumping on the big bed; they came close to their older sister, and they hugged her firmly:

- We love Dindin!! We love Dindin!!
- And I love you too!!

The little twins continued their joyful jumps on the bed. At her 5th bite of the cake, Dalya rejoiced:

- This strawberry charlotte cake is really delicious! ... I have never tasted a cak...

Dalya stopped for a moment:

- One second ... one second ... Mother never cooked this cake before?!

Turning toward the little twins, Dalya asked them with a curious voice:

- Ari ... Adi ... where did you take this cake from?

Except that before the little twins could answer, a deafening scream shook all the walls of the grand Mansion.

- AAAAAAAAAAAAAAAAAAAAAAAAAAAAAAAAHHHHHHHHHHHHHHHHHHHH!!!!!!!!!!!!

When the Cook, Mr. Ferrero Lutché entered the kitchen of the grand Mansion, he intended to double check that the oven door was locked. But what he found in the kitchen ... far exceeded his imagination. The Cook took a few steps inside the kitchen, his legs trembled, his hands were paralyzed, his eyes were confused, and his heart had stopped. The Cook was struggling to breathe, to think and to speak:

- What is ... but ... who ... it's ... who ... but ...

In few seconds, as soon as they heard the scream, the head of the grand Mansion, the Gardener, Cristelle and Igor, they all appeared on the kitchen door. They were all in pajamas and night robes. And they were all shocked by what they found:

- Good Lord!! ... But what happened?
- It's as if a storm passed through here!!
- Who could have done this?
- I've checked all the doors!! Everything is double closed!!
- I haven't heard anyone come in here!! How did such a thing happen?

The kitchen of the Grand Mansion was upside down, entirely. All the chairs were removed, all the spice jars were opened and overturned, the kitchen towels and cloths were all dirty and crumpled, the ground was covered with spilled milk and oils, drawers were opened without any exception, all the vegetables were scattered on the table, all the fruit seemed to be bitten ... never the kitchen of the grand Mansion has been in such a state!

On the upper floor, in her bedroom, Dalya froze when she heard the deafening scream that shook the entire grand Mansion. And immediately, Dalya asked again her little sisters, with a trembling voice:

- Ari ... Adi ... where did you take this cake from?

The amused laugh and accomplice glances between the little twins, didn't reassure Dalya. She knew that the scream was that of the Cook, Mr. Ferrero Lutché, and it came from the lower floor; which means the kitchen. For a long second of silence, Dalya observed the plate she was holding, and she asked the little twins in a worried voice:

- What did you do again?

The little twins hurried to defend themselves with all their strength and energy:

- We do nothing at all!!
- We just search fruit for Dindin ...
- And we found cake ... we tasted cake just a little.
- Good cake ... yes ... very good ...
- So we took just the cake!!
- And after looking for forky ...
- Forky hard to find!
- And we took forky ...

273

- That's all!!
- We touch nothing more!!

All the arguments of the little twins only increased Dalya's worry:

- Please tell me that you didn't turn the kitchen of the grand Mansion upside down!

The little twins announced in a serious tone:

- Not at all!! We just took the cake and forky for Dindin!!
- That's all!! Just cake!! We touch nothing more!

Despite being sure of the disaster caused by her younger sisters, Dalya couldn't help but have an uncontrollable laugh. And for several minutes, the three girls, sitting on the big bed, laughed aloud, all while eating the cake.

Some moment later, Dalya stood up from the bed:

- It's time I take you back home ... it's late.

The little twins came down from the bed too. Dalya went toward her bedroom's door:

- Come on, I will walk you to the annex house ...

Except that the little twins walked toward the opposite side of the bedroom, and they announced with a cheerful voice:

- Yes!! Back home!! Back home!!

Dalya was holding her bedroom's door wide open:

- Come on now, the annex house is this way ... follow me.

The twins stepped a little more to the opposite side of the room:

- Yes this way!! This way!!

Dalya was confused of what her little sisters wanted, she explained to them:

- Where you are going is toward the bathroom and the dressing room ... the annex house is over here ... we will go down to the hall and go out through the front door of the grand Mansion ... come on, follow me!

Except that, the little twins had another plan. In front of the refusal of their older sister, the twins walked toward Dalya, and they pulled her by her pajamas to the opposite side of her bedroom.

- This way home, Dindin!! This way home, Dindin!!

Being forced to follow them, Dalya explained:

274

- No, there is only the bathroom and the dressing room here ...

When the twins reached the wanted place, Dalya affirmed:

- You see now? ... there is just the bathroom and dressi...

Before she could finish her sentence, Dalya was surprised by her little sisters' moves. Ari and Adi walked toward a gray marble wall separating the bathroom and the dressing room. They easily opened a large square on the wall, and they disappeared inside of it. Dalya immediately followed them:

- But ... what is this? ... A passage in the wall? ... How did you know about it? ... Where does it lead?

The little twins laughed joyfully, they seemed to know that passage since a long time. It was a long, well-built corridor. Several torches were lit at the slightest step. The little twins advanced into the passage and Dalya followed them. Several steps and stairs later, the little twins stopped in front of a small door. They discreetly pushed it outward, and within seconds, Dalya and her sisters found themselves ... in the annex house!

Dalya barely repressed her surprise, for fear of waking up her parents. The little twins went up straightaway to their bedroom. Dalya put her little sisters into bed and she covered them, while whispering:

- Will there ever be a day that passes without your fooleries?

The little twins burst into malicious and accomplice giggles, while kissing their older sister:

- Good night Dindin!! Good night Dindin!!

Dalya closed the door of her younger sisters' bedroom, and so as to not get noticed, she had to take the same way back home. When she stepped inside the secret passage between the annex house and the grand Mansion, Dalya's mind was invaded by hundreds of questions:

- A secret passage! ... I would have never guessed it if Ari and Adi didn't open that door ... Yet I lived in this bedroom for a year!! ... I wonder how long since the twins knew of this passage ... are there any other passages in this grand Mansion? ... Cristelle never told me about any secret passage ... perhaps she doesn't know about it? ... And mostly why are there secret passages in this house? ... What could it be used for? ...

Chapter 56

What he took

Sunday, December 04th, 1892. At the grand Mansion.

It was dinner time. Cristelle undertook to bring the dinner tray to Océanie's bedroom. When Cristelle entered, Océanie didn't take off her gaze from the fire in the chimney, still lying down on her bed. Since several weeks now, Océanie was always lost in her thoughts. And if we didn't force her to eat, she wouldn't touch the food.

While putting down the dinner tray on a bedside table, Cristelle smiled:

- There is an excellent oat soup, tonight! ... I know you love it, Océanie ... and the Cook prepared you buttered bread slices.

Océanie continued to observe the flames of fire in the chimney. Despite her lost and silent state since several weeks, Cristelle still wasn't used to Océanie's silence. Cristelle sat on the edge of the bed near Océanie, and she put the soup bowl in Océanie's hand, to force her to eat:

- It's oats soup with honey and cramberries on top ...

Océanie didn't move, her gaze focused on the fire in front of her bed. Some tears rolled down on her cheeks. She seemed to have lost her senses and reason. Days and nights, Océanie was silent, crying until damaging her eyes. Her condition was only getting worse, despite the doctor's remedies and the employees' cares. Occasionally, Océanie would repeat the sentence "he took everything", but none of the employees of the grand Mansion could understand what Océanie meant by these words. Nobody uncovered the mystery of what could have possibly put Océanie in such a state, to the point of wanting to end her life.

So then, with a heavy heart, Cristelle took back the soup bowl from Océanie's hand, and she decided to help her eat. Océanie opened her mouth and swallowed unconsciously, without tasting or even knowing what she was eating.

After several minutes of silence, Cristelle finished to feed Océanie. And before Cristelle took away the dinner tray, Océanie murmured:

- I am an idiot ...

Cristelle jumped. It was the first time in weeks that Océanie pronounced these words. Cristelle came back near the edge of Océanie's bed. And strangely, Cristelle felt that she would soon discover Océanie's mystery. In a kind voice, Cristelle encouraged her to speak:

- What makes you say that?

With tears flowing down her cheeks, Océanie said in a trembling voice:

- Because I believed him ... because he took everything from me ... I am an idiot ...

Cristelle firmly held Océanie's hands:

- No Océanie, you are wrong, you are not an idiot! ... you may have made a mistake by trusting someone ... but that doesn't make you an idiot ... certainly not!

For some long seconds, Océanie looked at Cristelle, and she asked:

- So why did he call me his darling? ... why did he play me? ... was I just a toy for him? ... yet he knew very well that I liked him ... he promised to stay with me ... he promised to settle in with me ... and yet he played me ... why?

Cristelle couldn't answer Océanie's many questions. Except that for the first time in weeks, Cristelle understood a little more clearly what happened; Océanie had a broken heart, she liked a man, and it didn't turn out the way that Océanie wanted. Yet, Cristelle tried to cheer up her friend:

- If you think a little more about it, you will find out that this man is not worth the trouble ... even if I don't know him ... I'm sure he is a nobody!

Océanie's tears flowed abundantly, and her voice trembled:

- He ... he made me feel that I am an idiot ...
- And I repeat to you that you are wrong to think so, Océanie! ... you are not an idiot!

Océanie looked at Cristelle, and she asked her imploringly:

- Will there ever be a man who would love me? ... will there ever be a man who would want to take care of me?

Cristelle replied without hesitation:

- But of course one day a man will love you! ... and not just any man! ... a handsome, kind and generous man, who will make you happy!

And a second later, Cristelle whispered with an amused voice:

- Except that for a man to take care of you, I can't promise you that ... men don't even take care of themselves ... so to take care of someone else?! ... for cooking, cleaning and doing laundry, I cannot guarantee you that a man will know how to do these housework ... if I didn't spend my days cleaning this grand Mansion, we would be living in a cave!

Amid tears, Océanie unexpectedly let out a sudden giggle. And it was the first time since several weeks that she laughed. Cristelle was glad she could finally relieve and help Océanie. Cristelle explained to her with a caring voice:

- All the employees of the Mansion were very worried about you ... you scared us when you climbed on the roof ... even Mademoiselle Dalya was trembling ... please, don't ever do that again, Océanie ... please ... nothing is worth that you end your life for!

Océanie replied in a calm but sad tone:

- But ... he took everything ... he took everything ...

It was the only sentence that Cristelle still didn't understand. She dared to ask:

- You are still healthy and young, Océanie ... and you have our support, of all of us, the employees and even Mademoiselle ... What do you mean by he took everything from you? ... maybe I can help you, Océanie ... tell me.

Océanie hesitated for a moment, and then she dared to tell everything to Cristelle. After long minutes of listening, Cristelle's head was dizzy, her throat tightened, her face became pale, her heart was trembling. When Océanie confessed everything to her, Cristelle was so shocked by what she had heard, she dropped the bowl of soup, which crashed to the floor. Cristelle suffocated:

- Good Lord!! ... He really took everything!!

Minutes later. In the kitchen of the grand Mansion, the Cook Mr. Ferrero Lutché was serving tonight's soup in bowls. The head of the grand Mansion Mr. Bûchebois had just finished setting the plates and cutlery on the table. When the Gardener came in from the outside door, the Cook greeted him with a wide smile:

- Just in time for dinner!!

The Gardener greeted him with a head bow, and he sat on his usual place around the dinner table, before turning toward the head of the grand Mansion:

- I stored the wood logs in the garage; to avoid that rain wets any of it.

Mr. Bûchebois exclaimed:

- Excellent idea! Lighting the fire with wet wood logs is a difficult task!

At this moment, Igor joined the employees around the table. And as soon as he sat down, the head of the Mansion announced to Igor:

- The wood logs are in the garage now ... I want you to recharge all the rooms; it looks like a cold night.

Igor jumped out of his chair, and exclaimed:

- Recharge the rooms now?! ... Before dinner?!

The head of the grand Mansion and the Gardener exchanged an amused laugh. Mr. Bûchebois reassured Igor:

- No, not now! …you will do it after dinner ... you will not survive any longer if you don't eat now!
- And dinner may cool down quickly! Completed the Cook while placing on the table, a dish of red beans and tomato sauce.

Igor served himself immediately, and between 2 mouthfuls of bread, he murmured:

- This is not a buffet either ... there's only soup, buttered bread, red be...

Before Igor could continue his lamentations, he received several knocks of cloths to the head, from the Cook:

- If my dinner don't please you … vieni e cucinalo al mio posto!!

When Cristelle entered the kitchen and sat down in her seat at the table, the other employees were all busy serving themselves dinner and eating eagerly. Cristelle took her spoon and she slowly stirred her soup with a lost and worried mind. While the conversation was lively around the table.

- Pass the salt please ... the soup needs salt. The head of the employees asked.
- I've already put salt in it!! Exclaimed the Cook.
- More salt brings out the flavor of food. Explained Mr. Bûchebois.
- The bread slices are delicious with the chopped coriander ... is it the one I brought you? From the farm of Mr. Pierrefonds? Asked the Gardener.
- Yes!! Delicious Coriander!! Exclaimed the Cook. Does he have any chives?
- He planted several this year. Replied the Gardener, between two bites. Mr. Pierrefonds sprinkles them with sugar water ...
- Sugar water? Igor wondered aloud.
- So that's why the coriander was fresh and so sweet!! Screamed the Cook.
- Delicious!! Really!! Said Mr. Bûchebois.
- Yes, that's what Mr. Pierrefonds told me the other day, when I got the earth pots from his farm. The Gardener explained. Mr. Pierrefonds has many ingenious tricks to make his herbs more tast...

When a voice interrupted the conversation of the employees of the grand Mansion:

- He took everything!

The 4 men turned around toward the maid Cristelle, and they noticed her pale face and her shocked state.

- Cristelle ... is everything alright? Mr. Bûchebois asked in a worried voice.

Cristelle put down her spoon, and she looked at the employees for a long second:

- He really took everything!

None of the employees could understand her words. Cristelle announced in a sad tone:

- I finally found out why Océanie wanted to end her life!

On this news, all the employees froze in their moves. The Gardener asked in a serious voice:

- How did you know it?
- Océanie spoke to me just earlier, after I helped her eat her dinner.
- She spoke?! Wondered the Cook. It has been many weeks that she is silent!! I thought she would remain in her state forever!
- So then ... what did she say? Igor grew impatient.
- Why did she go up on the roof? Asked the head of the grand Mansion.

Cristelle took a long breath, and she announced her discovery to the employees. After several minutes, the Gardener lay back on his chair, with a serious and grave face. The Cook lost his words and went mute for the first time in his life. Igor held his head in his hands, he couldn't believe his ears. And the head of the grand Mansion crossed his arms; he never before appeared so worried and disturbed. All the employees became silent and they froze in their moves. It was difficult to recover from the news that Cristelle had just told them. The maid of the grand Mansion lay back on her chair, she repeated in a shocked state:

- He really took everything ... he really took everything ...

No one dared to eat dinner that night, in the kitchen of the grand Mansion.

Chapter 57

The Music performance

On Monday, December 05th, 1892. The morning. In the Royal Georgetown College.

It was the last exam that Dalya had to undergo this semester, and it was the most difficult one. In Music class, the exam was that each student had to play the melody in front of the entire class, and will be graded by Professor Haîyang. Despite the many hours of practice and encouragement from her friend Amira, Dalya was anxious and stressing.

In the Music classroom, all the students had arrived in advance. Some were adjusting their instruments; others reread their Music notes one last time. Dalya settled near her friend. Amira gently cleaned her violin with a silk cloth. And feeling her friend's worry, Amira reassured her:

- You played so well, the last time we practiced ... don't stress, it will be alright!

Dalya pulled out her flute and the melody paper to review it one last time:

- It's too late, I already stress.

Amira whispered to her with an amused tone:

- If you succeeded the Latin course ... then you can succeed anything in your life!

Dalya smiled; she gathered her courage and energy for this last exam. When a tall silhouette entered the classroom, the students went silent.

- Good morning everyone!

Professor Haîyang put her briefcase on her desk, and she continued:

- It is the day of your exam ... as I announce your name, please play the song melody I gave you ... The Philosopher Stone ... breathe a long shot ... play slowly ... and mostly, do your best to give the best performance possible!

Professor Haîyang sat behind her desk, and then she called the first name on the list:

- Amira Mounier.

Amira and Dalya exchanged an accomplice smile. Then, Amira took on her violin on her shoulder with one hand and her violin's bow in the other hand. She breathed a long shot, and then began to play. Under a complete silence, Amira played perfectly. She touched all the notes of the melody, without making the slightest mistake. Eriem and Gael were not thrilled

281

with Amira's performance. But Dalya was so happy about it. In all their previous rehearsals, Amira played beautifully well...

- Excellent Miss Amira ... I didn't expect any less from you ... 19/20!

When she finished, Amira's cheeks were all red and she displayed a happy smile. Professor Haîyang continued:

- Gael Benoble.

Raising his trumpet, Gael took a long breath, and then he played the melody with skillfulness. He missed a few notes, but his performance was pretty good. His presentation lasted only a few minutes, too.

- That's very well, Mr. Gael. Try to slow down next time. 17/20!

Eriem and her court showed off proud and arrogant smiles when Gael joined them.

- Salman Elpacha.

The student stood up with an average size harp. And barely had he touched it, Music notes invaded the silence of the classroom. Salman was a prodigy of this instrument, that's what Amira had explained to Dalya one day.

- Excellent Mr. Salman ... excellent ... 18/20!

Dalya's turn approached, and she was stressing increasingly. All the students had given a perfect and exemplary performance. Dalya doubted her ability to play as well as the other students.

- Eriem Eyelord.

With an arrogant and haughty air, Eriem settled behind the grand piano in the classroom. Her fingers ran through the piano keys so quickly and skillfully. She even played with her eyes closed, focusing on the Music notes. Her performance was exceptional.

- Remarkable Miss Eriem ... it was your best performance yet ... bravo ... 19/20!

All eyes followed Eriem Eyelord who joined her court, showing off a proud smile.

- Dalya Bouvard.

Hearing her name, Dalya jumped. Amira whispered to her friend:

- Do exactly as in the rehearsals ... breath and play slowly ...You can do it! You can do it!

Dalya stood up. She breathed slowly, and then she lifted her flute. Professor Haîyang straightened up on his chair to better listen. Amira smiled encouragingly to her friend. All the other students went silent, everyone was curious to see if Dalya Bouvard would succeed in playing a Music melody ... or not.

Dalya focused her eyes on the flute. And as soon as she uttered the first note, Dalya continued to play slowly and as the best as she could. She was aware of her many mistakes, some wrong notes and other forgotten ones. Dalya could clearly hear the laughs and whispers of other students. But Dalya was determined to finish playing the song, even though it was imperfect.

When finished, Dalya was all breathless and her cheeks were red. Instantly, Eriem and her court burst into an amused laugh. Gael imitated Dalya, who choked to blow the flute. A few whispers were heard:

- She butchered the melody!! Everything was wrong!!
- It will take her 10 years to learn playing the flute!!
- Did you see how she was blowing? One would have thought she would choke on her flute!
- I have never seen such a performance! It's scandalous!

When all of a sudden, a noise forced silence upon all the students. And it was a strange noise. All the students were surprised and shocked to see Professor Haîyang ... applauding!

Everyone was confused and curious, including Amira and even Dalya. They all watched Dalya play badly the melody, yet nobody understood what the teacher was applauding. Professor Haîyang answered:

- I applaud your determination, Mademoiselle ... despite that you are a beginner, you have worked hard and decided not to give up ... your playing is certainly not without mistakes and forgotten notes ... but your performance is more than what I've expected ... 10,5/20!

Dalya was shocked and surprised by Professor Haîyang's grade and comment. She was so sure to get a zero!

Back to her seat, Amira whispered all happy to her friend:

- Congratulations!! You passed!!
- But ... I made many mistakes ... I forgot many notes ... I didn't play the tune correctly ... I distorted much of the melody ... I didn't d...

Amira interrupted her:

- The Professor gave you 10,5/20!! It's not the best grade in the class, but you have passed this course ... so don't try to understand more than there is!

While Dalya Bouvard was delighted and surprised she didn't fail her exam, a discreet proud smile displayed on the lips of Professor Haîyang. The performance was imperfect, certainly ... but thanks to the sound of the played melodies, Professor Haîyang could weigh the strength of Dalya's fingers. Professor Haîyang's smile confirmed that the fingers of Dalya Bouvard have been reinforced ... not to play the flute instrument, but for an entirely other thing!

Chapter 58

35 300 dollars

The same day, Monday, December 05th, 1892. The evening. In the grand Mansion.

Océanie was lying down on her bed, observing the fire in the Chimney in a worried stare:

- *What should I do now? ... It took me a lifetime to collect that sum of money ... they urgently need it for this winter ... what should I do now? ... What do I tell them? ...*

When the bedroom door opened, Océanie paused in her thoughts. Cristelle walked toward her, carrying a tray:

- I prepared for you hot chocolate ... and the Cook affirmed to me that these muffins were delicious!

Océanie thanked Cristelle with a sad smile. She would always be indebted to Cristelle and all the employees of the grand Mansion, for taking care of her during her illness. When Cristelle put the tray on the bedside table, another silhouette entered the bedroom.

- How are you feeling today, Océanie? Asked the head of the grand Mansion.

But before Océanie could answer, Cristelle exclaimed:

- But she is so much better, Monsieur Bûchebois! Look at her pink cheeks that are appearing!
- Your recovery is reassuring, Océanie. The head of the grand Mansion smiled.

A silhouette appeared in the doorway:

- There will be fish soup with vermicelli, tonight for dinner! The Cook announced proudly.

A voice appeared behind him:

- Soup again! Are you serious? But I need something to chew! Protested Igor, who entered the bedroom with an upset step.

The Cook stared at Igor with an angry look:

- Oh! ... Sorry not to cook a buffet for you ... your Highness!
- I've lost so much weight these past weeks! Exclaimed Igor.
- I brought some oregano ... I've put it on the kitchen counter. Announced the Gardener, bowing his head to greet the employees of the grand Mansion.

All the employees of the grand Mansion surrounded Océanie's bed. And given their hesitant faces and nervous giggles, Océanie understood that the employees wanted to say something important. Sitting on the edge of the bed, Cristelle was the first to dare talk to her. Cristelle cleared her throat and she said in a calm and serious voice:

- Océanie ... all the employees of the grand Mansion took a decision, about you ...

Océanie's heart stopped beating, she became pale and trembled:

- I ... I will go back to work ... tomorrow, I will do my housework tasks ... I cannot be fired ... I have nowhere to g...

The head of the grand Mansion interrupted her in a firm voice:

- We never thought of dismissing you, Océanie! ... It's absurd!
- Rest well, take all the time you need! Continued the Cook in a kind tone.

Océanie lay back down on her bed, somehow reassured to keep her job. Cristelle continued her explanation:

- Our decision does not concern your work ...

At this moment, Océanie observed the employees in a confused look:

- I ... I don't understand ... what's happening?

At that moment, Cristelle turned around toward the other employees of the grand Mansion. With an accomplice look and no words needed, all the employees knew what to do.

Instantly, Cristelle took out of her apron's pocket a coin purse, and she put it on the bedside table near Océanie. The head of the grand Mansion Mr. Bûchebois moved a few steps forward, and he put an envelope on the bedside table. The Cook Mr. Ferrero Lutché took out of his apron's pocket a velvet purse, and he placed it on the bedside table. The Gardener Mr. Weil Rosenwald walked toward the bedside table, and he put a purse wrapped in a cotton cloth. Igor took out of his pocket a small box, and he placed it on the bedside table.

Océanie froze in her place, lost and confused at what was going on. All the employees smiled at her with a compassionate look. Cristelle explained to her:

- We have gathered all our savings ... and we offer them to you!

The head of the grand Mansion said:

- Cristelle informed us you have lost all the savings that you have collected, since so long, to help your parents build a new home ... and we are all very sorry that you had this incident...

The Cook became angry instantly:

- Because of a thief!! ladro!! sciocco!! stupido!!

Of all the possibilities, never Océanie could have believed that the employees of the grand Mansion would help her, by offering her their own savings. Océanie whispered in a trembling touched voice:

- But ... that's a lot of ... all your savings ... it's ... I ... it's ...

Océanie lost her words; she blushed, and tears ran down her cheeks. And for once, the employees of the grand Mansion were not worried or sad in front of Océanie's tears.

Immediately, Cristelle held tightly Océanie's hand:

- It's not much ... it's not the entire amount that you have lost ... 11 300 dollars, that's all we have for now ...

The Gardener affirmed in a sure voice:

- But with a little more time, we can manage to get you the 24 000 dollars, so that you can send them to your parents, even before the summer seaso...

At this precise moment, a little voice appeared and startled all the employees gathered in Océanie's bedroom:

- I have them!

All the employees' eyes turned toward a little silhouette, standing at the door. Dalya Bouvard walked inside the bedroom, with slow steps, toward the bedside table, and she placed a purse near the others. Dalya exclaimed in a happy voice:

- The amount is complete, now! 35 300 dollars!!

The employees of the grand Mansion exchanged a confused and shocked look. Cristelle dared to ask:

- But ... Mademoiselle ... 24 000 dollars?! ... all that money?! ... How did you get it?

Dalya didn't expect to justify her help, she hesitated for a moment. But before she could say a word, Igor jumped:

- Selling ahead prepared soup ... at the market in front of the Toscana restaurant!!

The Cook asked Dalya with a surprised tone:

- You worked every Saturday at the market ... to get money for Océanie?

The head of the grand Mansion could not contain his shock too:

- You peeled vegetables and sold ahead prepared soup ... to get money for Océanie?

Dalya just smiled, unable to find the right words to say. Cristelle asked:

- Mademoiselle ... how did you know about the money that Océanie lost?

286

This question was easier than the previous ones, Dalya smiled while addressing Océanie:

- It was a pure coincidence ... I heard your conversation with Mr. Henrik one day, and I noticed you giving him a little rectangular package. At first, I didn't know what it contained. But after some time, I understood it was money. And a large amount of money!

The head of the grand Mansion exclaimed:

- You knew about it all this time, Mademoiselle?

Dalya continued in an intimidated tone:

- Yes ... but I didn't dare to speak to anyone about it ... and when I heard that Mr. Henrik used all Océanie's savings, to buy a house for himself and his family, I didn't dare to confront Mr. Henrik and tell him to return back the money. I preferred to work to give you back the money you lost, Océanie ...

After this confession, the employees of the grand Mansion were struck by lightning and paralyzed with shock. The head of the grand Mansion and the Cook exchanged a surprised look. The Gardener crossed his arms, occupied in his thoughts. Océanie became pale with astonishment. Igor had become mute. And despite her shock, Cristelle was curious to know:

- But ... Mademoiselle ... 24 000 dollars is a big amount of money ... and with all your sales in the market kiosk, it would have taken you at least a year to collect this sum ... how did you get it, in such a short time?

Dalya jumped joyfully:

- I've had one of these lucks, Cristelle! ... In the 2nd week of our work, me and my friend Amira ... the Headwaiter of the Toscana restaurant, in front of the market ... the Headwaiter appeared in front of our kiosk, and he made an order of 2 400 bags of diced vegetables!

The Cook didn't believe his ears:

- 2 400 bags?!

Dalya confirmed:

- Yes! 2 400 bags of diced vegetables!
- That's ... that's quite some luck, Mademoiselle!! Exclaimed Cristelle.

Holding her laugh with difficulty, Dalya continued:

- A quite strange luck ... because the Headwaiter insisted on paying 10 dollars a bag ... it exceeded by far our selling price of 5 cents ... and since we had an urgent need of money, Amira and I, we didn't hesitate to accept the offer of the Toscana restaurant!

Océanie asked with a lost voice:

- But ... 2 400 bags, it's an enormous work task ... and your exams and homework and courses at school? ... how did you do it?

Dalya smiled at her:

- Amira and I, we worked after our school classes every day, for weeks ... we prepared all the bags in Amira's house ... her father Mr. Jacob Mounier, and even the vegetable seller, Mr. Choux, they helped us prepare this order!

A long second of silence followed Dalya's explanation. The employees were trying to understand all what was revealed that night, in Océanie's bedroom. The head of the grand Mansion was the first to break the silence, thinking aloud:

- 2 400 bags ... 10 dollars a bag ... that's how you gathered 24 000 dollars so quickly!

Dalya smiled proudly:

- Exactly!! ... and the Headwaiter promised the vegetable seller, Mr. Choux, that he would pass more orders of vegetable diced bags, each time the restaurant will need any... even if I and Amira will not be present ... Mr. Choux is glad to have found a new source of income!

The little Dalya Bouvard was happy she could help Océanie. After all, it is because of Dalya's family member, that Océanie lost her savings.

The head of the grand Mansion and the Cook exchanged puzzled looks. Cristelle and Océanie didn't believe their ears. The Gardener froze standing in his place, leaning on the wall. Nobody found any words to say. All the employees were surprised by the gesture of the little girl. All ... except Igor. He let out a mean and arrogant laugh:

- An Heiress who works at the market, peeling vegetables and selling soup bags!

Dalya looked at Igor, and she spontaneously replied:

- Work is not a shame, Igor ... and yes, an Heiress proud to work at the market, peeling vegetables ... to help a person who has lost her money.

At this instant, Igor's smile faded away. As if lightning struck him, Igor wasn't expecting this answer at all. None of the employees of the grand Mansion did expect this answer. But this is what's special about Dalya Bouvard ... spontaneous and disarming answers.

The Gardener turned toward Dalya, displaying a proud smile:

- What you have done, Mademoiselle, is a very generous gesture.

Since their first meeting, the Gardener was sure to have seen right in this strange little girl. She was much more than ordinary.

Océanie's room plunged into an amazed silence. For so long, the employees of the grand Mansion underestimated and misjudged Dalya Bouvard. And for the first time ever, the head of the grand Mansion doubted his formal protocol and rigid attitudes. For the first time ever, the Cook doubted what his ears heard that night. For the first time ever, a shame cloud floated over the Igor's head, and he felt very small. For the first time ever, Cristelle was in admiration of the little girl's generosity and empathy.

And for the first time ever, Océanie laughed and cried simultaneously; she was touched by all the employees help, and mostly by the gesture of Dalya Bouvard, the Heiress of the biggest fortune in the Country. Océanie murmured:

- She worked at the market ... peeling vegetables ... to help a maid!

At this moment the snow Panther entered inside Océanie's bedroom, and slipped between the gathered people, toward the bed of the employee. The snow Panther approached Océanie who was still lying down on her bed, and with a tender gesture, the animal placed its paw on Océanie's belly, emitting a long happy meowing. The snow Panther, Séraphine was delighted that Océanie has well recovered.

It is true that Mr. Henrik took the 35 300 dollars ... he took all Océanie's savings ... he took her confidence, her self-esteem, her laugh ... Mr. Henrik took almost everything ... except one thing; the solidarity of the employees and the little Dalya Bouvard.

Present or absent, the Excelbox still teaches you lessons ... thanks to the cares, the recipes, the remedies, and especially thanks to the human kindness ... in a few days or a few weeks ... the heart will always heal!

Chapter 59

Magnificent

Tuesday, December 06th, 1892. In the house of the French neighbors, Les Poirier.

Dalya thought about visiting Mrs. Glorina and Mrs. Marianne Poirier, on her way back from school. When Dalya knocked on the back door of the kitchen, Mrs. Glorina opened and she exclaimed cheerfully:

- What a nice surprise to see you today, Mademoiselle!! Come on in!!
- I wanted to see you ... before the ...

Dalya's throat tightened, she struggled to finish her sentence. But Mrs. Glorina understood the little girl's anxiety, and she continued Dalya's phrase in a serious tone:

- Before the Challenge in a few days.

Mrs. Glorina hugged Dalya tight, and she affirmed with a determined voice:

- You will succeed, Mademoiselle!! I am sure of it!!

Dalya sadly and nervously smiled while hearing these words. She thought that if Mrs. Glorina knew about the disappearance of the Excelbox, the woman would have changed her opinion about the success of the Third Challenge. But as impossible as the situation of the Third Challenge may seem; Mrs. Glorina's words were comforting for the little girl.

When Mrs. Glorina released Dalya, the woman regained her cheerfulness and her usual energy:

- You did well coming here, today. Mrs. Marianne Poirier asked about you last night.
- Is Madame in her bedroom?
- Yes, and she will be happy to see you. Get ahead of me.

Dalya left the kitchen, and she walked toward the great woman's bedroom, on the upper floor. And as usual, Dalya took off her shoes in front of the door, at the corridor, before going inside the bedroom of Mrs. Marianne Poirier.

The daylight of this afternoon embellished the bedroom of a refined French luxury. A huge bed with wool blankets, silk pillows, lace curtains, a large lit fireplace, several chandeliers and bright lights illuminated the room, a big table in fine wood, and luxurious divans. The bedroom exuded calmness and a contagious serenity.

Seated in front of a table, Mrs. Marianne Poirier was drinking hot tea, while reading a book. The great woman smiled when receiving Dalya.

- Good evening Madame!

The great woman put down her book, and she invited the little girl to sit in the chair next to her, and serve herself some tea. Dalya complied:

- How are you today? ... It was a bit cold this morning ... winter is close ... a blow of wind almost made me fall off the sidewalk, earlier ...

The great woman smiled tenderly and inclined her head. There was no need for many words to understand how much Mrs. Marianne enjoyed the visits of the little girl.

- At school, the concierge Dadès is getting ready for the upcoming snow fall ... he prepared the salt to sprinkle on the stairs ... he also took out the shovels to clean the school's entrance ... I proposed to help him clean the school next week ... next we...

When suddenly, Dalya stopped talking. Her smile faded away, her heart tightened, and she became pale. Because next week, Dalya doubted she would return to school. The Excelbox was missing, and the clues were incomprehensible. Next week, Dalya's life would change for the worst. And this thought made Dalya tremble.

With a single glance, Mrs. Marianne guessed the reason of the little girl's anxiety. The great woman took a pencil, and wrote on a paper, which she handed to Dalya:

Everything will be alright

Dalya forced a smile on her face. But her anxiety betrayed her:

- It's just that ... Madame ... things don't look that good for this Third Challenge ... unfortunately, I cannot pass it ... I cannot ...

The great woman observed Dalya for a long moment. Then, with a slow move, Mrs. Marianne extended her hand toward a small wood box which was placed on her bedside table. Dalya understood the request, and she stood up to bring the box to the grand woman. As soon as received, Mrs. Marianne opened the small box; she pulled out a small paper, and she handed it to Dalya:

I cannot

Immediately, Dalya recognized the handwriting and the context of this little note. She straightened up on her chair, surprised and astonished:

- This is your writing! ... It's the answer you gave me when I proposed you write a simplified guide about the nursing profession, for schools and hospitals ... This note is 2 years old ... You kept this note, all this time?

Mrs. Marianne smiled and gently held Dalya's hands. The great woman will never forget the support of this little girl; how she revived her from the disease, and helped her enjoy life, once again.

And as unpredictable as it was, touched by this note and gesture, Dalya felt encouraged for the upcoming Third Challenge ... as impossible as it may be!

Mrs. Marianne Poirier and Dalya Bouvard exchanged an accomplice smile, before enjoying their cup of tea.

Several minutes later, when Dalya left the bedroom of the grand woman, a voice interrupted Dalya, as she walked down the corridor.

- Mother asked about you, last night.

Dalya discovered that the voice came from Richard Poirier's Office. The office door was always closed, except on that day. One would think that Dalya was expected and awaited. A young man was sitting at his desk, working on a stack of files. Dalya entered the office room and she replied to him:

- Yes, Mrs. Glorina informed me. I've had tea with Madame, just a few minutes ago.

Richard Poirier was well aware of Dalya's presence with his mother, since earlier on. But that was the only sentence and excuse that Richard found to speak to Dalya. He noticed the unenthusiastic voice of Dalya, despite she tried to hide her stress.

When Dalya turned around to leave the office, Richard stood up quickly from his chair and he moved toward Dalya:

- I ... I should receive some books of the author Steve Havel, next week ... if you have some free time ... you can come pick them up.

Dalya was surprised by the offer and delighted to read more of her favorite author:

- Other books by Steve Havel?! ...Thank you! ... It is among the best books I've read, up until today ... I would love to read more of this author! ... Thank you so much!

Richard smiled, pleased and proud to notice that Dalya's voice tone was more cheerful. For many days, Richard had eagerly searched more books by this author. The young man continued:

- The author is lucky to have you as a passionate reader.

Dalya smiled:

- In any case, next week Madame and Mrs. Glorina are expecting me. Madame made me promise her that I will come and help build the gingerbread Christmas house.

Richard let out a surprised laugh:

- The gingerbread Christmas house? ... really! ... I have not seen or tasted this cake, since a very long time!
- Madame insisted on making it this year, she will help build it, too. Mrs. Glorina has already made a sketch of the walls and the roof of the house. We will also build a garden in front of the house. I will create miniatures, flowers, people and many...

While Dalya was explaining Mrs. Glorina's plan for the gingerbread Christmas house, Richard observed her. He was well aware of Dalya's effect, not only on his mother, but also on the gloomy routine of this house. Richard was happy to hear that his mother was participating in new activities.

When she finished her explanations, Richard replied:

- I am eager to see the gingerbread Christmas house ... it promises to be well built!

Dalya continued:

- And mostly delicious!!

Richard smiled:

- Certainly!

Advancing toward the Library, Richard pulled out a book and he asked in a calm voice:

- I understand that your birthday is close, Mademoiselle. Isn't it?
- Yes, December 12th ... in a few days ...

Richard pulled out a second book from the Library:

- And from what I understood ... your birthday is also the day where you have to answer to some Challenges?

Dalya came close to the Library. And although Dalya seemed to read the book titles on the row, her mind was preoccupied with something else. She replied in a natural voice:

- That's right ... the Challenges were indicated in the Will of Mr. Governor.

A few seconds of silence settled in Richard's office. The young man put the books on his table desk, and he searched for any words to say. Richard clearly felt Dalya's nervousness and the crushing weight of these Challenges on her little shoulders. Dalya observed the books in the Library, with a lost worried stare. When, Dalya's voice interrupted the silence of the room:

- I am not sure I can do it again this time.

Richard was surprised by her words. Since the first time Richard met her, up until this day, Dalya had always displayed a determined and a natural confidence. It was the first time ever that he was in front of an uncertain and an anxious Dalya. Richard dared to ask her:

- Why do you say that?

Dalya failed to hide her nervousness:

- Because ... honestly ... I don't even know how I succeeded the first 2 times!

Immediately, Richard answered:

- And yet ... you have succeeded the first 2 times.

A discreet little smile appeared on Dalya's lips. Richard Poirier was well right; although she didn't know how and why, Dalya had managed to pass the two first Challenges.

While still standing near her, in front of the Library, Richard Poirier said:

- I have met the Late Mr. Governor ... Iskander Balthazar ... on many occasions before. At important meetings and private parties.

At that moment, Dalya looked at Richard. The young man took a 3rd book from his Library, and continued:

- I didn't know the man, personally. But after meeting him several times, as part of my work, I can assure you that the Late Mr. Governor certainly didn't choose you by any whatsoever chance or mistake.
- How do you know that? Dalya asked all curious.

Richard looked at her:

- Iskander Balthazar must have recognized something special in you ... which led him to leave you his entire fortune, although at strange conditions and Challenges. And besides that, Mr. Governor must have been sure of your great abilities.

The encouragement's words of Richard Poirier filled Dalya with strength and energy. Richard continued with an amused smile:

- ... your great abilities ... except in pastry!

At that moment, a laugh escaped from Dalya:

- Yes ... I admit that pastry is not my strong point ... I have been attentive and eager to learn from Mrs. Glorina, but I still have a hard time separating the yolk from the egg white.

Richard and Dalya both shared a laugh. But despite this little moment of laugh, a difficult Challenge was awaiting for Dalya, and it weighed on her. She observed the books in the Library, and thought aloud with a worried voice:

- Mr. Governor should have chosen his nephew ... it would have been easier for everyone ... Mr. Ferdinand Edelmen is more qualified than me ... I am just ... I am just ... I am just ...

At this precise moment, both Dalya and Richard's voices completed this sentence, simultaneously:

- ... Ordinary.
- ... Magnificent.

Suddenly, a traffic jam of words happened. Dalya thought she heard another word. She turned toward Richard Poirier, all confused:

- What?

Richard didn't realize that he had spoken aloud. The young man immediately pulled himself together, and he cleared his throat, trying to look as natural as possible:

- The bouquet of flowers is ... is magnificent ... Mrs. Glorina picked it from the garden ... Magnificent flowers.

When Dalya turned around, she noticed that the vase contained bland and dry roses, certainly several days old. She didn't understand Richard Poirier's comment.

Some moments later, after Dalya greeted him and left his office, Richard approached the large windows of his office. He observed with all his attention, the little silhouette leaving his home and walking the road back to the grand Mansion.

He ... Richard Poirier ... the brilliant young man, the hard worker, the prodigy son, the youngest employee of the Government ... he ... Richard Poirier ... for the first time in his life, he was losing his words, he was becoming clumsy, and his throat tightened ... even worse, he was intimidated. And in front of who? ... In front of a 14 year's old little girl, who sold fruits and vegetables at the market. A little girl with a disarming naturalness. A little girl ... how did he describe her, again?

The exact word occupied the young man's mind. While observing the little silhouette of Dalya Bouvard, through his office windows, Richard Poirier thought aloud:

- Magnificent.

Chapter 60

Chess Pawn: the weak Queen

Wednesday, December 07th, 1892. In the Law Firm. The end of the afternoon.

The Chess game is fascinating. Because, it's not enough to master the best game strategies, to win the game. Oh no ... in the Chess game, you will need more than that to succeed.

The Lawyer, Mr. Ernest Laszlo announced in a calm voice, while moving his pawn:

- The soldier ... one square in front.

Sitting on a chair in front of him, Sloan Wilfrid replied:

- The Tower ... 2 squares to the right.

Mr. Ernest Laszlo didn't waste a second:

- The Knight ... in L to the left.

After a few seconds of thinking, Wilfrid decided:

- The soldier ... one square in front.

Mr. Ernest Laszlo let out a bored sigh:

- The Bishop ... 3 squares on the right ... and you lose your pawn.

With a slow confident move, the Lawyer took Wilfrid's Tower, and he placed it near the other white pieces he won and crushed, since the beginning of the Chess game. Mr. Ernest Laszlo lay back on his chair, bored not to have a worthy rival. As usual, Sloan Wilfrid didn't see this attack coming. For a few seconds, Wilfrid seemed shocked to have lost an important pawn.

At a moment, Mr. Ernest Laszlo asked in a calm tone:

- The Third Challenge is in few days ... isn't it?

Wilfrid pulled himself together and replied:

- Yes ... next week, Mr. Ernest.

A little evil smile displayed on Ernest Laszlo's face:

- December 12th will be a very special evening ...

Sloan Wilfrid observed for a long second, the Lawyer sitting in front of him. The words of Ernest Laszlo, his unusual smile, and his icy calm, didn't predict anything good ... it was clear that the little Dalya Bouvard was the Lawyer's target!

At this precise moment, while thinking about Dalya Bouvard, a strange idea settled in Sloan Wilfrid's mind. A piece in the Chess game appeared in the middle of the army; the Queen. In all the previous Chess games, Sloan Wilfrid had never used this pawn before; the Queen!

Sloan Wilfrid stretched out his fingers and he was about to play the Queen pawn. Suddenly, Mr. Ernest Laszlo let out an amused laugh:

- Wilfrid ... Wilfrid ... I will give you a tip this time, in order to avoid you a humiliating loss, the upcoming seconds ... the Queen is a useless pawn!

Curiosity invaded him, and Sloan Wilfrid asked:

- If the Queen is a useless pawn ... then, why does she appear in the Chess game?

The Lawyer, Mr. Ernest Laszlo relaxed back on his chair, and he explained his logic:

- The Queen is a stopgap ... she is the weakest pawn of all ... notice that she is the only female of all the board composed of 15 male pawns. Her place is always in the second rank ... in the back ... using her would be a waste of time and energy.

After a few seconds of hard thinking, Sloan Wilfrid doubted his choice. Having read very little about the strategies of the Queen's pawn in his manual, Sloan Wilfrid didn't know much about the Queen pawn, her moves and her role.

Under the cocky smile of Mr. Ernest Laszlo, Sloan Wilfrid hesitated and decided not to use the Queen. Sloan Wilfrid continued the game:

- Soldier ... soldier pawn ... one square in front.

Immediately, Mr. Ernest Laszlo made one single unexpected move. He moved his Bishop diagonally 6 squares, and ... he swallowed the white king of Wilfrid, announcing in a proud icy voice:

- Checkmate.

Chapter 61

A weapon

The same day. Wednesday, December 07th, 1892. The end of the afternoon.

The same day. Wednesday, December 07th, 1892. The end of the afternoon.

When Dalya walked out of the school Library, her friend Amira was waiting for her, outside near the exit doors of the school. And when she noticed Dalya, Amira smiled:

- Did you finish?

Dalya joined her:

- Yes ... I returned all the books that I have borrowed from the Library ... it's pretty clear that I will not come back to the college next we...

Amira interrupted her friend, in a determined tone:

- You will find that box ... everything will work out, Dalya ... you'll see!

At 5 days from the Third Challenge, the Excelbox was still missing, despite the incessant search of the employees of the grand Mansion. Dalya forced a smile on her face:

- We must do the shopping task that the Cook Chef asked us to do ...

Amira jumped joyfully:

- And this will be our last detention task!

The two girls continued their road toward downtown. Hours before, for their last day of detention, Chef Shang had ordered Dalya and Amira to buy a spice from a new store.

Several minutes later, Dalya and Amira arrived in front of the alley indicated by the Cook Chef. The alley was long, dark and empty, with several door stores closed. When they crossed half the alley, Dalya stopped:

- I think we are at the wrong address ...

Amira, who followed her friend, hesitated to move forward, as well:

- I think so, too. There are no spice shop in this street ...

Just as Dalya and Amira made a u-turn in the alley, 3 men appeared out of nowhere and they blocked the way. The 3 men were of the same Asian origin, they wore black clothes. And although they looked thin, the 3 men appeared tough and strong.

- Pleased to meet you ... pretty demoiselles ...

Dalya and Amira froze in their place. The man's voice, their amused smiles, and their postures blocking the alley ... none of this reassured Dalya and her friend.

Gathering all her courage, Dalya held firmly Amira's hand, and she stepped forward to clear a path through the 3 men. Except that the men didn't move at all, completely blocking the alley.

- But where do you think you are going? A man asked with a mocking smile.

Dalya tried to keep her calm and not reveal her fear:

- We have nothing to give you ... no money, no jewelry ...

One of the men let out an amused laugh:

- Oh! ... that is wrong, demoiselle ... you have many things to give us ...

At this sentence, Amira stepped back behind Dalya. She trembled, her throat tightened, her cheeks turned all red. The situation didn't predict any good. Dalya struggled to keep her composure, and she exclaimed in a defiant tone:

- Let us through!
- It will not be that easy, demoiselle ...

At this instant, fear invaded Dalya's entire body:

- What do you want from us?

The 3 men exchanged an accomplice look, and one of the man replied:

- How about having a little fun?!

Immediately, one of the 3 men grabbed Amira's arm and he pulled her to his side with a brutal move. Amira screamed. Dalya tried to defend her friend, but one of the men abruptly pushed her, and Dalya fell on the ground. Straightaway, Dalya stood up:

- Let her go, right now!!

A man laughed:

- Or else what? ... Do you think you are of a size to challenge 3 men?

With a quick look, Dalya vainly searched for an emergency exit, but the alley was empty, no one would hear her screams, and they were alone to face 3 men. While Dalya's brain was thinking of a solution to this situation, a man came close to her with slow steps:

- I'll make you a deal ... demoiselle ...

While Amira was held by one of the men, Dalya had no other choice but to listen to the man's offer. He continued in a calm cold voice:

- Here's what I suggest ... Do you see that point, there, in the middle of the plank?

Dalya turned around and looked at the place indicated by the man's finger. A small dot painted in blue on a wood plank. The man explained:

- If you touch this point ... 3 times in a row ... right on target ... we will let you go unharmed, you and your friend.

Dalya still couldn't understand what the man wanted her to do:

- Touching this point?

The man walked up to Dalya and he gave her a strange item:

- Yes ... shoot these 3 arrows with an arc ... shoot 3 times in a row, and you would be free.

Dalya stepped back:

- But ... but I can't ... I can't do it!

At that moment, the man who was holding Amira's arm, he pulled out a knife from his pocket and he put it on Amira's neck with a brusque move. A scream of pain and fear escaped from Amira. Dalya jumped:

- I swear I can't do it!! I swear!!

The 3 men exchanged an amused look, and one of them smiled:

- Have you any other choice?

The man tightened the knife on Amira's neck, her cheeks became red, her face turned pale, and she lost her voice to even scream. Dalya could clearly notice the traces of the knife-edge on Amira's skin. At this moment, Dalya realized that her only way out, was to shoot the arrow toward the point.

- Take your time ... demoiselle! The man informed her with a mocking tone.

Dalya's entire body was shaking, she took the arc and the arrow, and she turned toward the indicated target. Her hand trembled so much; she dropped the arrow before even putting it on the arc. The 3 men laughed aloud:

- She will amuse us!
- We should have given her an apple instead of an arrow to launch!
- It's the painting you should reach ... not the ground!

Dalya took back the arrow. She noticed pain tears streaming down Amira's cheek; the knife was squeezing her neck. At this instant, Dalya regretted having dragged her friend into the alley, and for having caused her 11 months of detention.

- We have the entire night ahead of us ... so no pressure! Exclaimed a man.

Except that the knife on Amira's neck was a pretty significant pressure for Dalya. She had to save her friend, and get out both of them alive, out of this alley. Dalya adjusted the arrow on the arc, and she froze to face the ordered target. For several seconds, silence filled the alley, Dalya forced herself to clear her mind, and she stared at the blue point on the wood plank. When the arrow was released and launched, Dalya closed her eyes and she prayed.

A long second of silence later, the man's voice exclaimed:

- Not bad ... demoiselle ... not bad ...

Dalya opened her eyes, and she was thunderstruck by what she was seeing. Her arrow had reached the little blue point on the wood plank ... right on target!

How did she manage to do it? Was it because of her prayer? Or by pure chance? Dalya had no clue about it. Without losing a minute, the man handed to Dalya a second arrow, with an arrogant smile:

- Confirm to me that it's not the beginner's luck that launched the arrow!

By hearing this comment, Dalya trembled. She noticed the frightened look of her friend Amira, still at the mercy of the knife placed on her neck. Dalya turned back to the target, for the second time. Her brain was paralyzed, her throat was tight, and her hands were shaking ... because to succeed for a second time in something that we have never tried before, it would need a miracle!

- Come on!! ... Hurry up!! The man was impatient.

Dalya raised her arc, and she adjusted her arrow. She stood motionless for several long seconds in her place, she stared at the target of all her attention, she slowed down her breathing, she tightened her fingers on the arc, she took a long breath ... and she launched the arrow!

The 3 men were thunderstruck. Dalya was paralyzed in her place. Amira let out a scream of shock ... the 2nd arrow had landed on the blue point, and was aligned side by side with the 1st arrow. The strength of the 2nd arrow was clearly more visible, it pierced the wood plank!

At this precise moment, Dalya realized two things ... first, it was not the miracle that help reach the 2nd arrow ... second, something was wrong with her!

The man walked a few steps toward the wood plank to confirm what his eyes were seeing. After a few long seconds, he turned toward Dalya and he exclaimed:

- Well ... well ... the demoiselle is talented, as it seems!

Dalya remained silent and confused in her thoughts. The man pulled out a third arrow and he handed it to her. In a brusque move, the man grabbed Dalya's arm and he whispered in a menacing tone:

- I said 3 times in a row ... if you miss this one, you and your friend, you will not get out alive of this alley!

When he released her, Dalya shivered. Her legs were no longer holding her, her face was pale, her lips trembled. A single arrow would determine the fate of Dalya and her friend. The two girls exchanged a look; and despite the knife was still placed on her neck, Amira encouraged Dalya displaying a discreet smile, although terrified.

Having no other choice, Dalya turned toward the target, for the 3rd time. She breathed a long shot to calm down the rapid beating of her heart, she lifted her arc, she placed her arrow, she pressed firmly her fingers, she maintained her standing balance, despite that her legs trembled, she stared some long seconds at the target .. and then, Dalya launched the 3rd arrow!

The seconds after that move seemed to be an eternity. Time stopped. Dalya's heart froze, her legs let her down and she fell to the ground, her hands trembled, her throat choked, her eyes were astonished ... looking at the 3rd arrow that had reached the target of the blue dot, and it had pierced the wood plank with a remarkable strength!

The man applauded in a slow movement:

- Well done, demoiselle ... well done ... I admit that I didn't think you were capable ... but I am pleased to spare your lives, both of you!

Amira was released immediately, and the 3 men disappeared out of the alley, without any more words or threats. Right away, Amira approached Dalya, and she noticed that Dalya was even more terrorized than her. Amira helped her get up:

- Everything is alright, now ... everything is alright ... breathe Dalya ... breathe slowly ...

It was only then that Dalya released the tears and the fear that she had repressed since earlier. And when Amira hugged Dalya in her arms, Dalya trembled crying:

- I ... I'm ... so sorry ... to have … dragged you ... in this ... I am ... so sorry ...

Amira tried to reassure her friend:

- Breathe Dalya ... breathe slowly ... it's over, now ... they left ... everything is alright, now ...

After many minutes, when Dalya finally recovered her normal breath, she exclaimed:

- I'm so sorry I've put you in such danger! I'm really sor...

Amira interrupted her friend:

- Nothing is your fault! How could you've known that these 3 men would attack us?! Don't be absurd!
- But ... we almost lost our lives!
- We are still alive, Dalya! Safe and sound!
- I really had no choice ... no other solution or a way to escape!

Smiling, Amira said in a compassionate voice:

- I know Dalya ... and I understand you!

Dalya was still trembling by what had just happened. And at that moment, Amira had a funny thought:

- And I admit ... fortunately, they choose you to shoot the arrows ... if they had chosen me, we would have not survived after the 1st arrow!

Despite the seriousness of the situation, a laugh escaped from Dalya. Amira laughed, while tying up her detached hair:

- In fact ... Dalya ... you never told me you were gifted at archery!
- Because I have never tried it before.

Amira froze for a moment, and she observed her friend in a confused and lost tone:

- Dalya ... you shot 3 arrows in a row, right on target ... 2 strong arrows even pierced the wood plank ... If you have never done it before ... so then, how did you succeed?

For a long second, Dalya Bouvard watched the wood plank pierced by 3 arrows, and she whispered in a worried voice:

- I don't know how I did it ... I really don't know ...

As much as Dalya didn't know how 3 arrows reached the target, Dalya also didn't know that 3 silhouettes were watching this incident from the beginning. In a modest house, a window was offering a full clear view on the alley. The 3 silhouettes observed the two little girls, with all their attention.

The Cook Chef Shang explained in a calm and confident voice:

- By cutting the rice in two, and counting the red lentils, her eyesight has strengthened ... by running to get groceries from downtown, and working on a slippery floor with a bucket of water on her head, her legs have gained strength and balance ... by shaking and shaping the dough butter, her arms have muscled, and she has mastered the archery moves ...

Approaching the window, the Cook Chef Shang continued:

- Her arrows pierced the wood plank ... her launch is strong.

And even though she was against the training of the Cook Chef and his brutal methods, Professor Haîyang could not help but to be proud:

- In my Music course at the College, playing the flute strengthened her fingers ... allowing her precision and perfect control of the arc ... her launch is precise.

At that moment, an old man approached the window. Master Fong Ka-Ho smiled and affirmed:

- She has a weapon!

Professor Haîyang and Chef Shang exchanged a proud look. And although the training was still at its beginning for this little girl, their first goal was accomplished.

A minute later, Chef Shang asked:

- What are your orders now, Master?

Master Fong Ka-Ho replied in a calm tone:

- Continue to prepare her.

Without taking his eyes off the two little girls walking along the alley, and returning back home, Master Fong Ka-Ho asked:

- What about the box?

Professor Haîyang answered with a confident voice:

- The box is well guarded, Master.

Before the two little girls disappeared from the alley, Master Fong Ka-Ho thought aloud:

- She has a weapon … she has a weapon …

The training was hard and painful … minutes of falls … hours of disappointments … days of practices … months of preparation … all of this was for one second of perfection!

Chapter 62

Clean hands

Thursday, December 08th, 1892. In the garden of the Grand Mansion. The afternoon.

Having trouble to focus on his files, Sloan Wilfrid stood up from his chair. It was needless to force himself to work, having his mind preoccupied with something else. Sloan Wilfrid decided to visit the grand Mansion. Passing by Lyor's office, Wilfrid knocked on his door:

- Would you like to join me? ... I am going to the grand Mansion for a quick visit.

Lyor closed his book, and he stood up:

- I'll go with you ... I have a book to check in the Library of the grand Mansion ... will you drop me home, on the way back?
- Certainly!

The two men left the Law Firm. On the way, Lyor was busy in his notes, and Sloan Wilfrid was strangely silent and lost in his thoughts. Sloan Wilfrid was worried, for once. The day of the Third Challenge was approaching rapidly. And the disappearance of the Excelbox has changed Wilfrid's plans.

When they arrived at the grand Mansion, Lyor walked straight inside the house:

- I will be right back ... I only need a minute!

When Sloan Wilfrid got out of the car, he noticed Dalya in the big garden of the grand Mansion. Sloan Wilfrid forced himself to smile and he walked toward her. As usual, Dalya was helping the Gardener in planting flowers. Her little twin sisters were playing ball with their little cousin Hugo. Ari and Adi were wearing pretty small blue overalls, and pink hats. The cousin Hugo juggled the ball with his feet, while adjusting his usual bronze blue scarf.

- Good evening mademoiselle!! Exclaimed Wilfrid in a joyful tone.

Dalya stood up and she greeted him:

- Good evening Monsieur Wilfrid.

Wilfrid smiled:

- I am delighted to notice that some habits have not changed!
- Mr. Gardener brought some white roses today. And I am helping to plant them.

Wilfrid approached a white rose, and he smelled it:

- Lovely smell!! Excellent choice Mr. Rosenwald!!

The Gardener greeted the Lawyer, bowing his head, and then he went back to work. The little twins exclaimed happily while chasing the ball with their little cousin Hugo.

Only one thing was missing in the garden of the grand Mansion. The snow Panther. Since many days now, as strange as it may seem, Séraphine stopped following Dalya everywhere, the animal even stopped sleeping in Dalya's bedroom. The only thing that the snow Panther did throughout the entire day, was lying down immobile on a garden wall, her sapphire blue eyes were focused toward the annex house.

At a moment, Dalya ordered her twin sisters and her little cousin:

- Wash your hands with the garden's hose, it time to go inside for snacks!

Ari and Adi exclaimed joyfully:

- Oki!! Oki!! Wash hands!!

Sloan Wilfrid asked Dalya in a serious tone:

- Are there any news ... about the box?

Dalya's face darkened and her smile faded right away:

- No Monsieur ... the employees and I, we looked everywhere in the grand Mansion ... in all the places and rooms ... there is still no trace of the Excelbox.

Sloan Wilfrid put his hands on Dalya's shoulders, and he looked her in the eye, while affirming with a sure tone:

- We will find a way out! ... There is always a solution to any problem!

And what was this solution to get out of this impasse? ... Honestly, Sloan Wilfrid didn't have a clue. But the Lawyer preferred to reassure Dalya, rather than worry her even more.

Before retiring, Sloan Wilfrid asked one last question:

- How were your exams at school?

Dalya was pleased to answer him:

- I had good grades in Mathematics, Physics and Chemistry ... in History and Geography, I was glad my grades were better than the previous semester ... and in Latin, I managed to have the average grade to pass, although this course was difficult for me ... I played a melody in the Music exam ... Professor Haîyang gave me 10,5/20 ... it's the first time in my life that I play a Music instrument!

But before Sloan Wilfrid can say a word, the little twins approached their older sister, and they proudly showed off their hands:

- Voilà! ... Clean hands! ...Voilà! ... Eat snack now?

At the sight of the little twins, Sloan Wilfrid became mute, the Gardener froze in his move, and Dalya's heart stopped. Dalya murmured in a confused voice:

- What ... what did you do? ... You ... I said ... I told you to wash your hands!

Ari and Adi exchanged a confused look, and they defended themselves:

- But we wash hands! ... Looky ... Looky ... Clean hands! ... Voilà! ... Clean hands!

Dalya approached her younger sisters:

- Yes, I can see that! ...Your hands are the only thing in you that is clean!!

Because a few minutes ago, when Dalya was busy talking with Mr. Wilfrid, the little twins left their balloon, and they decided to play with the mud that the garden's hose formed. After only a few seconds, Ari and Adi were entirely soaked in dark mud, up to their ears. And although they looked like two little black flies ... the twins made sure to wash their hands, all the same:

- Looky Dindin!! Clean hands!! We washed our hands!!

The cousin Hugo adjusted his blue bronze scarf, and he whispered in a hesitant tone:

- I tried to stop them ... sorry ...

Dalya smiled kindly at her little cousin:

- Don't be sorry, you had nothing to do with it, Hugo!

And addressing her little sisters, Dalya exclaimed in an angry tone:

- But why do you always act like pests?

Sloan Wilfrid failed to hold back his laugh; he confirmed the little twin's answer:

- They are right on this one, Dalya ... their hands are clean!

Ari and Adi jumped joyfully, because Sloan Wilfrid defended them:

- You see!! Frite also said our hands clean!! We Zentil!! We not pests!! We clean hands!! Looky Dindin!! Looky!!

At that moment, a silhouette joined them from inside the grand Mansion. Ignoring Dalya as usual, Lyor Laszlo spoke directly to Sloan Wilfrid:

- I am done! ... The book I was looking for is not in the Library of the grand Mansion. I still have to look for it in the National Libr... but ... what is ...what is th...

Lyor stopped in front of the little twin, he didn't understand why they were soaked in dark mud from head to toe, and only their hands were clean. But it's been long ago since Lyor Laszlo gave up understanding the strange behavior of these two little twins.

While observing Adi and Ari with a disgusted look, Lyor Laszlo continued:

- I'll wait for you in the car, Wilfrid ... I don't want these black flies to touch me.

The effect that this sentence had was remarkable. Ari and Adi exchanged an accomplice glance and a mischievous laugh. And the sooner said the sooner done. The little twins ran toward Lyor, screaming full lungs and stretching their hands to hold Lyor in their arms:

- RIRI!! RIRI!! RIRI!! RIRI!!

Lyor jumped and he stepped back immediately:

- No no no!! Go away!! Stay where you are!! Don't touch me!! I don't want any mud on me!! Stay away from me!!

In an instant, the little twins ran behind Lyor, and he was forced to run too in order to escape from them. The Gardener and the little cousin Hugo laughed aloud at this scene. While observing Lyor Laszlo and the little twins, Sloan Wilfrid asked Dalya with a serious voice:

- Do you think Ari and Adi will catch him up?

Dalya laughed:

- I hope so!

Chapter 63

Fudges

The same day. Thursday, December 08th, 1892. Later in the evening. In the house of the Lawyer Sloan Wilfrid.

In the living room of his house, Sloan Wilfrid sat in front of the fireplace. The living room was a refined place, perfectly reflecting the elegant taste of Sloan Wilfrid. Several chairs of purple velvet, gray curtains, a Library filled with books and colorful birds' figurines, and a big bright beautiful chandelier shining a thousand lights.

The December cold forced us to enjoy the fireplace warmth. Except on that night, Sloan Wilfrid was concerned neither of the cold nor the hot. Being known for his calm nature, the young Lawyer was stressed out and he worked his brain hard to find a solution to a problem.

- *There are only 4 days left ... we are short out of time ... I reread the Will of Late Mr. Governor a hundred times ... there is no way out or exception in this Will ... I cannot delay the Third Challenge of December 12th ... and the Challenge must absolutely happen along with this box ... but where did this box disappear?*

Wilfrid seemed worried at the turn of the events.

- *And what if someone had stolen the box? ... It is a hypothesis ... but it's not possible ... The employees of the grand Mansion assured me that no thief entered the house ... and if this thief is lucky to get through the snow Panther, anyway! ... so then, why did this box disappear right now? ... In the most crucial moment?*

Except that, it was not the only worry in Wilfrid's minds.

- *Ernest Laszlo is preparing something nasty ... I can feel it ... is he involved with the disappearance of that box? ... I don't think he would dare to steal the box, he risks his credibility and his career ... but the strange visits he recently received at the Law Firm, it smells nasty ... he perhaps may not have stolen that box, but I'm sure he will use all means to prevent Dalya to pass this Third Challenge ...*

The tea that the house housekeeper, Mrs. Potts has prepared for him, failed to calm Sloan Wilfrid's nerves.

- *I promised to protect her!! ... I thought of keeping her away from her abusive parents, and by letting her stay at the grand Mansion, the box disappeared!! ... I should have assigned a police officer to guard this box!! ... This little girl doesn't deserve that ... she doesn't deserve to return to her old life ... I promised to protect her!! ... I promised her!!*

A feeling of frustration invaded Sloan Wilfrid all of a sudden.

- *What can I do to help her? ... I cannot let her down, just like that! ... I have to find a solution! ... I have to help her! ... But how? What should I do?*

Suddenly, a silhouette entered the living room and interrupted Sloan Wilfrid in his thought.

- Well, I would have never believed to see you forget to eat the chocolate Fudges!

Mrs. Potts was an old woman, short size and chubby, rosy cheeks and a kind printed smile on her face. A small purple cap on the head, long white hair tied in a bun, and a pink maid apron around her waist. Mrs. Potts watched over Sloan Wilfrid since a long time, caring for him like her son.

It was only at that moment that Sloan Wilfrid noticed he hadn't touched the plate of chocolate Fudge that Mrs. Potts had placed for him near his tea. And because Sloan Wilfrid has always been obsessed with this delicious cake, Mrs. Potts was very surprised to see that the plate was still intact.

- You're not yourself these days ... you must have a great concern that worries you, to forget eating Fudges!

Sloan Wilfrid lay back on his chair, and he forced himself to smile. For taking care of him since several years now, Mrs. Potts knew better than anyone the young Lawyer's mood. Mrs. Potts filled a cup of tea, and she handed it to him with a kind smile:

- Does your concern include a little girl named Dalya Bouvard?

Mrs. Potts guessed right. She sat on the chair in front of Sloan Wilfrid, and she sighed:

- It's been many nights now that you don't sleep and eat well. Your dark undereyes are proof!

Sloan Wilfrid drank some tea, and he announced to Mrs. Potts in a grave voice:

- The Third Challenge is in 4 days ... the box that will allow her to pass the Challenge, disappeared ... I feel a conspiracy against her from the Lawyer Mr. Ernest Laszlo, but I don't know what he is preparing ... I don't know how to help her.

Mrs. Potts poured herself a cup of tea, and she answered in a calm tone:

- It seems to me that this little girl was chosen by the Late Mr. Governor ... I heard saying that she is very polite and kind, toward everybody.

Sloan Wilfrid confirmed, with a sad sigh:

- She is, yes!

Mrs. Potts smiled tenderly:

- So then, if Mr. Iskander Balthazar chose her ... that must be for a very good reason! ... Therefore, it is useless to worry about her fate. The kindness of this little girl will come back to her and protect her!

Thanks to her wisdom and contagious calm, Mrs. Potts managed to appease Wilfrid's nerves. She continued with a confident voice:

- And don't worry about people who want to dismiss her from her heritage ... no matter their tricks, they will not succeed in undoing the last wishes of the Late Mr. Governor ... Goodness always triumphs, my son! The Will of the generous Governor may be a small piece of paper written on this earth ... but it is always the heaven that handles the last wishes of the soul!

Wilfrid smiled:

- That is well right, Mrs. Potts ... they cannot undo his last wis...

Suddenly, gently and discreetly, a strange idea infiltrated Wilfrid's mind. The young Lawyer repeated aloud:

- Undo his last wishes ... undo his last wishes ... undo his Will ...

When abruptly, Sloan Wilfrid straightened up on his chair, and he screamed:

- THEY WANT TO UNDO THE GOVERNOR'S WILL!!

In front of the confused stares of Mrs. Potts, Sloan Wilfrid explained in a surprised tone:

- The visits that Ernest Laszlo received at the Law Firm, and the urgent messages! ... Mr. Strauss ... Mr. Jean-Pierre ... Mr. Marius ... Mr. Quentin ... Mr. Eliott ... These five men were present at the legalization of the Late Mr. Governor's Will! ... All these names were on the list that I've noticed on Ernest Laszlo's desk! ... Ernest Laszlo called them all to cancel the Will!!

Mrs. Potts tried to follow the thread of informations:

- But ... how ... they cannot cancel the Wi...

Sloan Wilfrid jumped out of his chair, and he interrupted her:

- Yes!! They can cancel it!! ... The presence of Mr. Strauss in this list means they will declare that the Governor was unfit at the signing of the Will!!

Her cheeks became all red, Mrs. Potts let out angry words:

- That Ernest Laszlo is a villain!! ... Using tricks to prevent an innocent girl from her right!!

Sloan Wilfrid collapsed on his chair, in a shocked state:

- I finally understood!! That's what Ernest Laszlo has been preparing for months!! That's how he will prevent her from passing the Third Challenge!!

Mrs. Potts put down her teacup in an angry move:

- But why does Ernest Laszlo insist to prevent this little girl from passing this Third Challenge? Why does he want to cancel the Will now?

Wilfrid explained:

- Because at the First Challenge, everyone has underestimated Dalya Bouvard. No one took this matter seriously. No one thought that she would succeed. We all thought, including myself, that it was a stroke of luck. At the Second Challenge, everybody thought that luck can never be repeated twice. Except that we were all wrong! And even royally wrong! Dalya Bouvard didn't succeed by any luck ... she passed the Second Challenge, by her own merit!

Mrs. Potts understood a bit more:

- And for this Third Challenge ... they think she might succeed ...

Sloan Wilfrid finished Mrs. Potts' sentence:

- For this Third Challenge ... they all tremble of it, Ernest Laszlo, the nephew and niece of the Governor, the entire Edelmen family, and all this friends ... Ernest Laszlo is willing to risk the credibility of his Law Firm and his entire legal career, to see Dalya Bouvard fail ... But on the other hand, he would be the savior of the biggest fortune in this Country!

After a few seconds of silence, Mrs. Potts affirmed in a determined tone:

- Now that you know what's preparing for this innocent little girl ... you need to help her! ... the last wishes of a dying man are a duty, my son!

At once, Sloan Wilfrid stood up, he took his coat and he headed toward the exit of the living room. At this precise moment, the young Lawyer knew exactly what to do and how to help Dalya.

Mrs. Potts exclaimed immediately:

- But where are you going like that? ... At this late hour?

Sloan Wilfrid returned back to the living room right away, and he hugged Mrs. Potts so hard, that the grand woman nearly lost her balance.

- Thank you for the boost Mrs. Potts!! Thank you, thank you, and thank you! ... I know how to help her right now!

The grand woman was all blushing. Sloan Wilfrid walked toward the exit of the living room, when suddenly, he turned around for the 2nd time and he approached Mrs. Potts. The old woman, with cheeks still rosy, asked in a curious tone:

-   What have you forgotten again, now?

Sloan Wilfrid emptied the entire plate of pastries in his pocket:

-   The Fudges, Mrs. Potts!! The Fudges!!

The grand woman watched Sloan Wilfrid leaving the house, with determined steps, and with a defense idea in his mind. Mrs. Potts couldn't help but laugh proudly, noticing the plate of Fudges completely emptied:

-   Now I recognize my son Wilfrid!!

Chapter 64

A goodbye gift

Friday, December 09th, 1892. In the annex house.

On this December day, the Safoubri family was preparing to leave Georgetown city, for their new home in Florida. Dalya had planned to say goodbye to her mother's family, before their departure. She put on her coat and walked toward the annex house.

Strangely, and since several days now, the snow Panther was lying down immobile on the garden wall, staring at the annex house, day and night. When Dalya walked near the snow Panther, she greeted her:

- How are you doing Séraphine?

Except that the snow Panther didn't even realize the presence of the little girl. The sapphire blue eyes of the animal were focused toward the annex house. All the employees of the grand Mansion, including Dalya, none of them understood the strange attitude of the snow Panther.

Dalya continued on her way. And before she walked up the entrance stairs, the little twins welcomed their older sister:

- Hello Dindin!! Hello Dindin!!

Dalya kissed her little twin sisters:

- Good morning Ari!! Good morning Adi!! ... I brought you your favorite candy!!
- Mici Dindin!! Mici Dindin!!

Immediately, her little cousin also appeared at the entrance to the annex house. Dalya smiled at him:

- Good morning cousin Hugo!!

The little cousin Hugo was wearing an elegant navy blue suit, a gray hat, and around his neck his usual scarf in blue and bronze lines, with a flying eagle stitched on the edges.

The little boy smiled, before informing Dalya:

- My parents and grandmother went Downtown with your father ... they are buying some last things before we leave ...

The little twins sat on the steps of the entrance stairs, enjoying their candy. Dalya approached her little cousin, and she said to him in a serious tone:

- Well ... I came especially to see you today, Hugo ... I wanted to talk to you about something important!

On this comment, the little cousin jumped, he became pale and anxious, and his voice was shaking:

- It's not me!! ... I don't have it!! ... It's not me!!

Dalya was surprised at her little cousin's reaction. She asked in a confused tone:

- What are you talking about? ...

The little boy became worried and he was trembling. Dalya didn't understand what could have caused the strange reaction of her cousin, she insisted:

- Is everything alright, Hugo?

The little boy pulled himself together quickly, and he tried to smile despite his anxiety:

- Yes ... yes ... all is good ... all is good ...

Although she was not convinced of this answer, Dalya didn't want to make her little cousin more uncomfortable. Dalya took out of her bag an item packed in a decorated paper, and she handed it to her cousin, displaying a kind smile:

- Like I said, I came especially to see you today, Hugo ... before you leave for Florida ... I have something important for you!

When the little boy took the item, and opened the decorated paper, he was surprised and confused by what he found. The little cousin exclaimed immediately:

- This ... this is for me?

Dalya smiled:

- Since you love cars so much, I thought a book about the mechanics of cars will be useful to you ... the words are explained very simply ... and I bought you also a notebook, with a set of pencils ... the seller assured me that this is professional equipment that only grand painters and artists use ...

At that moment, the little cousin seemed thunderstruck and amazed by this gift. He was not expecting it at all. The little boy lost his words, while consulting the notebook and the pencils' set. Never someone had given him a gift, never someone was interested in his drawings.

Hugo's parents were always too busy to be interested in him, his mother Claudine was always busy envying other people, and his father Henrik was always busy courting other women.

It was the first time in the little boy's life, that someone was interested in him and his cars drawings. Dalya hoped that this gift will please the little boy:

- I hope to see your notebook filled of car drawings, when we visit you, one day in Florida!

The little cousin Hugo looked at Dalya, and he smiled, all touched by her gift:

- Thank you ... thank you, very much!!

On the steps of the annex house stairs, the little twins enjoyed their candy, while Dalya watched her little cousin Hugo flipping with amazed eyes, the book of the cars mechanics.

Except that ... Dalya Bouvard didn't know, that she wasn't only offering a simple goodbye gift ... she was offering way more than that!

Chapter 65

A meeting of Macarons

Saturday, December 10th, 1892. At night.

A few minutes before 11 PM, a meeting was getting prepared at the house of Mr. Jean-Pierre. The living room of Mr. Jean-Pierre was an exuberant luxury. Golden divans, Lace curtains, Crystal chandeliers, Persian carpets, Porcelain vases, refine wood tables.

Mr. Strauss and Mr. Marius were sitting by the fireplace, discussing the latest political rumors. Mr. Jean-Pierre was reading his newspaper. Enjoying his tea calmly, Mr. Ferdinand Edelmen seemed relaxed and calm, for once. While Mr. Quentin tasted the Macarons offered with tea.

The quiet living room was interrupted by the arrival of the Lawyer Mr. Ernest Laszlo and Mr. Elliott. Immediately, Mr. Jean-Pierre closed his newspaper, and he greeted them with a delighted smile:

- Good evening Ernest ... Good evening Eliott ...

Ernest Laszlo and Mr. Eliott greeted the other men, before sitting down on the luxurious living room divans. Ernest Laszlo asked in a serious tone:

- I assume that no one is aware of your presence here, gentlemen?

Mr. Marius replied with an amused tone:

- Not even our wives!

A wave of laughs invaded the living room. Ernest Laszlo continued:

- Excellent ... excellent ... I want to finish this matter in the greatest discretion.

Mr. Strauss asked:

- And I presume that all the documents to be signed are in order?

Mr. Elliott stated with a sure tone:

- Yes, all the documents that you need to sign tonight, are ready ... after your signature, Ernest Laszlo will legalize them at Court, tomorrow morning ... and the good news will be official tomorrow afternoon!

Mr. Marius was curious:

- And did you find a judge who will agree to legalize these documents?

Ernest Laszlo answered with a calm confidence:

- Yes ... a young judge, very ambitious to become a magistrate.

Mr. Elliott addressed his friend:

- Jean-Pierre ... you will take good care of this young judge ... he would have done us an invaluable favor!

Mr. Jean-Pierre smiled:

- Certainly!

Mr. Strauss spoke to the nephew of Late Mr. Governor:

- Your fortune will finally be returned to you, Ferdinand Edelmen!

Mr. Marius laughed:

- Finally!! ... it was about time!

All eyes were turned toward Ferdinand Edelmen; he put down his teacup and he replied in a proud tone:

- And I can assure you that I will not forget the people who helped me get back my fortune!

Mr. Jean-Pierre relaxed on his chair:

- It is your right, Ferdinand ... this fortune should have been given to you, 2 years ago ... if it wasn't this judgment error of your uncle Iskander Balthazar ... we have done nothing more than correcting his mistake!

Ferdinand Edelmen displayed an arrogant smile:

- I thank you all!

Mr. Quentin took a Macarons:

- Ernest Laszlo ... you did a great job!! Bravo!!

With a cocky grin, the Lawyer Ernest Laszlo bowed his head:

- I did only my job, as a Lawyer ...

The nephew Ferdinand Edelmen turned toward his friend Lawyer:

- Ernest ... you have worked for months to gather all the documents and necessary people, to cancel the Will ... it's a remarkable job!

One could almost say that the Lawyer Ernest Laszlo blushed.

A question slipped in the mind of Mr. Jean-Pierre. He picked up his cup of tea, and he asked the Lawyer in a serious tone:

- Ernest ... I don't mean to spoil the definite success of your plan ... I wonder if you have thought about another backup plan in case something goes wrong?

Silence invaded the living room. The Lawyer Ernest Laszlo replied in a calm confident voice:

- Certainly, Mr. Jean-Pierre ... I always think of a plan B ... and I am happy to announce to you all, that a couple of days ago, I was informed of the box's disappearance.

All eyes were surprised by this news. Mr. Marius thought aloud:

- This strange box has disappeared? ... and therefore without the box, there will be no Third Challenge ... and without a Challenge, the Will is then canceled!

Ernest Laszlo displayed a proud smile:

- Exactly! ... my initial plan is to cancel the Will by declaring Iskander Balthazar unfit while writing it ... if my original plan doesn't work, for anyhow reason ... it will be canceled by the disappearance of the strange box!

After a long second of a shocked silence, a wave of laugh invaded the living room.

- This is great news Ernest Laszlo!
- Why didn't we think of that before?
- Everything in its time. We would have awakened suspicions toward us!
- I admit it is genius! It is really a smart idea Ernest!

The Lawyer Ernest Laszlo and the nephew Ferdinand Edelmen exchanged an accomplice look. Mr. Jean-Pierre stood up from his chair and he announced:

- Now that this case has been exceptionally well prepared, by our prodigious Lawyer Ernest Laszlo ... I propose that we sign the papers immediately, in order to be done with this matter, once and for all!

Mr. Quentin replied in an amused tone:

- I'll sign anything you want ... as long as you serve me these delicious Macarons!

The living room was covered with a victorious laugh. All the men laughed aloud, not only because of Mr. Quentin's humor, but because of their successful plan.

When suddenly, an outsider voice joined the conversation:

- And I quite agree with you, Mr. Quentin!! For having tasted them before, these Macarons are divinely delicious!!

Instantly and abruptly, an icy cold silence fell on the living room. All the men froze in their places, and their smiles disappeared immediately. All eyes turned toward the living room door. A tall big silhouette was standing there. And it was not just anyone ... The Congressman Yolan McKlain himself!

The Congressman was very elegant as usual in a purple suit. Large size, a chubby belly, the Congressman McKlain had an imposing and intimidating allure.

And just like all the other men present in this living room, the Lawyer Ernest Laszlo couldn't believe his eyes, he pulled himself together with difficulty:

- Monsi ... Monsieur the Congressman?

The Congressman didn't wait to be invited. He walked inside the living room with a confident step, and he sat down on a divan, under the shocked eyes and the silent mouths of all the present men. Mr. Jean-Pierre was the first and most courageous one to ask:

- Mr. Congressman ... to what do we owe the honor of your visit?

Congressman Yolan McKlain stared at all the men, with a defiant and threatening look, and then he answered with a natural voice:

- My invitation card to this meeting must have been lost in the mail!

The heart of the Lawyer Ernest Laszlo, stopped beating. All the men became as pale as marble. And while they all displayed a natural face, they all trembled at the idea that the Congressman could discover what they were up to do that night. The Lawyer Ernest Laszlo decided to take control of the situation. He took a long breath of air, and he claimed with an arrogant tone:

- I allow myself to correct you, Mr. Congressman ... this is not a meeting ... given our busy schedules, it has been a long time since we have met ... Mr. Jean-Pierre had the courtesy to invite us for tea tonight.

Congressman Yolan McKlain was a man of great character, fair and honest, but intimidating when necessary. He observed for a long second the Lawyer Ernest Laszlo, with an intense stare, before asking:

- Am I wrong, then? This is not a meeting?

Mr. Marius dared to confirm:

- Certainly not! We already have enough meetings in our day jobs!

Mr. Jean-Pierre said in a trembling voice:

- It is a simple evening between friends ...

Mr. Quentin stated:

- Just over tea and Macarons!

The Congressman relaxed in his chair, displaying a cheerful smile:

- Well then ... I was misled, for once!

At that precise moment, the laughs that occupied the living room were nervous and uncomfortable laughs. The Congressman Yolan McKlain served himself a Macaron, and he declared in a natural voice:

- In any case, it seems to be a nice evening between friends.

All the men exchanged relieved glances. The Congressman continued in a calm tone:

- And I am reassured to have made a mistake ... because if it had turned out that this meeting was about the Will of the Late Mr. Governor ... if it had turned out that you were all gathered to sign the annulment of the Will, certifying that Iskander Balthazar was unfit when signing it ... if it had turned out that you were up to something to change the course of this heritage ... then I can assure you that the consequences of your actions would have been paid ... very very highly!

Instantly, a heavy silence weighed on the living room. The Congressman ate a Macaron:

- But ... fortunately, I am wrong, am I? ... This is a simple evening between friends, isn't it?

Although he trembled to the bones, Ferdinand Edelmen asked with an arrogant tone:

- Where did you get these ridiculous informations from, Mr. Congressman?

The Congressman Yolan McKlain answered right away:

- A little bird called Justice informed me that something is getting prepared against the Will of the Late Mr. Governor ... and I am happy to see that the generosity, the kindness and the integrity of Iskander Balthazar, still serves him, even though he is no longer of this world!

Everyone was struck by this answer. The tension in the living room became heavy and frightening. After the Congressman's revelations, no man dared to speak or move or even breathe. The Congressman Yolan McKlain was a man who knew how to explain perfectly well his message:

- I am confident that all the men present here, will follow the last orders of Iskander Balthazar ... I am reassured to know that all of you will apply the Will of the Late Mr. Governor, as it is ... am I not right?

For a long intense minute, the Congressman stared at the men present, one by one, with a defiant and threatening look. Without anyone daring to raise their eyes or protest or speak. Then, the Congressman turned toward the Lawyer, and he said with a calm cold voice:

- This is the second time I straighten you out, Ernest Laszlo ... the second and the last time!

This menacing tone made the Lawyer tremble and became all pale. Ernest Laszlo lost his voice, like all the other men in the living room. The Congressman Yolan McKlain took another Macaron, he lay back on the divan, and he announced in a more cheerful voice:

- These are really delicious Macarons! ... we should organize meetings between friends more often, don't you think?

Chapter 66

The employees of the grand Mansion

Sunday, December 11ᵗʰ, 1892. In the grand Mansion.

That night, dinner in the kitchen of the grand Mansion, took place in a heavy and tense silence. Even though the Cook had prepared a delicious dinner, and Océanie has well recovered. Silence occupied the dinner table, the employees of the grand Mansion moved their spoons, but no one dared to say a word.

When suddenly, the Gardener stood up from his chair, he took his dinner plate and cutlery, and he left the kitchen. All the employees exchanged a curious look; everyone was surprised by the Gardener's attitude. But everyone knew where the Gardener was heading to.

Turning around a carrot with her fork for the 54ᵗʰ time, Cristelle got tired and she lay back on her chair. After some seconds of thinking, Cristelle decided to stand up, she took her plate and cutlery, and she too left the kitchen, by the same door the Gardener took before.

Without the need of thinking any second, Océanie got up too, she held her dinner plate and cutlery. And before she would leave the table, Océanie took the bread basket with her, and she left the kitchen.

Igor was the only one eating dinner with appetite, that night. Igor was forced to get up and follow Océanie, only because she carried the bread basket that he still needed.

The only ones who remained in the kitchen were the head of the grand Mansion Mr. Benjamin Bûchebois and the Cook Mr. Ferrero Lutché. The two men exchanged a confused look, surprised by the unusual attitude of the other employees. The head of the grand Mansion put down his fork, and he lay back on his chair:

- Lutché ... is it possible that we were wrong?

The Cook sighed, crossing his arms in front of his still full plate:

- Perhaps ... yes ...

In the luxurious dining room, Dalya ate alone what could be her last dinner in the grand Mansion. She did the best she could to find the Excelbox, but without any success. Her mind was worried and anxious. Dalya could barely notice what she was eating. When a voice interrupted her thoughts:

- Good evening.

Turning around, Dalya was surprised to see the Gardener Mr. Rosenwald standing at the door of the luxurious dining room. Dalya noticed that the Gardener was carrying a dinner plate and cutlery. The Gardener asked in a respectful tone and somewhat hesitantly:

- If ... if Lady Dalya allows me to join her ... tonight ... for dinner.

Dalya jumped instantly:

- Of course, Mr. Gardener ... I will be very pleased!

The little girl was happy to have some company for once, in this too big luxurious dining room. The Gardener walked inside, and he sat on a chair, displaying a happy discreet smile.

Barely a few seconds later, a second voice interrupted Dalya and the Gardener's dinner. The maid Cristelle approached Dalya, and she asked with a nice smile:

- May I join you ... Lady Dalya?

Dalya smiled back at her, and she invited her to sit:

- Absolutely, yes! I am glad to have company for dinner! ... Please come in!

Cristelle and the Gardener exchanged an accomplice smile; they were both proud to have made the little girl happy, perhaps on her last day in the grand Mansion.

Before Dalya could take her fork and finish her dinner, a third silhouette stood on the door of the luxurious dining room.

Dalya Bouvard was surprised to see Océanie and Igor. And just like the Gardener and Cristelle did before, Océanie and Igor were carrying their dinner dishes and cutlery. Océanie came close to Dalya with slow steps; she addressed the little girl with a trembling voice:

- I ... I was very rude and mean to you, since the day you arrived at the annex house ... you have even endured a slap because of me ... and despite everything that I have done to you, you saved my life, and you worked in the market for me ... so then, for your kindness and goodness, I will be eternally grateful to you ...

But before Dalya could say a word, Océanie made a move that surprised everyone present in the dining room. For the first time ever, Océanie Shell bowed in front of the little girl, and she affirmed:

- Lady Dalya Bouvard.

As always, the spontaneity of Dalya surpassed her. Immediately, the little girl stood up, and she hugged Océanie so tightly, while exclaiming in a happy tone:

- I am so glad you are well recovered, Océanie!

When Dalya released her, Océanie displayed a happy smile, and tears flow down her cheeks. Océanie was touched by the little girl's spontaneous manners.

When Igor made one more step toward the table, to sit and finish his dinner, he received a harsh leg kick from Océanie. Igor's voice screamed of pain:

- LAAAAAAAdy Dalya!

Dalya laughed; she was reassured and happy that Océanie regained back her usual dominant character. When they all sat around the big dining table, Dalya was delighted by the employees' gesture, and she was mostly happy to have some company for dinner, that night.

A few minutes and a few bites later, a voice cleared its throat at the door of the dining room. The head of the grand Mansion displayed a serious face. All the employees sitting around the table became silent and immobile. Mr. Bûchebois stepped inside the dining room, and he addressed all the employees, in a cold voice:

- Never ... in all my years of service ... never have I allowed the employees to eat at the same table as the Masters of the place!

The employees exchanged worried looks. Dalya searched for words to soften the upcoming anger of the head of the grand Mansion. When Mr. Bûchebois continued:

- However ... when the Master of the place is a little girl gifted with an exceptional generosity and a rare nobility of the heart ... when a Heiress dares to work in the market to help a house maid ... I must admit that never … in all my years of service ... never have I witnessed such a gesture.

Then, as unexpected as it may seem, the head of the grand Mansion, Mr. Bûchebois bowed:

- It was a great honor to serve you ... Lady Dalya Bouvard.

The little girl was not the only one shocked by the attitude of the head of the grand Mansion. The employees expected reprimands instead of a curtsy bow. Dalya was touched by the words and the respect of Mr. Bûchebois toward her. Dalya didn't hesitate to stand up, and she firmly hugged the old man.

- Thank you, Monsieur Bûchebois! ... I was delighted to spend these months with you, here in the grand Mansion.

Mr. Bûchebois was intimidated by the spontaneous hug of the little girl. The serious formal head of the grand Mansion was also disarmed and softened by the manners of the little Heiress.

When suddenly, a loud scream surprised everyone:

- SURPRISE!! SORPRESA!!

The Cook Mr. Ferrero Lutché entered inside the dining room, he was carrying a big plate; it was a chocolate cake, with strawberries and white cream. The Cook addressed Dalya in a joyful tone:

- We wish you a happy birthday ... buon compleanno ... Lady Dalya Bouvard!

In all her life, Dalya never had a birthday party or even a cake. At that moment, tears rolled down her cheeks, words failed her, and a smile of gratitude displayed on her face, Dalya was touched by the employees' surprise and gestures. And instantly, all the employees of the grand Mansion ... Mr. Bûchebois, Mr. Ferrero, Mr. Rosenwald, Cristelle, Océanie, Igor ... they all stood up and they happily sang in one voice:

- Happy Birthday ... Lady Dalya Bouvard!

Well ... well ... what do we hear now?

A little girl, selling vegetables and fruits ... called a Lady!

At the First Question, she was named Lady ... by one.

At the Second Question, she was named Lady ... by two.

Here at the Third One, Lady was pronounced by most.

It seems that one doesn't become Lady only by wealth, rank, or Law.

Apparently, dear reader ... a little girl, selling vegetables and fruits ... she became a Lady ... only by a Noble heart!

Chapter 67

A busy morning

Monday, December 12th, 1892. The morning, in the grand Mansion.

Dalya could barely sleep one hour of the entire night. One and only question tormented the little girl's mind all night:

- *How to pass the Third Challenge ... without the Excelbox?*

When Cristelle knocked on the bedroom door, Dalya got up from her bed. Cristelle entered the room, and she exclaimed:

- Good morning, Mademoiselle Dalya!

Cristelle's voice tone was nervous, but the maid tried to appear cheerful, despite her anxiety. When she put the breakfast tray on a table, Cristelle affirmed with a sure tone:

- It promises to be a beautiful day, Mademoiselle!!

Dalya tried to smile:

- Good morning Cristelle ... thank you for the breakfast.

While the maid Cristelle was opening the curtains, a little silhouette entered the bedroom, at that moment. Amira Mounier couldn't be absent, on such an important day for her best and only friend. Amira displayed an encouraging smile:

- Good morning Dalya!!

Even before Dalya could answer, Amira hugged her friend so tightly, and she ordered her:

- Now ... Hurry up, Dalya!! We have a busy day today!!

Dalya observed her friend with a confused look:

- Professor Canfield said that I could skip school for today ... I don't have any classes ... so why a busy day? ... and how come you are not at school?

Before leaving the bedroom, the maid Cristelle exclaimed in a determined voice:

- It sure is a busy day for everyone!!

Amira immediately headed toward the dressing room, and she took out Dalya's clothes of the day:

- I asked Professor Canfield for permission to skip school and be with you here ... we both don't have any classes, today ... but we have a Third Challenge to pass!

Dalya sighed:

- Without the Excelbox, the Third Challenge is impossible!!

Amira put the clothes on the bed, and she answered with a positive lively tone:

- Perhaps ... but you still have the clues, Dalya! ... don't forget that they are important too! ... come on!! ... get dressed and eat your breakfast ... we will study the clues in the Library of the grand Mansion! ... come on!! ... hurry up!!

In front of Amira's contagious enthusiasm, Dalya decided to follow her friend's plan. After all, the Third Challenge was until tonight, and Dalya had nothing better to do during this entire day. Dalya got dressed quickly, and Amira forced her to eat breakfast, even though the stress was already filling her stomach. Then, Dalya and Amira left the bedroom.

Before coming down the stairs of the grand Mansion's hall, Dalya heard the employees talking down the stairs. Cristelle's voice was clear and determined:

- So, I will research all the rooms of the upper floor ... and ...

Océanie continued the sentence:

- ... and me and Igor ... we will take care of the living rooms ... we'll search in every corner! ... including the fireplaces!

The Cook stated:

- I will look again in all the kitchen shelves and the Pantry!

The head of the grand Mansion thought aloud:

- This box shouldn't be so far from here ... I will recheck the attic, and also the roof ...

The Gardener announced:

- I will search in the garage, around the grand Mansion, and the entire garden!

All the employees understood their task, that day. They all seemed determined. Cristelle exclaimed in a decided tone:

- This box has to be found today! Before midnight! ... we must find it!

Everyone in the grand Mansion, seemed busy with a specific task. The only silhouette that remained calm and immobile was the snow Panther. Since several days before, the animal's attitude didn't change at all; Séraphine stared at the annex house, day and night. And this morning as well, the snow Panther remained motionless and focused toward the annex house, through the windows of the living room. Séraphine didn't care at all about what was happening in the grand Mansion.

Amira opened the Library door. Dalya followed her inside, and she asked in a lost tone:

- What should we do now?

Right away, Amira sat down at the desk, she pulled out papers and pencils, and she thought aloud:

- First, we write the 4 clues that you have received ... it seems to be questions ... next, we try to find all the possible answers to these questions ...

When Dalya sat near her friend, Amira continued:

- The 2 previous Challenges were questions ... you had to give one word as an answer ... so then, can the Third Challenge might be a question too? ... Is it possible that you will have to give one word as an answer?

Dalya lay back on her chair:

- I am not sure ... but, probably yes ... the answer of the two previous Challenges was about lessons that I have learned.

Amira repeated aloud while noting a sentence on her paper:

- Third Challenge ... a lesson learned ...

For a few seconds of thinking, Amira reread some sentences on her paper:

- The clues are all questions ... and their answer is often related to a period of time ... maybe the answer to the Third Challenge is ... a period of time ... time ... hours ... minutes ...

Dalya straightened up from her chair and she pointed at the numbers on Amira's paper:

- But the numbers below the clues ... what are they about?

December 12th promised to be a long, busy and tense day.

Chapter 68

The Challenge

Monday, December 12th, 1892. The evening.

The grand Mansion was lit up with its entire splendor. All the lamps and chandeliers were shining bright; the luxurious living room was filled with seats, divans, and comfortable chairs. The present people were talking and waiting for the start of the evening's event.

Tonight, the grand Mansion was preparing to host the most anticipated event of the entire city of Georgetown; the Third Challenge of Late Mr. Governor Iskander Balthazar's heritage.

It was 10:00 PM, and several people were already present in the living room. The nephew and niece of the Governor, Mr. Ferdinand and Mrs. Honoré Edelmen, had settled comfortably on the luxurious divans; surrounded by their friends, talking in a cheerful voice and enjoying tea. Usually anxious and nervous, Mr. Ferdinand Edelmen seemed curiously relaxed and calm. The piercing laughs of his sister, Mrs. Honoré, indicated that the Edelmen family was waiting for a happy announcement, on that night.

The housekeeper of the French neighbors, Mrs. Glorina insisted to attend the event this evening, to encourage the little Dalya Bouvard. Mrs. Glorina held her bag tightly and with an anxious move, failing to hide her anxiety. Mrs. Glorina was sitting next to two men, Mr. Jacob Mounier and Professor Canfield. Amira's father and the Professor were discussing the latest news about the Royal Georgetown College.

A few chairs away, next to a window of the living room, Professor Haîyang stood still discreetly. The young woman needed to be present at this crucial Challenge. Professor Haîyang displayed a calm and serene appearance. And every two second, Professor Haîyang watched the garden, through the living room windows. It looked like as if Professor Haîyang was waiting for the arrival of a visitor...

And for once, Lyor Laszlo was relaxed and Sloan Wilfrid was anxious. Lyor sighed in relief while coming out of the car:

- This will be the last time I attend this ridiculous Challenge! ... I am relieved that my father will handle this affair entirely!

Sloan Wilfrid came out of the car without saying a word. Lyor had noticed the strange and tense silence of Sloan Wilfrid during their entire car trip. But before Lyor could ask him the reason for his worry, Sloan Wilfrid walked with hurried steps, inside the grand Mansion.

In the hall, Dalya was sitting on a chair; she was surrounded by the employees of the grand Mansion, and her friend Amira Mounier. Sloan Wilfrid was eager to know:

- So? ... Any news of this box?

The head of the grand Mansion announced in a sad tone:

- We looked everywhere, Monsieur ... we didn't find it.

Sloan Wilfrid cleared his throat, and he addressed Dalya with a kind tone:

- I will see if I can gain more time for you, Mademoiselle ...

When a famous man entered the hall of the grand Mansion, Dalya and the employees turned around. Sloan Wilfrid was the first to welcome the man:

- Good evening Congressman McKlain!
- Master Wilfrid ... I am glad to see you, on this evening!

As usual, Congressman McKlain was elegant in a dark blue suit, he still had an intimidating allure as always, and he was followed by 2 men. Sloan Wilfrid approached the Congressman, and he whispered to him a few words. The Congressman listened attentively, and then he replied discreetly, and in a serious tone:

- Law is the Law, Master Wilfrid ... and I am here to make sure the Will is applied precisely as it is! ... Rest assured!
- Thank you, Congressman McKlain. Wilfrid answered, before stepping away to let the Congressman and his 2 men, enter the living room of the grand Mansion.

Sloan Wilfrid returned back to Dalya and the employees, and he affirmed:

- We have until midnight to find a solution! ... Congressman McKlain will ensure that the Challenge does not end until after midnight, not a minute before!

Cristelle asked in a worried tone:

- What can we do?

Océanie thought aloud:

- But ... we have searched for days ... everywhere!

Sloan Wilfrid insisted:

- This box cannot just evaporate! ... Search again and again! ... In all places and corners! ... This is the biggest fortune of the Country! ... Our future of all of us depends on this box!

At that moment, the Gardener affirmed in a decided tone:

- Understood, Monsieur Wilfrid! ... We will divide just like this morning ... Cristelle, take care of the Library ... Océanie and Igor, go back in the rooms ... Ferrero, recheck the garage ... Bûchebois, you take care of the kitchen ... and I will search in the other living rooms!

Immediately assigned, all the employees of the grand Mansion disappeared from the hall, everyone toward their indicated place. Dalya's legs couldn't hold her anymore, she sat on a chair, and Amira immediately joined her. Sloan Wilfrid knelt in front of the two girls:

- I need you to stay here, in the hall ... None of these present people should know that this box has disappeared ... I will return to the living room, to keep the situation under control.

Dalya whispered in a trembling voice.

- What if ... what if we cannot find the Excelbox? ... what will happ...

Sloan Wilfrid interrupted Dalya:

- I prefer not to think about it, for now. I only worry when it's necessary! ... Right now, we must stay calm and find a solution!

10:45 PM.

The living room of the grand Mansion was complete with people; everyone was eagerly awaiting the start of the Third Challenge, which seemed delayed. Dalya paced up and down in the hall of the grand Mansion, her heart was getting increasingly tighter, her legs were anxious, and she was shaking. Amira tried to calm Dalya, the best she could:

- There is still more than one hour ... Mr. Wilfrid will find a solution ... He promised you! ... at the worst case, the Challenge will be delayed for another day ... and there is the presence of the Congressman ... nobody will dare to sa...

When suddenly, Amira was interrupted by a cold voice:

- You look worried ... little veggy seller.

The Lawyer Ernest Laszlo came close to Dalya, with slow step, displaying a diabolic smile, and he asked:

- Where is this strange box?

This simple question made Dalya's heart tremble. Dalya didn't dare to answer, let alone move. She froze up standing and she became pale. Immediately, Amira jumped out of her chair and she came near her friend to help her. And although her voice trembled, Amira gathered all her courage, and she addressed the Lawyer:

- Are you looking for ... for the bathrooms, Monsieur? ... It's ... that way ... to the left.

Ernest Laszlo stared at Dalya, with a diabolic look. The Lawyer's amused smile, was oddly frightening. Amira and Dalya were both paralyzed standing, one next to the other, not daring to move or say a word.

332

At this moment, Sloan Wilfrid appeared in the hall of the grand Mansion, and he did his best to divert the situation:

- Mr. Congressman has asked after you, Mr. Ernest Laszlo ... He wishes to discuss the new project of the migration Law ... he wanted to have your opinion on this matter.

While ignoring the words and the presence of his employee Sloan Wilfrid, the Lawyer Mr. Ernest Laszlo spoke to Dalya with a clear menacing tone:

- No box ... no heritage ... you may have succeeded 2 times, and that is quite enough. Tonight, I will escort you myself into your rat hole!

When he turned around and walked toward the living room, Mr. Ernest Laszlo let out an evil laugh. Sloan Wilfrid watched the Lawyer for a long second, before affirming:

- He knows about it!

Dalya and Amira exchanged a confused look. Sloan Wilfrid explained to them:

- Ernest Laszlo knows about the disappearance of the Excelbox!

At this statement, Dalya jumped:

- Is he the one who took it?

Ernest Laszlo sat near the Congressman, and he was talking in a formal and calm tone. Without taking his eyes off Ernest Laszlo, Sloan Wilfrid thought aloud:

- I doubt that it was him who stole this box ... he just knows that the Excelbox disappeared ... Ernest Laszlo can do trickeries sometimes, to circumvent the Law ... but never something illegal ... He wouldn't dare to steal that box ... he risk much more than his reputation and his career.

After several minutes of a heavy and tense silence, Dalya asked in a trembling voice:

- What do we do now?

Sloan Wilfrid didn't have any answer to this question. It is true that the young Lawyer has tried all his best to gain more time for this Third Challenge. However, Wilfrid had no plan B. And for Sloan Wilfrid to lack of ideas for the first time in his life, it meant that the situation was alarming and desperate. And as strange as it may seem, at this moment of despair, Sloan Wilfrid did the only thing he could think of, he did the only thing he had left to do. The young Lawyer looked up to the hall ceiling, and he whispered a prayer with an imploring murmur:

- We need a miracle tonight ... and I promise to stop calling people by nicknames!

In the living room of the grand Mansion, the voice of the Lawyer Ernest Laszlo announced:

- 50 minutes remain!

11:10 PM.

Dalya's heart stopped beating. Her body was shaking, her throat tightened, her cheeks turned red and breathless. Amira felt that her friend Dalya was about to faint, so she helped Dalya to sit down in the nearest chair.

At this moment, the Gardener appeared in the hall, accompanied by the Cook. Océanie came down the stairs at a rapid pace, followed by Igor. The head of the grand Mansion entered from a back door. Sloan Wilfrid was impatient:

- So ... has anyone found it?

All the employees of the grand Mansion remained silent and confused. No one dared to answer this question. Sloan Wilfrid decided to return to the living room, to try and gain a little more time. While Dalya remained motionless and terrified, sitting on a chair in the hall, surrounded by her friend Amira and the employees of the grand Mansion. They were all silent and devastated by their failure to find that box. Dalya whispered in a crushed tone:

- In a few minutes, it will be done ... my life will be over ... in a few minutes ...

At that moment, a loud voice was heard from the living room. The Lawyer Ernest Laszlo laughed:

- Is it really necessary to make us wait until midnight?

Congressman McKlain affirmed with a decided tone:

- The Will is very clear, Ernest ... midnight is midnight ... not one minute before, not one minute after!

Mr. Ernest Laszlo turned toward the nephew Mr. Ferdinand Edelmen, and he whispered:

- I can guarantee you that 40 minutes more or 40 minutes less, will not change the situation tonight!

The nephew Mr. Ferdinand Edelmen laughed aloud, and he asked in a mocking tone:

- There is no need to waste more time ... we should name the true Heir now!

And the Lawyer Mr. Ernest Laszlo confirmed his friend's idea:

- It is clear that this little veggy seller, will not pass the Challenge tonight!

Except that Congressman Yolan McKlain was an intransigent and upright man, to the big relief of Sloan Wilfrid. The Congressman insisted in a formal voice:

- No announcement will be made before midnight! ... with or without the Challen...

When all of a sudden, a piercing scream shook everyone present in the grand Mansion. The maid Cristelle appeared from the front door of the grand Mansion, and she screamed with all the strength of her lungs:

- FOUND IT!! FOUND IT!! FOUND IT!!

Cristelle entered the hall, screaming and jumping, without caring about anyone:

- FOUND IT!! FOUND IT!! FOUND IT!!

And without being able to contain themselves too, all the employees of the grand Mansion jumped and screamed in a single wave. The head of the employees Mr. Bûchebois exclaimed:

- I knew that this box will appear!! I knew it!!

Océanie trembled with happiness:

- Finally!! We did it!!

Igor exhaled a long breath:

- It was about time!! It took us days!!

The Cook and the Gardener laughed and shared a hug. And instantly, Sloan Wilfrid jumped from the living room, and he landed in the hall. The first thing the young Lawyer Sloan Wilfrid did, was to raise his eyes up to the hall ceiling, and he murmured in a grateful voice:

- Thank you! ... And I will stop sticking nicknames to people ... I promise!

The maid Cristelle approached Dalya, and she explained:

- I was searching at the Library and ... I noticed a shadow moving outside in the garden ... when I came outside, I couldn't see who it was ... but I found these items on the front door!

A silhouette sitting in the living room, was interested in the scene that was happening in the hall of the grand Mansion. When Professor Haîyang stretched her neck and noticed the strange box intact in one piece, the young woman turned around in her chair, displaying a relieved and a satisfied smile.

Immediately, Dalya took from Cristelle's hands the Excelbox. At first glance, the box seemed safe and sound. Cristelle handed to Dalya 2 other items; a scarf, and a small note.

It was a pretty stitched scarf in soft cotton, with lines of blue bronze colors, and flying eagles stitched on the edges. By examining the scarf closer, Dalya thought:

- This scarf belongs to my little cousin Hugo ... why was this scarf with the Exce...

When suddenly, Dalya jumped:

- This is ... this is the scarf that was given to me by the Dean of Merchants, Mr. Kenan Einsenberg, as a birthday gift, last year ... I thought I had lost it, I searched for it everywhere ... and all this time, my little cousin Hugo was wearing my scarf?! ... But how and why my little cousin took this scarf? ... how did he get inside the grand Mansion? ...

Ideas became increasingly clearer in Dalya's mind:

- The secret passage! ... My little twin sisters ... Ari and Adi entered my bedroom through the secret passage ... that's how my little cousin Hugo took my scarf, and the Excelbox too!

At this precise moment, a little silhouette joined the few people gathered in the hall of the grand Mansion. The snow Panther approached Dalya Bouvard, with slow confident steps. Séraphine observed the little girl with a calm serene stare. Dalya thought aloud:

- All this time, the box was in the annex house! ... That's why Séraphine was observing the annex house, day and night! ... Séraphine knew it was there!

Her friend Amira Mounier finally understood too:

- The snow Panther stopped following us everywhere, on the same day that this box disappeared!

The employees of the grand Mansion exchanged confused looks. The head of the grand Mansion exclaimed:

- The annex house? ... It's the only place we haven't searched!

The Gardener caressed the snow Panther's head:

- Mighty Séraphine!! ... This little one knows so many things!

Igor sighed:

- And Séraphine didn't think to tell us that, a bit earlier? ... I spent hours with my head buried in the chimneys! ... I smell only wood dust in my noise, since many days!

A laugh of relief and amazement, invaded all the people present in the hall. Amira Mounier remembered that Dalya had received another item with the scarf and the Excelbox:

- What is written on that paper?

When Dalya unfolded it, she was shocked:

- It's ... It's the 5th clue!!

How long before a heart will bow ?
Guided by the lights,
Do you think we will stop ?

The 5th clue seemed as mysterious as the previous ones. Except that several other questions appeared in Dalya Bouvard's mind, she thought aloud:

- How and why this clue came out of the Excelbox? ... Why did my little cousin Hugo took the box and my scarf? ... Why did he gave them back to me tonight?

Dalya Bouvard was confused and lost. It happens that sometimes, some answers are slow to reach us.

At this moment, and while Dalya Bouvard was preparing to pass her Third Challenge in the grand Mansion, a train was leaving Georgetown city, heading toward Florida. On board of the train; there was a diabolic grandmother and her unbearable smell, an Uncle with a name and manners the same as pigs, a madly jealous Aunt, a husband womanizer and profiteer, and ... a little calm boy.

In the train leaving Georgetown city, the little boy Hugo was reading the book of the cars mechanics that his cousin Dalya offered him. And for once, he smiled proudly. One, because he returned items that he had taken from the grand Mansion. And two, because he helped his father to also return an item belonging to the grand Mansion...

While watching the scenery outside the train window, Aunt Claudine asked her husband:

- Henrik ... the purchase papers of the new house... you put them in your backpack, didn't you?

Mr. Henrik said, continuing to read his newspaper:

- Yes, my darling ... certainly...

Claudine exclaimed joyfully:

- Me too, I will have a new home, like the one of Augustine ... Me too, I will have a large garden, like the one of Augustine ... Me too, I will have many rooms, a living room and a big kitchen, like those of Augustine ... Me too ... Me too ... Me too ...

At that precise instant, the little boy Hugo smiled proudly. Because he was the only one in the train compartment, to know that the purchase papers of the new Florida home ... These papers were far away, carefully hidden in a corner of the garden in the grand Mansion ... waiting to be discovered ... some day.

Mr. Henrik continued to read his newspaper, in a serene confident air, displaying a sneaky and arrogant smile. Mr. Henrik didn't know that a good lesson of honesty, was waiting for him in Florida. As for his wife Claudine, will she ever heal from her jealousy? ... let's hope so ... let's hope so ...

And as for the grandmother, Mrs. Medusa Safoubri and her adored son Duroc ... the unbearable smell, the diabolic stares, the pigs' manners, and the despicable character ... the grandmother and her adored son, what was waiting for them, at the end of these pages? ... you don't want to know ... you really don't want to know ...

11:33 PM.

In the hall of the grand Mansion, Sloan Wilfrid interrupted Dalya in her thoughts:

- Mademoiselle, you only have half an hour left to pass this Third Challenge!

Dalya looked at Sloan Wilfrid, with a terrified stare:

- But ... I ... the clues are incomprehensible ... I can't do it ... I tried to understand the clues, me and Amira ... but we failed ... I can't do it …

Sloan Wilfrid approached the little girl, and he said in a confident voice:

- The Excelbox did not appear for no reason, Dalya!

On this point, Dalya had to admit that the young Lawyer was well right. Surrounded by the employees of the grand Mansion, and her friend Amira Mounier, Dalya Bouvard could clearly read on every face present in the hall, sincere encouragements and a great support.

Sloan Wilfrid ordered Dalya with an enthusiastic voice:

- Look a Challenge right in the eye ... and give it a wink!

And as unlikely as it was, this sentence made Dalya smile. She held firmly the Excelbox in her hand, and she headed toward the living room ... and the Third Challenge began!

11:35 PM.

Dalya settled on the chair behind the desk, in front of everyone present. And immediately, she asked the question of the Third Challenge. And the Excelbox was delighted to provide an answer. After a light burst from the strange box, a small paper appeared on the rectangular opening:

The First helps to start,
The Second helps to ahead walk,
Oh ... but it is the Third that helps through cross.
My Third Question is
In one word, what it is ?

Dalya's heart tightened. She knew that the Third Question would be to provide a one word answer. But still, Dalya hoped to have an easy and clear question.

Instantly, Dalya wrote down on a paper, all the clues she had received:

Clue 1: How long before a heart will be born? 16, 1
Clue 2: How long before a heart will dare? 20, 9
Clue 3: How long before a heart will heal? 5, 14
Clue 4: How long, the pressure, a heart will bear? 3, 5
Clue 5: How long before a heart will bow? Guided by the lights, do you think we will stop?

Dalya lay back on her chair and she thought aloud:

- All the clues are asking the same question ... and the answer is about time ... hours or months or years ... time ... a phase ... a period of time ...

While the little Dalya Bouvard was using all the neurons in her brain to find an answer, the young Lawyer Sloan Wilfrid followed her with all his attention. The employees of the grand Mansion remained standing, at the living room's door, they seemed all anxious and worried. The housekeeper of the French neighbors, Mrs. Glorina tightened so hard her purse; it almost ripped off, without her noticing. Amira Mounier felt her throat strangled and her cheeks blushing, while sitting in front of her friend Dalya. Professor Canfield watched Dalya with a serious look. And Professor Haîyang who had been discreet until this moment, she stretched her neck to better observe her student. The Lawyer Mr. Ernest Laszlo and Mr. Ferdinand exchanged worried and confused looks. Their plans A and B have failed; the two men were in a difficult situation for the 3rd time!

Of all the people present in the living room, only the Congressman McKlain seemed to manage to keep his calm.

For some long minutes, Dalya reread the clues several times:

- The Third answer is about a time ... but each clue indicates a different time ... I need only one period of time ... one period ...

At this moment, the Lawyer Ernest Laszlo couldn't contain his anxiety. Ernest Laszlo stood up to inform of the remaining minutes, in a last attempt to blur the thinking of Dalya Bouvard and make her lose more time. Ernest Laszlo announced with an arrogant voice:

- Only twe...
- SIT AND SHUT UP ERNEST!!!

The Congressman screamed with such a strong voice, that the living room windows trembled. Congressman McKlain shot the Lawyer with in a menacing look, easily suspecting his ruse. A few chairs away, Sloan Wilfrid was happy of the Congressman's presence. The Challenge was already hard enough without the tricks of Ernest Laszlo.

In the middle of her thinking, a small detail caught Dalya's attention:

- The numbers! ... What do these numbers mean? ... Certainly not the location of a book ... We have looked everywhere Amira and me ... 16,1 ... 20,9 ... 5,14 ... 3,5 ... maybe these numbers indicate hours ... 4:01 PM ... 8:09 PM ... or something else ... it's not clear at all! ... I need more lighteni...

When suddenly, Dalya straightened up from her chair:

- The 5th clue ... guided by the lights ... the lights ... the lights!

And gifted with a good memory, Dalya remembered a small important detail:

- One of the clues of the Second question ... 26 lights illuminate our minds ... the lights referred to the 26 letters of the alphabets ... is it possible that ... the same word ... is it possible?

Dalya took another blank paper and she wrote all the clue numbers:

- 16 ... 1 ... 20 ... 9 ... 5 ... 14 ... 3 ... 5 ...

And without a second of hesitation, right below the numbers, Dalya wrote:

- P ... A ... T ... I ... E ...

All the present people watched Dalya, in a focused and stressed air. Professor Canfield crossed his arms. Amira had a hard time to breathe. Mrs. Glorina tightened harder her fingers on her bag. Professor Haîyang observed the little girl with complete focus. The employees of the grand Mansion exchanged worried looks. Sloan Wilfrid straightened up on his chair, keeping his eyes focused on Dalya. Ernest Laszlo was paralyzed in his chair, not daring to move or speak. Ferdinand Edelmen and his sister became increasingly worried. And the Congressman continued to observe Dalya, without losing a crumb of the ongoing scene in front of him.

Immediately and abruptly, Dalya Bouvard jumped out of her chair:

- Patience!! The numbers refer to a word ... the word is Patience!!

Forcing herself to be calmer, Dalya took back the clues and she thought in a low voice:

- **Clue 1: How long before a heart will be born?** ... a baby is born at 9 months ... it's a quite example of patience ...

While reading her paper, Dalya remembered an unusual incident, and a discreet smile displayed on her lips:

- **Clue 2: How long before a heart will dare?** ... For a heart to dare, it will only need some time ... and some patience ...

At this moment, Dalya remembered an episode in the school canteen, between Gael and the student Esteban ... that day, Esteban didn't dare to defend himself ... so Dalya insisted to intervene and stop Gael, although it cost her a 4 months detention ... Except that, strangely, some 6 weeks after this incident, a stranger dared to provide Dalya with a complete vocabulary Latin cards ... and these cards helped her pass the exams ... is it possible that this stranger could be Esteban? ... For a heart to dare, it will only need some time ... and some patience ...

Reading the 3rd clue, Dalya thought in her head:

- *Clue 3: How long before a heart will heal?* ... I asked for this clue to help Océanie ... her recovery required Cristelle's cares, the doctor's remedies, the recipes of Mr. Cook, the help of all the employees of the grand Mansion, entire days of work in the Saturday market ... and certainly patience! ... Her healing was a long way!

Dalya breathed a long shot, and she continued her research:

- *Clue 4: How long, the pressure, a heart will bear?* ... Certainly not as long as people think ... patience has limits!

In the living room of the grand Mansion, the only person who didn't care the slightest about the Third Challenge; was Lyor Laszlo. Even worse, while everyone stared at Dalya in a focused anxious look, Lyor Laszlo was reading a book!

Dalya observed Lyor, for a second. Several days ago, Dalya remembered that after Lyor Laszlo had decided to give up being her legal guardian ... she was curious about Lyor's relationship with his father ... and witnessing the reprimands and cruel critics of the Lawyer Ernest Laszlo toward his son Lyor, Dalya could well understand that Lyor couldn't bear such pressure ... certainly not for long as Lyor thought he could ... patience has limits!

And for the last clue, Dalya read:

- *Clue 5: How long before a heart will bow?* ... A heart can change his belief and attitude in a year or in a minute! ... And it surely requires some patience!

At this moment, Dalya looked at the employees of the grand Mansion. Their attitude has oddly changed, comparing the first day and the last day of Dalya Bouvard in the grand Mansion. It took several months for the employees to understand her spontaneous manners, and her natural language ... for the heart of the employees to bow, it took one year!

... And thinking about her little cousin Hugo, it took him one minute to decide returning back the Excelbox and the scarf with it ... for the heart of a little boy to bow, it took one minute!

Dalya thought about the question of Third Challenge:

- The First helps to start ... Courage helps to start ... The Second helps to ahead walk ... Perseverance helps to ahead walk ... Oh, but it is the Third that helps through cross ... Patience helps through cross ...

While thinking of all the people and the events that took place this year ... Dalya have learned that it is thanks to patience that many incidents have been resolved.

Patience helps you cross through the most difficult times of your life ... Patience always heals your heart ... your Patience allows someone to dare come out of his shell ... Patience makes you stronger and more resistant while facing pressure ... Patience allows you to tolerate rejections and receive respects afterward ... Patience helps you through a training of several months, to launch 3 perfect arrows ...

Patience ... dear reader ... trust Patience, it will help you cross through so much more challenges than you think.

11:50 PM.

Dalya looked up at Sloan Wilfrid, and she clearly announced:

- I have an answer!

Sloan Wilfrid jumped out of his chair and he approached Dalya:

- Are you sure about it?

Dalya replied with a trembling voice:

- Honestly ... no.

At this moment, Sloan Wilfrid smiled at her:

- It's always better this way!

11:57 PM.

Sloan Wilfrid inserted the paper of Dalya's answer in the rectangular opening of the strange box. Under the eyes of Congressman McKlain, and all the other present people in the living room of the grand Mansion. Immediately, the Excelbox lit up with all its glory. A powerful light invaded the glass cage; the gold wrought vines shone in a thousand lights, the inside clock needles were close to that night's date.

A second later, the Excelbox provided a piece of paper ... all the present people, were waiting with great anticipation and worry. The employees of the grand Mansion came closer a few more steps. Amira Mounier felt her throat choking. Professor Haîyang straightened up to better see what will happen. Mrs. Glorina covered her eyes with her hands, unable to bear the intense moment. The Congressman straightened up on his chair, more curious than he thought he would be. Sweat appeared on the forehead of the nephew Ferdinand Edelmen. His sister Mrs. Honoré Edelmen became all pale. And the heart of Dalya Bouvard ... stopped.

The only one, who dared to move, was Sloan Wilfrid. And his hand trembled while taking the verdict paper from the Excelbox. He read the content, without any clear emotion on his face. Sloan Wilfrid was paralyzed, reading the judgment in his hand.

Because you must remember an important thing ... dear reader ... life is a remarkable Chess game. You can master the rules and techniques ... you can handle your opponent's pawns and moves ... you can be smart and talented ... however, it happens that sometimes, you will be surprised by some Chess game finales.

Recently, during a late afternoon, the Lawyer Ernest Laszlo affirmed that the Queen was a weak and a lonely pawn. And on the advice of the Lawyer, Sloan Wilfrid didn't dare to unite with the Queen, in order to win the game. Mr. Ernest Laszlo was somehow right. The Queen is perhaps the only female pawn in the entire male Chessboard; the Queen's place is and always will be in the second rank. Except that the Queen is not a pawn to be underestimated ... she is be feared.

At this instant, Sloan Wilfrid looked up, not towards Dalya Bouvard ... but towards someone else; the Lawyer Ernest Laszlo. And after a long second, Sloan Wilfrid smiled at Ernest Laszlo, and he pronounced a word for the very first time ever:

- Checkmate!

Dépôt légal : 2021MO0760

Cover design & Print by ALPHA PRINT

www.alphaprintmaroc.com